P9-DCD-697

The Breath of Dawn

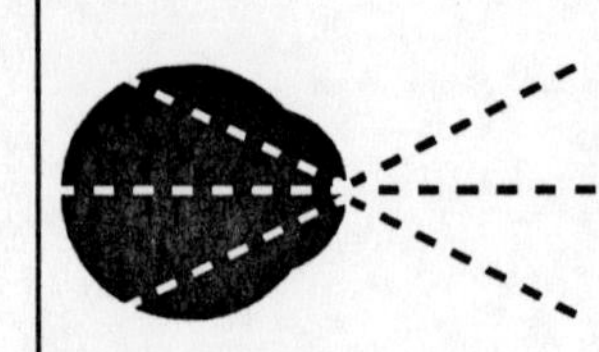

The Breath of Dawn

Kristen Heitzmann

THORNDIKE PRESS
A part of Gale, Cengage Learning

Detroit • New York • San Francisco • New Haven, Conn • Waterville, Maine • London

Thorndike Press, a part of Gale, Cengage Learning.

Thorndike Press® Large Print Christian Fiction.
The text of this Large Print edition is unabridged.
Other aspects of the book may vary from the original edition.
Set in 16 pt. Plantin.

LIBRARY OF CONGRESS CATALOGING-IN-PUBLICATION DATA

Heitzmann, Kristen.
The breath of dawn / by Kristen Heitzmann.
pages ; cm. — (Thorndike Press large print Christian fiction)
ISBN 978-1-4104-5539-0 (hardcover) — ISBN 1-4104-5539-4 (hardcover) 1. Widowers—Fiction. 2. Single women—Fiction. 3. Family secrets—Fiction. 4. Large type books. I. Title.
PS3558.E468B84 2013
813'.54—dc23 2012044212

Published in 2013 by arrangement with Bethany House Publishers, a division of Baker Publishing Group

Printed in Mexico
1 2 3 4 5 6 7 17 16 15 14 13

To Everleigh Grace,
my joy and delight

*But seek ye first the kingdom of God,
and his righteousness;
and all these things shall be
added unto you.*

Matthew 6:33 KJV

Prologue

Seeing Morgan standing still as stone beside the freshly opened earth, Noelle St. Claire Spencer believed a man could shatter. One touch, and he might crumble and blow away. Ashes to ashes. Dust to dust.

Heat emanated from his tiny infant, who slept unaware that her daddy looked as close to the grave as the wife he buried. *Jill.* Noelle tightened her hold on the motherless babe, feeling her own little boy press tighter against her legs, as he sensed a magnitude of loss he hadn't before encountered. With one long arm, Rick held his family and one tiny part of Morgan's in mute protection.

Tall, silent as a sentry, his eyes mirrored the pain in hers. How did this happen? No, not how — why?

Her throat swelled with tears, her mouth sour with the bitter taste of grief, as she looked into the baby's face. Would she carry even a vague memory of the mother who'd held her inside, nestled and crooned and stroked her, anticipating moments of wonder and delight? Who would tell her?

She could see the silence growing in Morgan — he who'd wielded words with the skill of an empire builder, who'd lived potently and vibrantly. Once before she'd watched him fade. Now he seemed colorless. He raised his face, needing more, another moment to hold on as the priest concluded the prayers over the casket. "We entrust this soul to God in the name of the Father and of the Son and of the Holy Spirit."

Those closest to the grave crossed themselves — except for Morgan, motionless. She touched his arm.

"Don't." His lips barely parted around the word.

Curled like a flannel-cocooned inchworm, his baby emitted a high-pitched mew. Morgan didn't turn. He stared at the curtain-draped hole and rasped, "Take her with you, okay?"

"To your house?"

"To the ranch." He cast a look at Rick, his taller, younger brother. "I'm no good to her."

Of course he'd think that. After everything.

"You come too," Rick said, solid, stoic. "Come back with us."

Morgan said nothing. The pain coming off him staggered her.

Rick told him, "We'll help, Morgan, but you have to come too. Your daughter needs you."

He might not realize the impact of those words, words Morgan had responded to for a different daughter, one he'd tried to save and couldn't. After losing Kelsey, Jill's death seemed cruel and excessive.

A shudder moved through him, sun glinting off new silver threads in his black hair. His indigo eyes looked almost black. His face was gray. He had one foot over the line with the dead. Only Livie held him. If he convinced himself that she and Rick were enough for his baby girl, he might quit altogether. Who wouldn't?

Her in-laws, Hank and Celia, stood ready to support the cause, but it was Consuela, his housekeeper, who moved toward him, her face revealing a heart breaking for all he'd lost. "You go with them, Morgan," she said, her nearly black eyes awash yet fervent, her jaw set. "You go, and you come back."

His breath seeped out. "Fine." He took a step and once in motion kept on until he reached not the limousine that had brought him to the cemetery but his wine-red Maserati GranTurismo, pulsing power and prestige as it sat on the graveyard road that barely contained it.

Noelle trembled at the thought of him behind the wheel. How many times had she and Rick expected the call that he had died driving drunk? When he actually did crash his Corvette, he'd been stone sober. And he lived. He healed.

Now it had been Jill and two friends on a moms' night out — their minivan concealed by the whirling, wind-driven smoke of a sudden wildfire — who'd been hit by a rushing fire truck. There had to be order in that somewhere, but she couldn't find it. She could only hurt.

Thin, soundless rain fell unobtrusively as she and Rick joined Morgan at his car. No baby seat, since he never drove Livie in the sports car. Had he parked it there anticipating an unencumbered exit?

"Morgan . . ." Rick started to speak.

The older Spencer bent and kissed his baby's head, then looked up. "I'll see you out there."

She expected Rick to argue, to make him fly back with them, but he only said, "Don't drive crazy."

A dark and humorless smile touched Morgan's lips as he climbed in. The license plate read MYGRLS — a reminder to come home to the ones he loved? Or a way to have them with him wherever he went. Now he had only Livie. Noelle clutched her protectively.

Tears streamed down her face as the engine roared and he peeled away. No lingering over food and sympathy with his family, business associates, and hundreds of friends and members of his community all waiting at the reception. Morgan wanted the road. In pain,

Morgan always wanted the road.

She looked up at Rick, whose gaze had landed on tiny Olivia.

"He won't leave her, Noelle. It's not in him."

Grief wasn't a feeling. It was a force, an entity, demanding entrance with the delicacy of a battering ram, and once that wall was breached, once the gates shattered, all hell would break loose. Morgan accelerated, as though speed formed a defense, as if flight could take him far enough, fast enough to keep the grinding pain from crushing him to dust.

Jill. He couldn't remember a time he hadn't loved her. Even the years apart, she'd been there, inside him, invading his memories, haunting his heart. Even in the anger, the betrayal, there'd been want. There'd been knowing she was in the world.

And mixed into every moment with Jill, there'd been Kelsey, the daughter he'd thought she aborted. The daughter he'd tried to save from leukemia. He failed then. What made them think he wouldn't now, with Livie?

He pressed his eyes shut, even though the Maserati topped a hundred and ten. Then he remembered the road wasn't his alone and opened his eyes. If he were to fly, he'd do it where no one else paid the price with him.

Plenty of places between California and Rick's ranch in the Colorado mountains.

He'd experienced that soaring after Kelsey died, a crash that broke his body in so many places he rivaled the Bionic Man, but it hadn't quit. In her collision, Jill died instantly. Gone so fast there'd been no pain, no prolonged suffering. Just gone. What he wouldn't give to know that trick.

Except for Livie.

In spite of the crushing pain, his heart swelled. Nothing he did, nothing that happened to him, it seemed, could stop that love. He might be no good to her, might fail her as he'd failed Kelsey, and now Jill, but nothing in this world could make him stop trying. Not this pain. Not the rest to come.

Jill smiled from the photo on his visor, caught unawares and unposed. Beside her, newborn Olivia, and then one of his only pictures of Kelsey before the angels carried her away. Bald and brave and otherworldly, she anointed him with courage, drops of mercy from a pain-perfected soul. His must be utterly grace-resistant to require, once more, this particular scourge.

Chapter 1

Quinn liked the way mountains made her feel small — not unusual at five three, a hundred and five, but beneath the towering peaks, she felt minuscule, practically invisible, almost invisible enough.

She stepped onto her narrow balcony that had no room for furniture but enough to stand and look out and become a human thermometer — valuable in a changeable weather place such as Juniper Falls, Colorado. And climbing over the railing and dangling would make the drop from the bedroom do-able — should that ever be necessary.

Nestled in her tiny cabin's A-frame peak, her bedroom held a full-sized bed, a closet with built-in drawers, the door to the balcony, and her. Also in the loft was the pint-sized bathroom, shower — no tub — in pale yellow tiles. She climbed down the ladderlike stairs to the living, dining, cooking room. In her cabin, she sometimes felt like Alice biting the wrong side of the mushroom. But it was hers.

What could be sweeter?

Bundling into her boiled-wool coat, she stuffed her dark, curling hair into the hood, went out to her F-150 pickup, and pulled out onto the dirt road. A foggy cloud sat hard on the valleys, revealing bits of grayed scenery — here the dark evergreen arms of trees, there a stone canyon wall with spring water frozen into phantasmal shapes.

She couldn't wait until it cleared. The chance to look through what sounded like a sizable estate before anyone else was an opportunity she wouldn't miss. It was her livelihood. Sometimes she drove hours just to have a look. It usually paid off with at least a few things — sometimes a big fat zero, and every now and then a treasure trove. The spark of discovery quickened in her now.

She'd lucked out that the estate was in the vicinity, only a few miles away. She didn't know the deceased. Having lived only six months in Juniper Falls, that applied to most of the live population as well. It also meant she'd barely plumbed the possibilities in the area.

Families with estates to settle could always list and sell the stuff themselves, wait for the right buyer or collector, package, ship, and insure, and deal with gripes while grieving their loved ones, but she'd found most were perfectly happy to let her make an offer and take all that on herself. For those who got greedy or sentimental, she left her card in case they changed their minds. Many of them did, and not too begrudgingly. She was making a living, not a killing.

She pulled up to the property, surprised to see a truck in front of the small ranch house. Two cars were in the garage, a blue-and-tan Subaru she guessed was the deceased's and a white compact marked as a rental. The truck might mean someone else was interested in the estate. Being new to the area, she didn't yet recognize all her competition. But she'd been promised first look.

She moved toward the house, her breath mingling with the fog. The doorbell gave a sort of short-circuit buzz that brought no one. Frowning, she stepped away and walked around the side of the house.

With the mist tightening her spiraled strands, she moved toward barely audible voices. Two women stood at a green metal fence jeweled with condensation. They turned as she approached.

"Hi there," said the one whose every blond hair must have been glued in place to hold in the mist. Her slicker barely accommodated her ample hips. "You must be Riley."

"Quinn. I'm Quinn Reilly."

"Oh, I had it backwards."

"It happens." Way more than it should.

"I'm RaeAnne." Her twang made the name sing. "And this is Noelle, from the ranch next to my mom's here."

The other woman had classic Michelle Pfeiffer–style beauty with silky golden-brown hair and natural grace. Caught up in her appraisal, Quinn startled at the snort that preceded a bony black face appearing through the fog. Casting a wary look at the whiskered muzzle frosted with age, she took a step back.

RaeAnne patted the horse. "Noelle's offered to pasture Matilda, for what time she has left. Poor old girl."

"We have a lot of pasture." Noelle stroked the skimpy mane. "And Vera loved this horse."

"She did." RaeAnne's voice tightened. "Even though she came with the house and Mom never sat a horse in her life."

"I'm sorry for your loss," Quinn said.

"Thanks." RaeAnne blinked. "But Vera lived independently and passed in her sleep. What more can we ask?"

Lacking an easy answer, Quinn nodded.

"Well, come inside."

RaeAnne's hips swung back and forth with her stride. Noelle barely touched the ground, and Quinn just walked. Saying she'd be back for the mare, Noelle left in the Chevy truck — not what she'd picture the woman driving, more like a silver Jaguar.

"Pretty, isn't she." RaeAnne pushed open the back door.

"You think?"

They giggled.

The house had the old-person smell she recognized from similar circumstances — stale and slightly astringent — but RaeAnne must have alerted authorities almost immediately, because there was very little death scent.

"Well?" RaeAnne cast her gaze around. "Kind of leaves you speechless, doesn't it?"

While she hadn't been buried alive, Vera'd had a lot of things. Quinn took in the packed tables, shelves, cabinets, hutches, and stacks. She could tell at a look that a lot of it didn't interest her. That left a lot of it that might. "What do you want to happen here, RaeAnne?"

"Well, there are a few personal things I'll hang on to. Some of it's just got to go, and for the things you want . . . whatever's reasonable, I guess."

"It can work two ways," Quinn told her. "I can purchase only what I might sell, which leaves you dealing with everything else. Or a flat rate buys whatever you don't choose to keep, and I'll resell or donate accordingly."

"That second way sounds great." RaeAnne seemed eager to separate from her mother's things. "I don't think the furniture will get you much. It's all secondhand."

And not antique, except in the kitchen. They haggled gently, the woman's genial nature and Quinn's own professional reserve keeping it civil. It wasn't about ripping people off. Though she imagined there were sharks in the water who preyed on the bereaved, it raised her hackles when people assumed she operated that way.

"Keep your stuff," she wanted to say when people questioned her offer, but she explained the process and the losses she took on things that never sold, not to mention her time. She did them a favor handling the whole lot and sometimes found hidden treasures — the hook for her.

In Vera's house, she recognized some popular and hard-to-find pieces. Her collector's guides and handbooks would help her know where to start the bidding or set the price. She'd learned a lot but still barely touched the surface of everything out there.

When they agreed, she gave RaeAnne her card with contact information and said, "I'll start with the knickknacks, if that's okay. You can reserve anything you want."

"Take them all. Just leave any jewelry for now."

"Okay." Jewelry was often excluded for value or sentimental reasons. She went back into the mist and brought in the lidded containers she kept stacked in the truck bed and cargo area to pack up and carry away the bits and pieces of a life.

After driving away with a full truckload,

Quinn stood in her gray steel edifice lit by hooded bulbs suspended from the ceiling and warmed by space heaters in each corner. The prefab barn was the reason she lived in a dollhouse — that and the selling price. The structure was perfect for collecting, storing, and packing the wares she fostered as each awaited a new home.

While she hadn't grown up thinking she'd be an eBay trader, over the last four years she'd developed a knack for finding deals as well as an eye for quality. It didn't tie her to any physical location and was virtually anonymous, except when she acquired merchandise. Not a bad fit.

Even so, hours of handling, photographing, and listing other people's stuff sometimes made her glaze over. She slid the door open to a dry dusting of snow — the tiny pellet kind that struck the mountains anytime from September on and frequently now, as October waned. She'd heard the wind but hadn't realized it brought a companion.

Fog, mist, a few moments of sun, and now this, all in one day. Weather in the Rockies. She stepped out and slid the door shut, wind tossing hair across her face as the phone rang in her pocket. "Hello?"

"Hi, Quinn, it's RaeAnne Thigley. I'm sorry, but I wonder if I could look through the things you hauled out. There's a locket I can't locate that means a lot to me."

"Oh." Quinn turned back toward the building. "You want me to bring —"

"Heavens no. I'll come to you."

"Um. Okay." She gave RaeAnne her address with a tiny twinge.

"That's it? No argument? No, 'I bought it and it's mine'?"

"Of course not. You said there were personal things you wanted."

When RaeAnne arrived, Quinn let her in and pointed to the storage containers. "Help yourself, though I'm pretty sure I didn't pack a locket. Unless it's inside something else."

RaeAnne's deep-set eyes pooled, tears beading on mascara-crusted lashes as dense as caterpillar fur. "You restore my faith — you and Rick and Noelle. People who know how to treat one another."

It seemed that since they'd parted, something more than grief had dampened RaeAnne's spirits.

"But . . ." RaeAnne waved a hand. "You don't want to hear my woes."

"I have two ears that work." Quinn pulled the lid off one of the containers she hadn't begun to inventory. She'd immediately unpacked the Hummel figurines in near-mint condition in spite of overcrowding in one of Vera's glass hutches. She had them set out on her long tables for photographing and knew for a fact none harbored jewelry. The little faces were as innocent as they appeared.

"I took off four days to handle Mom's affairs, and I just found out I've been put on notice at work. What kind of world is that?"

"What do you do — national security?"

That got a laugh. "I work for an advertising company."

"Ah, very time sensitive." Quinn pulled the next container down and sat on the cold floor since all the table space was taken with the porcelain peasants. "No one covering you?"

"That's the problem." RaeAnne hunkered down a little less easily. "My overeager assistant. I've had some health issues this year, and he's filled in more than I wanted."

"But if you're back tomorrow . . ."

"How can I be? I haven't found the locket."

Quinn cocked her head. "It means that much?"

"It means everything. My dad's picture's in it." She looked up. "A picture I've never seen . . . as I've never seen him."

"Seriously?"

RaeAnne nodded. "Mom said when she died I could see him, and not a day before. Now she's gone and he's nowhere to be found." Tears welled up again. "She might have directed me to it in her last moments if I'd been there, but obviously . . ." She spread her hands.

"Maybe it's in a safe deposit box or with a lawyer."

"She banked online and never made a will,

except what she wrote out by hand. It said, 'Everything to RaeAnne — obviously.' " She laughed softly. "That was Vera in a nutshell."

"There might be a letter in the paper stacks, telling you where to find it."

"Maybe. But that could take months to sort through."

Quinn reached into her container. "Well, let's start with what we have."

After searching the remaining bins, RaeAnne rocked up to her feet with a groan. "I'll have to ask for an extension. If it ends up being permanent, we'll just have to make do."

"You can't lose a job over this. I'll find the locket, now that I know what I'm looking for. I'm already sorting the rest."

"Quinn, it could be anywhere. I mean *anywhere.* I found a ring tied up in a sock."

"Oh." She hadn't planned on scrutinizing every item of clothing and sheet of paper.

"I know it's too much to ask." RaeAnne pulled a tissue from her pocket and dabbed her nose. "But I could give some money back for the extra time."

"I might find it first thing tomorrow."

"And it could take weeks. If I didn't have to come back and clean the place for sale, I'd give back all you paid and call it even."

If there were things squirreled away, the sorting alone would be monumental, but considering she had more time than money, Quinn said, "That's fair."

"It is? Would you do it? Just having it off my hands . . ." Again the tears pooled. "Between Vera's arrangements and the house and my job, I'm a wreck."

"You don't look a wreck." Every hair was still in place.

"I've lost six pounds worrying. And yes, I can afford to, but I'm more likely to have a stroke than a heart attack from all this."

Quinn touched her arm. "Be kind to yourself. This isn't easy."

RaeAnne dug into her purse and retrieved the bills they'd exchanged earlier. "You sure?"

"Are you?"

They laughed.

"If I fly back tomorrow, will you keep me posted?"

"The minute I find it, you'll know. And if it's right away, we'll renegotiate."

"Oh!" RaeAnne grabbed her into a hug. "You are the sweetest thing."

Enveloped by the warmth and sincerity, Quinn returned the hug, touched and intrigued by the woman and her tale. Such gestures were beyond the scope of her job, but somehow it felt right.

The next morning, dressed in black jeans, ankle boots, and an embroidered kimono-shaped sweater from a different estate, she paused in front of the Alpine Patisserie, with blue shake-shingle roof and white letters etched on the glass. At the window table, she saw Noelle, elegant in designer jacket and jeans — no mistaking that quality.

The man sharing the parlor-style table fit her perfectly, polished, urbane, and way too handsome, with nearly black hair and fine, angular features. He wore his well-fashioned clothes with as much ease as Noelle. A matched set.

Reaching behind the table, he brought up the last thing she'd expected — a fairy child, maybe two years old, with dark wispy hair and such precious features Quinn stopped, hand pressed to her heart. They were a family. Nothing amazing in that, so why did she feel such pathos?

When the little girl leaned in to kiss her daddy's mouth, something almost piercing —

"Going in?" a rugged guy in a Stetson asked while the young boy with him hung back by his arms to open the door.

She hadn't decided yet, but the little guy held the door so earnestly, she said, "Thanks."

Red-faced with exertion, the kid beamed, then ducked in when the man took over the door. Heading for the counter, Quinn scanned the menu board, catching with the corner of her eye the newcomers joining Noelle and her husband.

The boy, who looked about four, ground the metal feet of a parlor chair over the tile floor like a file on a washboard and slid into place at the table. The man removed his hat, bent, and kissed Noelle, a hand wrapping the back of her neck in a brief, telling gesture. What?

Quinn stopped pretending to read the board and ordered hot green tea. Captivated by the three adults and two children, she carried the mug to a seat with a view. She'd always been an excellent people reader. Not, as it turned out, that it mattered.

She squeezed the tea bag by its string around the spoon, then set both on the table. The little girl spoke earnestly to the man who held her. Quinn could have sworn she was his child, their features and coloring so similar.

When Noelle asked the boy his choice, he cried, "Chocolate crepes!" The kid could have a career in broadcasting.

"Choc-late crepes," the fairy child mimicked with far less volume and precious pronunciation.

Noelle went to the counter and placed their order. When she turned with the tray, their glances met. "Quinn? Hello."

Sipping her tea, Quinn raised her fingers in a wave, then lowered the cup when Noelle stepped toward her. "Your kids are cute."

"Oh." Noelle glanced over her shoulder. "The little girl's my niece, but that rascal Liam is mine."

So the little girl was the first man's, and Noelle really was with the rancher. Thus the truck, not the Jaguar. "Liam looks like his dad, his expressions especially."

"And every bit as determined." She laughed softly. "Want to join us?"

Quinn looked at the overcrowded table. "I'll just finish my tea and run. I'm cleaning out Vera's house."

"That's a project."

To say the least. "How's Matilda?"

"Not much fazed, I think. Our properties adjoin and the grass tastes the same on our side. But if she does prefer the other, it won't be a problem. My husband, Rick" — she tipped her head his way — "made RaeAnne an offer on the land."

"What about the house?"

"She'll sell that separately."

"Mommy!" Liam hollered.

Noelle cast another glance over her shoulder. "Better feed my starving child."

Quinn watched her and then, more openly, the little ones. If the girl was her niece, then the first man was her brother, or married to her sister. She couldn't get a clear view of his ring hand. But when the husband, Rick, said something, the other man's expression shifted. Brothers. They were brothers. Quinn sat back and sipped, an unfamiliar sensation in her chest.

■ ■ ■ ■

Morgan frowned. Rick's attempt to interest him in the slight, dark-haired woman irritated him almost as much as Noelle's ever-present concern. "For future reference, Rick, my own eyes work just fine." Though small, the woman would never be inconspicuous.

"They don't see three inches past Livie."

"What else is there to see?" He spoke over his daughter's head as she dipped a fingertip in the chocolate.

"Me, Uncle Morgan!" Liam declared.

He frowned at the kid. "Who are you again?"

"Liam!"

Noelle shushed him. "Don't encourage it, Morgan. This shouting is not cute."

Morgan grinned. "Oh yeah. Little Will."

"Wil-li-am. Liam!" He pressed the side of his hand into the middle of the crepe, oozing chocolate out both ends. "I'm not little Will. I'm Liam."

"Don't play with your food." Rick nudged his hand off the crepe.

"Livie does."

"Livie's two."

Producing a tiny fork-spoon from his pocket, Morgan gave it to his daughter. "Tools are what separate us from the animals."

"That and opposable thumbs," Rick said.

"And the ability to reason," Noelle rounded it out.

"Hands work better." Liam gave the crepe another karate chop.

Morgan had to smile at Rick getting a kid more headstrong than he. Olivia on the other hand was perfect — sweet-natured and affectionate, with an impish streak like a vein of silver and a gold dusting of feistiness. Why would he ever look past that?

"I'm just saying," Rick said, lowering his voice, "at some point that little girl's going to want a mother."

Not to put too fine a point on it. For almost two years now, Livie had shared Noelle with Liam as a sibling would, though no sibling had yet . . . Or had one . . . He narrowed his eyes. "Something you guys haven't told me?"

"How did you do that?" Rick leaned back in his chair.

Morgan rubbed Livie's back as she switched her little fork from one hand to the other, testing proficiency. "You say go get a life; you mean yours is moving on."

"I didn't say go get a life."

"No, you wouldn't. But that's the point, isn't it?"

Noelle touched his hand. "It's not because I'm pregnant —"

"But you are." Had they gone four years between children because of him and Livie?

"What's pregnant?" Liam stuffed a drippy end of chocolate crepe into his mouth.

Living on a brood ranch, he presumed the kid had an inkling, but neither parent offered insight.

Noelle leaned in. "We want you to be happy."

Her version of happy. He didn't contradict. His second book, *Ten Spectacular Ways to Fail — and Why CEOs Choose To,* had flown up the bestseller list faster than *Money Magic by the Success Guru.* There was no reason to believe his nearly completed work-in-progress would do any less.

Like Beethoven, the subject of TSO's metal rock opera, Morgan Spencer brought forth brilliance from agony, birthing as great a fame and wealth as the "vaporous wizard," who refused signings and tours, as he had being the turnaround specialist who took corporations from ashes to blazing suns.

Everything he touched thrived — except the people he loved, and he'd be damned, literally, before he lost Livie. *"Jesus loves you,"* Kelsey had told him in the letter he read after she died, in the crash when he almost joined her, in his heart even now. But that love had an edge so sharp, blood spilled before he ever felt the blade.

The past two years, with help from Rick and Noelle, he'd been everything Livie needed, present and more than accounted for. But he'd disrupted their lives long enough. He tuned back in to their conversation as Rick said he had fencing to tear out from the new pasture.

Noelle lowered her cup. "RaeAnne took your offer?"

"Yep. Now she just needs to dump the house."

The house. Morgan tipped back in his chair as a thought occurred. Out of sight of Rick's log complex, but close enough if Livie needed Noelle. His real home waited in Santa Barbara, but for now . . .

CHAPTER 2

Morgan parked the Range Rover that replaced his Maserati during inclement months in front of the house he'd come to see. Unlike Rick's western log house and cabins, this single-level ranch was nothing special, a rectangle with a peaked center, probably a low cathedral ceiling in the living room. Not looking for permanence or even investment, he only cared that it was livable in this step toward independence for his daughter and himself.

If not for Livie, he'd have thrown himself into the all-consuming milieu where he turned coal into diamonds — to hear the pundits tell it. Instead he'd put to paper the tenets of his success and welcomed their use by any and all.

Maybe he would return to the corporate world, but it could not be traumatic for Livie. And so he got out and surveyed the house. No sign indicated a listing yet, and he'd just as soon make an offer without real estate agents. His lawyer could handle the details. The bell made an asthmatic wheeze he wasn't sure carried anywhere.

Trying the door when no one came, he found it open and called, "Hello?" He'd like a quick look to make sure nothing ruled the place out.

The woman who exited the bedroom caught him by surprise. It was the one from the bakery. "You're RaeAnne?"

She looked equally taken aback. "Quinn."

He took in the elfin features, the dark tumble of hair moments from jailbreak from its clip. "Does that come with a first name?"

"Quinn Reilly. Quinn for my grandpa's favorite hound."

"You're named after a dog?" And admitting it.

"Not just any dog. A bluetick hound with a nose like none before or since."

"Huh." In spite of himself he ran his eyes down her slight figure in jeans and threadbare sweatshirt that reminded him of one he wore on his balcony when he didn't care if the salt air drifted in.

"Did you want something?" She placed her hands on her hips.

"To see RaeAnne about the house."

"Oh. She flew home. I have a number though."

"That would be good." He looked around. "Can I walk through?"

"Not easily. I'm going through Vera's stuff."

"I just need a sense of the place, to see if it works."

"For you?" Surprise found her eyes, though he didn't know what difference it made to her.

He cocked his head. "Is that a problem?"

"Not for me. I'm just doing a job."

He nodded. "I'll take a quick peek and get out of your way."

She shrugged and went back to the bedroom; at least he thought there was a bed under the heaping clothes. Quinn pulled a pair of pants from a drawer and checked it methodically — pockets, lining, seams — then added it to the pile on the bed.

"Looking for something?"

"I'm . . . sorting."

"Thoroughly."

She cast him a look. "Yep."

He found her laconic approach to conversation interesting. He hadn't experienced many women who said less than necessary. Taking a quick cruise through the single level that would keep life with Livie simple, he returned to Quinn, still sorting clothes. "Is there a basement?"

"A cellar." She sat back on her heels. "I understand it's not habitable."

"Oh?"

"This house was built on the foundation of an asylum."

"No way."

She shrugged. "That's what RaeAnne said. They sent people up the mountain to 'rest their minds.' "

Not at all sure he wanted to live over an asylum, but diabolically intrigued, he said, "Have you seen it?"

"No."

"Want to?"

"No."

He leaned on the doorframe. "Aren't you curious?"

"I see plenty of cellars."

"Not haunted."

She rested her palms on her thighs. "Do you see all this? RaeAnne's mother kept every piece of clothing she ever owned."

Rick had not noticed her for nothing. She had a sort of spark. "Come explore and I'll help you haul those clothes out."

She cocked her head. "You're scared to go alone?"

"I could use a shield."

She narrowed her eyes. "Do you have a name?"

"Morgan."

"Does that come with a first name?"

A smile tugged the corners of his lips. "Morgan Spencer. Now come on, let's see that cellar."

Reluctantly, she rose.

He swung his arm. "Lead on."

She raised what might have been ordinary eyes but were instead espresso brown with lighter starbursts around the pupils. "I'm not going first."

"Scared?"

"The one in front gets all the spider webs."

Something opened up in his chest, something like amusement. "Okay. I'll take the webs. Just show me the way."

"I don't know it."

"What?"

"I've been going through the stuff, not exploring the house."

"Might be stuff down there."

She shuddered. "That's creeping me out."

Since he hadn't seen a door elsewhere, access was probably in the kitchen. The room had very little floor or wall space with all the tables, hutches, cabinets, and a rolling dishwasher. The linoleum popped and crackled like little firecrackers under their feet.

She enclosed herself in her arms. "You know, I'm not —"

"Can't back out now," he said. "We need a nose like none before or since."

"All right. I thought I saw something . . ." She leaned around a massive mahogany hutch. "Is that a door?"

He leaned too and saw it. "Now see, you're living up to your name."

Head tipped, she slid him a look. His mouth twitched.

Together they angled the hutch away from the wall, and with a yank, the door opened to stairs much older than the house. "Cool," he said as a musty draft drifted up. He tried the old wall switch to no effect. "Hmm."

"No doubt there's something in here to use." Quinn pulled open drawer after drawer until she found a flashlight, banged it a few times to get the lamp on, then flashed the dim beam.

"That should work." Taking it, he stepped onto the stairs, pushing a stringy spider web aside. "They seem sturdy, but tread carefully."

He could feel her close behind him, her creaks immediately following his. Thick dust without footprints coated the stairs. The iron railing wobbled but held. Nearing the bottom, he shot the light wide. "Whoa."

She gripped the back of his shirt. "Are you kidding me?"

The space was filled with iron beds, carts, commodes, rubber tubing, and unidentifiable paraphernalia.

She tightened her grip. "Are those chains?"

He focused the beam on a bed rail. "I think you'd say shackles."

"I'm beyond freaked."

He took the final step down.

"Wait, wait, wait. We're not going in."

"Don't chicken out now." He trailed the light slowly across the darkness, pausing on a glass-faced cabinet near the wall. "Check that out." He felt her straighten, interest kindling as the light ran over dusty bottles on the inner shelves. "Tinctures of newt and eye of bat?"

She shifted her grip to his arm, excitement trumping concern. "Can we get to it?"

"I thought we weren't going in." Swinging the lantern beam to illuminate her face, he eyed her, all pent-up energy and impatience.

"Do you think we'll die?"

"No, but squeeze any harder and I might lose that arm."

"Oh!" She looked down and let go.

He swept aside a dust-coated cobweb and moved between two beds stacked sideways on his right and three to his left.

"Who would build a house on top of all this?" Her voice sounded thin.

"Someone who didn't want to dig and pour a new foundation."

"With all these things inside?"

"Know what it'll take to clean it out?"

"No. But I guess I'll find out."

He half turned.

"I bought the contents of the house, so it's my problem."

He pushed through several carts, the wheels of one wailing like a ghost. "You could contact a museum."

"Like anyone would want this junk." But when he illuminated the drug cabinet, she moved past him and wiped the glass with her sleeve. Didn't make much difference as far as he could tell. The glass itself looked milky.

She pulled the metal knob. "It's locked. Think we can carry it up to the light?"

She seemed serious. The cabinet was his height though narrow, hardwood and beveled glass. "You'd be risking the contents."

"Not if we keep it tipped just right."

He shrugged. "High or low on the stairs?"

She looked over her shoulder. "I guess realistically I better take top."

"Good call." It put her backward for the climb, but he'd bear the weight. "Just a sec." He stuck the flashlight into his waistband in back, sending an insipid light to the ceiling that prevented total darkness as they dislodged the cabinet. They pushed it through the path he'd made, then hoisted it up each riser, the bottles jangling against each other.

At the top, they brought the cabinet into the scant remaining floor space and slowly righted it. Even so the bottles tinkled and tumbled. "I guess a locksmith could get it open."

She fingered the knob and keyhole. "I have a whole box of skeleton keys someone collected for about two hundred years."

"Long-lived."

"I mean the keys date back —" She caught the joke and said, "One of those might work."

He dragged his thumb through the dust

along a crease. "Or you could leave it sealed. Let it keep its secrets."

She turned. "Why?"

"It's been in the dark a long time."

"Don't you want to know what's in the bottles?"

Turning pensive he asked, "What'll you sell this for?"

"I have no idea. I don't usually handle furniture."

"I'll give you a thousand dollars — as is."

"What?"

"I want to keep it here in the kitchen."

"It's not your kitchen."

"It will be. I'm making RaeAnne a cash offer."

She crossed her arms in clear frustration. "We brought it up to see inside."

"One thousand five hundred, intact with the bottles."

"Are you insane?"

A smile twitched. "Think I belong down there? In the shackles, maybe?"

Her expression left no doubt. "I want to open it."

"Then refuse my offer."

She squirmed in the trap. With almost no context, he couldn't guess which way she'd go. But he could nudge. He took out his checkbook, wrote one thousand five hundred dollars to Quinn Reilly, and tore it off. "That's the deal, take it or leave it."

She snatched the check. "I'm not showing you anything else before I see it myself."

"Fair enough," he said. With the exercise ended, the ache inside returned like a guard who'd looked away for a second, then resumed scrutiny.

Watching him leave the kitchen, Quinn had the same sensation she'd experienced outside the patisserie — desolation. One moment those indigo eyes probed and teased, the next they caved in like bad ice, leaving fathomless black water.

She moved down the hall and jumped when he came out of the bedroom behind a heaping pile of clothes. "What are you doing?"

"I told you I'd haul these out."

"I didn't think you meant it."

"I wouldn't say it otherwise." His lackluster tone had a razor-thin edge.

She watched him carry armful after armful of clothes to his Range Rover until at last he came back inside, rubbing his hands from the chill.

"That's all I can fit. Where do you want them taken?"

"There's a church in town that sends them to a mission."

He nodded. "I'll drop them with Pastor Tom."

"You know him?"

Now the edge found his eyes, but in truth,

Morgan didn't seem like a man who'd know the pastor by name.

"Right." She broke the stare. "Thanks for your help and . . . purchase." She'd been too flabbergasted to haggle.

"You're welcome. Hope you find what you're looking for."

She hadn't admitted to searching, but he'd obviously analyzed and drawn conclusions. If she was smart she'd do the same. Maybe he didn't have fifteen hundred dollars and his check would bounce. That suspicion seeped in with an acidic burn.

She still had possession of the cabinet, so it wouldn't matter except in principle. Still, she couldn't stand dishonesty, hated it almost as much as cruelty. Being the victim of lies as a little child had first baffled, then demoralized her. Now it infuriated her to encounter even senseless, supposedly harmless deceit.

Bundling into her coat, she hurried to her truck and drove home, parking not at her little house but the big metal storehouse barn on the side of the property. Chafing her chilly hands, she fired up her laptop and searched Morgan Spencer.

Moments later, her jaw fell slack. "Oh. My."

Videos, images, articles, and blogs. Awards, events, international corporate news. She read one business article about his second *New York Times* bestseller. *Elusive corporate specialist Morgan Spencer avoids the public eye as his fame and success crescendo. . . .*

Quinn gaped. She'd clung to a world-famous mogul. Huffing a laugh, she shook her head. She should have charged five thousand.

With his head to the steering wheel, Morgan sat alone in the night, clutching his baby's monitor to his chest, the engine unturned in the Maserati that would fly if he let it. Outside in the car was as far as he could go, and that only because the lights of the monitor would show what he might not hear over the pure-pitched speakers throbbing words he knew by heart from countless repetitions.

A life leaving nothing behind. No dream to echo in time.

Hours ago, he'd typed the final word of his third book and sent the file without once looking back to revisit what he'd written. He'd laid out the core of his philosophy, everything that made his zenith shine. Whoever could reproduce it, let them. Let others save the world.

Visions and dreams dismembered. Nothing remembered. Everything lost in this night.

Once, he'd fed on the cool certainty, the razor-sharp focus and adrenaline of the contest, recognizing potential and turning disasters around, seeing problems and finding solutions no one else saw. Now it was all ashes in his mouth, shades laughing softly in the night wind.

A few strides might get him the sympathy of his brother and even Rick's wife, but no matter how close they were, in the end, it was his own effort to put one foot in front of the other, step by step by step.

All his successes, yet he hadn't seen it coming. Almost two years, and still the stealth and shock of death rocked him. The lyrics had ended, and in their place came the caring platitudes.

"What could you do? You weren't even there."

He'd been useless to his wife and worse than useless to Kelsey, his vigorous bone marrow damaging one organ after another when she had nothing to fight back with.

"You did all you could. It was out of your hands."

The hope had been a slim one, but he'd believed. He was golden. He'd save her, and then he and Jill could know her. Only he hadn't. Morgan Spencer wasn't God. If he were, Kelsey would be here, *Jill* would be here.

Instead . . .

The piercing-clear moon showed his face in the rearview mirror. The kings of the earth rise up and the one enthroned in heaven laughs.

CHAPTER 3

Vera's second bedroom smelled of ancient sachets and floral body powder, a whisper of spring on an autumn day. No guessing what color the room was painted or if it had a window. Quinn pressed between folded piles of textiles, including bolts of fabric and batting for apparently unfinished projects. It made her think of Grandma Pearl's quilts, none fashioned from store fabric but from dresses and shirts no longer worn. Maybe she got her penchant for salvaging and recycling from the woman she'd loved only second to Pops.

Without the pocket doors on the closet, she'd have never gotten to the clothes inside. She pushed them into their slots and dug her fingers between hangers packed so tightly the polyester had nearly fused. Better insulation than a prairie soddy, but she had to wonder, what made the woman fortify her home this way?

Gripping a wooden hanger, she used her

weight to pull a woolen blazer free. The first in a battalion of forgotten clothes, it yielded only a grocery receipt. On the receipt she read a penciled reminder to call Ray. RaeAnne, she assumed — Vera's bright ray of sunshine.

With that first chink in the wall, the next hangers offered less resistance. In the chartreuse dinner jacket she felt a lump in the cuff of one sleeve. Turning it up, she found the lining held closed by a safety pin. She removed the pin, and a pearl earring fell into her hand.

Though RaeAnne had relinquished everything but the locket, originally she said to leave all jewelry, so this find needed clarification. Quinn took out her phone and called. "Sorry to bother you at work."

"Please, bother me." RaeAnne's throaty twang brought a smile. "Did you —"

"I haven't found it."

RaeAnne made a long, heartfelt sigh.

"But that ring you found in a sock isn't the whole story. I just found an earring pinned inside a sleeve." As she spoke, she felt the other cuff, but didn't find the match. "It's a good-sized pearl, but I don't know whether it's real."

"I doubt it. She only ever bought costume."

"You went through the jewelry she had accessible." Quinn fingered the earring, thinking. "But this was hidden, and I'm wonder-

ing why."
"You can't ask why with Vera. She just did things."
"You said she had all her faculties."
"No old-age issues. But she wasn't what anyone would call typical."
"Maybe someone gave it to her, someone important."
That gave RaeAnne pause. "There's only one?"
"So far."
"Maybe you could hold onto the things she's done something stranger than usual with."
"Okay." She laid the jacket on the pile. "I'll keep those objects together, and you can make a decision when I'm done." She didn't want RaeAnne to come out of the situation with regrets from choices made in haste. Or grief. Or the anger and disillusionment of unresolved issues.
Getting back to work, Quinn realized as the clothes went down in size they increased in style and elegance. At size twelve, there were vintage designer gowns she would definitely sell through her online store. Easier to believe the pearl real when paired with a gold lamé gown. Vera would have looked quite the dame in that.
The pockets of the polyester pantsuits with slinky Qiana blouses and wide '70s lapels yielded nothing more interesting than hand-

kerchiefs, emery boards, and ticket stubs, but the hem of a shoulder cape had been loop stitched over a Venetian-glass necklace. Holding it to her chest, Quinn pictured Vera in a gondola with the opera-style cape over her shoulders and the beads glittering in moonlight. She imagined the man in the locket perched beside her on the cushioned seat.

"Do you like the necklace, my dear?" she asked the empty room.

"I *adore* it."

Laughing, she placed the necklace with the earring. Everything had a history, even if no one knew it. Confident she'd find the locket secreted like the necklace and earring, she resumed her search. Piece after piece of clothing moved through her fingers, but no locket. Not pinned into any cuffs, not sewn into any hems. It was not in the lingerie drawers of the dresser, not in the trunks that produced every conceivable linen from embroidered pillowcases to Christmas stockings to latch-hook rugs.

The matching vanity yielded lipsticks and sticky brown, mostly evaporated perfumes. The bottles might have value to product-line collectors, so she carefully packed them into a container and loaded it into her truck with the usable clothing and fabric goods. The brilliant sunshine had produced a vibrant October day she took a moment to enjoy, breathing deeply of the piney scent before going back in. She was getting a sense of Vera that should be helping the quest but so far hadn't.

Size-ten shoe boxes bricked the wall floor to ceiling, double deep. All held shoes, except those filled with clothing tags and tags with tiny bags of spare buttons and beads and tags with receipts stapled on. Tags and receipts she dumped, but she could probably match the novelty items to things from the closet, which would add value.

From the toe of one pink leather pump, she drew a butterfly pin studded with blue stones of differing hues. Lifting the butterfly on her palm, she watched the light glitter through the stones like sunlight on an aqua sea. "Butterflies shouldn't be locked in boxes," she told it. Nor should things that matter be hidden behind heaps of camouflage, like a heart sealed by ever-thickening walls.

She moved into the kitchen, shook and sifted open containers of oatmeal and cornstarch and baking soda while she sorted and boxed the canned and dry goods for a charitable donation. She checked and emptied the containers in the fridge and freezer, something RaeAnne would surely have done if she hadn't been absorbed in finding the locket.

With her arm pressed to her forehead, she glanced at the asylum cabinet, brooding in the center of the floor. She could almost hear it calling, "Open me." What if the locket was in there? Vera knew about the cellar, might have known about the cabinet. She couldn't imagine her down there at eighty-two with hips wider than RaeAnne's, but perhaps when she was younger.

Quinn pushed her hair back and looked once more at the milky glass panes obscuring the contents. It belonged to Morgan — as is. But she might search everywhere else and find it was in the cabinet all along. Shouldn't she rule it out? Her fingers itched.

She'd brought the skeleton keys with her — in case Morgan changed his mind, but how would she know? Since he'd seen what he needed of the house, he wasn't likely to return before she finished. The locket might be inside one of the bottles, and there was no way she could check without leaving signs of tampering. She groaned. Why had she taken the check? Immediately her sense returned. Fifteen hundred dollars was why.

She'd spent the previous evening photographing and listing items that didn't require research. Everything from the cellar would. How much for shackles? She shuddered, casting a glance at the door. She'd have to go through it sometime, but she'd felt a creepiness down there, and going alone into dark, confined spaces violated her safety code.

With Livie holding his finger, Morgan entered Rudy's general store, a dark-stained wood-plank exterior with green roof that reminded him of Lincoln Logs. Inside was a magical place for a little person who loved fishing flies as much as toys. As always, she ran to the case that held them arrayed like jewels, pressed her little hands to the glass, and stared in. Moving from one end of the long counter to the glassed end, Rudy bent and peered at her through the display. A superb judge of character, Livie didn't jump back but studied him in kind.

Wordlessly, he pulled one of the drawers toward himself. With big, blunt fingers, he took one brilliant bead-and-feather fly out and stood up tall. Livie's eyes followed him, her chin tipping up and up. He bent over and lowered the fly. Morgan almost stopped him, then realized it had no hook. Why would Rudy make a fishing fly with no hook? But then he knew.

Livie stretched out her hand, and Rudy laid the thing on her tiny palm. Rapt, she scrutinized its form and design, the iridescent colors. No scientist in a lab could have researched it more thoroughly.

Morgan met Rudy's eye, both their mouths twitching. He said, "Like that, Livie?"

"*Like* it, Daddy." She held it higher for him to see.

He and Rudy hadn't discussed her fascination, yet the burly mountain man had obviously prepared this for her next appearance.

"It's awesome, Rudy. You're an artist." How those big hands made something so intricate, delicate, and minuscule, he didn't know.

"Just a hookless fly." But pleasure lit the yellow-green eyes beneath shaggy russet brows. Morgan took out his wallet, but Rudy waved him off. "Seeing her face is enough."

He slid the wallet back, not insulting Rudy with an argument. Cradling the fly in both hands against her chest, Livie trailed behind him like a pint-sized shadow as he picked up the items he'd come for and laid them on the counter. After paying, he crouched in front of Livie. "Would you like to tell Rudy something?"

She studied him a minute, then looked up at Rudy. "Thank you this fly."

Rudy grinned. "You're welcome, little miss."

Livie giggled. "No li'l miss. Livie."

"Oh." Rudy looked astonished. "Well, now I know."

Smiling, Morgan gave him a wave and led her out by a finger. Moments like these seemed to crystalize and hang in the air like something wonderful, just out of reach. He buckled his daughter into her seat, kissed her forehead, and laid his hand over hers still holding the fly as though it might spring into the sky. "You're pretty special, you know."

"You special, Daddy."

He placed another kiss in her hair, inhaling

her scent, and then stepped back and closed the door. A truck pulled up to the pumps at the other end of the lot. Quinn slipped out and moved toward the pump controls. In another life, he'd have greeted her. Since she didn't see him, he got into the Range Rover and drove away.

Early the next morning, Quinn got back to it. Ordinarily she'd have the furniture picked up as is, but because of the locket, she scrutinized the underside linings, fingering every pillow, unzipping the sofa cushions, feeling down between the seats and sides and backs. Seven ten-dollar bills rewarded her search. But no locket.

She drew the line at cutting into the stuffing. Vera's hiding places had been amateurish and noninvasive. No sense ruining things that could be used by others. She was feeling good about her progress — until she entered the dining room. There Vera had reached true hoarder status, or suffered an avalanche of mail and subscriptions.

The thought of going through everything felt like a preview of hell. She narrowed her eyes. Was that assistant really champing at RaeAnne's job, or had she taken one look in the room and run? Quinn went in, and squealed when a mouse skittered from behind one stack to another. Not surprising her first rodent encounter at Vera's happened in the room most wildlife friendly.

It wouldn't bother her except that cute, tawny-colored mouse with creamy cheeks was a deer mouse that could transmit hantavirus. Because of that, she kept a misting bottle of bleach water in her truck. Heading out for it, she paused when Noelle's truck pulled up, though it was her husband, Rick, who climbed out wearing a dark brown vest over a heavy shirt. At this elevation, she'd have wanted sleeves on that jacket. Except in the heat of summer, her arms were always cold.

"Hi." He approached her, bearing a trace of stable scent. "I'm Rick from the next ranch over."

She nodded. "We met at the bakery — except for names, though Noelle told me yours. I'm Quinn."

"She told me yours too." His eyes creased. "I'm just letting you know I'll be taking down the fence back there."

"Joining yours and Morgan's properties?"

Rick frowned. "Morgan's?"

"You know . . . the house?"

"What does the house have to do with Morgan?"

And of course she realized her mistake. "You should talk to him, I guess." She got the bleach sprayer and bandanna from the truck and started back in.

"Are you saying Morgan's buying this house?" He seemed not only puzzled but annoyed. Or maybe it was worry. Rick was not easy to read.

"I'm a little caught between here."

Apologizing, he fit his lanky form back into his truck and drove around the house, through the pasture gate to the tumbledown fence. Quinn tied the bandanna over her mouth and nose, went inside, and applied a fine mist around the perimeter of the dining room to quell any dust-borne virus. Half an hour later, when she went to the kitchen sink to wash her hands, she saw Morgan in the pale golden pasture working beside Rick with, seemingly, no harm done.

Morgan didn't have Rick's rustic edges, but seeing them together again, the similarities stood out. Morgan shook his head at something Rick said, and Rick shrugged. Just two guys, brothers. And yet there was something compelling in their interaction, a sibling substance of respect and affection. Not always a given, she well knew.

Feeling like a spy, she took a step back and bumped her heel into the foot of the asylum cabinet. She thought again how the locket could be in there. This was her chance to change Morgan's mind, but she'd have to tell him RaeAnne's tale to get any traction, and she felt protective of something so sensitive. Admitting that wasn't the only reason she wanted a look, she left the kitchen with her word intact.

She'd given the bleach time to work and started sorting and clearing. Though it was a mild solution, the fumes made her eyes water. The dust made her sneeze. The bandanna helped with both, but she was relieved to step out of the dining room when her phone rang.

Sadly, it was RaeAnne hoping for good news. After finding the earring and pin, they had both believed yesterday's clothes would yield the locket, but now she told her, "Sorry, not yet. I'm attacking the dining room now, and then, of course, there's the cellar."

"Do you think it could be down there?"

"Anything's possible." She described the cabinet she and Morgan had found, hoping RaeAnne might say, "Quinn, you have to look inside." But it didn't happen, so she said, "There are any number of places it could be down there."

"I had no idea. Oh, Quinn, I don't know what I'd do without you."

The job had certainly expanded. "It's okay."

"Can you use that stuff in the cellar for your online store?"

"I have no idea. I mainly sell collectibles." She peered through the dining room doorway to the cabinet. She'd been after the bottles until Morgan claimed it. And speaking of that, "Did you get an offer on the house?"

"I meant to tell you, it's sold."

And his brother had no idea.

"We close in November."

"That was fast."

"Full price too."

Naturally.

"Isn't that a godsend? Real estate is hardly moving these days. And in an out-of-the-way place like Juniper Falls, I thought it would take forever."

Out-of-the-way was exactly why she'd landed in Juniper Falls. "Do you want any of what's in the cellar?"

"What on earth would I do with it?"

"Sell or donate to a museum? It could be valuable."

"You know, I'll just leave that to you." Her voice caught. "Quinn, what if you don't find the locket?"

She wished she could assure her. "You've gone this long without knowing, RaeAnne. Would it be so awful to keep it that way?"

"Feels like it." She sniffled. She'd just lost her mother and had counted on seeing who her dad was.

"I'm doing my very best."

"I know that. I could see you would."

Quinn stared at the still-heaping dining room. "If you think of anything else your mom might have said, or any peculiar ways she had that might shed some light . . ."

"I've been racking my brain. She had plenty of peculiar ways, like moving to that mountain at seventy. Can you imagine?"

Quinn leaned against the wall. "I guess old

age is as good a time as any to do something. There's so much less to lose."

RaeAnne said, "I never thought of it that way. You have such interesting insights."

A knock at the kitchen door startled her. "Oh. Someone's here. I better go."

"Okay, but —"

"I'll let you know the minute there's news." Ending the call, she admitted Morgan, holding his bleeding hand. "Yikes."

"It looks worse than it is," Morgan told her, "but can I use the sink?"

"Your sink? In your kitchen?"

Not quite, but close enough.

She emptied and removed a basin, then turned on the water. "How come Rick didn't know?"

He hissed as the water streamed over the gash running from the web of his thumb across the pulpy part of his palm.

Leaning in, she winced. "Barbed wire?"

"Rick's pulling it out so the horses won't get cut."

"Guess you didn't think about gloves." She turned his hand under the stream for a better look, her hair brushing his cheek. "When was your last tetanus shot?"

He drew a husky breath. "I'm up to date, Nurse Reilly."

She darted a look. "And cranky. Does blood make you dizzy? I knew a six-and-a-half-foot lavender farmer who fainted at the sight of it, especially his own."

He hissed again when her ministration ran the water over the jagged end in the web. "I don't intend to faint." Holding his teeth aligned, he reached for a paper towel.

"Don't." She pulled it away. "Let me get a fresh roll." She ripped the plastic off a new roll of towels. "I've been all over the house with that other." She tore off two sheets and quickly folded them, then reached for his hand, briefly drying the back side before pressing the packing to his palm.

His chest was not functioning correctly. "I could do this, you know."

"It's hard one-handed while you're streaming blood."

"I think I've got it now."

She looked up, almost right under his chin and close enough he could tell the starbursts in her coffee-dark eyes were amber. She slid her hand off as he took over the pressure, then turned off the water. "If your buying the house was a secret, I'm afraid I blew it. I assumed your brother —"

"It's no big deal." Finally taking his eyes from her face, he noticed the bandanna around her neck. "You riding herd?"

She gave the scarf a little tug. "On mice."

He didn't want her to be cute and funny and helpful and caring.

"The bandanna's in case of hantavirus."

Good. He made a slow nod. Think of disease. Mice. Scat.

Her chin had a soft point that rounded up to the base of her lip. His eyes felt hooded, because they wouldn't rise any higher.

"Are you okay?"

He must have run a lot of blood down the drain to feel so light-headed and tongue-tied.

"Lean against the counter."

"I don't need to." But he did it, keeping pressure on his throbbing palm and glad for the pain.

"So I brought the skeleton keys I mentioned to try in the cabinet." She motioned toward the box on the big mahogany hutch.

He welcomed the distraction. "Did you find one that works?"

"I didn't try any. It's your cab—"

At the sound of Rick's truck, he pushed off the counter and moved toward the door. "If it matters to you, go ahead."

"That's not what I —"

He pulled open the door and stepped out.

"— meant."

It wasn't quite a slam, just an awkwardly closed door.

Rick eyed him when he got in the truck. "Stitches?"

"Probably."

Doc Bennington was older than Moses and no plastic surgeon, but he could still stitch up a slashed palm. As long as the hand worked, what was one more scar?

Rick dropped him off at the faded blue Victorian house Doc retired in and practiced from. With no office help, he didn't take appointments or insurance, which put some people off — thankfully. There was only one patient ahead of him, a woman with a howling cough that sounded like a wolf-seal crossbreed. After that, Doc took a look at his palm, probed and stretched, and finally tacked it with several stitches, using a numbing agent that would have put down a horse.

He wrote a scrip for antibiotics and painkillers they filled at the drugstore-minimart. Back at the ranch, he found Noelle reading to both kids on the brown leather couch in the slanting sunrays through the great room window. Livie's intense expression revealed astonishing concentration, but Liam immediately jumped down and ran to him.

"What's wrong with your hand?"

"Alligator bit it."

Liam's eyes got big. "Where is it? Can I see?"

"Nah. Took one taste of Uncle Morgan and flew away."

"Alligators don't fly."

"They don't? Must have been a pterodactyl."

"Can I see?" His brown eyes widened even more.

"Too late — it's gone." Morgan roughed

the kid's head.

Noelle's fair brow furrowed with concern. "What happened?"

"Just a cut."

"Five stitches," Rick supplied, coming in behind.

"I want to see the pterodactyl," Liam bellowed.

"Uncle Morgan's imagining things," Rick told him.

"Nuh-uh. He said."

"Sometimes grown-ups exaggerate." Rick patted Liam's head. "So, Morgan. Something you want to tell us?"

Question courtesy of Quinn Reilly. "Oh yeah," he said. "I bought a house." He settled in beside his tiny girl.

Noelle turned with just the mix of surprise and worry he'd expected.

"Livie and I are moving to Vera's. I'll get Consuela out here to keep house and cook." He hadn't expected to leave them speechless.

"But . . ."

"You guys need your space. This'll help me wean Livie from this situation without too abrupt a change, while I figure out what's next."

"That wasn't necessary, Morgan." Rick planted his hands on his hips.

"Yeah, it is. She's two years old."

Noelle said, "That's still a baby."

"Thus the halfway house."

She caressed Livie protectively, wondering, no doubt, if something she'd said or done prompted his decision.

"It's not you. Or Rick. It's just time."

She nodded. "You'll still be close."

"For a while. As soon as Livie's ready, we'll go home. You have another focus now." Noelle was the only mommy Livie knew. But it wasn't working anymore. She was an only child, not the middle offspring of this combined effort.

Unconsciously Noelle touched her belly. Imagining who she'd bring into the world this time? Jill had speculated endlessly — boy or girl, fair or dark, lively or calm, smart, of course, and beautiful.

Her pregnancy had been a breeze, hardly a moment's discomfort until she got big enough to need backrubs, a role he accepted wholeheartedly since he played such a small part in the rest of it. The memory formed a furrow between his brows.

"Down to the right. Now up, up . . . okay over to the left."

"Your whole back, in other words."

"Just where the baby pushes."

"Here?" He squeezed her neck.

"Well, if you insist."

"Baby pushing here?" He squeezed her ankle.

"Just a little." Giggling, she'd taken the whole body massage.

Livie climbed into his lap, pushing up and

wrapping his neck. How did she always know? She caught his face and kissed his mouth, her precious lips rough with a tiny beaklike sucking callous from her likewise calloused thumb.

He hugged her close, breathing her baby scent. Noelle was right. She was still so small. But he was right too. Standing up, he swayed, a little woozy. Doc Bennington was of the old-school mindset that pain meds should render you senseless. "Livie and I will be taking a nap. If anyone hears her wake up and I don't, please barge in."

He felt their stares as he'd felt Quinn Reilly's. As he'd felt . . . her. Intensified, no doubt, by blood loss and painkillers.

CHAPTER 4

Long after Morgan left, he remained on her mind. Not her business, Quinn told herself, since his bleeding hand bore a wedding ring. Even if his marriage was in trouble, as the sadness and isolation might indicate, it didn't involve her.

Given her own situation, getting involved would be doubly unwise. She shook her head with a self-deprecating laugh. Not to mention who the man was. She didn't even understand what he actually did. Author, sure, but turnaround specialist?

With a sigh, she locked up and went home. Tempted to get online and read more about him, she avoided her computer in the barn and went into the house instead. The little she'd gleaned was enough to know about someone off-limits. He'd made that clear, leaving like that when she had only tried to be helpful. That handsome rose had thorns — not big flesh-ripping thorns, but the little ones that pricked an unsuspecting finger that throbbed for days. He could at least have thanked her for the use of the sink . . . his sink. Almost.

She tipped her head back with a groan. She'd gone into the house to stop thinking. At this rate she might as well work on Vera's haul. But no, she'd eat first. She slid the iPod she'd acquired, already loaded with someone's songs, into the dock and touched a playlist. As LeAnn Rimes started in with "Blue," Quinn wondered what kind of music a corporate mogul listened to.

Enough! Turning up the plaintive lament, she grabbed a whisk and used it as a mic, certain no one could tell her voice from LeAnn's. In her kitchen, no one said otherwise.

After vegetable chowder and crusty, chewy bread, she went out back to the warehouse, valued and listed the perfume bottles online, and then chose a DVD from the stacks. She went back inside and watched it in bed with the small DVD player on her lap. Almost every sale had DVDs, and since she hadn't watched movies growing up, these last four years she'd worked through people's collections before listing them online.

It was a bit haphazard but was culturally educational. Anything too stupid, gross, or violent, she closed back up and moved on. Beyond that, she'd enjoyed everything from Disney's *Aladdin* to *Schindler's List.* Now teary from *Finding Neverland,* she snuggled into the covers and had only just dropped off when her phone jarred her awake. She pushed aside her blanket and snatched it up. "Hello?"

"Did you hear?"

She stiffened. "Hannah?"

"He's getting out."

The words doused her like ice water.

"He's getting out and you'll pay for what you did."

Quinn pressed a hand to her racing heart. Hannah was only repeating what she'd heard — the original far more chilling. *"You'll pay for this,"* delivered in a tone so cold it freeze-dried her bones. Had she thought prison would rehabilitate him, that he'd leave her alone when he got out?

It hadn't even been the full five years. Good behavior? Bribes? Lies? Her voice shook. "Hannah, how did you get this number?"

The signal ended. She clenched her fists. Only three people from her old life had her cell phone number, and while none seemed inclined to use it, neither would they give it to Hannah. Or would they?

Her nails made painful dents in her palms. Releasing her fists, she pulled up the rose-colored comforter. The last person who slept beneath it hadn't died, merely included it in their moving sale, but still, she shivered.

With vigorous strokes, Morgan toweled his

hair and face. He hadn't anticipated Consuela's negative response — in loud and colorful Spanish. Yes, the climate and terrain would be a shock, but he paid her to meet his household needs. She was doing that in Santa Barbara, but right now he needed her in Juniper Falls.

Brushing his teeth, he studied his reflection. She would call him gaunt and scold him for not eating. Good. Consuela loved a cause. He lathered and took up his razor. She knew his expectations, his preferences. She knew . . . everything. It would only be until Livie understood the two of them were a family of their own. But if that was his goal, why bring Consuela?

He frowned. This practice of questioning himself had never been part of his makeup. Until Jill died, every decision — good and bad — had been clear and purposeful. Then he let her go out, encouraged it, assuring her he and Livie would be fine, everything would be fine.

He closed his eyes. They weren't fine. How could they be? But he slowly pulled the razor along his jaw. Keeping up appearances.

"Daddy?"

"Coming, peanut."

Twenty minutes later, he'd dressed Livie in a long-sleeve Onesie and tights, minuscule blue jeans, a fuzzy loopy sweater, coat, hat, gloves, and boots. Satisfied his little girl was better fortified than an armored truck, he started out from his cabin to the main house. Golden leaves drifted on the frigid morning air, small gusts tossing them up.

He'd watched quite a few seasons on the ranch over the years, on visits to refresh between high-powered consultations and the year spent healing in body and spirit after Kelsey died, when he'd launched his Vette over a cliff — unintentionally. He'd loved that Corvette.

He should be healing now, and maybe he was. It was just that Livie took so much. . . . No, she didn't take it. He gave. Whatever was inside, he poured into her. And maybe that was the best healing could get.

Livie curled her arms around his neck, chattering. Her vocabulary dazzled him. Everything about her dazzled him. He answered her queries with the smile growing on his face. She'd be okay. They'd be okay. This change was a small one.

He hoped Rick was making breakfast, since Noelle's cooking was an exercise in diplomacy. Unfortunately it was Noelle in the kitchen, stirring oatmeal. He kissed her cheek, then settled Livie into her little seat. Liam came roaring in, flying a fighter jet over his head, and chaos reigned until Noelle provided his cereal.

He was simply high octane. Constructively channeled, he'd do fine. Noelle, on the other hand, looked a little green.

"How are you feeling?"

"Lousy." She sighed. "How well am I hiding it?"

He gave her a sympathetic pat. "Where's Rick?" He half listened while he tied the bib around Livie's little neck, provided a spoon and the small bowl of oaty-mush. She didn't know the difference.

"Want some?"

"Just coffee." Noelle's brew would be trial enough. His mouth watered thinking of Consuela's meals. How had he gone so long without her? Or was his appetite only now awakening? The sooner he got that ball rolling, the better. But rolling Consuela was like opening the tomb — it took supernatural power.

"Maybe I'll have Consuela cook for you too, give you a break."

"What about your house in Santa Barbara? If she comes here, who will keep that?"

A good question. She'd held down the fort out there over all his absences, not only this extended one. "I'll have to figure that out, I guess."

As soon as Livie finished eating, he bundled her up and carried her out the front, where she decided it was better to walk. Leaning on the rail while she one-stepped the stairs up and down on tiptoes, he heard someone's approach. Through the aspen and spindly pines, he watched Quinn coming cross-country from Vera's.

With the drug worn off and no current blood loss, he had no reason for the tightening in his chest, the constriction in his throat. It must be guilt for overreacting, for leaving so rudely.

It didn't stop when she got there, when she crouched down beside Livie on the stairs and said, "Hi, sunshine." Or when she tipped her head and added, "She's stunning, you know. You'll be fending off strapping young men with a stick."

"Didn't realize that included scrappy young women." What was with the edge?

"Ha-ha."

Taking that as a joke showed a tendency to see the best in people, including insolent men. As she straightened, Livie watched with keen and innocent interest, another barometer in Quinn's favor.

"Is this where you're living?"

"Until I move."

"Right. As it happens, I was coming to ask Noelle how to find you."

He waited.

"Salvation Army's coming for the furniture, but I thought one or more of the old hutches and cupboards in the kitchen would look better with that asylum cabinet than something new."

He narrowed his eyes. "Are you hustling

me?" Buying the cabinet had been an experiment. Now she was hitting him up for more?

"I mean I won't have them take anything you want to use."

"Oh." He'd misread her intention, but she didn't back away or rise to the accusation, only corrected his error. This woman held her ground, unobtrusively. "We'll come have a look." He scooped Livie up, since her little strides would take two weeks to reach the house he had not begun to think of as his. Probably never would. It was a world between worlds. A waiting place.

Quinn walked quietly, in the mode he'd first encountered instead of yesterday's chattiness. She'd taken a clue from his rudeness then and now, and he felt a hint of remorse. There was no excuse for discourtesy, especially when she was only taking care of business. As they went in, he noticed the progress she'd made in the rest of the house. While it was still overcrowded with furniture, she'd radically reduced the clutter. Hard worker, Quinn Reilly.

Livie said, "Down, Daddy."

He glanced at Quinn. "Do you mind?"

"That's your call." She pulled the woolen cap off her curly hair. The stuff had a mind of its own but looked soft and shiny. "Remember, I bleach-treated the dining room for the mouse droppings."

"I'll keep her out of there." He did wonder,

though, how risk averse Quinn was — a sort of thought he hadn't entertained for quite a while. Appetite and curiosity. Had his brain begun the slow, grinding churn of a frozen engine starting again after long disuse?

She led the way to the kitchen. "I'm sure you won't want all of this, so pick what stays, and they'll take the rest."

He took Livie's hand and followed Quinn to the kitchen. The asylum cabinet stood exactly as he'd left it. The box of keys still perched on the counter by the sink. "Any luck with the lock?"

Quinn folded her arms. "I haven't tried."

That surprised him, especially since he'd freed her to. "Could be good to have a key."

"It could."

Quinn looked down at Livie, still enraptured by his child. He couldn't really blame her. While he was not that guy who used his daughter as a babe magnet, Livie didn't know it. She just shined.

"I'll keep that big mahogany hutch." He pointed to the piece they'd pulled away from the cellar door. "To block the cellar back up, so Livie won't even think about it."

She peeled a sticky note from a pad and stuck it to the wood.

He looked at the other pieces, some pressed oak, some painted but still showing good bones. "Why don't you sell the furniture? You could get something for these antiques."

"I'd have to haul and ship it." She indicated her small stature. "Not happening."

"No one to give you a hand?"

"I'm a sole proprietor."

Didn't mean she couldn't get help, but he let it go. "How's it going downstairs?"

"I haven't started."

"Not to rush you, but my closing is scheduled for the end of next week."

She raised her brows.

"It's an uncomplicated sale. No liens or financing."

"I'm not sure I'll have the cellar emptied by then."

"We can work on it." He almost said *together* before recalling he needed life simple.

"I still have to deal with the dining room and clean everything for your walk-through."

"You're cleaning too?"

"I traded RaeAnne service for stuff."

He looked around. "Then you ought to sell these antique cupboards and tables. Take pictures and post them at Rudy's general store. I bet they're snatched up in a few days. People like local pieces, and these have obviously been around a while."

"How would I deliver —"

"Post them for pickup. Or use your truck. I'll help you load."

"With your injured hand?"

He looked at the bandage on his palm as though it had just appeared there. Doc's treatment was hazy, but not Quinn's. "It's stitched shut."

"How many stitches?"

"Enough to hold it through eternity."

"Or until you get them out."

"Or that." A smile touched his mouth. "Doc doesn't work halfway. I'll be fine."

She chewed her lower lip. "I'd have to search comparable pieces for pricing."

"Or just decide what you want." From the wallet in his back pocket he took a blank check and wrote it for six hundred dollars. "For mine."

She looked from the check to him. "I already sticky-noted it to stay."

He set the check on the table. "That's no more than it's worth." He'd intentionally kept it reasonable yet high enough to induce her to try the others. She'd be cheating herself otherwise.

"Why do I feel bad?" A search of her face showed she did.

"Because of what I said, about hustling me. But I came here intending to buy, not take."

Still hesitant, she nodded. "I guess I will post the others at the store, if the guy'll let me."

"He'll let you." He didn't imagine many people turned Quinn down, and Rudy was even less likely. Before he started looking for reasons to stay, he said, "I'll see you around," and let his daughter and himself out the back door. They started across the pasture through the trees. This time, she could take as many tiny steps as she wanted.

Quinn looked at the second check Morgan Spencer had written her and wondered if it would be worth more as a collector's piece from the elusive success guru than at face value. The thought of auctioning his signature brought a laugh. Maybe she'd be awestruck if he wasn't so starkly human.

She looked out and saw them under the trees — Livie staring up the white bark of an aspen to the wealth of golden leaves, Morgan staring at his child as though she were worth far more than gold. Quinn pressed a hand to her heart. How could his wife leave them? Or had he left her? No, he'd have taken off the ring. Either he hoped to reconcile, or else . . . That wasn't possible. And if that was the case, the sorrow made sense, the loss in his eyes.

She backed away from the window when he sent a glance over his shoulder. The last thing she wanted was for him to see her watching. She went out the front door to her truck. Using the camera she kept there, she photographed the antiques, drove to her place to price the items and print the pictures, and brought them to the general store.

"Sure you can hang the pictures," the brawny guy behind the counter told her.

"Tape them to the window by the door. I'll point them out and spread the word."

"Okay. Are you Rudy?" And when he nodded, she said, "Thanks, Rudy."

He must have done a good job of talking them up, because, within the hour, a woman bought two of the hutches for displaying her porcelain dolls, and a couple hours later, Rudy called to say a friend of Vera's wanted the pressed-oak cupboard but couldn't pick it up.

She told him, "No problem," and for the second time that day, sought Morgan at Noelle's ranch. Dressed in a collared shirt and khakis, he came out on the porch as she pulled up and powered down the passenger window. "Did you mean what you said?"

"I always do."

"Then I could use you."

He reached inside for a coat, then moved down the steps and let himself into the truck. Not a huge man, he still seemed to shrink the space. "First sale?"

"Third, actually. The first things were picked up."

"You must have priced them to move."

"Anything's more than I would have had." She pulled out. "The oak cupboard's going to a woman right in town."

The thing was heavier than sin, though, both of them struggling. "If you pop your stitches I'm going to feel bad."

He flexed his hand. "I know where to find the doc."

Together they shoved the cupboard on the packing blanket onto the tailgate and into the bed. "This —" she huffed — "is why I don't sell furniture."

He eyed her. "You're pretty strong for your size."

The unaccustomed warmth was out of proportion to what might not even be a compliment. It just felt good to have someone in her corner. "If Minnie has stairs, we're in trouble."

Minnie did have stairs, but the cupboard stayed on the first floor in the kitchen, where they got it after removing the door at the hinges. She absolutely would never sell furniture online.

Going back outside as the sun sent scarlet flame across the rosy sky, Morgan raised his head. "Hear that?"

She said, "Elk." The screeching bugle was unmistakable.

"Someone's proud of himself."

"That noise would make me run."

His mouth pulled sideways. "Good thing you're not a lady elk."

She cast him a glance. "Thanks for not calling me a cow."

The corners of his eyes crinkled as he pulled the truck door open.

She left him at Noelle's and went home

herself. The more she saw of him, the less she could imagine his alter ego. Without the Internet pictures proving his fame, he'd be just a guy — a devastating guy with as much baggage as she.

Watching Quinn leave, Morgan turned at the sound of hooves as his brother cantered into the yard on his fine roan stallion. A dark rust color and perfectly proportioned, Destiny had great bloodlines, and Rick knew how to make the most of it. With his expert training, Destiny's foals brought top dollar.

Man and beast halted by mutual consent with a stilled power awesome to behold, especially knowing how many times Rick had landed in the dirt and gotten back on to accomplish it. "Was that Quinn's truck?" he said.

Morgan nodded.

"Problems with the house?"

"I helped her move something."

Rick dismounted. "It's a huge undertaking for one person. You ought to help her out."

"I just did."

"I mean —"

"I know what you mean."

Rick stroked the horse's neck. "It is your house." He was saying more than that.

"Not yet." Unlike Rick, Quinn hadn't made his helping personal. At one time their playful repartee would have prompted an invitation for more. Either she read his boundaries or the edges warned her off — a good thing either way.

Noelle came out with Livie and called them for dinner.

Rick said, "I'll just see to Destiny," and headed for the stable.

Morgan joined Noelle and reached for his child. "Hey, jelly bean."

She smiled. "Not jelly bean."

"Sweet pink cotton-candy bean."

"You . . . green jelly bean."

"No, that's Liam. I'm black licorice." He made his voice growly.

"Don't like *licrish.*"

"But I do." He dove for her neck with his mouth. Recalling the delight Quinn took in his little girl — whether he invited it or not — a smile touched his lips. She got points for spunk. And pure good taste.

Chapter 5

Given the guilt Rick had spooned on like sugar when it was really cayenne, Morgan took his little girl the next morning for a drive to Vera's house. Quinn hadn't requested any more help, and her truck wasn't outside, though it could be in the garage, given the bitter weather. He jogged through windblown ice flecks from a sullen sky that ached to do worse. The truck was in there, so he fetched Livie and banged on the front door.

He'd intentionally come when Rick and his family were otherwise occupied so they wouldn't get ideas and feel freer with advice than they already were. His younger brother's nudges irritated him, even when they sometimes happened to be right. Clearing out the house was a big job for one person.

Quinn opened the door tentatively, then, seeing them, pulled it wide and spoke to his child. "Hi, you." She gave Livie a puckish smile, then raised her gaze. "If you really don't want people falling for her, you ought to keep her locked up."

"No use. She'd shine through the cracks."

Her eyes sparkled. "No doubt. So what did you want?"

"Just seeing if you need help with cupboards or anything."

She gave him a puzzled look. "I do know where you live."

And thanks to Rick, he now felt stupid, a feeling he had little acquaintance with and less affection for. "Any luck with your search?" He glanced into the dining room still heaped with paper. She'd made progress but not a whole lot.

"The best I can say is I haven't lost my mind."

Kind of endearing how committed she was to someone else's cause. How would Rae-Anne even know if she scooped the whole mess out with a bulldozer?

She said, "I'm not bothering with the unopened mail. Anything else could be relevant."

"Sold any more cupboards?" He moved on to the kitchen.

"As you see, we're down to one hutch besides yours and a couple of tables. I'll probably let the Salvation Army have the rest."

He eyed the pieces and agreed. "Let them."

"What are you doing for furniture?"

"Getting some." He set Livie down.

"Mmm. Well, unless you want to dive with

me into the dining room . . ."

"Not happening."

"Yeah. If I don't finish the stacks today I'm coming back with matches."

Again the amusement caught him. She wasn't trying to be funny, she just was. "Any luck with keys?"

"I told you, I haven't —"

He walked over to the box that surely held every size and shape of skeleton key made. Reaching in, he grabbed a handful and tried them one by one.

She rolled onto the balls of her feet, eager in that childlike way she had, like Livie waiting for ice cream. "What are you going to do if it opens?"

He cast a glance over his shoulder. "Show you the bottles you're dying to see."

Hyperextending her fingers, she bounced the tops of her palms together, hardly containing her anticipation. He doubted the contents could be that exciting, but the ongoing experiment with Quinn was certainly entertaining.

From the corner of his eye, he saw Livie crouch and then creep under a rickety dropleaf table. Bending, he saw the hole in the baseboard she was making a beeline for. Every speck and crevice fascinated her, which was why she picked up more lint and fuzz than a Swiffer mop. "Don't go there, Livie." He bent under the table, caught her by the waist, and hoisted her to the surface.

Quinn squealed.

"What!"

"That's it!"

"It's what?" He looked down at the gold thing clutched in Livie's little fist.

Quinn reached out and spoke sweetly. "May I have it?"

He knew from experience it wouldn't be that easy. But Livie floored him by dropping the item into Quinn's hand.

"It *is* it. I can't believe it." Her excitement animated each word. "I search every nook and cranny —"

"Not every cranny."

"A mousehole? That's diabolical."

"Unless you're two. Then it's irresistible."

Quinn squealed again. "Thank you, thank you, thank you." She kissed Livie's cheek. "You've saved me from the dining room."

"She doesn't comprehend the magnitude of that gift." Morgan said, toting his daughter to the sink and washing her hands.

"I can't begin to express it."

"You gave it a pretty good shot." Killing a laugh, he dried Livie's and his own hands with paper towels. "Is the photo inside?"

Quinn went still. "You know about the photo?"

"RaeAnne told me. At length." Especially how overwhelmed she was by Quinn's willingness to search, and wasn't she just the sweetest thing, bless her heart.

Quinn stared at the locket. "I guess to be sure, I have to look."

"To be sure," he said. She was dying to look. "Go ahead."

She pressed her nail into the seam, freeing the latch with her other thumb. The locket sprang open and revealed a photograph in one side, a lock of hair in the other.

"Wow," she breathed. "Do you think that's her dad's?" She pointed at the hair.

"DNA would tell."

She looked up, her striking eyes making contact. "Morgan, she could actually know."

Emotion welled visibly in her over this thing she'd done for a practical stranger, something he and Livie had played a part in. A strong conspiratorial energy passed between them. They stood a long moment, basking in whatever this was; then he forced a neutral tone. "You should call, tell her you have it."

She drew a breath. "I will. Right now." Clutching the locket to her chest, she pulled out her phone.

As Morgan moved out of the kitchen with Livie, she called RaeAnne at work, laughing at the prolonged and muffled squeal. "Morgan's little girl found it in a mousehole in the kitchen. A mousehole, RaeAnne. I'm sorry, but I would not have looked there."

"Are you sure it's the one?"

"It has a man's photo."

RaeAnne breathed hard. "How does he look?"

"I only glimpsed it to make sure he was there."

"Oh, I can't take it. If he's a horror I want to know."

"He's not." She laughed. "And there's something else. A lock of hair."

"For real?"

"Looks real. I'll mail it —"

"No! What if something happens in the mail?"

"I package very securely. I can FedEx it overnight, if you want."

"Is that the one that crashed in that Tom Hanks movie *Castaway*?"

Quinn scratched her jaw. She shipped items all the time, and yeah, things happened, but hardly ever. Still, with the possible DNA . . . "What do you want to do?"

RaeAnne groaned. "I can't take time off. Randy's breathing down my neck — in a predatory way. If I don't bring this project in on time . . ."

"I'll keep it safe until you decide."

"Oh, Quinn, what would you do?"

"I'd say send it insured — except compensation won't matter if it's lost."

"Have you had things lost?"

"A very tiny percentage, but yes, it happens. I'd hate for it to wash up on an island

and be used for cooking oysters."

RaeAnne laughed, a hard nervous release. "Oh, Lord, what should I do?"

She couldn't say. But then she thought of Morgan and his resources. "Let me check something and get back to you."

"I don't know how to thank you."

"It may not pay off."

"I'm just so blessed you'd try."

A lump formed in her throat. It had been a long time since someone had considered her a blessing. "No problem." Heading for the living room, she said, "Morgan," then looking around, called, "Morgan?"

It seemed he'd used up his words and left before he turned into a real boy. Luckily for her, she knew where he lived.

Noelle joined Liam, who'd answered the door with greater eagerness than a butler and only slightly less noise than a watchdog. Surprised to see Quinn standing there, she smiled broadly and said, "Hi."

"I hope I'm not bothering you."

"Not at all. Come in."

Stepping inside, Quinn looked up and around the high-ceilinged space dominated by the huge stone fireplace with a half-log mantel. "Wow. Feels like a giant honeycomb."

Noelle scrutinized Rick's handiwork. The pine log walls and ceiling were like a golden beehive, in spite of the colored throws and watercolors she'd used to soften it up and add color.

"Do you play?" Quinn indicated the grand piano in the corner.

"I do." Music had been a huge part of her life, to a detrimental degree at one point, but now she rejoiced in the gift. "You're welcome to join us Saturday evenings for praise and worship." She didn't know if Quinn shared the faith, but it never hurt to offer.

"Mom-my."

When Liam gave her hand a tug, she said, "I'm making this one hot chocolate."

"With marshmallows!"

"Would you like some?"

She hesitated a moment, then said, "Sure. Thanks."

Noelle led her to the kitchen. "It's great what you're doing for Vera . . . well, RaeAnne. Cleaning that place out."

"It's a win for me, too, a wealth of things for my online store." At the puzzled glance, Quinn added, "I'm an eBay trader."

"Oh. I've heard of eBay but haven't used it, I'm afraid." She had charge accounts that her father funded with Neiman Marcus and Bloomingdales, and individual boutiques, even if she needed so much less than it once seemed in New York.

"It's like other online shopping sites, except an endless cyber auction."

"Sounds like fun."

"It's a business," Quinn said. "I sell things I buy from estates like Vera's. Though I have to say, I didn't anticipate the escalation of that job."

Noelle handed her a mug as Liam made whirlpools in his with hard, pointed breaths. "Please sit."

Quinn took one of the high stools around the center counter, sitting diagonally from Liam, who perched as usual on his knees. He could reach just fine if he ever sat, but he'd been assembled with a rear wiggle button.

She joined them without a mug of her own and answered the unasked question. "Punky stomach. I'm four months pregnant."

Quinn's eyes lit. "Congratulations."

She formed a wan smile. "It's a joy and a challenge. These first months anyway. The sight and smell of almost anything . . ." She shook her head, then ruffled her son's hair. "Liam's still considering the situation." She eyed him indulgently, but he was busy trying to sink a marshmallow with his finger. "He'll let me know when he approves."

Quinn said, "I'm not sure my sister ever did, but we were eleven years apart. Not likely to become best friends."

"That's substantial. I'm an only child. After my mother died, my father raised me with fear and trembling. Tutors, dance, music, art, and equestrian training, with chauffeurs and a security detail to get me everywhere and back safely."

Quinn cast her a knowing look, as though she'd guessed as much. It must be more apparent than she knew, since Morgan had guessed the same at first glance.

"It wasn't easy for either of us. That's why I feel so deeply for Morgan and Livie." Love and fear were uneasy bedfellows.

Quinn cradled her mug. "Can't be easy single parenting in any circumstance."

Noelle nodded, unsure how much to say. Morgan had resented Rick's nudge, yet he and Quinn seemed to have connected at Vera's on their own, a conjoining of interests in the house, Quinn for RaeAnne and Morgan in his disconcerting decision to move there.

"I was hoping he could help me with something."

"Well." She'd obviously realized what everyone learned sooner or later. "Helping's what Morgan does best."

"Is he here?"

"His car's here. Second cabin down." After the first months, he'd moved there and insisted on paying the rental rate for a cabin plus expenses. Rick accepted the deal, saying Morgan had to do things his way.

"Well, thanks for the cocoa." Quinn gave Liam a wave and smiled when he said bye into his mug with marshmallow clinging to his upper lip.

■ ■ ■ ■

As she hurried through the early twilight, Quinn's breath made a cloud that curled around her cheeks. The ranch nestled in a valley surrounded by pink granite crags dressed up with conifers and aspen. The log cabins seemed to grow out of the pale grasses and red gravel of the yard. Low airy foliage bore the remainder of red and orange leaves, dulled now by the passing light.

The dry heads of wild flowers rustled as she neared the second of three cabins, larger than the first by maybe a bedroom, but not as large as the third, family-sized. One front window spilled light onto the porch. She'd approached him for help before, but not in his own place nor asking anything he hadn't offered.

Their interactions had run the gamut from playful to shuttered, so there was no way to anticipate her reception. She had to wonder why he'd gone without a word, after the excitement of finding the locket. Maybe Livie'd had an accident or . . . something he couldn't mention with a quick good-bye. Maybe walking out and slamming doors was his typical departure, though he hadn't slammed anything this time and the first could have been an accident of his injured hand.

When she knocked, he called, "Come in."

Sure he didn't realize the knock was hers, she said, "It's Quinn."

After a pause, he said, "Door's open." He looked up from his laptop when she entered, his fingers hovering over the keyboard. Sitting on the couch, dressed in a gray V-neck sweater and faded jeans, he could be any guy — but wasn't.

"I'm not stalking you."

One tiny muscle at the corner of his mouth flickered, but he'd apparently lost his former congeniality. His eyes had a blue blaze she hoped related to whatever he was working on, since the look had teeth.

"Sorry if I'm interrupting."

He didn't say otherwise.

"I would have done this at Vera's but you left." When he still didn't answer, she drew a bolstering breath. "It's about the locket. Rae-Anne's afraid it will be lost in the mail. She can't come out for it. So I thought you might have a way . . . to . . ." *do what regular people can't.* The words formed, but she couldn't say them.

"To . . ."

"Accomplish it?"

"Don't you ship things all the time?"

"Yes! I do. And I would, but there's the *Castaway* thing."

He frowned.

"Packages washing onto a beach, being

used to open coconuts?"

He said, "I'm sorry — how is this my problem?"

She blinked, feeling beyond foolish. "It's not. But I imagine you get things done in ways the rest of us —"

"The rest of you?"

"People who aren't Morgan Spencer."

"Aha." He sat back. "You've been busy."

"That first time we met. I wanted to know if your check would bounce, so I searched you." How did he make his eyes so flat? "And found the business articles and stuff. You know. Your books and the . . . thing you do." She sounded thirteen. Where was the conspiratorial connection, the easy parlance? Hadn't they faced a spooky cellar and solved a mystery and —

"Leave me the locket. I'll get it to RaeAnne."

Deep freeze. "I was going to package it . . ."

"Leave me the locket."

If helping was what he did best, he could work on his presentation. But then, who did she think she was, petitioning someone like him? He could swat her off like a fly, and basically had. She took out RaeAnne's treasure and set it on the table where his feet rested. A little deeper and she'd make a full bow. She straightened and walked out.

Morgan watched the door close behind her.

Part of him recognized his rudeness, but the rest had felt her in his home like high noon on sunburned skin. He didn't want to react to her. He'd realized that mistake at Vera's and scrammed. Then there she was, invading his space, his privacy. She'd searched him? Thought he'd rip her off?

And yeah she'd interrupted something. His assistant, Denise, had threatened resignation, claiming he could set up an automatic rejection on the corporate Web site if he continued to avoid the high-level consultations that required his on-site involvement. For most of two years, the recession had provided plenty of lower-level rescues he'd handed off to his second-string players, giving cyber support as needed.

Nothing international or encompassing enough that he'd have to leave Livie. In addition he'd written the books. Turning in the last one had felt like an abdication, a transfer of power. Or was it simply a cop-out? How many would take what was on the pages and actualize it?

His team called the books advertising. Even an instruction manual like the newest couldn't infuse that something God had wired into him. He was no Steve Jobs, but in his little piece of the universe he seemed to be unique.

And Denise had a point. It was what he did — in the life when any of that mattered. Still, her insistence grated. That on top of Consuela's threatened defection suggested wholesale mutiny. And he hadn't seen it coming. As he hadn't anticipated Quinn's impact. With creeping incrementalism, she'd invaded not only his thoughts and feelings, but now his environment.

"Daddy. Eat a fishy." Livie climbed onto the couch with him.

He accepted the goldfish cracker Livie raised to his lips and thanked her. Lowering her sippy cup, she gave him a milky kiss. He pulled her in for a hug, certain she could sense his unease. Would it kill him to accept one request, make one physical foray into the field?

He looked at the locket lying on the table, recalled the fun of finding it. What Quinn researched was public domain. She'd done nothing anyone else couldn't. So why did it feel personal, as if she'd made an assault and occupied him? Heat rushed through his skin as nerves or blood vessels pulsed.

"Daddy." Livie gripped his chin and turned his face.

"What, honey?"

"That a mad face, Daddy."

"Is it? What should we do about that?"

"Make it happy." She pressed her finger into the side of his mouth, stretching his lips.

He held the smile in place. "Is that better?"

She flashed her chipmunk smile.

He kissed her soft dark hair, a downy cloud of curls around her head, not unlike Quinn's in toddler form. "Eat your blueberries."

Instead she plucked one cracker-dusted berry through the spill-proof lid of the snack dish and fed it to him.

"Mmm. Yummy."

Livie popped one into her mouth and chewed vigorously. He couldn't bear to think of leaving her for any amount of time, but maybe he owed her just that. He reached for the laptop and responded to Denise. *You're not going anywhere. Choose ONE project and set it up.*

He didn't imagine her doing a Snoopy dance. More like rolling her eyes and thinking, About time, loser. He shut down the laptop and snuggled his little girl, hoping he'd taken one healthy step in the right direction.

Quinn left Morgan's, feeling chastised by the high-powered professional. Good intentions she had, but good judgment? Not lately — as Hannah's phone call reminded her. *"He's getting out and you'll pay."*

She had pushed that call out of her mind, but this scuffle with Morgan brought home how things could turn on a dime. She thought she'd found a good place to be, an innocuous occupation, some potential friends. A man . . .

She sighed. Not even dreams put her and

Morgan in any real-life involvement, but having no illusions didn't mean he hadn't impacted her. He and his precious child. Why couldn't she get them out of her head?

After pulling up the garage door in the steel barn, she parked inside, got out, and looked around, disheartened at the thought of losing her merchandise. She couldn't take much if she had to leave, nothing if she had to run. She didn't think Markham could find her. She used a store name for her business, so even if someone told him what she did, he wouldn't recognize it as hers. Her mother knew she'd bought a house, but Quinn hadn't told her where. She had sent no cards or letters, had no landline phone with a number in any directory. It should be okay.

She chose a DVD that had no chance of having a romantic thread and stepped outside. Her breath made a thicker fog now, as twilight gave in to dusk. She entered her little house, darkness covering every inch of the A-frame. It crawled over her like smoke. What if he was waiting for her? Would anyone notice if she went missing? RaeAnne might call to thank her when she got the locket. Morgan would want the stuff out of the cellar, but he could take care of it himself.

Would anyone check her house? Would anyone know where to look — or care? When they found her remains, Noelle might say, "My goodness, if only I'd known." But she didn't know. No one did. Except the ones who'd been there.

Swallowing hard, she switched on the light. Nothing jumped except her own skin. The place was so small, she could see everything, including the loft, from the door. Someone could be in the closet or bathroom, but they'd have to make it down the steep stairs to jump her. She checked them anyway.

Back in the kitchen, she tried to think of something for supper. At this rate her lip might be the only thing she chewed. God said it wasn't good for man to be alone. It was worse for woman. She should get a dog.

A dog could sense trouble. A dog could go in first and growl and raise its hackles. A dog would bark at night if someone tried to get in. And most of all, she wouldn't be alone.

Trembling, she took cheddar, tomato, and whole wheat bread from the fridge and assembled it for toasted cheese. The money from Morgan would buy a dog. Not a puppy — she needed help now — but not too old either. She was depending on it. Just an unfortunate soul who'd lost a family and had no companionship. She'd check the nearest shelter and let the animal choose her. She'd know when it was right.

Noelle straightened from the toilet and wiped her mouth. Swishing mouthwash almost started the reflex again, but she resisted and crept back to bed. Rick held the cover up, concern etching his face. As she settled in, he worked his thumbs and fingers up and down her back in slow, deep circles.

She murmured, "If we ever split up, I get your hands in the settlement."

"We're never splitting up."

"Lucky you. You get to keep your hands."

"I wish I could do more."

She rolled to face him. "It's only nine months of misery." She pulled a grim smile. "I'm four down."

"That's the spirit."

Settling her head in the hollow between his chest and shoulder, she said, "What do you think of Quinn?"

"Who?"

"You know who." She squeezed his arm.

"What am I supposed to think? I've seen her twice."

Morgan, she was sure, had an opinion — or the old Morgan would have. Rick had an opinion, too, somewhere deep inside, where he kept thoughts in appropriate order. At first she'd found that so strange, his faith-guided life. Now it was a pillar she clung to when dreams and memories seeped in.

"I like her. I'd like to know her better."

"You think she needs a friend."

"You feel it too?"

"No." His eyes crinkled with sun-weathered skin, even in winter. "I just know you."

"Well." She ran her hand over his lean muscled arm. "What about inviting her to Thanksgiving dinner?"

"Who's cooking?"

She started to scold him, then realized he was referring to the morning sickness. The thought of preparing a turkey almost sent her back to the bathroom. "Not that, then. I wonder if she rides."

"You can't ride pregnant."

She sighed. "Right."

"Why don't you go visit while she finishes at Vera's?"

"I could. She did ask for Morgan's help with something."

"Sorry she had to ask. I suggested he offer."

She sighed. "Do you think he'll ever . . . you know . . ."

Rick fingered a strand of her hair. "I don't know. It was always Jill."

"Because she was out there, somewhere. Now that she's gone, he could start fresh."

Rick shrugged. "Maybe." He kissed her shoulder. "Get some sleep now."

But before she dropped off, Quinn came to her heart again. "Okay," she breathed, though not to Rick. This was more than a hunch. It was a nudge.

CHAPTER 6

He felt like a reptile coming out from under a rock, blinking in overbright sunshine, cold wind standing his short blond hair. He felt like a predator waking to thoughts of prey, to hunger and awareness. He felt shame. He felt fury. He felt vengeful and powerful.

Thinking of Quinn, he felt prophetic. She couldn't know what she'd unleashed, couldn't see the storm rising, couldn't grasp the judgment coming where she would be sorted and discarded. He was Markham Wilder, and he'd promised she would pay.

With the locket found, Quinn had hauled all the paper out of the house with rejoicing. That left — she sighed — the cellar. Armed with a small, high-powered Maglite and a battery-operated lantern, she opened the old door.

Maybe it was false bravado going into a dark, haunted vault. She certainly had no desire to join the ghosts in perpetual lament if she got murdered down there. But the job needed to be done, and she refused to let Hannah's threat keep her from it. While Markham might be out, might be looking, nothing would lead him to Vera's. She was probably safer in this cellar than her own bed.

Morgan had cleared the worst of the webs on the stairs, so creaky step after creaky step, she made it down and hung the camp lantern on a high rail. Drawing her shoulders back, she took a look around. The cellar probably hadn't been used for patient care, and any screams she imagined were the stuff of movies.

This was storage, maybe a furnace and generators and boilers. There — she saw something that could be just that, a monster of a machine. She moved past the stacked beds to check out the cracked dial of a monstrosity right out of *The Shining.* That puppy could blow the roof off.

It was not functioning, thank goodness. It was also not going up the stairs. Something cold passed over her shoulders. She spun, light and shadows jerking around her as the lantern handle squeaked in the metal hasps. Wherever the draft came from, she didn't want to feel it again. She moved back in the other direction.

For the next hours, she filled plastic bins with bedpans and other junk. She carried each load to the rented trash container and went back down. The rubber tubing left a powdered residue on her latex gloves as she stuffed another bin for the trash. She shuddered at the large metal box filled with hypodermic syringes, but that was nothing to the frisson that shot up her spine when she discovered the stiff gray straitjacket. She shrieked when someone spoke behind her.

"I'm so sorry!" Noelle called from the top of the stairs.

"No. It's okay." Pushing the medical mask down under her chin, Quinn pressed a hand to her chest as her heart stopped pinging like a pinball against her ribs. "Just jumpy."

"I can see why." Noelle descended warily. "This place is creepy."

"Yeah. I was pretending otherwise, but the creep factor's pretty high down here." She turned the straitjacket for Noelle to see.

"Is that . . ."

"Unless someone had really long arms." Quinn bent the stiff fabric and laid it in one of the plastic tubs for possibilities.

"What will you do with it?"

"Morgan told me I should contact a museum."

"Morgan?"

"When we found all this."

"You and Morgan."

"I guess he didn't tell you."

Noelle shook her head. "The house is a touchy subject."

"Why?"

"When he learned I'm pregnant, he decided Livie's too much for me. I don't want to be the reason he thinks he has to leave."

"Is that a big deal?" Quinn sat back on her heels.

"No. But he's been with us almost since she was born, and . . ." She cast a glance around the cellar. "This just isn't like him."

"Oh, the rest of the house is nicer."

They laughed.

"So." Noelle rested a hand on her chest. "I was going to invite you to Thanksgiving dinner before you made other plans —"

"You were?"

"Yes, but Rick asked who's cooking, and you know my condition."

"I'll cook. I have a turkey fryer the previous owners left in my house." Cook their Thanksgiving dinner? When Morgan had all but dropkicked her?

Noelle stared. "I absolutely wasn't asking you to cook."

"Maybe by then you'll be past the worst of it."

She looked dubious. "I'm not sure I could even be in the kitchen."

Quinn shrugged. "The fryer goes outside. It's a big vat of peanut oil —"

Noelle clamped a hand to her mouth.

"Oh, sorry. Forget that. Don't think about any of it. I'll make it all."

"I'd feel dreadful."

"For including me?"

"And making you do the work. How can that be right?"

"Gives me somewhere to be on Thanksgiving." She threaded her hair back. "And here I was thinking of getting a dog."

Noelle tipped her head. "Are you really up for all that work?"

"I like work. Being still makes me . . ." She'd almost said anxious. "I get bored without something to do."

"No wonder you get so much done."

"Wouldn't know it down here."

"Do you want some help?"

Quinn rose. "I have no idea what's down here. Given the biowaste I've already discovered, it could be toxic."

Noelle placed a hand on her stomach. "Thanks for considering that."

"Thanks for the offer. But you probably should get out."

"Well, if you're sure."

"I'll look forward to Thanksgiving." She pulled the mask back over her mouth and nose. The invitation had taken her by surprise, but now a flood of memories almost brought tears. Cooking and baking, preparing the feast with her family. It was weeks away and she could hardly wait.

When she had nearly filled the rented Dumpster with rusted, mangled, crusty refuse, broken carts and wheelchairs, hardened red-rubber water bottles, and stained vinyl mattresses, some that looked melted, there was hardly a discernible difference in the cellar. Every piece of furniture and equipment in the place must have landed down there, regardless of condition.

No matter. She'd done all she could stand for the time being. As she drove to the crossroad in the shafting light of the golden autumn afternoon, her eye caught on kids and adults in costume. There must be a Halloween festival in the town center. On a whim she pulled over, got out, and watched the little ones cavort.

The smell of kettle corn and freshly cut pumpkins reached her as she moseyed in, keeping to the fringes for observation since she wasn't properly costumed. A pumpkin-carving station, beanbag toss, and apple-dunking trough reminded her of her own childhood. At the higher elevation the apples rested on shredded paper instead of floating in water that would have chapped little cheeks raw.

Booths held jams, jewelry, and handcrafts, mostly geared to the children. Grown-ups carried pails of candy or crackers or raisins for the little ones who approached them with "Trick or treat!" Good idea bringing the treats to one place instead of the kids trooping all over the mountainsides in search of handouts.

Across the way, she saw Rick in fancy wrangler chaps, vest, and Stetson, Noelle beside him in a flowing velvet gown, with crown and wand. Liam was a crocodile, Livie a pumpkin with adorable tam, black tights, and boots that lit up when she danced around. Trailing behind them, Morgan rivaled Jack Sparrow for best pirate ever. She wouldn't have recognized him except for the others, but children seemed to. He made them stand for inspection, circling with a hard eye, before drawing gold foil chocolate coins from the deep pockets of his embroidered coat to drop in their containers.

Caught up in the little drama, Quinn jumped when a child screamed and laughed in turns as a full-grown mummy teetered his way. Her heart warmed and tugged at once. Oh, to be young and innocent enough that scary was fun. She closed herself in her arms and went home.

Morgan came out on his porch the next day as Noelle approached his cabin. Liam ran to her, blabbing the things Uncle Morgan let him do on his Halloween sleepover, like shaving with cream and a razor — blade guarded, of course. She whiffed Morgan's aftershave on Liam's rosy cheeks when she chucked her son's chin. "I didn't know you had a beard, little man."

"All shaved off!"

"Well, we wouldn't want you shaggy."

In haste, Livie double-stepped the stairs behind him. "Mine all shave off too."

Noelle laughed. "We certainly wouldn't want *you* shaggy."

"She's a bearded lady," Liam declared. "Bearded lady, bearded lady."

"Enough, Liam." Noelle hugged him, then rose. "Thanks, Morgan." He'd relieved her of the Halloween candy after-party.

He nodded. "Sure."

"So." She tipped her head. "Why didn't you tell me your house has a haunted cellar?"

"Haunted cellar!" Liam hollered. "Can I see it?"

Morgan canted his head. "What were you doing there?"

"Inviting Quinn for Thanksgiving. A back-handed invitation if there ever was one, since she'll be cooking dinner."

"You're not serious."

"Why not?"

He shook his head. "That's . . . weeks away."

"People make plans. I wanted to catch her before anyone else." Or make it seem that way. Asking last minute would imply she obviously had nowhere else to go — which Quinn's eager acceptance seemed to indicate. "She's deep-frying the turkey. Should be . . . interesting."

His mouth pulled. "To say the least."

"You don't have a problem with that, do you?"

"Deep-fried turkey?"

"With Quinn coming."

"It's your house. Have whoever you want."

"Morgan."

He picked Livie up. "Denise is setting up a consult. Will you keep Livie if I go play guru?"

"Of course." Her spirit soared. "Morgan, it's great you're going back."

He shrugged. "It's time."

"Speaking of time, I'll take Liam and nap now."

"No!" Liam stomped a foot, looking like one of the stallions his daddy bred. "Four-year-olds don't nap."

"Four-year-olds on high octane do." Otherwise he'd collapse right before dinner and not want to go to bed.

"What's high octane?"

Morgan said, "Race car fuel."

Liam's eyes lit. He started his engine and ran for the house.

"Thanks," she told him. "He doesn't realize napping is one of God's great gifts." Even if he only had quiet time it would help, though Liam burned enough energy he almost always succumbed. "Shall I put Livie down too?"

He thought a moment, then said, "Yeah, there's something I need to do."

■ ■ ■ ■

At Vera's, he noticed Quinn had the door propped open in spite of the cold, probably to facilitate hauling things to the commercial Dumpster in the yard. Inside, the furniture had been removed, and he walked into the empty house, trying to place himself and Livie there.

He'd keep the crib Rick built that converted to a bed, but he needed to order everything else. Consuela could outfit the kitchen — provided he got her on a plane. He might have to personally escort her. Maybe bodily. He entered the kitchen and saw another open door. Apparently Quinn was braving the cellar again. Gutsy little thing.

"Quinn?" he called from the top. He heard shuffling, and she came to the foot of the stairs. Though an attempt had been made at pulling her hair back, it didn't make a big difference. Put her in a Tinker Bell costume and she'd be a dark elf ready for mischief. He had to work for words — something he'd rarely experienced.

"No more pirate?"

Either she'd read his mind on costumes or seen him in action. "You saw?"

"Aye, matey. Quite by accident."

His mouth twitched at her accent. "Not bad."

He descended. Some of the musty smell had dissipated and her orange-and-vanilla-scented shampoo or lotion or body wash reached him. He searched her face for signs of pique from their last encounter. It appeared safe to proceed. "I hired a private courier to hand deliver RaeAnne's locket."

"Oh. I never thought of that."

"If he survives the flight, she'll have it today."

She cast him a half-amused, half-irritated look.

"And I apologize for the other night. I was curt."

"I caught you at a bad time. And invaded your privacy."

He shook his head. "I have no privacy. I pretend I can hide, but there's no such thing."

Something that looked like fear moved through her eyes, but she masked it. "Saving mega corporations and writing bestsellers doesn't help, I guess."

He acknowledged that, then changed the subject. "You've made some progress down here."

"Already filled the Dumpster once. Straitjackets, hypodermics, lots of rubber tubing."

"I hope it wasn't all that way."

"The docile ones probably sat in the sunshine and drooled."

Again she surprised him. He hadn't met many women as cynical as he.

She rested her hands on her hips. "So what did you want?"

"I came to discuss Thanksgiving."

"Discuss?"

"I need to warn you my family might be setting us up." He caught a wash of disappointment in her face. Not a reaction he'd expected.

"Forewarned is forearmed." Hoisting the clanking storage tub, she said, "Excuse me. More bedpans."

He moved aside and stared as she mounted the stairs. Pretty good power-to-mass ratio. And if he wasn't mistaken, she'd just firmly dissed him.

He looked around the dimly lit cellar, up at strings of cobweb adrift on spectral breaths — or the draft of Quinn's return as she pressed past without a word.

"The other thing," he said, "is Noelle's challenged in the kitchen."

"I know. She's pregnant."

"That too."

"Too?" She glanced up.

"Basically, she's an awful cook. I love her, but that's the bare truth. The less she has to do with the meal, the better."

Quinn raised her eyebrows.

"Just saying. Rick's not bad, and I'll do what I can. But we'll *spare* Noelle."

"Okay." She actually seemed fine with it, in spite of his warning.

"Can I help you here?"

She stood for a moment, tapping her chin with a gloved thumb. "I guess we could remove the beds crowding the stairs."

"Moving furniture is kind of our thing."

She shot him a glance, but no, he hadn't meant *thing*-thing.

He cleared his throat. "They won't be light."

"That's why you can help."

Otherwise not so much. A refreshing change, though in fairness, her other request had been for RaeAnne. He unbuttoned his shirt sleeves and rolled the cuffs. They gripped the bed nearest the stairs and, straining hard, dragged it off the lower one. She rearranged her grip and, stepping onto the first stair, wobbled a little, then righted.

This was not going to work. Even if he bore the brunt as he had the cabinet, the bed was the kind of heavy that loosened joints. She'd never remove them all. "Do you have a plan for these?"

"Not immediately."

"Then set it down." He eyed the two dozen or so iron beds, some with shackles, some missing springs. He couldn't imagine a market for them, and it shouldn't fall on her to deal with it. "If we consolidate the beds, you can get at whatever you want down here and leave the rest."

"I thought you needed it cleaned out."

He shrugged. “I’ll keep the hutch over the door so Livie can’t get in.”

“I wish you’d said so before the bedpans.” She wrinkled her nose.

He raised an eyebrow. “No collectors for those?”

“Ugh. There might be.”

She turned toward a giant old boiler. “Since that’s not moving, either, let’s pack the beds over there.”

He nodded. “Bring the lantern.”

Light beams swayed as she carried the source, illuminating something in the far corner — a different sort of bed or seat, an old generator, and electric cables. Behind him, Quinn made a strangled sound as recognition registered.

He clasped her arm and said, “Some cultures drilled holes in skulls to let evil spirits out. Seems barbaric, but they were acting within their understanding to relieve mental suffering. Electroshock was part of medicine’s search for cures and answers.”

“It’s so . . . *One Flew Over the Cuckoo’s Nest.*”

“That’s how it’s been portrayed. And maybe how it was. But the purpose wasn’t torture. This isn’t Auschwitz.”

“I can feel it though. The horror.” She shot a glance behind her, as though something repulsive brushed her.

“Forget this.” He turned her. “Let’s seal up

the cellar —"

"No." Steel came back into her arm, her shoulders. "These were real people."

"They're gone now."

"But where? And what happened here?" Urgency pulsed in her throat. The starbursts in her eyes seemed alight with fire. "Why does it feel so bad?"

He searched her face, seeing real distress. It was a lot of old junk in his mind, but it obviously triggered something in hers. "I don't know. But I know someone who might. A historian." He hadn't thought of Dr. Jenkins in ages. "I can contact him if you want."

"Yes." She nodded after a moment. "I want to know."

Her scent reached up to him again, her arm warm in his hand. She was so — His mind hit the wall like a crash dummy.

"Morgan?"

Turning his back, he pressed a fist to his chest where the ache felt like a heart attack no defibrillation would return to normal function. It wasn't that. He knew.

"What's wrong?"

Beads of sweat pearled on his forehead and trickled down his temples. It hurt to draw breath. Hands clenched, he tried to will it away.

"Morgan." Fear raised her voice.

He hadn't had an attack for more than a year. Why now? In front of Quinn?

She tried to get around where she could see him but couldn't get through.

His throat felt like sawdust. "Just give me a minute, okay?"

"Are you sure? Because I'd really hate a dead body down here with everything else."

That forced a laugh and eased the stricture in his throat. Now he needed his chest to stop pounding, the dizziness and sweating to pass. "I promise not to die." He turned enough for her to see he meant it.

Face twisting, she said, "That was callous. What if you really are dying? Are you?"

He swallowed. "No."

But she hovered as though he might keel over in spite of his promise. He jutted his chin toward a beige metal file cabinet. "Have you looked in those drawers? Might be answers in there."

"What?" She turned. "No, but —"

"Go see."

She frowned at him, then went. Squeezing between two metal desks, she reached the file cabinet and pulled one drawer after another. By the hollow drag he could tell they were empty. "Nothing but dust," she said, until she reached the bottom drawer. "There's some crispy Scotch tape in this one." She felt inside. "Something's stuck to the top. I think it's a key."

"To the medicine cabinet?"

"It's not a skeleton key." She peeled it loose

and held it out.

Breathing easier, he leaned with one arm on a bed frame and said, "Could it go to the desks?" They had locking center drawers.

She tried it in the first desk drawer and then the other. That one opened. He watched her grow still, and then in the dim light of the lantern, she removed a journal. Their eyes met. Once again they connected in discovery. The constriction released his chest.

"Could be your answers." He almost had his voice under control again.

She held it nearer the light. "It's not connected to the asylum."

"How do you know?"

"The name on the plate is Veronica Greenwald. Same as the mail upstairs."

He made a slow nod. "Guess the old gal got down here after all."

Quinn eyed Morgan, aware he'd diverted her attention. He seemed mostly recovered from whatever it was and obviously didn't want to talk about it. Maybe he had episodes that altered his moods and caused these symptoms. If bad enough, that could make him a recluse, though she was beginning to think that was some kind of publishing hype.

He nodded at the journal. "What will you do with that?"

"I'll have to call RaeAnne. There are other items she hasn't decided about."

"You could surprise her."
"Send it?"
"Take it."
"In person?"
"It'll cost less for me to send you than to hire another courier."
As if she would begin to ask that. "It's not your responsibility."
He sent her a look.
"I had no idea you'd go to such extremes last time. I didn't know there were such extremes."
He hung his hands on his hips. "Look, Quinn. There are no secrets here. I can afford to fly you to RaeAnne."
"But why would you?" It didn't make sense that he'd take offense at her previous request and now want to help in any way.
He must have read her confusion, because he said, "I was dealing with other things the last time. It came out on you, and I'm sorry. I'm happy to facilitate this process."
She looked away from his searching gaze. "There might be more things Vera hid down here. There's no sense doing anything before I'm finished." Then she turned back. "When are you moving in?"
"Not as soon as I thought. I'll be out of town for a week or two." He scanned the cellar. "Take your time and don't stress over this. Okay? As far as I'm concerned, it's finished."

Didn't she wish. "Okay."

He checked his watch — a Rolex? Cartier? Crown jewels? — and said, "I need to go. Let me know what you decide and . . . be careful down here. I don't want a dead body either." Something passed through his eyes that marred the humor.

She gave him a little shove. "Would you go, please?" She pulled the crushed medical mask from her pocket, where she'd stuffed it when she heard his voice. But she didn't go back to work. The cellar felt creepy again, and even though he was only repeating her words, it was too close to the fears plaguing her since Hannah's call.

She took the journal up to the kitchen, studied the red leather cover and nameplate. Didn't Vera realize someone could have hauled this off without knowing it was there? Or had she wanted that? At any rate it wasn't as weird as hiding the locket in a mousehole. On the other hand, no thief would look there. Maybe Vera knew exactly where her treasures were but died before she could tell RaeAnne. There was a lesson in that.

So now what? Morgan's offer troubled her on a lot of levels. He seemed to want to pay for anything he did for her, buying the furniture and flying her to RaeAnne. His mixed signals were harder to roll with than she made it seem. And when he'd suffered whatever it was, just now in the cellar, she wanted to wrap him in her arms and make the bad thing go away.

The other thing that troubled her, the point that worked its way in like a splinter under a nail, was an airline ticket would put her name on a manifest. She couldn't tell if that concern was paranoia or being careful. If Markham was looking for her, she might be no safer in her bed than on a plane, except she wasn't advertising her location at home.

She clenched her fists, furious the man could still be impacting her life and decisions. If Morgan offered again, she'd do it. Markham was out. He was angry. But he was not omnipotent.

Chapter 7

Morgan went home and showered off the sweat and dust and unease. Nothing like what happened in the cellar to underscore the foolishness of letting down his guard. Avoidance was the best defense he'd found — since he'd been sober. And drinking wasn't an option since Kelsey's arrangement with God made it impossible.

Long before bourbon or vodka or gin could infuse his blood, he'd be puking it up, an instantaneous reaction he'd quit battling. The best guess the doctors had was that sobering up and boosting his immune system for the bone-marrow donation had created a sensitivity to alcohol, an allergic reaction. But Kelsey had prayed for him to get sick when he drank, and frankly that was more believable. From his dying child's lips to God's ear.

Coming out of the bathroom clean and dressed in fresh clothes, he watched Livie kneeling on the floor and drawing lines and circles with a red crayon on a paper and telling him what they were, because they looked so much like lines and circles. If Kelsey's death hadn't reunited him with Jill, he wouldn't have Livie. He wouldn't have this heartache, wouldn't have this joy. Why did every bright cloud have a dark lining?

"Come on, honeybee. Let's have dinner."

He gave her Cheerios and grapes and sat with her while she ate. Then he took her to the main house and snuggled with her in the overstuffed recliner. In seconds, Liam found the side not occupied and burrowed in. Morgan took a deep breath and settled his soul.

If someone had told him he'd be spending Saturday evenings with Rick and Noelle in praise and worship, he would have scoffed mightily. But he knew what happened when the mighty scoffed. With Rick leading on guitar and Noelle playing piano, he sat among their friends, the two dozy kids plastered to his chest.

". . . He will raise you up on eagle's wings, bear you on the breath of dawn . . ."

Voices blended and soared, faithful hands swayed. He turned his face and kissed the top of Livie's head, gratitude coursing through him. For this child he'd offer praise and worship and supplication to God. He breathed her scent like incense burned on the altar of his heart.

When he opened his eyes, Rick had lifted the guitar strap over his neck and laid the instrument in the case. The fire had burned to coals and both children slept soundly. The joy and serenity the guests carried out were real, but he couldn't entirely get there. He'd come so far from the reckless ne'er-do-well, but, like freedom, courage was another word for nothing left to lose.

Rick peeled Liam off and carried his sleeping son up to bed. Noelle looked better than she had in days — praise did that for her. Funny, considering she'd been highly allergic to religion when she arrived, making his cynical faith look pious. She whispered goodnight and brushed a hand over Livie's damp hair.

Wondering how he'd make himself get on a plane and fly miles away, he bundled his sleeping daughter warmly for their trek to the cabin. Inside, he laid Livie in her crib, stood another moment watching her breathe, then went to his own room and turned on the monitor so he could hear her breathe all night.

Since Morgan would be out of town, Quinn gave herself a break from the cellar. She focused on listing the collectibles, decorative items, small furnishings, and vintage clothes. She had gathered as much from Vera's as she might have from multiple sources. In spite of everything she had to wade through, Vera's estate was, in fact, a gold mine.

All the work she'd put in would be well accounted for, and she should have felt great. But looking around her warehouse, she realized she'd collected enough merchandise to suffer an actual loss if anything happened, if not in expenditure, then at least in potential sales. Frowning, she reminded herself again that the chances of being located were small.

Except for secure things like the IRS records and her PayPal account, she practically lived off the grid. While law enforcement had ways to subpoena those records, an individual shouldn't. If she had no contact with people who already knew next to nothing, she'd be as invisible as a person could be with real bones and blood and attitude.

It wouldn't hurt, however, to follow up on the possibility of a dog. Leaving off for the day, she headed for the nearest animal shelter, more appropriately called a rescue, since it was run privately and the dogs showed their former circumstances in hung heads, drooping tails, and low growls. Breathing the scent of fur, feces, and fear, even though the kennels were clean and spacious, she moved from one to another, making herself available and searching for a spark.

With small, lacy snowflakes falling around her, she crouched at the end of a run, and the brown, bristly dog at the end pulled one lip back. It was more a twitch than a snarl. Reflex, not intention, but with the same result. She stood up and moved on.

Maybe they sensed her ambivalence, because none approached when she crouched at the ends of their runs. It might have been different if they were loose in the yard, but because of their unpredictability, they didn't mingle with each other or new prospective companions. She would have to come back several times before having actual contact. Her heart went out to them, while at the same time she wondered how appropriate her situation would be toward their restoration.

What if there was danger, if they had to flee, to keep moving from place to place? How would the animal handle such insecurity? She had to wonder if she could count on a dog even the rescuers called unpredictable. Without even one coming close enough to pet, she admitted adoption would be a mistake.

"I'm sorry," she told the stocky man with a broad, generous face and a brace on one leg who'd let her into the kennel area. "We'd have to trust each other and . . ."

"That comes with time," he told her. "Usually."

She nodded, believing it. "But I might not have time. And it wouldn't be fair to expect more than they can give."

He eyed her solemnly. "Are you in some trouble?"

She returned his concern with a smile. "I hope not." Then she looked at the kennels.

"But I think they have too much of their own to add any of mine."

He said, "If things settle out for you, keep us in mind."

"I will. Thank you."

It wasn't going to be as easy as she'd thought. Since she'd never had a pet, her assumptions could be completely wrong. Maybe that magical bond she'd imagined was only that — imaginary.

Disappointed, but confident in her decision, she went home alone. Since she wasn't a loner by nature, she gave herself kudos for handling solitude these last four years with equanimity and grace. The grace, she knew, didn't come from her, but dealing with it did.

His assistant, Denise, met him at the resort hotel in LA, where they'd all gather for a state-of-the-corporation session, announce his return, and prepare to move forward. He needed to connect with the team members who'd been actively working projects and the bigger talents who came on for the high-level clients he handled personally. He had to know if they could still commit the time, focus, and energy required to right sinking ships in an economy as unforgiving as a shark in bloody waters.

None had been static during his hiatus. Some would have positions they preferred to keep, places to hunker down and wait for the world to turn around. He wouldn't blame them. He'd been hunkering himself.

Coifed like a dame from a film noir in knee-length tight skirt and fitted blazer, blond hair swept into a tight twist, Denise joined him in the conference room at their disposal for the week. He slanted her a glance. "These are preliminary meetings, Denise. One-on-one to get the pulse of my team. We don't need to be quite so formal."

"The pulse, Morgan, that they need to feel is yours. The world isn't even sure you're alive and kicking."

He wasn't either. As with his engine, the gears were rusty.

She pressed a finger to her chin. "I've held off contacting Belcorp until we know your own people are on board."

As with a quarterback returning from a season-ending injury, they'd want to know he hadn't lost his nerve. Could he make the hard calls that led to victory?

He tapped his pen on the knuckle of his thumb. "That's what this week is for. I presume you have prospects and arrangements for a second week if it comes to making replacements?"

She nodded. "Believe it or not, there are people in the wings who would kill for a spot on your team."

"I hope it won't come to bloodshed."

She flushed.

He tipped his head. "Don't do that."

"What?"

"Shy away from anything to do with death. It is what it is."

She drew herself straight. "I won't, then. But others might."

He nodded. "Not your concern."

She consulted her tablet. "I've sent you the interview schedule and all pertinent information I could find for each member. Let me know when you need something else."

"You are amazingly good at your job."

"It's nice to have one — in which I do something."

A part of him quickened, a part that once felt vital. It might feel better if leaving Livie wasn't eating a hole inside. He could talk to her every hour if he wanted, see her via Skype morning, noon, and night. He used to know what was appropriate, and yes, he realized that wasn't.

"Morgan?"

He looked up.

Denise repeated herself. "Glen Conyer?"

"Send him in." This had been his life, most of it spent without Jill, and Jill in none of it to come. He pushed that from his mind. "Glen." He stood.

"Morgan." The man's hair had thinned and the scalp shined through it at the top. "Man, it's great to see you." They grasped hands. "We doing this thing?"

He cocked his head. "Some of that's up to you."

The ace accountant had small irises so the white showed all the way around as he said in all seriousness, "Say the word. I'm in."

Since she'd left the cellar with Vera's journal, Quinn had not gone back down. It wasn't a decision as much as a reluctance that came over her every time she thought of doing it. Instead, she'd scoured the house, even using paint from cans she'd found in the garage — which was incongruously uncluttered — to touch up walls and trim. The windows shone, the wood floors gleamed. There wasn't much she could do about the ancient gray-speckled kitchen linoleum that popped and crackled, but it was clean.

She felt good knowing Morgan and especially Livie would have a fresh start in the house. With the cellar blocked off, it would be a normal house Morgan could furnish and inhabit in comfort. The kitchen appliances were a little sad, but he'd figure that out. Now, as she had done each day before leaving, she reached into the key box on Morgan's hutch, drew a scant handful from the remaining keys at the bottom, and approached the medicine cabinet.

She pulled one from the collection in her hand and tried it in the lock — gasping when it turned, though others had too. But this time she felt the lock release. Squealing, she did a happy dance and then reached for the knob. With excitement feeding anticipation, she stared through the milky panes of the cabinet, one motion away from satisfying her curiosity — and stopped.

Morgan had told her she could open it. He'd tried the keys himself so she could see the bottles. Yet as much as she wanted to, she didn't want to alone. Together they'd discovered the cellar, together carried the cabinet. They'd found the locket and the journal, cringed at the bad stuff downstairs and sparred over the contents of this cabinet until she couldn't imagine opening the doors without seeing his face. After everything, where was the fun in going forward without him?

But she groaned. He was out of town. She didn't know when he'd be back. She knew he wasn't thinking of her, or the cabinet and whatever was inside. He might not even care when he got back. He'd wanted it left alone. She straightened her arm and started to pull the door — then stopped again.

She should break the spell he'd cast the night he dared her to take his check. And that, of course, reminded her that it was his. Sighing, she removed the key and stepped back from the cabinet and the promise of the old bottles. It was history. It was answers. And she may as well stop arguing. However it had happened, he was in this with her. And she wanted him there. So she would wait.

His welcome home consisted of Livie breaking into uncontrollable sobs as he entered the great room. "Hey." Surrounded by Rick, Liam, and Noelle, Morgan dropped to his knees and clutched her so tightly neither could breathe.

"I miss you, Daddy."

"I missed you too, honey. But here I am, and here you are." He scooped her up and swung her from side to side. "Shhh." Cupping the back of her head, he kissed her crown again and again. "It's okay."

If he'd been going to work and coming home regularly, it wouldn't be so traumatic. But before he left, they'd been together almost every minute. Her heaving chest against his made him feel both helpless and whole. "I'm here, honey. I'm here." Two weeks had been too long. "Livie, please. Please," he rasped.

The sobs slowed, her tiny chest shuddering, her chin shaking. He kissed her wet, salty cheeks, her damp eyelashes brushing against his skin. He begged Noelle, "Tell me it hasn't been like this."

"Not until now. A few flurries, but no flood."

He rubbed Livie's back. "That's my girl."

"Jelly bean," she whispered in his ear.

"Sweet pink cotton candy," he whispered back, heart squeezing.

"Want some dinner?" Rick said.

He could smell whatever one of them was making, and it wasn't bad, but he said, "I think Livie and I have a date." There was no fast food in Juniper Falls, no McPlay Place, and the parks were cold and getting dark. But she loved the spiral-sliced flash-fried potato chips at the Roaring Boar Pub and Grill. Food was served all day, and it was too early for the kind of drinking that accompanied the live music — though "live" was debatable for some of the bands in the winter months.

He bundled her up, and after the short drive, they stepped into the warm scent of barbecue and beer. He'd spent a lot of time in this place, even had a date here with Noelle before Rick. It was a local treasure, but he didn't come in much anymore, and the hearty greetings of the crowd told him he'd been missed. But since the outing was all about Livie, he nodded his head at a small corner booth where they'd be out of the way.

"Sure," the bartender, Scotty, said, indicating he'd serve them there. A bad case of acne had cratered his cheeks like shriveled balloons, but his friendly nature and quick hands made him great behind the bar and at the tables. His tips reflected it.

As Morgan turned with Livie toward the

table, the door opened and Quinn entered. Blinking in the dimness, it took a few moments before she noticed them, then her face lit. He felt a kick in his stomach. The last she'd seen, he was imitating a heart attack. Now it seemed he might have one of another kind. Not. Good.

She pushed her hair back in what had to be a continuous quest for order and said, "You're back."

He managed, "Just."

She tickled Livie with a single finger, then said, "I've been hoping to tell you, I found a key."

It took a second, and then he answered, "To the cabinet?"

She nodded, eyes shining.

"Was it everything you wished for?"

She folded her arms. "I haven't opened it."

He frowned at her, confused, as this was the cabinet she'd quivered before like a puppy for a bone.

"I was going to, but it seemed like you should be there."

The earnestness in her voice caught him unprepared. "Oh."

Her smile dimmed. "I'm catching you at a bad time."

"No. Yeah." Silver-tongued devil. If the team could see him now.

She waved a hand. "Don't worry about it."

"Listen. I'm having a date with my daughter. Can I meet you there in an hour?"

"Sure." She backed up a step, then headed for the bar. He stood long enough for her to start placing a to-go order, then walked with Livie to the booth.

Carrying the paper bag that held her order, Quinn left without looking back. Seeing Morgan after two weeks had lit her like a torch, and she'd shown it, but he was there with his little girl. The thought of a daddy-daughter date made a lump in her throat she couldn't seem to swallow. She put her truck in gear, wishing she hadn't extended the invitation. But for all practical purposes, she'd finished at the house and he'd be moving in. It might be her last chance to open the cabinet.

Why hadn't she just done it?

At the intersection, she crunched a homemade chip, waiting for a car to pass, then moved through. She parked outside of Vera's and ate in her truck, watching snow fall and thinking about Morgan spending an hour with his little girl, one-on-one, as though no one else in the world mattered. She bit into the usually mouth-watering pulled-pork sandwich that now left her taste buds uninvolved.

She'd spent time with Pops — fishing, talking, following his hound through the woods — time stolen from chores and service and studies. Her father had no time to waste, but

Pops made time, and truth be told, she preferred it that way. With Pops there was no lesson behind every single thing she was expected to bury in her heart.

She got out of the truck. It had been a bright and sparkling day, but clouds were now scudding across the dimming sky. The air was dry and cold but not yet frigid. If enough clouds gathered, it wouldn't be a question of whether but how much it would snow. At these mountain elevations it could do that in August if it tried. In November, it didn't have to try.

She let herself into Vera's — Morgan's — house and did a slow tour. No one would believe that weeks ago the walls couldn't be seen, and the floors were reduced to paths and patches. As frustrating as some of it had been, she wasn't complaining.

She had the money from the antiques, and her warehouse held more collectibles than ever before. The completed auctions had ended quite profitably. She'd already shipped out a number of Hummel and other figurines, decorative plates and glassware, and blessed Vera for caring for them. Where those things were concerned, she'd been a conscientious collector. It felt good dispersing those treasures to others who would love them. In this throwaway world she liked to think of things passing from hand to hand with care.

That made her think of Vera's journal and

Morgan's offer. She'd been waiting to see if she would find anything else, but even now the thought of looking in the cellar sent a shiver up her spine. To Morgan it was finished, and she was glad to call it quits. Maybe he'd send her with the journal, or maybe she'd send herself.

The best part of all was giving RaeAnne her dad. It had been a wonderful day meeting RaeAnne and Noelle in the fog. She smiled thinking of it. From the moment of RaeAnne's *"Pretty, isn't she,"* something had clicked between them. Noelle seemed nice, too, she thought, then jumped when the doorbell made its grinding wheeze.

She'd completely cleared her head, but the calm she'd accomplished vanished when she opened the door to Morgan and his daughter. She was only human.

"Well, Livie. How was your date?"

Livie giggled. "I have chips."

"Chips are the best. Guess your daddy's a keeper."

"Daddy a keeper." Livie pressed a hand to his cheek, speaking into his eyes.

Yeah, make her a puddle right here on the floor. Getting the nerve, she lifted her gaze to Morgan.

He was staring, mouth slightly ajar, around the house. "You didn't just clean."

"A little paint and repair. It's good to go."

"Quinn, this . . ." He looked down at her.

"This is more than your deal with RaeAnne."

"No, believe me, I came out just fine."

"But I . . ."

"You helped me sell the furniture, which I wouldn't have earned anything on. And this one found the locket and saved me from paper-stack hell." She touched Livie's head with a little hitch in her ribs. "I just wanted it to be nice."

"Nice." He cocked his jaw. "Yeah. It's nice." He had a great way with understatement.

"So. Are you ready?"

He set Livie down, and as she ran around the big empty room, they went into the kitchen. She picked up the key from the hutch and held it out.

But he shook his head with a slow blink. "You do it."

She'd been so right to wait. Drawing a breath, she inserted and turned the key. She pulled the knob, but the door wouldn't budge. Morgan tugged the other knob and that door groaned open. Clutching his arm, she leaned in to see.

On the top shelf were tiny bottles with glass spires. She took one out and examined the white paper label that read Delysid (LSD-25) *D-lysergic acid diethylamide tartrate.* SANDOZ LTD., BASLE, SWITZERLAND.

It looked like a perfume bottle, but she couldn't see how to open it. Morgan closed it into his hand and took it away. She looked up. "What?"

"It's LSD."

She searched his face.

"They're ampules of psychedelic drugs. You don't want to break it open. It might absorb through your skin and send you on a trip you weren't planning."

Jaw falling slack, she turned and stared at the cabinet filled with LSD and who knew what else. "I sold you illegal drugs?"

His mouth pulled as he replaced the bottle, closed and locked the cabinet. "We didn't know."

"But . . ." She felt completely flummoxed. "LSD in a mental hospital?"

"What do you think it was developed for?"

"I don't know." She glared at the cabinet. "I thought we'd find . . ." Herbs? Chamomile tea? "Something interesting and historical, not illegal."

"I warned you the mystery might be better than the truth."

She paced two steps and back. "What are you going to do?"

He said, "I'm thinking."

While he thought, she decided. "I have to give your money back."

"Stop." He said it like she was being silly, but she wasn't.

"You paid me five hundred dollars for LSD. That's a drug deal."

His eyes crinkled. "Don't worry, SWAT's

not closing in."

"This isn't funny. We should call the sheriff."

He leaned his arm on the cabinet, looking in. "Let's hold off."

"Why?"

"I want to show someone. After Thanksgiving, we'll turn it over."

She searched his face. "We leave it here for the next week and a half?"

"No one knows it but us."

"I just . . ."

He clasped her shoulder. "It'll be okay."

Heart suddenly skittering, she turned to see Livie, performing a little skip that hardly lifted her from the floor. Her cuteness was calming, as though nothing could be too wrong in the world. "Okay." If Morgan had a plan, she'd leave it to him. "See you for Thanksgiving."

Chapter 8

Deep-frying a turkey took about half as long as roasting one, according to the directions. The unopened fryer had been in the pantry of her A-frame, like the weirdest housewarming present ever, when she moved in. It had sprung to mind when Noelle invited her, so she hauled it over with the pumpkin pie and cornbread pudding she'd baked the night before, along with the fixings for the rest.

With her boots compressing last night's snow with a crush and squeak in every step, she reached the door. Rick greeted her with warmth in his brown eyes and a hint of solicitude. "For the record, I think you're getting the weak end of this invitation."

She looked up around the boxed fryer in her arms. "Honestly, I'm glad for something to do."

"Can I take that?"

"I have it, but you could grab stuff from the truck. The turkey's in a brine bucket."

He held the door for her to go in, as he had

on their first encounter. Though she'd spent time with Morgan and Livie since then, she still barely knew Rick or Noelle or their rambunctious Liam. The day could be interesting, but she was looking forward to it.

She passed through the kitchen and out the back to a snowy patio, where she unpackaged the big stainless vat. The peanut oil Rick brought her glugged into it in a golden stream. While that heated, she would start on the side dishes. She'd brought a variety of vegetables to roast in olive oil and garlic — squashes, onions, carrots, and yams without the gooey stuff that choked going down.

Since a deep-fried turkey would leave no drippings, and canned or powdered gravy should be illegal, she had to improvise on the potatoes too. She chose mashed with butter and sour cream. She'd have included chives but guessed the little ones wouldn't like it.

Back inside, she found Rick waiting for instructions. Noelle had warned her she might not make it to the kitchen, and according to Morgan, that was a good thing, so she'd take what help she had. She turned over the bag of potatoes, and, tall and rangy like a classic cowboy, Rick stood at the kitchen sink and peeled.

Just as she was starting to feel strange in someone else's kitchen with someone else's husband, Morgan came in, as darkly handsome as ever. At the hitch in her ribs, she shifted from his face to Livie's tearful one.

He said, "She disagreed about the need for a coat."

As she wore an adorable red coat with black embroidery and hood fur, it appeared her daddy won the discussion — and paid the price. He looked almost as crestfallen as his child.

He stood her on a chair and said, "Now we can take it off."

Livie gripped it at the neck with a forbidding frown, and Morgan laughed grimly. "Liam's rubbing off."

"Oh sure," Rick said from the sink. "Blame it on my son."

"It's human nature to emulate the older."

"Keep telling yourself that." Rick carried a colander of peeled and rinsed potatoes to the counter by the stove and asked, "You want these cut?"

"Quartered, please."

"I'll do it." Morgan set his daughter on the floor. "You should check on Noelle, Rick. She's coughing." There seemed something a little ominous in the way he said it.

Rick nodded, obviously sharing the concern. "Show him the sharp side of the blade, Quinn."

She looked from Rick to Morgan, not sure where the joking ended and truth began. "I'm sure you know how to use a knife."

"Eh." He waggled his hand. "Consuela

never lets me near one."

"Consuela . . ."

"My cook, who's coming out soon — if I have to hog-tie her."

"You don't cook at all?"

"I make a mean bowl of Cheerios. Don't I, punkin?" He patted Livie's head.

"Make happy Cheerios, Daddy. No mean Cheerios." She had discarded the coat and forgotten their tiff.

Quinn slid diced onions into the roasting pan. "How old is she?" She had surprisingly never asked. "Because I just don't think she should talk that well."

Morgan said, "How old are you, Livie?"

She held up three fingers, then added four from the other hand.

"She's twenty-six months. Last week she learned sentence structure, and now she's working on her PhD."

"I believe it." The child had changed in just the little time since they'd discovered the contraband.

He scooped up her coat and hung it over the chair before pushing up the sleeves of his slate blue — cashmere? — sweater.

She said, "You want an apron?"

"Did you really ask me that?" He leaned on one arm, masculine in every aspect.

"I did."

"No thanks. No apron. Ever."

She shrugged. "They're your clothes."

He pulled a paring knife out of the drawer and took hold of a potato.

"That's too little. Use this." She gave him the knife she'd finished with. It might be an act, but he was confirming Rick's assertion. "You must have done this before."

"Nope."

"As a bachelor?"

"I ate out."

"Growing up?"

"I have four sisters. And a mother who's never bought takeout." He made a careful slice. "You think I got near the kitchen?"

"But you're the oldest, right?"

"How'd you know that?" He accomplished another slice. In fairness, wet peeled potatoes were tricky.

"The way you teased Rick and how you said sisters."

He cocked an eyebrow.

"You said it like they were puppies. Older sisters, it wouldn't be that way."

"That's insightful."

She turned on the oven to preheat. "I always wanted a big brother."

"Oh yeah?"

She had no idea why she'd told him that, especially since she hoped he didn't volunteer to fill in. "I probably wouldn't if I had one."

"Depends on the brother. Did Rick pay you for the food?"

"No." She wiped the counter with a damp cloth.

"He plans to. There's no way you're cooking and paying."

She rinsed the cloth in the sink, wishing he hadn't brought it up. It made her feel like help. "So, is Noelle okay?"

"She's lousy at pretending she's fine. I think she and Liam are getting sick, and that's especially bad for Noelle." He glanced down to where Livie was pulling pans and bowls from the lower cabinets.

"I making soup, Daddy."

"Okay, sweetie." He cut another potato.

Glancing at the clock, Quinn said, "Time to stick the turkey in the fryer." She bent for the five-gallon bucket holding brine and bird.

"Better dry it off first."

When she looked at him suspiciously, he said, "I know what happens when hot fat and liquid meet. That's physics, baby." He took the other side of the bucket. "Let me help you with that."

She held the turkey as together they poured the brine into the sink. That close, his scent enveloped her, a musky cologne and baby shampoo.

"Grab some paper towels," Morgan said, hoisting the bird barehanded out of the bucket.

They patted it dry, like a big stiff baby from a sink bath, and then she swabbed the cavity and pushed the pronged tool through. Morgan said, "I'll carry it. You lift the fryer lid."

Out through the door, to where the fryer had melted the snowpack from the patio, he carried the pale, bumpy turkey that would turn out a rich brown, according to the pictures. Checking the thermometer to make sure the oil was hot enough, she said, "Three minutes per pound," and calculated the time as he lowered it in.

"How big is the bird?"

She told him.

"Good. There are two more joining us."

"Oh?"

"I invited Rudy from the general store."

Something in his tone and the way he looked aside caught her up short. He'd warned her this might be a setup. Was this a countermeasure?

"And the professor." At her puzzled look, he added, "The historian?"

"Oh. Great." They could talk asylum over turkey. He'd told her about that one, but Rudy? Apparently for this setup, he'd brought in a ringer.

Morgan watched Quinn make quick work of the potatoes and get them boiling. She slid the pan of vegetables into the hot oven. He wasn't sure what he'd said or done, but she seemed to close off, her motions hard and tight.

Looking into the dining room large enough to accommodate the family and guests in cabins at full capacity, he saw Noelle had already set an artistic table. There couldn't be much, if anything, left to do, so when male voices carried in from the great room, he said, "Come and meet them."

"You go ahead." Quinn took out another onion and some stalks of celery and began to cut them to within an inch of their lives. "I've got this now." She never looked up, but the vegetables suffered.

"Come on." Scooping Livie up, he herded Quinn toward the other room. "You know Rudy, right?"

"He let me tape up the cupboard pictures."

"Right."

Although Livie had found Rudy fascinating in the store with the counter between them, face-to-face, she wasn't so sure. Quinn looked minuscule next to the great bear with russet-colored beard, ponytail, and gaps for two lower teeth that made his broad smile a jack-o'-lantern. His heart was just as big and just as open. For that and other reasons, Morgan considered him a friend.

"Rudy, this is Quinn. She's responsible for the feast."

Her clipped greeting and closed body language surprised and bothered him. Rudy deserved better. And then it struck him that she thought he'd brought Rudy in to run interference. It must have sounded like, "Check out the little lady, and she cooks too."

She said, "I need to finish the stuffing," then turned and stalked to the kitchen.

His disappointment in her shifted to frustration with himself. He didn't usually make such mistakes. He cocked his jaw as Noelle came down the stairs and greeted Rudy warmly in spite of her pallor and the shadows under her eyes. If Rudy had suffered Quinn's chill, it was alleviated now, but the situation still required finesse.

When Rick took Rudy out to see the new crossbow he kept locked in the barn, Morgan leaned in to Noelle. "Can you check on Quinn? Something's up and . . ."

"You want *me* to solve it, Mr. Mojo?"

"Not solve, just check. It might be nothing."

Her eyes narrowed. "If you sense something . . ."

"Just go in, woman to woman, and feel it out." He set Livie down, and she made a beeline for the ark-shaped toy chest, seeming a little lost without Liam. "Make sure she's comfortable with the situation."

"She was excited when I invited her. What aren't you telling me?"

"Sometimes things get misconstrued. And I might be wrong altogether."

"Hmm." Casting a backward look, Noelle moved into the kitchen.

He knelt down with Livie and helped her raise the hinged roof of the wooden ark Rick had built for Liam. Though he'd constructed all the buildings and most of the furniture on the ranch, this was the first toy he'd fashioned. As the whim struck, his brother had added creatures until it was almost as packed as the real thing.

Livie reached in and withdrew a giraffe, then the elephants, lions, bears, beavers, kangaroos, and rabbits. Partly because of this set, she could name and make all their sounds by eighteen months. If she didn't know the sound, she gave them a word. Rabbits said nibble, alligators chomp.

Liam liked to line the creatures up along the roof ridge and knock them off with Ping-Pong balls, then Livie picked them up and said, "You all right, rabbit? All right, frog?" Now, with no threats to their well-being, she spread them on the floor. "Daddy, want squirrel?"

"I would love squirrel." He pretended to eat it.

"Don't eat it." Giggling, she tried to find it in his mouth, but he produced it in his hand. Then, of course, she fed him every other critter in the ark.

That's how they were when Rick and Rudy came in with Dr. Jenkins.

Just watching Quinn exhausted her. Noelle

sighed. "I'm so sorry this was all left to you."

"Oh no." Quinn hand-mashed butter and sour cream into the steaming pot of potatoes. "Both Rick and Morgan helped."

"Morgan? In the kitchen?" Feeling light-headed, she sank onto a stool.

"He cut potatoes and got the turkey into the fryer."

She fought a wave of nausea. "That's something, I guess. But I wanted to get to know you, not put you to work."

"You did?" Quinn flicked her a glance.

"I do. And I'm so sorry, but I can't . . ." She stood abruptly. "Forgive me." As stoically as she could, she went to the half bath off the laundry room and heaved.

She washed her face at the pedestal sink, rinsed out her mouth, and mortified, returned to the kitchen. "Ugh," she said grimly. "Don't begin a friendship in the early months of pregnancy."

"Well, it does break down walls." Quinn sent her a smile, but there did seem to be some effort to produce it.

Noelle pressed the back of her hand to her forehead. "I don't want to alarm Rick, but I'm pretty sure Liam's not the only one coming down with something."

"Alarm Rick?" Quinn put the lid on the potatoes.

"He gets very concerned, because when I first came out here, I got really sick. It almost killed me."

Quinn paused. "Wow."

"I'd moved out of the ranch and was living in a hovel. I had a broken leg and couldn't work or pay the rent. My utilities got turned off."

Quinn's face showed clear disbelief. "I'd have thought —"

"With my rich daddy?" She spread a hand. "I was proving myself independent. Instead I caught pneumonia. If Rick hadn't brought over my mail and found me incoherent, I'd have died."

"Thank God he did."

Yes, but she remembered his face. "He was *so* angry."

"Why angry?"

"Because I hadn't asked for help. Or taken the help he offered." She touched her fingers to her throat. "Unfortunately, that weakened my resistance, and anytime I catch something it worries my husband."

"He seems very kind." A hint of wistfulness touched the words.

"He's everything I didn't know I wanted." And more.

"I know what I want." Quinn's intense, long-lashed eyes burned. "Honesty."

"That's it?"

"It's no small thing. Even unintentional lies and well-meaning plots can wound." She grabbed mitts and opened the oven. The smell of roasted vegetables and garlic wafted out, wonderful and torturous. "That's why I'm disappointed this invitation was a setup."

"What do you mean?"

"Morgan and me. And now he's foisting me on Rudy." Her voice hitched.

Noelle blinked. "Quinn, my invitation had nothing to do with Morgan. I wanted to spend time with you."

"But he said . . ."

No wonder he looked guilty. "He's mistaken."

With a spatula, Quinn turned the glistening vegetables. "He believed it enough to bring a spare."

Noelle shook her head. "I don't think that's what he's doing. Although he might try to protect you from an awkward situation, if he really thought that."

Quinn slid the vegetables back into the oven without comment, and yet not without emotion. Color that might not be heat from the oven found her cheeks. "Is it awkward for him?"

"It doesn't seem to be. He's concerned about you."

Quinn raised her eyes. "Me?"

"I believe your feelings on the subject were apparent."

Quinn blew out a breath. "Great."

"Good thing we're all about honesty here." She smiled.

■ ■ ■ ■

Going out with a platter for the turkey, Quinn shot a glance over her shoulder.

"I'm not stalking you," Morgan said, amusing himself by using her disclaimer. "Just timed the turkey too."

"Oh." She noticed the roll of paper towels he held. "Good idea."

While she made a bed of the towels, he raised the crispy bird from the grease, letting the peanut oil run back into the fryer. They rolled it back and forth on the paper, then moved it to the platter. With some difficulty, he detached the utensil while she gripped the platter.

Morgan took it from her, nodding. "Can you get the door?"

"I could also get the turkey."

"Humor me."

"I doubt I'd be the first."

He cocked his head, eyeing her as she pulled open the door and motioned him in. Still seated at the counter, Noelle watched them beneath hooded lids. She might not have intended to throw them together, but it didn't stop her speculating.

In a voice raspier than moments before, she said, "I can't believe it, but that looks good enough to eat."

"True praise from a pregnant woman."

Quinn smiled. When the thermometer gave a perfect reading in the breast and thigh, she said, "I guess we're ready."

With Noelle's help, she got the feast on the table while Morgan summoned everyone.

"Dr. Jenkins!" Noelle gave a hoarse cry. Delight overtook her face when she saw the graying academic. "What a fantastic surprise! It's been much too long." She beamed at Rick.

"Not me," Rick said. "It was Morgan."

Morgan shrugged. "We have something to discuss. This seemed a good time."

Rick stood at his chair. "We'll all catch up, but first let's bless this food." Instead of bowing his head, he raised his hands and looked heavenward. " 'Praise the Lord, all you nations; extol him, all you peoples. For great is his love toward us, and the faithfulness of the Lord endures forever.' "

Rick's jubilance reminded her of King David dancing into the city under the scornful eye of a scoffing wife, though no one at the table scoffed. That Rick should be more expressive with God than she'd seen him with people touched her.

"Thank you for your bounty, for all that nourishes and enriches us, for this food, and for Quinn, who prepared the feast. Bless her and all she does, in Jesus' name. Amen."

Blinking tears from her eyes, she slipped into her chair. What did she have to feel testy about? This was wonderful.

But the plates had barely begun passing when Liam shuffled into the room, coughing and flushed. Dismayed, Noelle lifted him into her arms, murmuring an apology as she stood. Rick made a move, but she waved him back. Given the matching flush on Noelle's cheeks, Quinn doubted either would be back soon.

They passed plates to Rick for crisp, succulent turkey, then heaped on potatoes, stuffing, cornbread pudding, and savory roasted vegetables. Rudy's homemade cranberry chutney and the crusty dinner rolls from the professor rounded out the meal. She absorbed the compliments like a sponge in the desert.

With a stirring in the eyes of someone who loves seeking and imparting knowledge, Dr. Jenkins turned to her. "Morgan tells me you've discovered the sanitarium remains."

She nodded. "He thought you might know what sort of place it was."

"As with anything, the stories are wide and varied. Vera might have told you some, but sadly, I hear she passed."

"Yes." She took a bite so delicious she almost groaned. Not bad, if she did say so herself. She caught Morgan's eye, and when he raised his own bite in a toast, she realized he'd plucked the thought right out of her head.

Dr. Jenkins said, "I made you copies of the

tales I've collected, bits and pieces of asylum lore." He presented a brief history, mostly dates of operation and the like. "I won't say more now, since some of it's not for tender ears or dinnertime."

"Good," Rick said. "I don't want to lose my appetite for a feast like this."

The professor shifted glibly on. "I understand you shop estates. Have you come across other interesting pieces over the years?"

She brightened. "The best was a cabinet of curiosities."

"Really." His interest piqued. "Those were private precursors to museums, you know, though with dubious provenance."

"This one had a stuffed dodo on a perch. The doors were lined with silk and velvet and displayed small framed photos of circus performers. The shelves held a jar of mummy dust, a sample of Sasquatch fur, arrowheads and grizzly teeth, a fossilized snail, and a glassed insect collection."

"Perfect." He smiled, delighted.

Rudy asked her to describe the dodo and she did, laughing. "Mostly I find decorative or useful things. Some quite beautiful."

"Ah, beauty."

She loved the reverence Dr. Jenkins gave the word. Their discussion followed a natural flow, drawing Rick and Rudy in as well.

About halfway through, Livie pointed her fork at the window. "It snowing, Daddy."

"Snowing hard," he agreed, the first thing he'd said since the meal began.

They all looked out.

"Guess we'll see what it does." Rick pressed a napkin to his mouth. "The forecast is all over the place."

Rudy sliced his turkey with gusto. "This morning it smelled like the mother of all storms."

He smelled the weather?

Rudy took a bite worthy of his frame. "This turkey's stupendous."

She smiled. "Only a few thousand calories in peanut oil."

"Don't you know it."

She laughed. When she had misunderstood Morgan's motives, she'd resented Rudy. Now she was enjoying him and the professor — even if she hadn't imagined Thanksgiving dinner with four men and a baby.

Chapter 9

Somewhere between chopping potatoes and finishing his pumpkin pie, Morgan knew he was in trouble. Noelle hadn't come back after taking Liam up to bed, but Quinn held her own with four guys, three of them engaging her with a conversant ease he couldn't seem to manage, yet every time she opened her mouth, he had to hear what she would say. He'd interacted with Quinn in other situations. But sharing this meal, listening, watching, was like a black-and-white movie being colorized — skin tones warming, hues deepening, brightening.

She reacted to something someone said, and her laugh had a throaty quality like the best actresses, not manly but feminine in a sexy way that kicked him. He wasn't dead. He was virile. And for the first time since he'd walked away from a hole in the earth, he remembered that.

A gust of wind slapped snow against the window like fat white hands pleading to come in. The storm had gained corporeal mass. He looked down the length of the table at Rick. Unless they wanted to give everyone the bum's rush, they should offer them rooms. One thing this ranch had was shelter in a storm. But that meant a night. And a morning.

Pulling his thoughts from Quinn, he focused on cleaning Livie up before she left her booster seat. Quinn stood too and started clearing plates.

"I'll get the dishes, please," Rick said. "Make yourselves comfortable in the great room. Morgan, can you light the fire?"

Rick had laid it earlier with thigh-sized logs in the gargantuan stone mouth, a fire that would burn for hours and set every face aglow.

"Morgan?"

"Yeah. Okay." He moved with their guests to the great room. Leaving Livie at the toy box, he flicked the long-neck lighter and touched it to the kindling at regular intervals. Heat pushed against his face, but he did a thorough job before straightening. It would burn evenly and well.

Rudy moved to the sideboard, where he'd set a bottle of Courvoisier on arrival. He poured a snifter and held it out. Morgan shook his head.

"Well, I know it's not the top shelf you're used to, but it's not rotgut either."

"It doesn't agree with me."

Rudy eyed him. "Courvoisier?"

"Alcohol. It no longer finds a home in my stomach." Rudy had surely noticed he spent little time at the Boar since returning, but he'd have no reason to know it cut across the board.

"How do you party?"

Morgan looked at his little girl. "Well, sometimes we put on funny hats and pretend we're animals."

Rudy guffawed, but he was still puzzling a change that profound. Quinn had followed the exchange, perhaps equally puzzled, but she hadn't known him before.

"I wouldn't mind a taste on the porch with my pipe," Dr. Jenkins put in.

"Too nasty on the porch, Professor." Morgan swung his hand. "Sit here on the hearth."

Eyeing the sizable aperture, Dr. Jenkins drew a burled pipe from his pocket. "I imagine there's a pretty good draft."

As they traded places, Rudy held a glass out to Quinn.

"No thanks. I have to drive."

The word pierced like a barb. Morgan said, "You're not driving. Look outside." He was near enough that the fire might explain sweat breaking out on his neck. Only it wasn't that, based on the matching rush of his heart. "You won't see what's coming."

"I can drive in snow."

"Not like this." His heart became a fist punching his ribs. Moms' night out. Sundowner winds igniting parched hillsides like flaming locusts, billowing smoke and ash into a blinding shroud.

He heard her voice through a tunnel. ". . . probably should leave now."

"You can't!"

Rudy and the professor stared discreetly.

"You guys either. We have cabins. You should stay."

Rudy shrugged. "It's a storm, Morgan." No snow would stop that mountain man. And if one went, they'd all go.

He clenched his hands. His airway constricted. He'd sound like a fool begging.

But Quinn looked out again and nodded. "Actually, a cabin sounds good."

He sensed her indulgence and didn't care. Anything to keep her off the roads.

"Daddy." Livie ran over and hugged his leg. It was just what he needed — to crouch down low and recover. He buried his face against her head. Two attacks within weeks and both about Quinn. There was nothing confusing in that. He concentrated on pulling air into his lungs, visualized his heart rate slowing.

When he came out of it, the professor was talking. He'd been talking, the mellow tone of his voice interspersed by draws on his pipe. Rick responded from the other side of the room, where his fingers plucked a stream of praise on his guitar. Morgan sat back on the hearth and held Livie between his knees, warm and breathing. She turned and kissed his mouth, then replaced his kiss with her thumb.

The sweat had dried, his racing pulse slowed. Quinn sipped from a cordial glass, proof she wouldn't renege. Rudy sat on the edge of a chair, all brandy-warmed and smitten. Had anyone checked on Noelle?

"I'll be right back," he told Livie's ear and unfolded himself from around her.

Rick's gaze followed him up the stairs with generosity and trust. His brother had depths not everyone attained.

Morgan put a knuckle to the door. "Noelle?"

"Come in." She sat reading in the wing chair, with a softly snoring Liam on her chest. Both were draped by a knitted throw. Mentholatum scented the air from a vaporizer in the corner, but over that lay the stale trace of illness.

He left the door open behind him for more reasons than one. "How are you guys?"

"Contagious."

When he sat down on the footstool, she slid the bookmark into her novel and set it down beside the hardly touched plate of food. "Is Quinn doing all right?"

"She's great. Rudy's a goner. The professor's entertaining everyone."

"I so wanted to see him." Her eyes made a slow blink and stayed half-mast.

"He'll be here in the morning. They're staying over."

"It's that bad out?"

He cleared his throat. "Seemed like it."

She caught his meaning. "Are you okay?"

"What's a little meltdown, right?"

Liam shifted in her arms, then settled. It took an act of God to wake him at the best of times. This wasn't one.

Her brow furrowed. "I wonder why that's started again."

"Damaged nerves refiring."

"Better than paralysis."

He stared at his hands, uncertain he agreed.

"It's not wrong to care, Morgan."

"It's not smart."

She tipped her head. "Go look in my top right dresser drawer."

With exaggerated reluctance, he rose and obeyed. The drawer held a few silk scarves, gloves, and a box he recognized.

"Open it."

He didn't need to. It held the eggshell he'd once given her to symbolize the walls around her heart.

"You helped me crack my shell, Morgan. Now you need to break out of your own."

His throat constricted. "I didn't miss her tonight." He looked over his shoulder. "It's Thanksgiving, and I should have thought, If

Jill were here . . ."

"She's not." A shadow crossed her face. "But you and Livie are."

He closed the drawer and turned. "I thought my heart was steel."

She smiled softly. "I never believed that for a minute."

He flexed and clenched his hands. "I don't know what God expects."

"He wants you to live."

That took so much more than drawing the next breath. It took a leap of faith he wasn't sure he'd land. After a while he looked up. "Can I get you something?"

"Hot cider would be fabulous."

"I can do fabulous." He took the dinner plate away. Descending, he passed by the others in the great room, their conversation a circular eddy buoyed on the strains of guitar strings. In the kitchen, he ladled Noelle a mug of cider. He was about to take it upstairs when Quinn asked to do it.

"She's worried about contagion."

"I never get sick."

"That's because you live alone. Here it's a merry-go-round — on again off again up again down again."

She took the cup undeterred. "The professor has a question for you."

Looking into her face, he heard Noelle telling him to live. He hadn't gone looking, but staring after Quinn, he wondered how painful a rebound might be.

In the upstairs hall, Quinn watched Noelle back out of a bedroom with crayon drawings taped to the door. Liam's room, she guessed.

Seeing her, Noelle whispered, "He might finally stay down."

They went into a room less rustically furnished than the rest of the house, with cherrywood furniture. Noelle dropped into a wing chair and draped herself with a multicolor throw made of fabulous shaggy yarns and ribbons.

"That's awesome."

Noelle smiled. "Last summer's art fair. Are you cold?"

"No." She set the cider on the Queen Anne table. "I hope you don't mind that I took over from Morgan."

"I'm glad you did. I feel awful leaving you to the guys."

She raised an eyebrow. "There's no shortage of testosterone."

Noelle laughed, then coughed torturously. "Excuse me." She shook her head. "This stuff kicks my butt."

Coming so surprisingly from sophisticated Noelle, Quinn couldn't stop her own laugh. "I'm sorry. I didn't expect you to say that."

"I got it from Liam."

"Liam?"

"I believe he got it from Morgan, but

Morgan's admitting nothing."

"Speaking of Morgan . . ." Quinn took the other wing chair and drew her feet up cross-legged. "I wasn't going to ask, but is he sick?"

Noelle sipped her cider and swallowed. "Not the way you mean."

"Twice now —"

"I know. Panic attacks." Noelle set down her cup and seemed to consider her words. "Morgan's intensely private right now, but I think, if you give him the chance, he'll explain."

He'd had the chance and passed, both times. "It's just kind of scary." Especially that first time in the cellar, though the ambience hadn't helped.

"I'm glad you agreed to stay."

"I got the feeling it mattered."

"It did." Noelle studied her a moment. "Until now, he wouldn't have cared enough to worry. You've made an impact."

Not what she'd intended, and yet . . . She tucked up a corner of the cushy afghan from the floor. "Would you like me to make a dinner plate for you?"

"I got some from Rick, and it was wonderful." Noelle sank back in the chair. "I'd kill for a slice of that pie though."

"Plain pumpkin or walnut streusel?"

"Ordinarily I'd say streusel. But with this throat . . ."

"One slice plain pumpkin coming up."

Quinn slipped out.

In the kitchen she cut a slice, but Rick came in and relieved her as though they were a relay team passing the baton.

He said, "I need to check in with her."

She could see the worry in his eyes. These Spencer men were long on protective genes.

Morgan lay propped on his side near a wooden ark with little animals all around him. As he stayed perfectly still, Livie perched an elephant on his shoulder. It toppled, and she tried three times before it balanced. Laudable commitment to the goal. When he raised his eyes, Quinn met them with a smile. He didn't look away.

Instead of retaking her seat, she sat on the floor with Livie, who immediately laid a giraffe on her knee. Quinn stood it up and made it say hi. Livie's face lit. Morgan crooked a brow. His animals were just sitting there. Hers talked.

Livie handed her a bear, and the bear had quite a bit to say to the giraffe. The corners of Morgan's mouth deepened. He slow-blinked when Livie took the elephant from his shoulder and stood it with the bear and giraffe. He mouthed *Traitor.*

She ducked her chin, laughing silently as the elephant joined the conversation. It wasn't her fault if he didn't know how to play dolls.

Across the room, Rudy looked from her to

Morgan and back. His shoulders rounded. "Well, I guess I'll take off." He stood up. "Quinn, it was the best turkey I ever tasted."

"I'm glad you were here for it." She meant that.

Dr. Jenkins looked out the darkened window. "Sure you want to brave it?"

"My Wagoneer'll plow through anything." Rudy pulled on his coat and wrapped a scarf over his face.

Still propped on his side, Morgan pivoted toward Rudy. "I wish you'd stay. You'll have better visibility in the morning."

Now that darkness had fallen, the drive through a blizzard on mountain roads would be treacherous.

"Gertie needs her milk."

"Gertie?" Quinn craned up to see him at closer range.

"His cat," Morgan said. They all knew she'd survive a night without milk. But Rudy was determined.

Morgan looked from the door closing behind his friend to her. Did he think she'd change her mind? She wouldn't do that when it obviously mattered, but she rose when Dr. Jenkins nodded toward her, drawing a manila envelope from his briefcase.

She sat down beside him on the hearth, biting a hangnail. "So truthfully, how tough is this material?"

He considered a moment. "Some success

stories, an interview with one of the directors many years after the fact, local legends, and as I mentioned, some horrors."

She nodded. "There's an electrocution bed in the cellar."

The skin around his eyes creased deeply. "You mean electroshock."

"Right. That."

"And the term is now electroconvulsive therapy."

"Now?" She stared, distressed. "It's still happening?"

"Oh yes, abuses coupled with the development of antipsychotic and mood-stabilizing drugs curtailed its use, but recently it's had a resurgence. A hundred to a hundred fifty thousand patients a year in the US alone — under rigidly controlled hospital administration."

"Why?"

"Quite simply, it works. Electrically causing the brain to seize can be efficacious when drugs fail. Along the lines of defibrillation for the heart. A sort of kick start to reestablish normal rhythm."

"But I thought, I mean . . ." She shook her head. "If you saw the thing . . ."

"I have." He drew on his pipe, realized the bowl was finished, and tapped the ash out into the fireplace.

"The one at Vera's?"

"Whenever possible I go to the source to

collect my tales."

She imagined him down in the cellar, his thin frame poised and observant, curiosity in his keen, intelligent eyes. "Did you feel it? The despair?"

"Ah, my dear." He tapped her hand. "It's all part of the human condition."

"Big chunks of that condition stink like dirty socks."

He laughed. "Unfortunately."

"So you know about the drugs?"

He raised his brows.

"In the old cabinet."

He turned to Morgan. "That's the discovery?"

Morgan nodded. "I thought we'd have a look. But we're not getting over there tonight."

She said, "It's LSD. And I don't know what else. Why would they give confused and suffering people hallucinations?"

"It was once something of a psychiatric cure-all, hailed as a remedy for everything from schizophrenia to criminal behavior, sexual perversions, and alcoholism. It was administered to enhance the psychotherapeutic discourse by lowering inhibition. Some practitioners used it in conjunction with metaphysical and guided supernatural journeys."

"That doesn't sound like medicine."

"Until recently, treating the mind had little

concrete science. Anything that seemed an avenue was given a try. Therapists took the drug themselves to gain understanding of the schizophrenic experience."

"They dosed themselves to know what crazy looked like?"

The professor smiled. "Precisely."

"So why is it illegal?"

"After years of research and experimentation, its use in psychotherapy was largely debunked. It didn't increase creativity or libido, and had no lasting positive effect in treating alcoholics or criminals or deviants. It did, however, cause adverse reactions. Acute panic, psychotic crises, and flashbacks, especially in users ill-equipped to deal with such trauma."

"Like people in mental hospitals."

"Precisely."

Listening across the room, Morgan rubbed his daughter's tummy with feather-light strokes as she lay beside him on the floor. "Any thoughts on disposal?"

"Given the legalities, I suppose the sheriff and hazmat. But I'd like a look first."

Morgan's eyes moved to her. "We'll go over in the daylight."

Awash with their shared adventure, she nodded.

"In the meantime," Dr. Jenkins said, "I hope the anecdotes I've brought won't prove too troubling."

Quinn shrugged. "I'm not even sure why I want to know. It's not my house, not my people."

"And none of that matters, does it?" He smiled.

She really liked his face — Gandalf in his gentler moments. "I guess not. But why?"

"Another part of the human condition. Compassion."

She felt Morgan's gaze wrap around her but didn't look. The emotions were getting difficult to manage.

Rick came downstairs and handed her a bag of things. "From Noelle. For staying over."

She peeked in at warm pajamas and towel, new toothbrush, hairbrush, and small toiletries that reminded her the ranch provided commercial hospitality. No wonder they were so congenial. She slipped the asylum envelope into the bag, then, hugging the stack, she looked at Morgan.

He'd risen from the floor and was dressing Livie in her coat. Must be the little one's bedtime. Maybe everyone's, especially with Noelle and Liam sick. She put on her own coat, wishing she'd worn something warmer than the soft, thigh-high skirt and sweater, black tights, and over-the-knee leg warmers. They covered the top of her ankle boots, and the coat was warm. That was the best she could do.

Morgan said, "I'll walk you to your cabin."

"You have your hands full."

"There's room for one more." He pulled a quilted blanket from the closet, draped one side over himself and Livie, and held the other end open for her.

Much closer than she'd intended to get, but when Rick opened the door to the swirling storm, she ducked in and pulled the other side of the blanket tight. Blinking and gasping, they kicked through more than a foot of new powder and wind-driven flakes to the smallest, closest cabin. Letting go of the blanket, she hurried inside, surprised Morgan and Livie came too.

"Rick doesn't rent these in winter, so let me make sure your water's on."

And heat, though it didn't feel like it. Shivering, she set down her load.

"Here, hold Livie."

The child was so slight, it was like holding a kitten. Livie studied her, unconcerned since their animal play but curious, while Morgan opened the utility closet and confirmed that the pilot on the water heater was lit. He reached around and turned the valve to allow the hot water from the heater to the pipes.

"That would have been frustrating."

He closed the closet door. "There's no furnace, but I'll get a fire going in the woodburning stove. You could hang with me until it actually warms up."

"I'll be okay. I just wish I had my computer

so I could check e-mail."

"So many friends wanting you?"

"Business, actually. There's always something."

He straightened from the freshly lit stove. "Can you check it from your phone?"

"I don't have Internet on my plan."

"Come use my laptop. I'll be putting Livie down. You're welcome to it."

She looked from him to the door. Was it worth braving the elements? Even though it was Thanksgiving, she had auctions ending and people might need answers. Plus her teeth were starting to chatter. "Okay. If you don't mind."

He wrapped the blanket around her and Livie until she felt like an Eskimo mama. "Watch your step, okay? I'll run ahead."

If he was trusting her with his precious cargo, she'd more than watch her step. Inside the blanket, Livie clung like a marsupial in a pouch. Quinn yanked the door shut, the storm ripping at her as she pressed into the wind. If Morgan hadn't lit his cabin's porch, they might have wandered in circles until she dropped like a frozen pioneer on the prairie.

She stomped her feet before entering, though it was pointless with the porch as snowy as everything else.

He pulled her inside. "Don't sweat it."

When he closed the door and unwrapped the two of them, Livie dove into his arms.

She didn't blame her a bit. "I hope Rudy made it home."

"I was thinking that too."

"Will the professor —"

"He'll stay in the house."

"That was an option?" After the second dash through the snow, her teeth chattered purposefully.

"Rick assumed you'd want privacy."

She didn't say she was sick to death of privacy.

"Stick a log in that stove, will you?" He turned away, telling Livie, "Come on, sweetie. Time to tuck you in." He started toward the bedrooms, then looked back. "My laptop's on the table."

"Thanks." A blast of heat hit her face when she opened the iron stove door, even though there were only coals in the bottom. The previous fire must have been substantial. She took a smallish log from the stack and propped it over the coals, took a larger one and wedged it over the first. She left the door open for air to feed the fire. The wood must have been seasoned, because it didn't take long before pine-scented flames shot up.

Before using his computer, she went to the window and watched the storm. The wind had teeth, and she'd have to face it again. Cold just thinking about it, she turned away and activated his laptop. It came right up, but she couldn't get in, so she went to the door of Livie's room. The little girl wore footed jammies that made her too cuddly to bear. Nestled in with her daddy, rocking and reading, the two of them entranced her.

Morgan glanced up.

"Password?"

"Oh. Sorry. It's easier for me to do it."

She stepped back. "I can wait."

"No, I'll get it. You finish the story." He held Livie up, and she took his place in the rocking chair, warm from his sitting there. Snuggling Livie into her lap, she picked up where Morgan had left off, reading a sweet little story called *Sam's Bath.*

Morgan came back and leaned in the doorframe. The laptop must have been ready, but he didn't interrupt her reading. Sam's ball went into the bath. Sam's bear went into the bath. Sam's cookie went into the bath. Uh-oh, here comes Doggy. Doggy goes into the bath!

"Just goes to show what greed'll get you," she told Morgan. "If Doggy had only resisted the cookie."

A smile tugged his mouth as he reached down and lifted Livie from the chair. Kissing her cheek, her neck, her mouth, he tucked her in. Quinn moved out into the hall, where the tenderness didn't fill her throat with the ache of tears. She had to stop this. Her situation was precarious enough without involving a man with a child and issues of his own.

Chapter 10

Quinn sat on Morgan's couch and delved into business matters that were no more emotional than brushing her teeth. He came out, pulling Livie's door behind him. He closed the stove doors, as well, and sat on the chair to her right, crossing his ankles on the table. She looked over, concentration dissolving. Seriously, who could think next to him?

"She doesn't cry or anything?"

He cocked his head.

"Livie doesn't cry about going to bed?"

"If she's overexcited, she might."

"Blizzards and strange women aren't overexciting?"

"You're not *that* strange." His mouth twitched.

From their first foray into the cellar, his sense of humor always caught her by surprise. "You've only seen my good side."

"Do the fangs come out at midnight?"

"You're mere hours from finding out."

She completed the last few communications, then sat back and sighed. "Thanks for that. I like to address things as they come up."

"You're conscientious."

Detrimentally. She indicated the laptop. "Do you need this?"

He shrugged. "Whatever's there can wait."

How could a man so laid back have accomplished so much? She crossed one knee over the other. "How was your trip? The . . . consulting or whatever?"

"Mostly whatever. The consult comes next."

She threaded her fingers under her chin. "How does that work? Do you advertise?"

"Typically clients come to me."

Of course they did. "And you fix their problems." That thought sank in. A professional problem solver.

"If the situation has promise, I tackle it."

"For a fee?"

"Or stock in the company."

She leaned toward him. "If it doesn't work, you lose too."

He pulled a slow smile. Only once had she seen that level of confidence in a man, but this time it was real.

"Then on to the next crisis?"

"If there's one handy."

He had the sharp-edged features cameras loved, the beard darkening his cheeks and jaw in a way two days would make scruffily sexy. She had only dated soft men deemed appropriate by her father and the elders, since the minister's family must be above reproach. She didn't desire reckless, dangerous men, but not one of them had moved her as Morgan did.

She straightened. "I better get back."

"Uh." He frowned. "I didn't think this through very well. I can't leave Livie —"

"Of course not." She stood. "Don't worry, I'll make a run for it."

He walked to the window. "Can you see where you're going?"

"I'll follow our tracks."

"I'd let you —"

"No, Morgan, I'm fine."

He hesitated, then gave a small nod. "Call me when you get there."

"I don't have your number." She took out her phone to add him and paled. Missed text message from a number not in her contacts. She pressed End, nostrils distending.

"What's wrong?"

She had to move the lump in her throat to talk. "Nothing."

"It's not nothing."

"Just . . . harassment." She turned to go.

With a deft motion, he took the phone from her.

"Don't."

He tipped up his glance. "I'm putting my number in your contacts."

"Oh. Okay."

After doing so, he handed it back. "Call."

Nodding, she pulled open the door and dove into the storm. It pummeled her as she staggered back along their tracks, step by lurching step, and all but fell through the door. If she'd gone home right after dinner, she might have made it. There was not a snowball's chance now. But why did she need to be home? She could panic just as easily in this warmed-up cozy cabin.

Shivering, she got out of her cold, wet things, spreading them around the tiny room to dry. Furiously she tossed her phone onto the forest green couch, wishing she hadn't seen the text waiting to be read. Anyone she wanted to hear from was in her contacts. An unknown number —

Maybe it was a mistake. A wrong number. She didn't believe that. He must have gotten her number from Hannah, who got it from someone it would hurt too much to suspect. Her parents? Pops?

Quaking, she slipped into the bedroom. She put on Noelle's pajamas, then ducked into the bathroom and brushed her teeth, looking at herself in the small rustic mirror. Not *that* strange, huh? If Morgan only knew.

Morgan! She rushed out, grabbed her phone, and called the number he'd entered. "Morgan. I'm sorry I forgot to call."

His pause could have been amusement or annoyance. The first, she thought, when he said, “Keeping me humble.”

“It wasn’t you. It was —” She almost blurted his name. “The storm, I guess. I hurried in to get warm and dry.”

“Uh-huh.”

“So . . . I’m warm and dry.”

“Good.”

“And I’ll see you in the morning.”

“Okay. Good night.”

“Good night, Morgan.” Her hand shook as she ended the call, hating herself for being a coward. She had a message to read. Chewing her lip, she opened and read.

You’re dead.

Yeah? She scowled. Find me first.

Tough words, but her chest heaved. Her hands shook. She climbed into bed and lay wondering if Markham could flush her out like a quail in a thicket. How? He wasn’t mafia, wasn’t law enforcement. He had no vast resources — anymore. He was a grifter, a con, a low-down cheating liar. A sociopath.

She’d seen through him, but of course, no one believed her. That had puffed his ego like a glutted sow. Her own family, and it was still Markham they believed.

She drew a slow, calming breath. He wanted her to panic, to make a mistake. But she wouldn’t. People had been misused, their trust violated — not that they hadn’t participated. Still, they’d been duped, and so, even though he was everything she despised, she’d played his game and won. Now she only had to stay alive.

Sitting on the porch bench in the dark, Markham scowled, even though he hadn't expected Quinn to respond. Texting threats felt silly, and threats of any sort meant nothing when he had no way to carry them out. He would. He had to. But how?

"Tell me everything you know." He spoke in low tones, so as not to alarm the woman beside him or alert others to his presence.

"I've told you." Hannah looked hurt. "Quinn only talks to Mother. I had to sneak to get the phone number."

"If she talks to Gwen, she must say something about her life."

"They hardly ever talk."

"But there has to be something in some conversation that can help."

She rubbed her head as though thinking hurt. "No one knows where she is."

"Or they're not telling you."

"Mother would tell me. We don't have secrets."

He'd seen the overweening relationship with both her parents but didn't believe for a minute they told her everything. He clenched his jaw, frustrated and more than a little angry. "Think. Has she gone to college, had medical care?" He wasn't sure if it was possible to hack education or health care records.

He'd have to hire someone, and his funds might not cover that kind of work. "Does she have a pet? A relationship?" Any detail could lead to something useful. There were plenty of searches he could do.

"She has a house."

"What?"

Hannah gulped. He'd spoken too boldly.

"Is she renting it?"

"No. It's really hers." She looked sullen. "Quinn had to call and brag."

The tightness in his chest eased. He looked into her teary eyes, masking his sudden excitement with simulated compassion. "That must be very trying."

" 'Let the one who boasts boast in the Lord.' "

"Exactly so." If his smile was dry, she didn't notice.

"Quinn should learn humility," Hannah said primly.

Oh, she would. Indeed she would.

Morgan had waited for Quinn's call, worried when it took so long. He'd stepped out the door and seen nothing but snow and the lights of her cabin, but they'd left those on when she came to his. Her call came shortly before he was about to bundle Livie back out in the storm to search. He'd been out of the game long enough to believe she'd forgotten him, but something told him it was more.

Harassment had degrees. He doubted her claim that it was nothing but had nothing to go on beyond that. He keyed the number he'd memorized at a glance. When a man answered, Morgan said, "Hey, . . ." He garbled a name. "How's it going?"

"What?"

"Oh man, I can barely hear you."

The man growled, "Who is this?"

"Who's this?"

The call ended.

He hadn't really expected the guy to give his name, but it was worth a try before going to the next level. He pictured Quinn's face, the fear quickly hidden behind bravado. It only punctuated what he already knew. She had guts. But why did she need to?

He'd almost sat beside her on the couch, close enough to touch. Instead he kept his distance, and had to wonder why. He thought of the eggshell in its box in Noelle's drawer. Nice move, turning his gift from so long ago around on him.

Yeah, Quinn intrigued him, amused him, attracted him. But he knew better, no matter what Noelle said. It hurt to care. So forget personal. Deal with what he saw.

He speed dialed the investigator he used to check backgrounds and search for anything untoward in potential projects. Richard Anselm had sniffed out crimes and vices by white-collar kings that instantly disqualified them from consideration. He'd find something if it was there.

As it was earlier on the West Coast, he caught Anselm awake and gave him the phone number to search.

"This connected to a corporate client?" Anselm asked without remarking on the substantial passage of time since they'd talked.

"It's personal. I'll tell Denise to keep it separate." And in the next call, he instructed her to pay Anselm's bill from his private account.

"Anything else?" she said.

"How's everything there?"

"Fine, except for Consuela. She's going to have a stroke if you keep insisting she move."

"Oh, come on. It's just a little while."

"She wants you here, not her there. Do you know there are about twenty-seven different kinds of devils? She's called you all of them."

"It's beautiful here."

"It snows."

"Hardly at all." He refrained from inspecting the window.

In the night, Noelle rose and tiptoed to Liam's room. His temperature was elevated, but it matched her own. While not exactly robust, she'd never considered herself infirm, until the pneumonia compromised her respiratory system. Pride before a fall.

Caressing Liam's cheek, she prayed he had Rick's constitution, and then, satisfied that he was sleeping as comfortably as possible, she crept back to her room.

"Is Liam okay?" Rick's voice was soft and alert.

She had tried to slip into bed without disturbing him. "I think so. He's sleeping." Her own throat felt like a war zone. Pain made a headband from one ear to the other and spread like a veil down her neck and over her forehead like a blusher.

He took her hand when she lay back down. "You're hot."

"You're not so bad yourself."

Smiling indulgently, he felt her face. "I'll get you more Tylenol."

She didn't argue. It wouldn't kick the headache, but it might reduce the fever. As long as she could breathe without a swamp in her chest, she'd deal with the rest.

The wind made a long howl and buffeted the window. Morgan had been smart to keep Quinn and the professor from leaving. It must have been a grueling drive for Rudy, though he might have stopped at the store and slept in his emergency apartment. That was a lot closer than all the way home. Dr. Jenkins, thank goodness, had no macho compulsions.

Rick returned, and she swallowed the pills, thanking him in a raspy voice. He climbed in and kissed her temple. "I'm trying not to worry."

"I know."

He spread his hand over her belly. She rested hers over it, knowing he was praying for the child as well. After a moment she said, "I think Morgan's starting to heal."

"Because he likes Quinn?"

"You saw it too?"

"I know my brother."

"It's been so long."

"It has."

Her voice rasped. "I like her too, Rick."

"Don't get your hopes too high. It's Morgan."

She pressed in close to him. Though wildly popular and successful, Morgan hadn't always made the greatest choices. "But . . ."

"You didn't see him the first time he lost Jill. If he's been numb and it starts to hurt . . ."

He'd been a teenager when they broke up. "He's different now. Refined." Rick knew she didn't mean dignified but tempered by fire.

"I hope you're right. It's just hard to see past old junk."

"We all have it. Except maybe you."

"That's convicting." He ran a thumb over her cheek. "Thanks for setting me straight."

For two people who'd started out so different, they'd found an amazing synergy.

He pressed his lips to her fiery forehead.

"I'm blessed to have you."

She wrapped her arms around his neck. "It's so mutual."

Through the interminable night, Quinn went over every other way she could have handled things and landed right back where she was. She could not have let it go, could not turn a blind eye once she knew. She was sure of that. It was the rest that gave her nightmares.

She opened heavy eyes to a dim light filtering into the room. Pushing up in the bed, she shoved the hair back from her face and looked at the window. She'd have looked out, but it was blocked with snow. Shivering, she pulled on socks and padded to the warmer room that held the wood stove. The embers in the base looked like dragon eggs that scattered into fiery butterflies when she added a small log.

Not knowing how long the hot water would last, she hurried in the shower, but her hair could not be quickly washed. There was too much of it. Thankfully, the stove had efficiently warmed things up by the time she stepped out. She dried her hair, hank by hank, with the towel, then dressed. Her watch read 8:16. She didn't know when the Spencers got up, or if Noelle would even leave her bed, but she was not hanging around with nothing to do except think depressing thoughts and read depressing tales.

She gathered Noelle's provisions and the envelope from the professor, pulled on her coat and gloves and opened the door, then shut it against the collapsing wall of snow. Not good. She looked around for a shovel but found only the scooper for the wood stove. The small kitchenette with tiny fridge, two-burner hot plate, and sink yielded nothing more useful than a saucepan. If she were buried in an avalanche she'd use it. As it was . . .

The drift outside was probably highest where it had piled against the cabin. So, what, she'd body slam through it? Sounded good. Another person might throw wood on the fire and hope someone came for her. But Morgan had Livie. Rick had a sick family. And she was not waiting around for help.

Leaving Noelle's items to be retrieved later, she stuffed the envelope inside her coat and cinched the waist, then pulled up and tied the hood snugly around her face. Steeling herself, she opened the door, blocking with her body the fresh cascade of snow. Blinking in the white glare, she pushed forward and realized how little body mass she had compared to the chest-high drift.

Though it only extended about six feet and gradually diminished, making a path with nothing but her hands would not be easy. Powder slipped under her coat sleeves as she worked, soaking and freezing her wrists. Her tights and leggings were soaked. She'd chosen the skirt and sweater for Thanksgiving dinner, not to become a human plow.

Once she was fully outside the door, she pulled it shut. Pressing her back into it gave more power to her arms and legs. After clearing about two feet, her biceps started to burn. At two and a half feet, her shoulders felt like hot coals searing into her neck. She paused to rest, leaning into the snow so even her downtime might have some effect.

Turning back would have been hard if not impossible, because the drift had collapsed behind her, filling in the gap. She straightened, raised her arms, and pushed again. If she were a prisoner of war, no amount of pain would allow her to stop. If her life depended on it, she'd have fought through anything. Unfortunately, she had only boredom and frustration driving this decision.

Once again she rested. And when she started again she beat at the snow less methodically, her motions jerky. Wind blew a choking layer off the drift into her face. She tucked her chin down and away, but it caught in her lashes and the hair escaping her hood.

"Quinn!"

She turned at the shout and saw Morgan. The drift at his door was only about three feet high. With Livie in a carrier on his back, he used a shovel to dig through it, then marched through knee-high snow to her massive drift. Working at the far end, he shoveled snow side to side until he broke through.

She said, "A shovel sure makes a difference." Brushing snow off her coat, she saw him staring. "What?"

"You didn't get my text?"

Thinking of texts could ruin her day. "I don't have the charger, so I turned off my phone."

"It said for you to call when you woke up and I'd dig you out."

"That would have been a good one to get." Though perfectly clear of clouds, the air around them glistened with ice crystals.

He brushed snow off her shoulders and back. "You're lucky it wasn't over your head."

"I'd have stayed put if it were."

"Not sure I believe that, coming from a human snowman."

"Snow girl!" Livie corrected.

"Yeah, punkin. Snow girl."

"Snow woman if we're getting technical."

"Yeah but size-wise —"

She socked him.

"Hey. I just saved you."

"I didn't need saving, but thanks for nothing." She packed a snowball and tossed it at his chest.

"Oh-ho-ho." He packed one, and since she had nowhere to run, she ducked past him, high-stepping through the partly shoveled snow. His throw hit her shoulder blade, and she swept up another snowy wad. Morgan was a crack shot, and his next one knocked the snow out of her hands.

"Hey."

"I don't want you throwing wild and hitting Livie."

"Oh sure. Hide behind the baby."

He pushed through and stopped chest to chest, a dark gleam in his indigo eyes. "Those are fighting words."

Her heart hammered as she reconsidered her position.

"Let me shed my precious cargo and I'll school you in warfare."

She had no doubt he would. "No thanks. I'm a pacifist."

"As I recall, you started this skirmish."

"You insulted my size."

He looked her up and down.

She narrowed her eyes. "Watch it."

"Or what?"

"You don't want to know."

"Uh-huh." He slid his arm around her back. "Making threats you can't back up?"

She raised her chin. "I can."

"Mmm. I'm pretty sure you can't take me."

She'd be lucky if she could talk without squeaking.

He roved her face with those penetrating eyes. He was no heartbroken dad. That disguise hid a consummate seducer. She put a hand to his chest and stepped back. It was that or give up breathing.

Eyes still heavy with portent, he pulled the shovel from the drift. "Follow me."

The demand amused more than irritated her, as they couldn't move more than three feet. He laid into a five-foot-tall drift between them and the main house.

Feeling extraneous, she said, "Want some help?"

He turned. "You can take Livie."

Together, they moved the carrier from his back to hers. The pack and whatever was in it weighed twice as much as his child, and after plowing through her own drift, she worked hard to stand up straight. How had he shoveled with Livie on his back?

Morgan cleared the big drift and a smaller one after it, then paused, looking up. "Somehow, I don't think you're leaving today."

She studied her half-buried truck and the drifts all along the drive, not to mention the roads. Even the sun blazing in an electric-blue sky would need time. "At least we have leftovers."

"I see you land on the rosy end of the attitude spectrum."

"Right in the reality middle. Things are what they are, so go with it."

He dug the shovel in. "Not a bad philosophy."

Livie leaned toward her ear. "Want to playammals?"

It took a moment to translate the unusually babyish word, but then she said, "Sure. And Daddy can make the elephants talk."

Shovel paused, he cast a look over his shoulder. She smiled. There were more subtle forms of warfare than he'd ever imagined.

From Liam's bedroom window, Noelle watched Quinn and Morgan in the snow. Her breath caught at their playfulness, something she hadn't seen in Morgan except with the children for a long, long time. When he reached around and held Quinn, she pressed a hand to her heart, hoping at last his shell might finally be cracking.

"Mommy," Liam croaked.

She turned and lifted him from his bed, cradling his head in the crook of her shoulder like a smoldering coal against her own feverish skin. He snuggled deeper. Sad to admit, she loved the tender stillness that came when he was sick. Since she never got to cuddle and hold him for long on healthy days.

They settled in the rocking chair, expertly shaped by Rick to fit her and their child, and thought about their conversation last night. Morgan had been through so much, and grief could manifest in many ways. While some people implied he'd left the spotlight to lick his wounds, it was in fact the opposite. He'd set aside his wounds to raise Livie with joy and constancy.

Maybe he'd wept in private, but she doubted that. She suspected his panic attacks were an outgrowth of restraint and avoidance. They'd been terrible at first, one reason he and Livie stayed in the house those first months. He didn't want to be incapacitated if she needed someone. After a time they'd tapered off, but not, she guessed, because he'd resolved the grief. More that he'd grown accustomed to it.

Perhaps their return was grief demanding acknowledgment and resolution. And maybe that meant he was trying to love again. She wanted him to have someone who loved and believed in him, who cherished him.

She lowered her head to Liam's and rocked. She'd felt no stirring yet from the tiny one inside but prayed her illness would not affect that new life. She prayed the infection would not become the prolonged ordeal she knew it could. She prayed Liam would heal quickly. And she prayed that what she'd just seen in Morgan would spread and grow.

CHAPTER 11

Quinn looked up when Rick came out of the house with a shovel of his own and watched the two men apply themselves in silent competition. When his path met Morgan's, they shared a look she couldn't quite catch but guessed well enough when Rick looked her over, fighting a smile.

"Morning, Quinn."

Leaning on his shovel, Morgan said, "She was taking the linebacker approach to clearing her drift."

Rick nodded. "We'll find you some dry clothes."

Let them laugh. She stomped off on the porch and followed them in, shedding Livie and the snowiest layers at the door.

As Morgan removed his child from the pack and toted her to the kitchen, Rick said, "Noelle should have something that'll work for you."

"Thanks."

The professor stood at the fireplace leaving

only a hint of pipe tobacco over the scent of woodsmoke. Quinn hugged herself at the cozy scene.

"I see you brought your reading." He nodded to the folder she'd uncovered beneath her coat. "Did you start it last night?"

"Not alone." She gave him a sheepish smile.

After her lousy night and the morning's exertion, she'd have preferred stretching out on one of the soft leather couches and snoozing. But she joined the professor at the fireplace, her tights starting to steam by the time Rick brought her a pair of black elastic-waist pants and a softer-than-owl-fluff gray sweater. Rick and Morgan and the professor looked as fresh as the new-fallen snow, and she felt more than a little bedraggled.

Excusing herself, she changed in the bathroom, rolling the ankles and sleeves. She'd found a matched set of exquisite lingerie tucked inside the outer clothing, the likes of which she had never felt or worn. Coming out, she smiled at Dr. Jenkins, the only one left in the great room. "Should we dive in?"

His eyes brightened in response. "I think we should."

They sat on the hearth, looking at the first of the anecdotes he'd collected. From the kitchen came the smell of sausage and onions. Maybe potatoes. Someone could cook. Her stomach rumbled. She'd only had one meal yesterday, and while it was a substantial one, she was ready for another.

"Ah yes," Dr. Jenkins said, scanning the tale. "The porcelain doll."

"Is this a good one or a tough one?"

"Interesting, I'd say. It's one of the oldest stories from early in the asylum's history. The woman believed herself a porcelain doll and refused to do anything that might chip or crack her."

"Like . . . move?"

"Very little. She sat and stared, very pretty, and just like a doll on a shelf."

"Did she talk?"

"If spoken to, but only in phrases like 'Don't touch I'll break.' Or 'Such a pretty doll.' When they wheeled her in a chair for meals and to take the sun, she never moved a muscle, and was easily posed, holding it sometimes for hours."

"How awful."

"And rather a waste, don't you think, since there was nothing physically keeping her from a full life."

"What could they do?"

"An orderly noticed she was more active in sleep than awake, and when the doctor questioned her during the restless episodes, she readily discussed her dreams while seemingly still dreaming. Apparently, as a child, she'd been imprisoned by rules and expectations and punished for the slightest infraction until safety lay in doing nothing but looking pretty. So she became a doll upon the shelf."

"What happened to her?"

"Unfortunately that isn't recorded. Perhaps divulging the dreams allowed her to discard her impression of herself as helpless, breakable, and inanimate."

While sad, the story wasn't too difficult to hear.

But the professor ruined it by saying, "Not all the accounts have happy endings. You'll find the most disturbing under the Hauntings section."

She looked up. "It's haunted?"

His eyes held a gleam. "What's a historical recounting without a few ghost tales?"

"You believe them?"

"As a historian I neither believe nor disbelieve. I merely record."

"But you must have an opinion."

He gave a little shrug. "I don't dismiss them out of hand. You asked me if I felt the misery in Vera's cellar. I can't say that I did. But on leaving, as I passed by one of the shackled beds, I felt a chill on my wrist as though something gripped it."

Quinn shuddered. "I am so not going down there again. What happened to the building? Did they tear it down?"

"After the fire."

She slowly raised her eyes. "Tell me it was closed before it burned."

He met her stare in momentary silence.

"The loss of life was limited to the very troubled soul who started it."

"Please don't tell me how." Quinn slid the papers into the envelope. She wasn't a coward, but the story of someone burning alive was more than she wanted to hear.

With an understanding nod, the professor drew on his pipe.

In the kitchen, Morgan poured a thermal mug of coffee he'd brewed strong with a shake of salt to counter the bitter preground beans.

Rick said, "If you didn't brew it dark as mud, you wouldn't have to salt it."

"If you bought decent beans, it wouldn't taste like hose water."

"Decent beans to you is handpicked on a volcano in Hawaii."

"Or Papua New Guinea or —"

"Yeah, yeah." Rick turned the sausage, onions, and potatoes in the large cast-iron skillet.

Morgan watched with greater awareness than before. His brother had learned his way around a stove — something he might have to do, at the rate things were going. "Consuela's resisting my invitation to join us out here."

"She's established out there, friends, church, community. Even overpaying her, as I'm sure you do, doesn't mean you can rip her up and make her grow here."

"Why don't you say what you think, Rick?" He sipped his brew. "Don't hold back."

Rick cocked a brow, amused.

"How am I supposed to eat?"

"Learn to cook." Rick cast him a look. "Or hire someone else."

"From the vast labor pool up here."

Rick turned down the heat and whipped the eggs in a blue crockery bowl. "There's Quinn."

Caught midsip, Morgan studied his brother. Rick could be infuriatingly hard to read. "She has her own business."

"With her own schedule that might work around meals for you and Livie."

"She'd be insulted."

"You pay well."

"It's not only about money." He cupped his daughter's head. "It's about fitting together. Consuela fits me. Us." Half mother, half saint.

"Yogurt, Daddy." Livie held up a spoonful.

He took the bite and gave her a grateful smile.

"She'll be there when you go back. This is temporary. Right?"

Right, but Quinn was . . . what? Adorable. Feisty. In trouble? Richard Anselm was working on it, but keeping tabs on his end couldn't hurt. He rubbed his jaw. "I guess I can give it a shot."

Rick turned the scrambled eggs with a slow spatula. "I doubt you'll find her as reluctant as you think. Just turn on the charm."

That used to be easy. Now it was like pumping from an unprimed well, except for the times he had no control, like when she washed his wounded hand. A fresh wave flooded at the thought. Maybe that was the problem. He didn't want to hire her. He wanted —

"I'm done, Daddy."

"Okay, punkin." He washed her up and watched her scamper off to the great room, where Quinn and the professor were talking. In seconds he heard Livie talking to Quinn and something tightened in his stomach. His little girl liked her.

Yesterday, he'd seen her cook. She'd prepared the meal as thoroughly and lovingly as she'd prepared Vera's house. Still, except what he'd experienced, he knew very little about her, and last night indicated something amiss.

On his phone he checked his e-mail, and sure enough, found the reply from Richard Anselm. The person harassing Quinn was named Markham Wilder. He had two minor fraud convictions, both deferred until an embezzlement conviction that, combined, sent him to prison. He'd served four of a five-year sentence, was released on parole, no violent offenses on record.

If she was involved with, married or related to someone like that, it could suggest a shady character, but he hadn't seen it. Quite the contrary. She went over and above to do her part and earn her way. Still, it wouldn't hurt to run a basic background check on her — nothing invasive, only cautionary — so he issued the directive.

With the rental cabins, guests were Rick and Noelle's way of life, and though the hospitality might be practiced, it seemed easy and sincere. Over breakfast, Quinn and Livie had to hold their own with the three men, but Quinn mostly ate and let them talk — the opposite of yesterday. She was hungry and still aching from pushing snow.

When the professor asked about Noelle, Rick sighed. "She's worse. Liam too."

She turned to Morgan. "I hope you and Livie don't catch it."

"They're practically quarantined."

Except for the trips they'd all been making into the sick zone. How she wished that was the worst of her worries.

He said, "You okay?"

"Yes." She smiled too quickly. "Think we can reach Vera's?"

"I'm not shoveling the way, though you could try your technique."

"Ha-ha. So what's the plan?"

"For what?"

"For today."

He tipped his head. "What would you like it to be?"

Her heart did a quickstep when his eyes stroked her face that way. He must not realize the impact or he wouldn't use it so indiscriminately. "Um, well . . ." Great. Stammering was so attractive.

He said, "I brought the laptop if you need to check your business."

Her business felt like one loose thread in an unraveling rope, but she said, "Sure. Thanks. I'll go quickly."

"No hurry." He lifted Livie from her booster. "We have talking elephants."

It warmed her that he'd neither forgotten nor wormed out of the promise she'd made for him. He had depth and maturity and an uninhibited playfulness not reserved for the kids alone. As Rick cleared the plates and mugs, Morgan brought his computer to the table.

She checked her auctions and e-mail. Hardly anything had changed since the night before. If she were home she'd probably list more items, but she didn't wish she was. Finished, she went into the great room to keep her own promise to play animals, but Morgan had just set Livie down to watch *Nemo* on the small TV in the kids' corner that also held a pint-sized table and chairs. She supposed Morgan's elephants could only talk so long.

He came over to her. "All done?"

"The transactions and communications are pretty quick. It's finding, researching, and listing the merchandise that takes the longest."

"I hope it leaves you some spare time."

"Of course."

"Because I want to ask you something."

She crossed her arms, puzzling over his tone.

From the long narrow table behind the couch, he picked up a carved wooden pinecone with a spray of needles on the end of a curved branch. "It appears my housekeeper is reluctant to leave Santa Barbara. I guess it's not fair to force it, so I wondered if you'd consider the job for the time we're here."

Surprise and then disappointment hit. What had she expected?

"Obviously, you'd be able to keep running your business. I just need cooking, housework, and maybe some care for Livie. We could hash out the details." He set the branch back down and aligned it at an angle. His voice softened. "You did an amazing job with the house. And yesterday's meal."

Her mind raced as she pictured working for Morgan. Not what she might have preferred, but who was she kidding?

"I know it's coming from left field."

"A little, yeah." She studied him for motivation but saw nothing ulterior. Unfortunately.

"I'm in a bind, and Livie's taken to you like a baby duck."

She looked over to where his daughter sat sucking her thumb and watching the baby fish in Nemo's ocean. Time with her would be a treat.

"I'll pay —"

"I don't want to be paid."

He frowned. "What do you mean?"

Seeing the opportunity, she raised her chin and dove in. "If I cook and clean, can you get me a fake ID? The kind that stands up to scrutiny, with a real social security number?" He'd admitted his request came from left field. By his expression hers wasn't even in the ballpark.

Hands on hips, he dipped his head. "Why do you think I can do that?"

"You have money. Resources. You make things happen."

"Legal things." He spread his hand. "I might grease palms, but I don't have underworld connections."

She slumped. It had been a stupid thought.

"Why do you need to change your name?"

She stared at the floor. "Someone wants to find me."

"The law?"

She shook her head. She didn't think so anyway.

"The guy last night?"

She nodded without meeting his eyes.

"Your husband?"

Now she did look up. "No. Yuck."

He pulled a side grin. "Okay, that's out of the way."

"I'm not married or battered or abused."

"But you're in trouble."

"I will be if he finds me." Why had she thought Morgan could change that?

"Is Quinn your real name?"

"Yes. I don't have a way to fake it either." She wished she hadn't brought it up. Now he knew, and there was no help coming.

He rested a hand on the back of the couch. "You want to tell me about it?"

"There's no reason to, if you can't help me hide." All he was offering was a job, and she didn't know if she could commit to that when she might have to take off. What if she was alone with Livie when Markham found her? She turned to go.

He caught her elbow and turned her back. "I didn't say I couldn't help. I said I couldn't get you a fake ID."

She searched his face. "Other than changing my identity, I'm not sure what would help."

"There's more than one way to change your name." He still had hold of her elbow, a warm, encompassing grasp.

"Aren't official changes public record?"

"Sure." He let go and crossed his arms. "How good is he at searching things out?"

"Better than I am at hiding them. He got my cell phone number." The slimy rat.

"How serious are you about eluding him?"

She took the phone out of her pocket and turned it on. As Morgan watched, she retrieved the text and held it out.

He blinked at the words, then looked at her. "Not an idle threat?"

"He just got out of prison." She hated the hint of fear that found her voice and felt a responding anger that Markham had put her in this position.

"You sent him there?"

"He sent himself." The anger pinched her brow. "I just . . . made his business known."

"So he's angry. Doesn't mean he'll risk his freedom to kill you."

Except the part that Morgan didn't know. "You're probably right."

"But you don't think so."

She swallowed hard. "I don't know what to think. But I'm ready to run."

"That's no answer."

"It's the best I've got."

He pressed his palms together in front of his chin. "Let me work on it."

Her heart skipped. "Really?" In Morgan's mouth those words were magic.

"I'm not making you a fugitive."

"Would I be?"

"Yeah, honey. Obtaining a false identity is illegal."

She knew that, but still . . .

Morgan studied her. For someone so gutsy, she seemed honestly spooked. And naïve. Death threats explained the first. Youth the second? "How old are you, Quinn?"

She frowned. "Twenty-seven."

A couple years more than he'd have guessed by appearance, a couple shy by demeanor. "How do you feel about matrimony?"

"I'm not against it."

"Ever been?"

"No."

"Well, I think that's our answer."

Her jaw fell slack.

Yeah, rusty in the charm department. "Here's what I'm thinking. We leave the country so there's no immediate US record, have a civil ceremony that's legal but not consummated. You'll have your new identity, and you can help Livie and me as long as we need it."

Shock gave way to dismay, the lines of her face falling as she searched his. "This is you working on it?"

While he hadn't rehearsed his pitch, he hadn't expected that adverse a reaction. "It's a good solution."

"As a problem-solving exercise?"

"You rated your problem pretty high."

She slumped. "I can't believe this."

This time when he touched her elbow she slid it away. "There's no risk and a full resolution of your identity crisis."

"No risk? There are vows involved."

"Civil vows can be as simple as 'Do you wish to enter into this union? Yes. Do you? Yes. I pronounce you husband and wife.' " Saying the words caused a slight hitch. Was he problem solving, or seeing something worth pursuing and pursuing it? Wasn't that his gift, recognizing and maximizing potential?

Her eyes darted between his as though she might catch something different in one or the other. It was pretty straightforward, though obviously not what she'd envisioned. At least it was legal.

She swallowed. "And then what?"

"Then whatever you want."

"Divorce?"

When she put it that way, it did sound harsh. "If you find someone else to be with, we'll take care of it."

Her face flamed. "This has to be the worst proposal of all time."

Not what he'd intended. He was offering her a chance, not an insult. "Think of it as a merger. A mutual achievement of goals."

She formed the most withering expression he'd seen in years. "Is it some antisocial genius disorder? You can only seem human so long?"

Ouch.

"I thought . . . This morning it seemed . . ."

The morning had been brilliant. And maybe it was as much about that as their situations. At this point, however, it didn't seem wise to say so. He spread his hands. "I've made my pitch. Swing or let it go by."

Chapter 12

Stunned and . . . wounded, she watched him take his daughter and walk out. Part of her realized he'd slipped into professional problem solving. Part of her regretted her attack. But the biggest thing she felt was dismay. Did she seem like someone who'd accept a merger for a marriage?

She pressed her hands to her face, feeling stomped. It wasn't his fault she'd imagined a spark. Too many times she'd made more out of something than he obviously felt. He'd shown her again and again in his curtness, his exits. Not. Interested.

"Rick?" Noelle's hoarse cry came from the top of the stairs.

Quinn dragged her face out of her hands to see Noelle coming down with Liam in her arms. "Rick's not here. They all went outside."

"Could you please find him?"

"Of course." She grabbed her coat and pulled on her boots. Outside, she followed the shoveled path that led to the barn and stable. Drawing herself up, she entered the long hay-scented space and halted just inside.

Holding Livie on his shoulders, Morgan was chatting with the professor while Rick broke a section of hay from a bale and forked it into the first of a dozen stalls. That one held a stunning buckskin with intelligent eyes. In the next stall, a fiery roan snorted and tossed its head, demanding the recognition it deserved. Overshadowed, a gray horse, possibly a mare by the smaller stature, waited her turn. That was all of them she saw before telling Rick that Noelle needed him. "I think it's Liam."

Immediately Rick's focus shifted.

Morgan said, "I'll finish here." And as Rick hurried out, Morgan lifted Livie off his shoulders and carried her over. "Do you mind?" as though minutes before he hadn't inserted a blade between her ribs.

She took the child, amazed when he picked up the pitchfork and worked capably around the horses. Rick was the cowboy, Morgan the mogul — or not.

Leaving him with the professor, she carried Livie back to the house, noticing in the barn a tractor with a plow blade. Maybe escape was possible — though the desire felt less pressing when Livie's little arms closed around her neck.

In the great room, Noelle had bundled

Liam in coat, hat, and gloves. Setting Livie back down by the cartoon, Quinn said, "How is he?"

"He needs a doctor."

"Can Rick plow the road?"

"There isn't time. He's taking Liam on horseback."

"Seriously?"

"There's less drifting under the trees."

"But where's the doctor?"

"In town. Dr. Bennington still practices even though he's technically retired." Noelle coughed wetly.

"What about you?"

"He'll send an antibiotic back with Rick. He keeps a big boomer on hand for me."

Now, that was small-town medicine. "Is there anything I can do?"

"Would you mind watching Livie? I'm trying to avoid direct contact."

"Of course. I'm happy to." And Livie didn't seem to mind. She had opened up to her, though not, as Morgan claimed, like a baby duck. No question which adult she was attached to.

Rick came downstairs and went out, apparently to prepare the horse.

"I'm sorry you've been exposed to this."

"I'm tougher than I look."

Noelle gave in to a cough. In chain reaction, Liam coughed too. They sounded as bad as they must feel. Happy to help but unsure entirely how, Quinn moved over by Livie. She could almost imagine nothing happened with Morgan, almost pretend she was making friends with Noelle, except she didn't pretend. She couldn't afford to.

Rick came inside, wrapped Liam in a blanket, and carried him out. Through the window, Quinn watched him hoist the boy onto the sturdy buckskin and mount behind him in a single motion. They set out through the falling snow. She hadn't thought about horses as transportation since reading Western stories as a girl.

"Do you mind very much if I go to bed?" Noelle rasped.

"Please do." Quinn saw her shaking, now that her child required no show of strength. "Can you make it up the stairs?"

She nodded. "Thanks."

As Noelle left, Livie looked up, her face tender with uncertainty and dismay. Quinn took the little waif in her arms with a rush of emotion that softened her belly. "He'll be all right, sweetie."

Livie gulped back tears, far more aware than Quinn had expected.

"Hey, we were going to play animals, weren't we?"

Livie nodded. Quinn led her over and sat. Instead of going for the ark, Livie settled into her lap, the soft curve of her back fitting snugly. Quinn reached into the wooden boat and brought out a cleverly carved aardvark. Seriously? Whoever made this set had talent and ingenuity.

"Aar-vark." Livie took the little animal.

Quinn made her knee a steady perch. "What does the aardvark say?" Whatever sound Livie gave it would be more than she knew herself.

Livie looked from the carving to her. "The aar-vark says, 'Hi, elephant.' "

Quinn burst out laughing. "Of course."

Morgan and the professor came inside, Morgan's gaze homing in.

Livie squirmed up and ran to him. "Playammals, Daddy."

She must have learned that phrase early and retained its babyish pronunciation while the rest of her diction improved. In no mood for a three-way playgroup, Quinn stood up and turned to the professor. "Should we dive back in?"

He looked over where she'd laid the envelope. "If you're up to it."

In a choice between Morgan and the grim stories of the asylum, the decision was easy.

Rick had promised to call as soon as he reached the doctor's. With her head swirling, Noelle waited and dozed and waited. At last the call came. "You were right," Rick said. "The little guy's dehydrated."

"His throat hurts too much to swallow."

Her own made a sympathetic response.

"You need liquids too. Doc said it's crucial to regulate your fever."

"I know." As an adult she could force herself to do what Liam resisted.

"Okay," Rick sighed. "I have to go hold him for an IV."

"Kiss him for me." She knew Rick would soothe their little guy as well as anyone could. And he was right that this new baby needed her body to cool down, needed oxygen and nutrients in her blood. *Please, God.*

She reached for the water bottle beside her bed and took a sip. She envisioned it going straight to the baby and took another. She fought a cough and took a third, then waited. Let it absorb. Let her stomach receive it.

At the tap on the door, she turned her head, expecting Morgan, but it was Quinn.

"I brought you some tea, if you can tolerate it."

"You're a godsend." Noelle rose to an elbow in the bed and took the mug. This woman she barely knew had graciously slipped into the situation and not only tolerated but took initiative, receiving the hospitality they'd offered her and looking for ways to bless them back.

Not beating a hasty retreat, Quinn stood for a moment, hesitant.

"What is it?"

"I don't want to bother you."

"You won't." Noelle motioned to the chair.

Instead of sitting, Quinn folded her arms. "Morgan asked me to marry him."

"He what?" Noelle stared at her over the steam rising, certain she'd heard wrong.

"I asked for help with something, and he needs a maid and cook. So he proposed. If you can call it that." Quinn jammed her fingers into her hair, trying to look stern but only managing distressed. "You might have mentioned he's crazy."

"He's not crazy." She moistened her throat with the hot tea, then setting down the mug, rose a little higher in the bed. She didn't want to say more than Morgan might be comfortable with, but this was more than odd, and Quinn looked troubled. "He's waking up. But it's like a foot that's gone to sleep. There's pain and awkwardness and uncertainty whether it will hold weight and function."

And as Rick said, *"If he's been numb and it starts to hurt . . ."* She reached up and touched Quinn's hand. "I don't know what you asked. But with Morgan, if you ask, he'll try to do it."

"By any means?"

"Within his personal parameters. He's not exactly conventional."

Quinn took that in without comment, then nodded. "I'll let you rest."

Pausing midsentence in his conversation with

Dr. Jenkins, Morgan watched Quinn come down from Noelle's room. He hadn't realized she might have developed feelings for him until he saw her reaction to his pitch. The concept had formed easily and immediately, though maybe he should have thought it through before presentation.

He wouldn't have entered a boardroom without considering every aspect. Even so, CEOs didn't usually care for the fix until, little by little, they realized the benefit and accepted the conditions. Professionally, he shared the risk and reward of each solution. This was no different.

She'd asked him for something illegal; he'd offered an alternative. And she told him what she thought of him — an antisocial genius who could only seem human so long. It had been a knee-jerk reaction he didn't take personally. In fact, he rather admired her spunk. Looking at her now, it was clear any comment would make the situation worse, so he said nothing.

She addressed the professor. "Noelle said there's less drifting under the trees. Think we could make it to Vera's on foot?"

The academic's face was pure indulgence. "Let's try," he said.

Morgan stretched out his legs. "We can't dawdle. It's almost time for Livie's nap."

Quinn half turned. "The professor and I could just go, if you need to take care of things here." She waved a hand toward Livie.

Such a nice dismissal, but he rose. "Want to go for a walk, Liv?" He dug her out of the couch-cushion choo-choo and got her coat from the closet.

Sighing, Quinn donned her own coat as he lifted Livie into the pack, slid his arms through the straps, and buckled the cinch strap. Quinn and the professor went out the door and he followed.

The snow wasn't as deep beneath the trees, but it also wasn't melting as in the sunny stretches. It was thick, fluffy powder that breezes wafted from the tree branches in sugary cascades. Kicking through it, he replayed their conversation.

He offered her a job. She asked for a new name. He suggested his, no strings attached beyond the aforementioned occupation. While unconventional, it wasn't as insulting as she made out.

She had searched him online and had some understanding of his station. There'd be a prenup if she took his offer, but she hadn't even asked for money. She'd offered to work for nothing in return for his crime.

That didn't mean the opportunity wouldn't sink in. She was shrewd enough to realize the upside. And his upside? Besides the facts that Livie had taken to her and Quinn could cook, she had a good work ethic. She was easy on the eyes. She had a sense of humor — not at the moment, but in general. He enjoyed her and wanted to help. And he didn't want her to run.

Watching her and the professor, laughing as they high-stepped through the snow, he felt the rich timbre of her voice carrying in the woods. While her situation might be serious, if she were terrified, she'd have taken the offer. Since she seemed less frightened for her life at the moment, they might have time to work into it, or come up with something else — an oddly disappointing thought.

"Let me down, Daddy. Want to walk."

He removed Livie from the pack and let her tramp through the trail the other two cut, helping her over areas still drifted. He'd been feeling Quinn out as much as anything, gauging the threat level. He'd learn what else he could about Markham Wilder from Anselm, and about Quinn herself. Hopefully she'd get past her irritation long enough to at least consider his offer.

Quinn waited as Morgan produced the house key, then opened and held the door. Electricity that wasn't purely static snapped when he touched her arm, extending the cabinet's skeleton key in his open palm. A lump filled her throat, remembering the last time they'd done this. She'd been so excited, and he'd seemed warm and real and connected.

"He's waking up, and there's pain and awk-

wardness and uncertainty."

No one could apply uncertainty to Morgan Spencer. He knew exactly what he was doing, all the time. She took the key.

In the kitchen the professor examined the cabinet. "I can't believe I missed this."

"It wasn't up here," she told him. "It was all the way at the end of the cellar."

He peered through the glass panes. "I see why it intrigued you."

"I was planning to sell the medicine bottles, before I knew what they were. Then Morgan bought it intact to keep in the kitchen." She unlocked the cabinet and opened the creaking doors.

Dr. Jenkins removed an ampule and studied it. "That is LSD. It was administered on small squares of blotting paper. There's actually art devoted to the blotting paper design."

Shaking her head, she reached in to a lower shelf and drew out some larger bottles, one labeled morphine and others that held powders and pills with no labels and looked much older. "This is what I was hoping for. Just old . . . whatever it is."

Dr. Jenkins said, "I wonder if this cabinet didn't stand right here once." He rocked his foot on the popping linoleum. "This room was part of the asylum."

She blinked. "I hadn't realized."

"It was, I believe, an examination room, also possibly a treatment area."

"And the cellar?" She glanced at the unobstructed door behind the hutch still angled out from her last trip down when Morgan's panic frightened and touched her.

"Not a dungeon, I think. Most likely storage and equipment." He turned. "Should we go down?"

"Why?"

"I wouldn't mind another look." Something sparkled in his eyes. "It might convince us both our imaginations got carried away."

Her heart started to thump. "Morgan has Livie." The child was prancing in the living room, listening to her own hollow footsteps. No way was that baby going down those stairs.

"Go ahead," Morgan said. "I'll stay up here with her."

She cast him a glance. She'd met him in this house. It had been his idea to explore the basement, his arm she'd clung to. They'd laughed; they'd cringed. From that first encounter, hardly a day had passed she didn't think of him. Silly, naïve fool.

She turned to the professor. "Ready if you are."

As she opened the door, Morgan said, "You'll want a light."

Morgan Spencer, covering the details. From the pantry, she took out the camp lantern and illuminated stairs that now bore countless footprints and few cobwebs. The railing was icy cold, as though the heat of the house had no power over it. She let go and marched down.

At the bottom, she noticed more of a change than she thought she'd accomplished. In the midst of the work it had seemed never ending, but after being away for a while, her progress showed. The professor joined her. Upstairs, Morgan closed the door, probably to keep Livie from getting curious, but still she shivered.

Dr. Jenkins took the cellar in. "Ah," he said, his glance falling on a shackled bed.

"Was that restraint necessary?"

"Who knows. Before effective medications, patients could be violent to themselves and others. In a dormitory situation, preventing injury probably came first."

She couldn't bear the thought of patients writhing as forces inside fought the shackles holding them down. She turned toward the darkened end of the cellar. "The electroshock apparatus is over there." She really didn't want to see it again — too Frankenstein — so she handed him the lantern, then realized if she didn't follow she'd be standing in the dark. Bracing her shoulders, she walked behind him through the detritus she had not yet organized.

He stopped beside the electrical generator with cords reaching to a metal band lying on the narrow pallet. Her insides shrank in as she imagined cries and whimpers. It almost seemed she heard them. "Why is this so horrifying?"

"Because it suggests torture."

A chill traced the bones of her spine. Morgan had said it wasn't Auschwitz. He was right. The intention wasn't to cause but rather relieve suffering. Without consciously willing it, she reached out and touched the pallet. "You say it works?"

"It can."

She drew a long breath and nodded. But as she turned away, a sense of malevolence choked her. As a child, she'd been told to stand against evil but had equated it with the wrongdoings of worldly people. This was no person, but a force. She breathed, "Jesus."

The oppression lessened, and even the darkness seemed lighter. She shot a glance at the professor where he stood eyeing the old boiler. Her throat felt raw. Maybe she was getting sick. Or else something evil had stripped her voice. *Jesus, Lord.* "Dr. Jenkins?" The words came clearly.

He turned, seemingly undisturbed, and said, "That boiler's a period piece."

She nodded.

"Are you all right?" He tipped his head, concerned.

"Did you feel something creepy?"

He looked around her. "Did you?"

"I . . . um . . . Imagination, I guess."

He studied her keenly. "Can you describe it?"

"I don't want to."

He seemed hesitant to let it go.

She rasped, "What?"

"You haven't read them yet, but more than a few of the anecdotes involve an evil presence. A ghost, perhaps."

"I don't believe in ghosts."

"Well, the individual who died in the fire . . ." His brow furrowed. "Some claimed she was possessed."

Quinn clamped her hands to her ears. It wasn't the professor's voice she blocked, but the whisper of laughter. "Let's get out of here."

"Of course." He took her elbow. "I'm sorry to have frightened you."

"It's not you." A chill like a deep freeze caused a bone-deep shudder. She half ran to the foot of the stairs and charged up and into the kitchen. When the professor joined her, she closed the door and said, "Help me push this."

Straining, they shoved the hutch back against the wall. Chest heaving, she moved into the sunlit living room, where Morgan stood with Livie making echoes. Forcing a calm she didn't feel, she said, "We need to go."

"Okay. Everything all right?"

No, but she couldn't say so in front of Livie.

Morgan glanced at the professor when she hurried to the door. The walk back was no stroll. She felt a serious need to flee.

Back at the ranch, she saw Rick running the plow. He must have brought Liam home and gotten to work, since there was a good portion of the drive cleared already. She went to the cabin she'd used, stripped the bed and got the towel, put them with Noelle's things into the bag, and hauled it all to the house. She offered to run the wash, but Noelle said no. Friends could cook but not do her laundry.

Still shaken by whatever had happened in the cellar, she used the snow shovel to finish digging out her truck. She needed distance and a chance to think. Nothing that creepy had ever happened before — except maybe with Markham. At times there'd been a vacancy in his eyes that something else moved behind.

"Quinn?"

She turned.

Morgan joined her at the truck. "Want to tell me what's wrong?"

"You can't live there."

"What are you talking about?" he said. "What happened?"

Eyes shut, she shook her head. He'd think her the crazy one.

He touched her shoulder. "You've spooked yourself. The professor said those stories —"

"It's not the stories." She stared into his face. "There's something there. I sort of felt it before. This time —"

He didn't laugh, didn't scoff. "Go on."

"Do you remember your panic attack?"

"I'm not likely to forget."

"Could it be —" She squeezed the handle of the shovel. "Was it from something down there?"

"No." His hand cupped the shoulder more firmly. "Not at all."

She drew a ragged breath. "Are you sure?"

"I had another one yesterday — if you recall."

So maybe it hadn't affected him, but still. "I can't think of you being there with Livie."

"And you, if you take the offer."

"No. No way." Her voice wavered.

He nodded solemnly. "Is that your final answer?"

"Yes. No. I don't know." She rested her chin on the foam-padded shovel handle.

He lowered his hand to her elbow. "I'm sorry I upset you. Maybe that contributed to something in the cellar."

She shook her head. The thing in the cellar was altogether separate. "I'm not upset. Only confused, I guess."

"My fault."

She wanted to ask if he really didn't feel anything for her, but that would be too humiliating. "I have to go."

"Okay." He held out a sheet of paper. "Here."

"What's this?" She read the heading, a trip itinerary and confirmation number. For a minute she thought he'd planned their foreign wedding, then noticed the destination. Dallas. And the date. "Tomorrow?"

"RaeAnne will meet you at the airport. You'll stay at her house, get your business done and have a little fun, then fly back on Monday morning."

She'd all but forgotten Vera's journal and the pieces of jewelry. She hadn't agreed to fly anything to RaeAnne, but seeing her, giving her the journal, would be awesome. And it would take her mind off Morgan.

"Out and back in three days," he said softly. "No hassle."

"You obviously haven't flown lately." Neither had she, but she'd heard. "RaeAnne's up for it?"

"She's ecstatic."

That forced a smile. "Okay. I'll do it." She relinquished the shovel and opened her truck door.

"Need a ladder for that thing?"

"Ha-ha."

He stepped back as she climbed into the truck. Yeah, it was a climb, but she didn't require a ladder. And for a man who was no more than five eleven or so, he was pretty mouthy about her stature. He stood beside his own vehicle as she started her sluggish engine.

Casting a glance out the window, she said, "Please tell the professor good-bye. And thank Noelle."

He raised a hand in farewell as she backed into the plowed area. The drive home was not difficult, snow melting on the streets as though it had only been kidding. She pulled into her mushy driveway and parked. Varied emotions held a caucus in her head. Had she imagined the horror in the cellar? Dr. Jenkins felt — or admitted — nothing. The stories had disturbed her, and maybe she had worked herself into a spook — like telling ghost tales in the firelight.

At any rate, she was home, except her house had shrunk. After the massive log walls and soaring ceiling of Noelle and Rick's, her A-frame seemed an overgrown tent. She climbed the steep stairs, dropped onto her back on the bed, arms splayed, and stared at her peaked ceiling. In a while she'd get to work, but at that moment she needed to process everything.

Her cell phone rang. Warily, she pulled it out. The same number as the texted threat filled the screen. She hit End, then coded in the carrier and told them she needed a new number. It pained her to think one of three loved ones had given her old number to Hannah. They had to have known she'd give it to

Markham. Or maybe they didn't realize the hold he still had.

She couldn't believe they would betray her — though, after everything, they might say the same of her. She had, by extension, testified against her own father. She had brought the ceiling crashing down upon the heads of everyone she knew. It was only a matter of time before her own head felt the blow.

Chapter 13

Teeth clenched, Markham hung up. He could send another text, but he was through with threats. It was time for action. Hannah had given him a trail to follow, a fruitful trail — as it turned out — with a solid destination. The rabbit hadn't hopped very far. For the first time ever, he felt the anticipation of the hunt, though the word sent a liquid feeling to his legs.

Against his will, he recalled days when a shotgun blasting squirrels meant meat in the pot. Not his gun, though. He'd been too sensitive, so they left him to skin and gut. Punishment for compassion. Blood on his hands. Its stench in his nostrils, its shame on his soul, shame he felt to this day. But he'd learned to use a knife.

He wrenched his thoughts back. He was not a violent man. He had intelligence. He had charm. He had sincerity that made men weep. He didn't need vulgar tools to bend the wills of others. He needed nothing but himself — once he got what belonged to him from Quinn.

Traffic had been snarled by a rollover accident, a semi caught by high winds, and Quinn arrived at the airport certain she'd be told to forget even trying to board her plane. Instead, the woman processed her respectfully and directed her to security, where she was channeled into a column that had no one in line, given a cursory security scan, and directed to her gate.

After the hellish highway, it felt miraculous. At the gate, she was greeted and escorted onto the plane, where they seated her in a form-fitting recliner in the section she hardly knew existed — first class. She dropped her head back, recalling Morgan's smile when he'd said no hassle. He was unreal, not simply that he had the means, but also the inclination, to make her trip as seamless as possible. It made her heart hurt.

That feeling dissolved the moment RaeAnne met her with a huge hug. "I just can't believe you did this. You and Morgan. I can't believe it."

"I'm having a hard time myself."

"When he called to ask if you'd sent the journal, then told me what he intended, I knew he was a man who gets things done."

"Tell me about it."

"Car's right here." RaeAnne bustled her

into her Camry. “Morgan must have emphasized fourteen times to be here when you walked out.”

“Oh?”

“He said he wanted it ‘hassle free.’ ”

Quinn shifted in her seat.

“You want to tell me what’s up between you?”

“Between us? Nothing.”

RaeAnne cast her a dubious look.

“He’s not normal, you know.”

“Sugar, he makes normal as dull as pancakes without syrup.”

Quinn fiddled with the bag that held Vera’s journal and the jewelry. “You’re getting your things, and that’s what matters.”

“I can’t wait. There must be something worthwhile in the journal, if she hid it in the cellar like that.”

“That’s what I thought. She kept everything, but she squirreled away the things that mattered.”

“The locket alone meant the world to me.” RaeAnne wove into traffic. “But now maybe I’ll understand why.”

“Not a bad-looking man, your dad.”

“I know! Can you believe it? I mean, Mom did some stage work, but he looks like a star.”

Quinn studied the woman beside her, hair the color of the blond lock saved with the photo. “Think he swept her off her feet?”

RaeAnne’s shoulders rose and fell. “I hope

it's in the journal. I really do."

"The way she kept it secret, there might have been a bad end."

RaeAnne nodded soberly. "I've assumed that my whole life. Anything else will be a blessing." She merged onto an interstate highway and settled back. "We have an hour on here, this time of day. Want to read it to me?"

"Seriously?"

"I can't wait until we get home."

Laughing softly, Quinn pulled the journal out of her bag, more than a little curious herself. Still, she paused a moment, before entering Vera's private world.

"Go on. Read."

And so she read.

"The thoughts and dreams of Veronica Greenwald."

RaeAnne sighed audibly.

"I want to make one thing clear. What goes in here, stays in here."

Quinn looked up. "Does that mean we shouldn't read it?"

"It means she kept it to herself long enough."

Feeling as though she had a duty to both of them, Quinn went on respectfully.

"I have never claimed to take the conventional path. Nor have I wandered through a rose garden. What ways I traveled in this life are my own, for good or ill."

Quinn turned to RaeAnne. "Sounds like she wrote this later on, as a memoir, not a diary."

"I hope she'll tell the truth."

"She has no reason not to, if no one was meant to see it."

"True." RaeAnne nodded. "Go on, please."

Quinn turned the page.

"My dreams as a girl were like any young lady of my time. Fall in love, raise a family. But then I discovered theater. Oh, what a howl everyone put up, and they were right, as eventually every one of their concerns came to pass. But I'm old now, and I don't regret the lights, the curtains, the thrill of opening night. I was never the star I wanted to be, but I had my share of accolades. And I had Raymond."

RaeAnne jerked the car. "Sorry."

"It's okay. Now you know your dad's name. And I'm thinking it was more than a one-night stand."

RaeAnne's chin trembled. "Makes me wonder if I knew my mom at all."

Quinn gave her the silence of her grief.

"I never knew the rest of the family that well. We didn't spend much time with them. I don't think Mom really fit, and I doubt anyone changed her mind about anything. I guess I wouldn't be here if they had." A tear formed in the corner of her eye.

"Want to read the rest privately?"

RaeAnne sniffed. "I'd like you to go on. You seem part of this somehow."

Quinn read on, page after page about Vera's first awkward auditions, people she met, advice she received — good and bad and some meanspirited.

"My hips were big, my bosom small, but I had talent. It was not a career for the weak-hearted, but I wanted it. How I wanted it."

Such a clear voice. Vera came alive on the pages, jumping out to sit with them and share her story in raw detail. Quinn read without pausing, but still they reached RaeAnne's house without another word about the mysterious Raymond.

RaeAnne showed her to a guest room done in china-blue chintz. "You'd get to meet my husband, John Carter, but he's traveling for work. Anyway, it's good. We can have girl time."

After all the time spent with men lately, that would be a joy.

"While you freshen up, I'll get us something

to eat. The way they starve people on flights these days is a crime."

"Actually I had a full meal. Morgan sent me first class. In fact it might have been some VIP first class I've never even heard of."

"O-o-oh." RaeAnne packed three notes into the single syllable.

"It's probably the way he travels all the time."

RaeAnne nodded knowingly.

"It's not what you think." She set her overnight bag on the trunk at the foot of the bed. "He wants me to work for him."

"Doing what?"

"Domestic. Maybe helping with Livie. That's his little girl."

"Oh."

Quinn laughed. "Stop that. He's not looking for love." He'd made that so very clear.

"I wonder what his story is."

Quinn stared out the window, wishing she didn't. "He hasn't offered. And I'm not asking."

"But you would sort of like to know, wouldn't you?"

She rubbed the back of her neck. "I'm not sure. Sometimes the less you know, the better." If she'd gotten this connected knowing next to nothing, how dumb would it be to learn more?

"That is almost never true. Take it from me."

"Once you learn something, you can't unlearn it."

"Well." RaeAnne tucked her purse onto a table in the hall. "Can I get you anything?"

"Something to drink, if you have it."

"Oh, I have lots. Come see what you like."

Quinn followed her through a kitchen with navy calico curtains and shiny red-and-white backsplash tiles. There could be no more evidence of their dissimilarity than RaeAnne's decorating — not that it was awful, only vastly different. She chose a flavored tea from the fridge in the garage off the kitchen that held only drinks and said, "Ready to tackle the journal?"

"Absolutely. I'm all for knowing."

They laughed. "I guess you don't need me to read."

"No, but I kind of like it. You have a theatrical voice yourself."

"Oh, please."

"No, really. It's nice to listen to."

"All right." They settled into her china-blue living room. Quinn found her place in Vera's story.

> "I'll never forget the production of *Oklahoma!* where I first laid eyes on Raymond."

She looked across at RaeAnne sitting rigidly. "This is it, I guess."

RaeAnne pressed a hand to her mouth.

"Don't mind me if I blubber."

> "He sang Curly, and I had only the part of Aunt Eller, but we were love struck from the first rehearsal, even though he was sixteen years younger than I."

RaeAnne pressed a hand to her chest. "What?"

After double-checking that she'd read it right, Quinn looked up. "That's not unheard of."

"It is in my world. Sixteen years? My mother, the cougar!"

It was kind of shocking, but Quinn shrugged. "They fell in love."

"Sure, but . . . maybe that's why she never told me. Do you think that's it?"

"You're pretty scandalized."

"All this time I imagined a . . . I don't know, age-appropriate man. She was thirty-six when she had me. He must have been twenty. Don't tell me that's normal."

"Maybe he made normal as dull as pancakes without syrup."

RaeAnne laughed, but it was more of a croak. "I don't think you'd be as cavalier if it was your mother."

Quinn pictured the wispy woman who'd married a minister. If there had been a dream in her mother beyond that, she'd never heard it. Her father had dreams, though. They'd made him ripe for picking. "Should I go on?"

"I don't know." RaeAnne gripped her hands. "I can't stop thinking my dad's only twenty years older than I am."

"Lots of people can say that."

"But my mom was almost forty."

"Well, that's a . . . discrepancy. On the bright side, your dad's in his sixties."

"Oh my goodness." She collapsed back into the couch. "He might still be alive."

Quinn let that sink in. RaeAnne had obviously not been thinking in those terms. Understandably disquieting. "Do you know the theater where she performed *Oklahoma!*?"

"I have all her playbills. They were tucked neatly in a drawer."

Go figure. "Then you could find your dad's name."

RaeAnne rocked her head back and forth. "This is too much. I'm a church lady. I know there's a right way and a wrong way of things. It's bad enough they didn't marry — now this. What am I supposed to do?"

"You don't have to do anything. You'd simply know."

"You're right. Oh my goodness." She gripped her head. "I'm so glad you brought it in person. I'd just die if I read all this myself, without John Carter here."

Quinn smiled. "Not sure what I can do that helps, but I am here."

The rest of the journal told of a short, sad

infatuation. Raymond had risen as Vera's star waned. He was gone before his daughter arrived. No wonder she never told the tale.

"Well, I guess that settles that," RaeAnne said. "Why would I want to meet him?"

"On the other hand, it's been forty years, give or take. He might have regrets of his own."

RaeAnne shook her head. "I am so in need of chocolate. Let's bake brownies."

Quinn laughed. "The cure for anything." Especially RaeAnne's concoction, a Ghirardelli mix into which she threw two handfuls of extra chips. They literally melted in their mouths.

After that comfort, they studied the odd pieces of jewelry Quinn had found hidden in the clothes. It was a good assumption the ring had also come from Raymond, so RaeAnne added it to the lot. She picked up the pin. "Mom loved butterflies. This would have meant a lot, even if it's only glass."

"It could be aquamarine."

"Sort of looks like something a *young* man would pick out."

Quinn smiled at RaeAnne's earnest face as she tried to come to terms with all she had learned.

"This has been one amazingly strange day," RaeAnne summed up.

At least the strange belonged to someone else for a change. And that reminded her.

"Did your mom ever mention something scary in her house?"

"Scary like ghosts?"

"I guess."

"Not that I remember. Why?"

"Seems like the place might have a few."

"Ghosts are like husbands," RaeAnne joked. "They show up when they want and make a lot of noise, then disappear when you need them." She spent the next few hours telling stories of floods and tornadoes and all the mayhem that only struck when John Carter was on the road.

After a whirlwind of laughing too hard and eating too much, Quinn left a dear friend in Dallas.

"Where's Queen?" Livie asked for the fourteenth time in an hour. They stood out in the yard on the hot post-Thanksgiving Monday that could have been May instead of November. Fifty degrees at least. Rick took advantage of the temperature shift and the melted snow to exercise the stock. "Where's Queen, Daddy?"

"She went flying in an airplane." He pointed across the yard. "What's Uncle Rick doing?"

"Riding a horsey."

"Yep. And I bet he wants to take you along."

Circling just close enough to hear, Rick glanced over. "Want a ride, Livie?"

Morgan hoisted her between Rick and the

saddle horn, thankful for the time he'd get without her asking for Quinn. According to the information online, the flight had landed in its morning time slot, and she was either finishing the two-hour drive or home already. He hadn't asked her to call but should have, because while he'd given her his number and memorized the number of the jerk harassing her, he hadn't gotten hers.

He could count on one finger the times he'd failed to get the phone number of a woman who mattered even fractionally as much as Quinn. The oversight unsettled him. It was like fumbling the first play of the game. Not that this was a game, certainly not to Quinn. And not to him. Not to the player on Monday night football either. When you were in the business of results, you didn't drop the ball.

He'd be flying out next week for the Belcorp consultation and wanted resolution with Quinn before he left. Maybe she would contact Noelle. Or Noelle could contact her. On that thought, he went inside.

Noelle sat lengthwise on the leather couch, propped on pillows, a Brandenburg concerto playing softly on the stereo, warm sunlight bringing color to her cheeks. Liam sat across from her, building with Legos. Not quite back to his rambunctious self, his quick improvement might mean a smooth recovery for Noelle too.

He asked if she had Quinn's phone number.

"You don't?" She feigned shock, but it was only partly feigned. "Your own fiancée?"

"Yeah, yeah."

She'd been ribbing him from the moment Quinn left. She didn't realize he'd been working on a plan since the idea occurred. Quinn's "final" answer had been equivocal, her criminal and work history background as clean as newly fallen snow. Didn't hurt to think positively.

Noelle relented. "She's in my contacts."

"Thanks." He located her phone on the arm of the couch, entered the number into his, and went out. The tension in his stomach kicked up a notch when the no-longer-in-service message came on. Changing her number might have been smart, given the harassment, but there was that thing she'd said. *"I'm ready to run."*

Whether the danger was real or not, her perception of it was. The idea that she might actually go caused a discomfort he didn't analyze but couldn't ignore. He closed his eyes and raised his face to the sun. After a while, he keyed another number, and when RaeAnne answered, he asked how it went.

"Just great! She got in fine and I saw her off this morning. We had the best time."

That sounded positive, but would Quinn have told RaeAnne her fears, or just pretended she was fine? "Do you have her phone number?"

"Oh sure. Just a sec." She gave him the one he'd already tried.

"Okay. Thanks, RaeAnne." When Rick rode in and handed Livie down, he said, "Do you know where Quinn lives?"

Rick shook his head. "I only saw her at Vera's. And here."

There had to be . . . And then he had a thought. She'd done business on his laptop. He could check his history, contact her through e-mail. Maybe. It was worth a try. "Come on, jelly bean. Let's find Queen."

Quinn parked the truck on the paved road, more willing to walk a ways to her door than leave deep ruts in the driveway. The day was beyond beautiful, springlike, melted snow dripping from the trees like raindrops. The wet ground smelled fresh, the air warm and clear. Mountain chickadees flitted in the dripping trees. Crows cawed. High above, a hawk or eagle made a silent gyre, as though no winged thing could be still on such a day in winter.

It was all for show, because tomorrow it would probably snow again. The next front could drop temperatures below zero. But today the mountains shone like a scene from *The Sound of Music.* After the time with RaeAnne, her heart felt light enough to sing.

She reached for her carry-on bag as her

phone indicated an incoming e-mail. She'd added a data plan on the new number, so she wouldn't need someone else's device to check mail again. Digging the phone from her bag, she brought the message up, slumping when she saw the sender. She was not eager to deal with Morgan.

Sighing, she took a look at the message. *Checking that you got back all right. Hopefully no hassle. Call, if you don't mind, to let me know.*

Not wanting to talk, she touched Reply. *Back fine. No hassle. RaeAnne's happy. Thanks.*

She hit Send and tugged her tote free. Before she had the truck door closed a new message came. *Can we talk?*

No. We can't. She didn't want to hear his voice. She wanted to hear the birds that had strangely gone silent. She looked into the bare sky. No eagle.

She trudged to the house on spongy ground and paused, key in hand, when she reached the stoop and saw the door hanging loose against the splintered jamb. Heart thumping, she nudged the door with her elbow, stared long enough to see her shredded couch, her books ripped up and scattered, her clothes hanging in strips from the balcony. Legs turning to jelly, she ran to her truck, shoved her bag inside, and cranked the engine.

Yes, Morgan, we can talk. If she could

breathe. The destruction in her house had taken time, energy, and rage. The message was clear. Markham wasn't only after what he'd lost, he wanted to hurt her. Driving to Rick's ranch, she forced the terror down and thanked God there was nothing at her place that connected to the Spencers.

Every ten seconds she checked her rearview, but no one followed. Markham should have waited for her there, knowing she'd see the wreckage and run. Not very smart for a prophet. *Please, God, help me.* Morgan had offered her a new name. It felt bad that she couldn't keep her side of the bargain, but she'd been found, and that changed everything.

She knocked at his cabin, but no one answered. She hurried to the house, and he came out, head cocked, before she reached the door. The warmth in his face almost undid her. She wanted the cold business proposal, the reasonable merger. She wanted the imperious look he gave her when he told her to leave the locket.

"I only requested a call." A breeze lifted the hair over his forehead.

"I know." She swallowed, making herself meet his eyes, which studied her curiously under the dark, angled brows. "But I came to say I accept the merger."

He stilled. "More threats?"

Of course he'd jump to that conclusion,

not missing a thing, even if she were half skilled at hiding it. "I need a different name." Admitting it brought tears to her eyes. If he changed his mind, she was on her own. She looked away, blinking hard. "If you didn't mean it, say so."

"I meant it." He clasped her shoulder. "But I thought you —"

"I overreacted. Now I've had time to think." She drew and released a hard breath. "Can we do it now?" She didn't want to look desperate. She tried to look decisive. Her other choice was to take off — but if Markham found her here, how would she hide anywhere?

Lightly gripping her chin, he lifted her face. Staring into her teary eyes, he said, "Okay."

No questions, no argument. The single word quaked in her chest. Was this the biggest mistake of her life? She pictured her little home destroyed. No. She'd already made that one.

Surprised but determined, Morgan led Quinn into the great room, where Noelle sat with Liam and Livie prancing, neighing, and pawing her. She had barely greeted Quinn with visible delight before he said, "I know you're not at full strength, but could you keep Livie for a few days?"

"Of course, but . . . what for?" She looked at Quinn and back to him.

This wouldn't go over well, but the shaking in Quinn's hands, the hunted look in her eyes proved he'd been closer than he knew in his concerns. She was ready to bolt, and this would accomplish what she wanted and keep her close. "We're getting married."

Noelle's eyes showed the shock he'd expected, though she was too well bred to gape. He'd already explained his side of the plan when she questioned his "proposal." He'd kept Quinn's issue out of the explanation, because frankly he knew too little and it wasn't his tale to tell.

"We'll be back as soon as possible."

She shook her head, at a loss for words.

He said, "Where's Rick?"

"With a breeder, discussing spring foals."

Livie stopped galloping and grabbed his leg. "I a horsey, Daddy."

"A fine princess pony." Kneeling down, he hugged and kissed her. "I have to go away for just a little while. Okay?"

When her face clouded, he added quickly, "Not as long as last time. I promise." He held her tightly when she started to cry. This would only add a little to his already planned absence, and on the back side Quinn could help with her care. That would be new and fun for Livie. But how did you explain that to a two-year-old? He handed her to Noelle, a default they both understood.

She drew Livie in but caught his arm. "Are

you sure this a good idea?"

"We're managing a situation."

"With marriage?"

"Trust me." He brushed her arm, a little offended that it wasn't automatic. "Solving problems is my *raison d'être.*" He looked into her face, reminding her of what she knew, at least what he hoped she knew. If he didn't trust this course, he wouldn't follow it.

He'd hardly closed the door behind them when Quinn said, "I don't want to cause trouble with your family."

"There's no trouble." Noelle was the least of his concerns. "Do you have a passport?"

"Yes."

"On you?"

"Always." The tiny hitch when she said it was telling.

"We'll need your birth certificate."

"All my important papers are in my truck. When I heard he was released, I got everything ready, in case I had to leave in a hurry."

"Good foresight." And because she'd said she was ready to run, he'd prepared as well.

Pulling his borrowed Tahoe back into position behind the steel barn, Markham Wilder continued his watch on Quinn's house. The supplies he'd purchased would keep him another day or two before he made another run into town. He opened a package of cheese-filled crackers and chewed in morose silence. Sooner or later she'd come home and find his welcoming tableau.

She might think she'd been robbed. Maybe her first thoughts would be of him. If not, her next ones would. Maybe she'd call the police, whatever law enforcement this place had. She'd try to have him arrested, but he wasn't stupid. He'd been wearing gloves. And even if some miracle on their part put him inside, he'd say he found the place wrecked and was afraid for her. Quinn wouldn't buy that, but he could sell it to the rest.

He chewed a cracker, contemplating the vandalism. The only part that bothered him was its spontaneity. He couldn't afford to act without thinking. Still, it sent a message, and he couldn't wait to watch her receive it.

He wanted to see fear on her face. Fear and regret, and even hope that she could make it right. She'd make it right, but that wasn't enough.

Like the people he'd eliminated before, Quinn had made him suffer. Because of her, he'd experienced the degradation of prison. He'd lost four years of his life. Because of her, his cache was gone. But not . . . irrevocably.

Chapter 14

Driving on autopilot, Morgan ticked off in his mind the things he'd put in motion and the things they would still need to do. At the small mountain airport, he parked the Range Rover and chartered a flight to New York. When the crew arrived, he motioned Quinn up the steps into the jet, half surprised she didn't balk. Since she'd been practically silent, he thought she might be talking herself out of the plan.

She only said, "Where will we go from New York?"

He told her, "You'll see," and Quinn-like, she let it go. That was either trust or resignation.

She'd already flown twice in three days and looked a little weary as she buckled in beside him. Shortly after takeoff she closed her eyes. Her hand slipped down her side, the strong yet delicate fingers dangling. For the better part of the flight, he watched her sleep, watched the dreams move beneath her eyelids, studied the peaked line of her eyebrows, the narrow bridge of her nose.

Some heritage less fair than traditional Irish had given her skin a bronzer tone that matched her brown eyes. Her boldly formed lips were parted slightly in slumber, the breath passing softly through them. One shoulder hunched beneath her tipped head, and he thought of how it had fit inside his palm.

She had clipped her hair into a black plastic claw, but spirals fell loose in a way he could hardly keep from touching. It was the first thing he'd noticed and the most persistent. He wanted to bunch his hands into her hair.

The thought startled him. Quinn would be his wife on paper only, physically off-limits, their hearts unengaged. His mind did violence to the concept, but that was the agreement. She stirred and made a small, soft noise. She'd accepted a merger, not a proposal. He didn't think for a minute her choice of the word accidental.

And still, he imagined running his thumb down the slope of her cheek, the line of her neck. His throat constricted. He needed to resist the attraction — and not only attraction but fascination. Appreciation. Things more lasting than chemistry, though he suspected that was there too.

If Rick hadn't prompted him to offer a job, would he have asked her out? Could he even consider dating? His mouth twisted wryly. No dating, only marriage. He shook his head. He'd taken risks in his life, but this was the closest to playing with fire he'd come in a long time.

Quinn woke when they landed in New York, something vulnerable showing through her composure, as though she sensed he'd been watching. Inside JFK she fidgeted while he found a flight to their destination and purchased the tickets. They'd leave at 6:15 p.m. and arrive in Paris at 7:30 in the morning.

The knot in her stomach must have shown, because Morgan reached over and squeezed her hand. "It'll work."

Maybe. But it wasn't only her life changing. It was his life too, even if she left. That thought actually hurt, not only the dishonesty, but a sense of real loss. "What was it you said, *raison* . . . whatever?"

"*Raison d'être.* Reason for being."

"You live to fix things?"

He nodded slowly. "Sounds arrogant, doesn't it?"

"No." She shook her head. "Not if the core is doing what people can't do for themselves." In Morgan's case, it wasn't only his vocation but his avocation.

"You do pretty well for yourself, Quinn. This is for both of us. Okay?"

A lump formed in her throat. He was

counting on her. She almost told him everything right there and would have, except she needed it so badly.

As the jet began its slow taxi, he said, "Do you have a middle name?"

"Erin."

"Quinn Erin Reilly. Black Irish?"

"That's what Pops — my grandfather — calls it."

"A little Iberian Peninsula in your genetics." He smiled. "Catholic?"

"Until Pops defected."

"The one whose hound you're named for?"

She nodded. "My father was out of the country when I arrived, and my mother wouldn't act on anything without him. Before she knew what happened, Pops filled out the birth certificate. My father insists it was to keep me from receiving the Christian name he would have chosen."

Morgan cocked a brow. "Pops on sketchy terms with heaven?"

She slanted him a look. "My dad became a minister in response to Corlin Reilly's rabid apostasy. In retaliation, he adopted the most rigid faith he could imagine and built a church around it."

"He could have changed your name."

"It was only one skirmish in their war." Though she'd always felt her dad gave up on her there and then, as if the naming gave her into the heathen's camp. And truth be told, she loved Pops. He was a little like Morgan, larger than life without trying to be. It did break her heart that he battled as hard with God as with his son.

As the jet surged and lifted, he said, "How do you feel about Erin?"

She adjusted to the vertical rise. "It's fine, why?"

"I think you should be Erin Spencer."

She frowned. "Why?"

"Not to put too fine a point on it, but Quinn glares like a spotlight."

She had intended to change her last name when they married. Now she'd be losing her first as well. Even if Quinn came with baggage, it was her connection to Pops and her past. "Just on the certificate, right?"

"Bank accounts, credit cards. We want a good paper trail."

Everything she needed and more. "Erin Spencer." A tear leaked from the corner of her eye.

"You were ready to buy a false ID. What if the name available was Brunhilda?"

That forced a grudging laugh. "Guess I didn't think it through. I thought I'd keep Quinn and — I don't know — be myself still." She pressed her fingers between her brows.

He reached over and drew her hand down. "None of this changes you." The kindness in his voice quickened her spirit. "When you look in the mirror, you'll be the same feisty female of diminutive stature, wayward hair, and winsome way."

He was teasing, in a good way, his hand on hers warm and firm. "And hey," he added, "we're nearly straight Irish on my mother's side. Erin's a blessed name."

His encouragement braced her like a fresh wind in her face. How did he know just what to say? Part of his *raison d'être,* she supposed.

"So I go by Erin too? I mean when we talk?"

"Talking with anyone. A clean break is safer."

Erin Spencer. Erin. "What about my passport and everything?"

"We'll get it figured out."

"How can you be so sure?"

His smile went all the way into his eyes. Devastating. She hadn't considered the greatest risk in all of this. Falling for him, heart and soul.

A rare snow was falling on the streets of Paris as the cab carried them from Orly Airport to the town hall, where Justine met them, kissing him on both cheeks and taking Quinn's hand between hers in a warm welcome. "You know there is nothing I wouldn't do for you, Morgan, but this haste has stretched even my influence."

"I know. Thank you."

An executive with Chanel, Justine was still

as long and elegant as when she'd walked the runway. She had wealth, prestige, and close family in both the National Assembly and the Senate. A favor from Justine Gaudet was no small thing.

"You must still have the blood tests, and there is a doctor just down the street to perform them. You have the documents?" Her voice softened when she specified, "The *Acte de décès*?"

"Yes." He'd brought Jill's death certificate.

"The sworn translator in this *mairie* will transcribe your certificates of birth, certificates of celibacy — that you are not married already to others — certificates of law, that you are free to marry and your country will recognize it."

He'd obtained the forms at the French Consulate in New York.

"The doctor will issue your medical certificates, and that leaves —" she made a slow blink and tipped her head — "the *attestation d'hébergement sur l'honneur.*"

He held her eyes. "I'm not asking anything you're uncomfortable with, am I?"

"Do you think I would hesitate when you did so much to disguise what could have been so bad for us?"

She had struggled six years ago when he saved her father's company, until she realized he had reorganized the power and reversed the corporate damage, without revealing the malfeasance caused by, as yet undetected, dementia that would have disgraced and destroyed the man.

Since he had lived in one of the family's properties through the completion of not only the consultation but also the reorganization itself, her sworn statement that he'd met the residency required for this civil ceremony was passably true. Also, at her august urging, the mayor would waive the ten-day posting of banns. Without her, the marriage would not have been possible so quickly, if at all.

"Jean will arrive soon, and together we will witness the union. Your French is so bad — *c'est vrais*? — we could hire a translator, but only the witnesses are required to understand." She smiled broadly.

He touched her arm. *"Merci,* Justine. *Merci beaucoup."*

She leaned in and kissed his cheek again. "It is my joy."

He turned and saw in Quinn's expressive face that she was confused and visibly anxious.

Justine spoke to her. "Your fiancé did my family a great kindness, and I am happy for a chance to return it."

Quinn nodded.

"So." She gave him an address. "To the doctor with you; then back here. You can walk if you don't mind the snow."

"You call this snow?" He took Quinn's hand, noticing she looked pale and skittish. "It's a basic blood test and general checkup. In our case, practically a formality. Justine has arranged everything. She's well connected, and her husband, Jean, even more."

"Were they — I don't know what to call it — clients?"

"I turned her father's company around, but there were personal and private elements that made it especially sensitive."

He felt her tension. From the moment they landed she'd looked faint. In the taxi, she'd chewed a nail to the quick and clenched and unclenched her hands enough times to work out her forearms. The prospect of marrying him must be daunting indeed.

The snow fell silently, disappearing upon impact. Around them, the city moved and breathed in a sort of hush, as though pondering his intention. You think you can marry this girl and pretend it's nothing? Put this woman in your life and keep her at arm's length?

Back at the town hall, with their blood test results and the rest of the documentation in order, Justine introduced the mayor, Henri Brun. He asked if there would be guests or other aspects to the civil ceremony. Did they need somewhere to change clothes? Having come straight from the airport in the clothes they'd worn to travel, his query made sense.

"We'd like it simple. An agreement," Morgan managed in French.

The mayor nodded. *"Mais oui. Je comprends."* Since he understood, they would begin.

"Wait." Quinn turned, her eyes intense, two spots of color on her cheeks. "I have to tell you something."

Seeing the seriousness, he asked everyone's pardon and went off to the side with her. "What's wrong?"

"He found me."

"What?"

"My house is trashed. Everything I had, my furniture, my clothes, ruined. It must have been when I went to Dallas. Morgan, he found me . . . and this might be dangerous for you." Tears sprang into her eyes. "I thought we could do this and I'd leave before you really got involved. But . . ." She closed her eyes. "That's not fair."

Taken aback, he processed not only the information but her timing. It must have been eating her up the whole time. "Who is this guy?" He had Anselm's version but wanted hers.

"A con. A professional grifter who duped my father. I caught him at it and testified. But he's out, and he wants me to pay."

"He's in Juniper Falls?"

"He was. Long enough to wreck my place. But, Morgan, nothing in there connects me to any of you. I promise. If he even took time to look. He probably just went ballistic."

Morgan chewed his upper lip. He would call and warn Rick, but they were in France now. It took courage for her to tell, but it didn't change the plan. He gripped her shaking hand and returned to the mayor and the witnesses, waiting curiously. When he'd reassured them it was no more than jitters, the ceremony proceeded.

After they had both said yes, Justine and Jean applauded. Then the mayor held out his hands and said in English, "You may kiss."

They could skip that, but he turned, slid his fingers around her neck, and touched his lips to the corner of Quinn's — Erin's — mouth. She went very still, and when he drew back, tears once again washed her emotive eyes, the starbursts seeming to scintillate. He should have made it a real kiss.

They signed the certificate Morgan and Erin Spencer, officially entering her name change, and were presented the *Livret de Famille,* the family book that recorded the wedding and had pages for births and deaths and all of their future children. For some reason the little blue book that Justine called the Holy Grail of French life hit him harder than anything. He'd thought keeping it civil meant keeping it simple. Now it seemed it might be the first of how many misconceptions.

Parting from Jean and Justine at the town hall, he and Erin went to the US embassy. He told them she'd lost her passport and ID. He provided all of his information and the marriage certificate with the Gaudets' signatures. After reasonably satisfying the consular officer of her identity and citizenship, a passport was issued to Erin Spencer with a slightly shell-shocked photo of his new wife.

Stepping out of the embassy onto the busy Parisian sidewalk, he felt his chest expand. "Been to Paris before?"

She stared as though he'd asked if she'd been to the moon. "That's all you have to say? After what I told you?"

"I'm processing that." He held up a hand for a taxi. "In the meantime, we'll start with the Eiffel Tower. It's magical in the snow."

She did not need magical. She had already experienced more than she could take. The planning he had put in before she'd even thought of saying yes, the arrangements made with Justine on the off chance she might agree, confounded her. Had he guessed, hoped, or just covered the possibility?

And then, when it all became real, she'd given him the chance to back out and he hadn't flinched. He'd gone forward knowing not all the details but the seriousness of the step they took. He had made her problem his own. Her heart melted faster than the snow on the crowded Parisian streets.

Because no buildings in the historical district came close to it in size, the tower stood as in a postcard. But the closer they got, the less true that seemed. From beneath, the symmetries of structure dazzled as the massive yet transparent reality transfixed her. The intricate almost lacy structure encompassed them, more massive than she could have imagined yet exquisite in detail — a complicated balance of beauty and strength, like the man climbing beside her.

"It was built as a temporary structure," he said, "and here it stands." His words resonated with parallel meaning as she climbed the first three hundred stairs of the tower, trying to get her mind around the step they'd taken.

They paused on the lowest observation level to enjoy that view of the city, then climbed three hundred more stairs to a higher view of the same scene.

"It's nearly as tall as the Chrysler Building," Morgan told her. "Or more if you count the antenna."

"Was it built as a lookout?"

"Gateway to the 1889 World's Fair."

And now it formed the gateway into her new life. It was like something out of a movie, her in a supporting role as the man beside her stole the show. Every expression, gesture, and comment stirred her. *Lord.* She knew it wasn't real, but it might take an act of God to convince herself.

Morgan motioned her to the lift. They crowded in with other tourists for an acrophobic view at the highest level. They exited the lift and moved to the rail. He turned her to face him. "One thing you told me needs to change, and one thing is wrong."

She swallowed the swelling lump.

"You're not leaving, and I am involved."

Snow swirled lazily, melting on her hat and gloves, making droplets in their hair and lashes. He crooked his finger under her chin, tipped her face up, and stared into her eyes. Drawing a ragged breath, she met his kiss and returned it, as his fingers slid into her hair. He murmured, "Erin," in her ear. Quinn might have stepped back. But Erin had made the vows. They held and kissed each other as the snow fell silently around them.

He had told her paper only. But he shouldn't have chosen Paris with someone so endearing after two years in purgatory. Stepping back, he said, "This city has that effect."

She nodded.

"We'll need to be careful."

She nodded again.

Taking her hand, he led her to the line for the lift. After a new batch of tourists got out, they entered and went down. Back on the street, he said, "You'll need some clothes."

A shadow passed through her eyes — recalling her wrecked things, no doubt.

"It's Paris. Even if your closet was full, you'd need clothes."

Her brow puckered. "I don't think that way."

Good thing, since he'd never gotten the prenup. Bern was going to chew him up. Attorneys did that when clients made particularly stupid moves. Problem was, he didn't feel all that stupid right now.

Watching Erin shop was like watching a puppy on its first excursion into the big outdoors. First affection and then attraction stirred when some of the things she tried revealed a figure the layers she typically donned did not. She refused to buy more than she could carry. But he arranged for the shops to send their purchases to the hotel.

As the snow turned to rain, they toured the Seine beneath a single umbrella he held over them with his left hand, his right arm around her back. For the moment, no one existed but he and this woman. While the Eiffel Tower had rendered her mute, the water and surrounding scene brought a thousand comments. He realized those were her two modes, reticent and loquacious, as the mood struck. A smile quivered at the corners of his mouth.

After viewing the grand Notre Dame Cathedral, they shared a pita Grecque from the winding road of Greek food stands. The savory chicken sliced from a rotisserie of meat, stuffed into a large pita with lettuce and tomato and creamy cucumber and garlic yogurt sauce, then filled to the top with crispy French fries triggered his salivary glands like those of Pavlov's dogs. In the Parisian manner, they forked the fries straight from the sandwich.

For dessert, pistachio macaroons, the round almond-flavored cookie with two hard halves and a creamy middle, had Quinn declaring, "I don't ever want to eat again. It'll take this flavor away."

He smiled. "You just wait."

"You think I'm that easy?"

He looked her up and down. She socked him. Chuckling softly, he moved her on.

Still groaning with pleasure, she said, "How can you expect me to cook for you?"

"Honey." He grinned. "I don't expect Paris."

The suite he'd booked in the Plaza Athénée had two bedrooms, a bath, and a tiny sitting area appointed in powder blue and white with ecru and ivory furniture. He tipped the bellhop, then checked his watch. With the eight-hour time difference, he could now call his brother and did.

Typical Rick, he opened with, "Have you lost your mind?"

"Not entirely."

After moments of restoring his equilibrium

and, no doubt, swallowing the many things he wanted to say, Rick asked, "What are you calling for?"

He told him about Quinn's place and asked him to keep a careful watch on things. The wave of fear that washed over had less power than he'd have expected, probably because he still didn't know the extent of it. Text threats and a hissy fit felt amateur. It seemed that someone intending murder wouldn't be that careless unless he was stupid. But it didn't hurt to take precautions.

"Someone's harassing her. I don't think it'll spill over on you guys, but watch for anything unusual. And don't let the kids out of sight, okay?" His stomach tightened, but no panic came. Amazing.

While he talked, Quinn went and stood at the window. After disconnecting the call, he joined her there.

She said, "I'm sorry."

"It's all right."

"I shouldn't have involved you."

The rain had stopped. Now every surface glistened with lights. "You gave me an exit."

Her brow furrowed. "Was Rick angry?"

"No."

"If you hadn't handled everything for Rae-Anne so easily . . ."

He turned her. "We're in this. We'll deal with it."

Her face flushed, though not, it seemed,

with anger, fear, or shame.

She said, “I can’t believe we’re here, that we actually got married.”

“That’s open to interpretation, given the understanding going in.” The paint on the window sash behind her had fixed droplet marks like the impermanent ones on the panes.

“I know. But now I don’t know what to do, or . . . how to be.”

Although the shadows of her lashes hid the starbursts, he knew they were there. “My fault. I blurred the line.”

Her hand on his arm trembled. “It felt mutual.”

So mutual, he’d lost sight of the limits. He drew a careful breath. “There’s always room for renegotiation.”

“That’s not being careful.”

“No, it’s not.”

“More like reckless.”

He nodded. “And less easily annulled.”

A coil of hair fell across her shoulder. “Do we need it annulled?”

“You might.” His gaze slid to her mouth.

“If I don’t?”

Here it was, the point of no return. Accompanied by vows, there’d be no going back. “The question is how real we want to make this.”

Her throat worked. “Do you want it real?”

“You’re asking if I want you.”

She flushed. "I didn't mean —"

"Of course I do. But I know it's not that simple. It would be more than a merger."

She raised her eyes, the starbursts in full view. "If I say yes?"

"I'll believe you."

Moments stretched. Paris breathed.

She rested a hand on his chest, but instead of stepping back as she had in their snowplay at the ranch, she moved in. "Yes."

Emotion rushed in as he tipped her face up and kissed her mouth. As her arms came around his neck, he lifted her and carried her to their room.

She could not believe the care and tenderness Morgan showed when he realized this was new. He said, "Are you sure?"

And she told him yes, though it was hardly more than a breath. Suddenly the Song of Solomon meant so much more than ever before. Gently and passionately he knew her, and afterward they lay in silence wrapped in something so profound she couldn't have found words anyway.

After a time, he rolled to his side, tangled his fingers in her hair, and said, "Erin Spencer."

It caused nowhere near the pang it had before, but still it sounded strange. "I hope I remember to answer to it."

"By the time we're done here, you will."

"But I liked —"

He touched her nose. "Quinn's the name of a bluetick hound. Erin, the emerald pastures that call to every Irish heart." He bent and kissed her.

"You're only half Irish."

"About five-eighths." He kissed her throat and the hollow beneath her ear. "One-eighth Welsh and another English, and the final Norman fraction the reason we're in France." He stroked her cheek and breathed, "Mrs. Erin Spencer."

It was a good thing supper was served in Paris so very, very late.

CHAPTER 15

Looking at Erin across the dinner table, Morgan felt torn, as though half of him belonged to Jill and Livie, and half to this woman he'd made his own. He hadn't foreseen the schism, though it seemed somehow he should have. He looked down when her eyes met his, seeing more than he wanted her to see.

"Did we make a mistake?" She spoke calmly, but he sensed turmoil.

"No."

"You're having second thoughts."

"No." He'd passed second thoughts several stages ago. "Just figuring it out." Being with her had touched and amazed him. But guilt had slammed in like a sledgehammer, and he didn't know which woman he'd betrayed.

She set down her fork. "Is it all right for me to know what happened to Livie's mom?"

He stiffened, then made himself answer. "She died. A tanker truck en route to a wildfire struck her vehicle while it was concealed in smoke." His chest constricted with the memory. "Livie was three months old."

The skin between her eyebrows pinched in. "I can't imagine that pain."

He blinked. "Thanks for realizing that."

"Now I understand why you didn't let me leave in the storm."

"I'm glad you stayed." They wouldn't be here otherwise.

She softly asked, "Can I know her name?"

This was crazy. How could they be here, doing this? "Her name was Jill. We fell in love in high school. We got pregnant and broke up. A good family adopted the baby, but she died of leukemia."

Erin's face crumpled. "Oh, Morgan."

He gave up the pretense of eating, sipped his Perrier.

"I shouldn't have brought it up." Her voice shook.

"It's natural. Under the circumstances."

She started to speak and stalled. His body language was shutting her down, but he couldn't stop it. He'd made love to her, his body worshiping hers. But the shell on his heart grew thicker every moment they sat.

"Dessert?"

She'd obviously noticed how little he ate, because she said no. When they got back to the suite, he lingered in the sitting area.

She yawned. "How are you not exhausted?"

He said, "I need to unwind." Once he'd have done it with a snifter of Courvoisier, the finest on the market. He'd have poured until the pain was no more than a dull, throbbing memory. "I'll join you in a while."

"Morgan . . ."

He kissed the top of her head. "Get some sleep."

Staunch little soldier, she turned and obeyed. He closed his eyes, tempted to follow, but in this mood intimacy would be a mockery. He went and sat by the window, taking in the cold Paris night.

Quinn would have known better, but Erin Spencer had taken over her mind, heart, and body. Though she hadn't known the specifics of his loss, from their very first encounters she'd seen the effects. When his eyes turned to steely plates at the restaurant, she'd felt the pain coming off him like blades that could slice if anyone got too close. And what he'd shared — was it even possible to come back from that?

In spite of her dazed condition, she slipped into a restless sleep, broken by whirling smoke and the lights and sirens of a rushing fire engine bearing down on her.

Near dawn, Morgan slipped into bed, pressing his chest against her back. He whispered, "I'm sorry."

"There's no need to be." She truly could not fathom the losses he'd experienced.

He encircled her with his arms and fell

asleep. She lay there absorbing the strangeness and uncertainty of what they'd done, before drifting into a dreamless doze.

They woke at nearly the same moment and the strangeness returned. What yesterday had seemed so natural, almost inevitable, now felt like poorly fitting clothes, pulling in all the wrong places.

Morgan brushed his fingers down her cheek and said, "Let's not dawdle."

She said, "Okay." And they rose and prepared for the day.

With only a shadow of the night in his eyes, Morgan sipped his coffee in the softly drizzling morning outside the corner café. While he showed no crippling melancholy, neither was he buoyant. Yet he made an effort. "Once you've had breakfast in Paris, the word never sounds the same again."

"That's unfortunate if we ever plan to leave." Erin — she forced herself to think that name — sipped her own.

"As there's a small child in need of her father, I'm afraid that's imminent."

"Of course." She was Livie's caregiver now — if Morgan wanted that. It was difficult to tell what he wanted this morning. We'll always have Paris, she thought wryly.

As she started to rise, Morgan reached around and pulled out her chair. "Want one more run at the boutiques?"

"No thanks. I don't know how I'm checking all I have on the plane."

"I'll have the hotel ship it."

"Won't that take weeks?"

"No, honey. There's airmail. Overnight, if you like. I'll leave a New York address, and we'll have it for the second leg." He squeezed her shoulders to soften the tease.

How would she know? She was no world traveler. And she only traded in the US.

He cast a lingering glance around. "Not much of a honeymoon, I guess."

"It was, though." She hadn't expected anything.

He shrugged. "Maybe when we figure things out, we'll come back with Livie."

"That would be nice." *If* they figured things out.

He took her hand and they made the short walk to the hotel. Two hours later, they were flying back to New York. Just over seven hours after that, they landed. She had the strange impression Paris hadn't happened. But it must have, because Morgan stopped the limo driver outside a jeweler. Surprised, she followed him to a case sparkling with diamonds.

"Sorry I didn't have these for the ceremony."

"I don't expect —"

He pointed to a pair of platinum wedding bands, the smaller of the two dressed with baguettes.

"Very nice," the jeweler said, unlocking the

case and setting the velvet box on the counter.

She was reaching saturation.

"Do you have one in her size?"

The jeweler took out a clip with sizing bands and tried two on before he found one small enough. He locked the case and went into the back, probably to a vault. He came back with a box, took the ring out, and examined the diamonds with a jeweler's glass, then handed it to Morgan to do the same. He showed him the card that certified the particular brilliance and clarity of each long rectangular stone.

Looking into her eyes, Morgan held the ring against the tip of her finger, where it glittered and shone more beautifully than anything she'd seen.

"Will you wear it?"

She swallowed the tears in her throat. "If you want me to."

"It's not very convincing otherwise."

Who were they trying to convince?

He turned back to the jeweler. "And for me?"

She hadn't realized, but somewhere along the way he'd removed his previous wedding band. As the jeweler fitted him with the counterpart to hers, she wanted to ask if he minded the replacement, but feared he might say yes.

He directed the driver to a hotel where she hoped they could light even for a short time.

She was so tired of travel, she felt it in her bones.

Morgan assessed her with a critical eye. "We'll need dinner, but how do you feel about room service?"

"Great as long as I don't have to decide anything."

"I'll order for us."

Hardly noticing the accommodations, she went into the bathroom and took a long shower. The door opened and closed, and when she got out, she found a plastic-covered hotel robe, extra small. She towel-dried her hair, then pulled the cushy soft robe on and sighed. Cinching the waist, she left the steamy bathroom to find a low bouquet of flowers centered on the table where two covered dishes waited. Had she taken that long?

Morgan held her chair and she sat. He took the other seat and studied her over the flowers, a colorful mélange of exotics. "Would you like to bless the food?"

That took her by surprise.

"It seems we have things to be thankful for." Before she could think what to say, he added, "Otherwise I'll say grace."

"Let's hear your grace."

He said the blessing and she smiled. "That was my grandmother's prayer. Pops couldn't cure her of it."

Smiling, Morgan lifted both lids off to reveal perfectly seared and seasoned rib-eye steaks and waffle fries, with glazed baby carrots, the green stems attached. Hunger punched her. "I haven't done anything but eat for days."

"You climbed six hundred stairs."

"And walked a few miles shopping."

"Some women would call that therapy. My baby sister, Tara, for one."

"Baby sister?"

"She's really nineteen."

"What's she like?"

"Me. Unfortunately."

"How? And why unfortunate?"

"She's a born clown. And an attention hog." He cut into his steak.

For the life of her, she couldn't apply either of those to him. She took a bite of her own meat and the flavor burst over her tongue.

"Mmm." Morgan sighed. "The French have us on pastries, but there's nothing like American beef. I told them to send up the best cuts in the kitchen."

"Naturally."

He cocked his head. "What's that mean?"

"Nothing. I didn't mean anything. It's just Paris, diamonds, this — I'm going to spoil." She hadn't meant to say it out loud, but fatigue had loosened her tongue.

His eyes narrowed. "You're supposed to feel special."

"But . . ."

"You can have bread and water when we

get home."

She stared at the delectable food. "I knew you were famous and rich, but living this way . . . It's uncomfortable." Where was this coming from — her dad's disdain for opulence, his fear that joy might actually be sin? Or a deep-seated belief that she didn't deserve it.

She must have hit a nerve, because Morgan got up and strode to the window that looked out on a million lights. He leaned on the sash without speaking.

"Morgan, I'm sorry. Please eat while it's hot."

"I'm not hungry." He spoke without looking.

Feeling bad for treading on sensitive ground and too fatigued and disoriented to make sense of it, she went into one of the two bedrooms and closed the door. Moving to the window, she looked out. Since their suite formed the corner of the building, she and Morgan might both be staring at the city — only in different directions. She sighed.

Moisture in the air haloed the lights of another place she didn't know. If she and Morgan hadn't joined, she could have disappeared into the vastness with her new name — Morgan's name. She groaned.

"Erin." He tapped the door.

Eyes closed, she blew a slow breath and opened it.

He leaned on the jamb. "It's an old argument I'm tired of, but that's not your fault."

How could it be old, when they'd only broached the subject? And then she realized.

"I'm not as rich as you seem to think. I've made money that makes money. I have a foundation that serves needs. And excuse me, but if I want to enjoy a steak with my wife, I can't work up too much guilt."

She looked at him, chastened.

"So, if we're done with that, will you have dinner with me?"

"Of course."

He stepped back, held her chair when she sat, and took his own. The food had cooled, but neither of them said so. She ate every bite, then wiped her mouth. "Thank you. That was excellent."

"My pleasure."

The words sank in. It was his pleasure to give. He didn't appreciate the gift criticized or judged. She put the used dishes back on the cart and rolled it outside the door. That was what they did in movies. When she went back in, she heard the water running in the shower. How had she come to be in a hotel suite with Morgan Spencer in the shower?

She sat down sideways on the couch and drew her knees up. Stretching her arm across the top, she rested her head on her shoulder, closed her eyes, and prayed for wisdom. She might have thought of that before they landed here, but fear had driven her. That was never good.

"I've made so many mistakes. Please don't let this be one."

"Do not let your heart be troubled. Trust in God." Those were the verses her grandma had used to soothe whatever woe she'd shared. *"Trust in God."*

She wanted to. But even that was muddled. Her mind went through the moments that had brought her here. The trial, of course. The nomadic journey to Juniper Falls. The fragile roots she'd put down there. Her first sight of Morgan and a sense of purpose that felt like a shifting in the stars. Before that her universe had been one thing; now it would be another.

She replayed each of their encounters, words, and expressions. Things he'd said, and things she surmised. She knew so little and sensed so much. Was there even a chance they could work? Tears burned behind her closed eyelids.

Morgan came out in a similar robe and sat down behind her. He brushed her damp hair back and kissed the side of her neck with clear, if subtle, intent.

"Morgan." She turned. "Could we get to know each other first?"

He rested his forehead against her hair. "If you want to *know* me, Erin, this is the way."

Catching the nuance he gave the word, she

half turned. "I don't mean biblically."

"But have you wondered why they chose that word? In bed, we are what we are. And when we come together, we are what we are together. Speaking for myself, knowing you is pretty awesome."

It was awesome. And she wanted him so much it scared her. But still she said, "Could we talk?"

With only a second's hesitation he said, "Sure," and settled her back against him.

Naturally, she could think of nothing to say.

He pulled a crooked smile. "Favorite ice cream?"

She elbowed him.

"You're making this harder than it has to be. Just picture Paris." He kissed the crook of her neck.

She groaned. "That was another world, another me."

"You're my wife. And for what it's worth, I'm —"

"For what it's worth? Do you think this is about you?"

"I'm not sure what it is."

She dropped her head to her arm. "I just feel . . ." Dazed. Confused. Scared. Paris had been a dream and a cold awakening. To experience such love, then such raw unresolved pain . . .

He stroked her arm. "There's no pressure.

We can sleep. We can talk. Whatever moves you."

She shifted around, circled his neck, and kissed him.

He raised his brows. "Interesting conversation starter."

"Do you think I'd have dared that a week ago?"

He tugged a piece of her hair with a contemplative expression. "I get it."

"You're this person I . . . okay, fantasized about."

Again the humor in his eyes.

"We had a snowball fight. A . . . turkey dinner."

"Don't forget the furniture moving."

"A haunted cellar and a drug deal."

"Way more interesting than dinner and a movie."

She loved the way he did that, catching the flow and spirit and letting it take them. He leaned in and kissed her long enough to still her doubts and quicken her heart.

"I don't want to mess up."

"Why do you think you could?"

Like the asylum's "porcelain doll," she'd been fed a heaping dose of stricture and criticism, something she'd successfully conquered until now.

He murmured, "Erin," in a tone that reminded her of all he'd done and why.

As she wrapped his neck again, her wedding band caught and scattered lamplight, infusing her uncertainty with hope and longing. It was possible. They could make it real, couldn't they? Maybe they already were.

Leaving Erin sleeping, he went shirtless to the window in the elegantly appointed sitting room, a sensation like vivisection once more destroying any hope of rest in the city that never slept either. He'd been swept up by her sweetness, her energy, the way she spoke, the way she laughed, that half-vixen, half-vestal cast to her eyes that called to everything physical inside him. Sex was easy — it was great. It was not the whole story.

It complicated. It claimed. It demanded an emotional, spiritual engagement or the beast stayed hungry. He recognized the void, but couldn't fill it from reservoirs drained dry and cavernous. And it was dangerous, dangerous ground.

He might live to fix, but God knew he could also break. He could destroy. He closed his eyes and saw, not his precious Livie, but the daughter he'd lost. Sometimes it seemed that single glance she'd sent through the thick hospital glass had emblazoned on his mind, eyes his color in a face swollen and peeling, a ravage of dying that ended heartbeats later.

Erin had no part in that pain. It was Jill's sorrow and despair that had joined and mingled with his, their love that found a way through. What would she think now? Did this betray her? He ground his fists into his sockets.

What would she say if she could answer? "I never loved anyone but you"?

He dropped his head into his hands, loss rising from his chest to his eyes, grief unexpressed like rusty water from a well. Corrosive. Toxic. These tears would not cleanse if they fell. He should have done this work before he tried again. It wasn't fair —

He stiffened when Erin's warm hand touched his clammy arm. He wanted to resist, to make her go. Instead he turned. "It's been two years. I thought I was past this."

"You've been everything for Livie. When did you grieve?"

He opened and closed his mouth.

She slid her hand down his arm. "You're cold."

She was right. His body felt rigid with cold, as though nothing could thaw it. He reached, and she pressed into him, warmth and softness and strength. He found her mouth and took it.

In his kiss, she felt the wound, the loss, the shattered pieces of him. When he pressed his face to her hair, she held him, feeling their age difference closing — feeling older even, stronger. She could almost see something breaking open inside him, something he savagely defended. "What can I do?"

"Nothing." He moved away, as though fearing his grief might devour her. He went to the sofa and sank down. "There's too much you don't know."

She sat down beside him, waiting.

"I'm not going to . . ." His voice trailed off.

"Talk about Jill?"

"About everything." His hand fisted. "Her, me . . . all that's come before."

They sat in the glow of city lights through the window, his reluctance an uninvited guest.

"I crashed on my bike once," she said, "and all these pebbles got ground into my knee. One was imbedded so deeply they missed it. A week later the infection had burned up and down my leg and the lump turned a streaky, fiery red." She tucked her foot up underneath her. "I thought I'd suffered enough the first time they pulled the stones out and demanded they leave it alone. Because I'd been indecorous, my father made the nurse leave it. Three nights later I woke, crying with pain only excising the wound could relieve."

A clear and simple message. "How old were you?"

She blinked. "I don't know, maybe four."

Feeling a faint spike of anger, he ran a finger over the knee protruding beneath her robe as though it might still bear the wound. Perhaps inside it did. Slowly, he worked into the silence she offered. "When Jill got pregnant, I'd have married her, but her dad said she'd aborted the baby, and I would never come near his daughter again." A rippling rage passed through the muscles of his jaw.

"The official version was a summer mission trip, but she went somewhere to have the baby, to give her up." Again emotion clogged his voice. "The adoptive family cherished her. Kelsey." His face twisted. "They called her Kelsey."

Her heart tugged.

"As I told you, she contracted leukemia. When she was fourteen it came out of remission with a vengeance. The only chance, since she had no siblings, was an allogeneic bone marrow transplant." He swallowed. "At best it's a half match with either parent. Jill's DNA didn't work. So she had to find me." His voice dropped to a hoarse whisper. "I wish to God I hadn't matched either."

She ached.

"It gets technical, but in essence my healthy bone marrow attacked her depleted body. She died from graft-versus-host disease." His voice turned to sand. "You can't imagine what it felt like knowing part of me was in there killing her."

"Morgan, I'm so sorry," she breathed.

"Sometimes I think, if I could destroy something so innocent . . ." He pressed his hands to his face like claws, then slowly drew them down. "I'm just not sure what's left. If

I can do — what good I can be to you."

Everything inside her softened. "Maybe I can be some good to you." Her eyes pierced his defenses.

Sinking back into the tale she'd told, he gripped her knee and said, "What kind of person makes a child pay for being afraid?"

Chapter 16

The Manhattan office Morgan took her to the next morning was beyond her imagining. Where did one even get such posh furnishings? The paintings on the walls were signed originals. Sculptures on the side tables should have been in a museum. People hustled about with purpose, making no sound on the Aubusson carpets overlaying the coral-toned marble tiles. Oiled wood and leather scented the cool air as they moved along the spacious corridor.

"Morgan." A man who perfectly matched his surroundings rose from behind a burled-wood desk when they were ushered in.

"Hello, William." Morgan and the silver-haired man shook hands warmly. "Thanks for receiving the packages."

"Of course. Ellen saw to them."

So this was the New York shipping address.

Morgan said, "William, this is my wife, Erin."

Now she received the warmth of his greeting, though there was steel in his handshake and a keen appraisal in his eyes. "I hadn't heard. Congratulations."

"We married in Paris," Morgan said, "and are just now getting back."

"Ah, Paris." His voice filled with nostalgia. "My summer there with Noelle has fondly lodged in my memories."

"This is William St. Claire," Morgan said. "Noelle's father."

"It's so nice to meet you." This gracious opulence was exactly what she had imagined Noelle came from.

William interlaced his fingers. "How's your little girl?"

"She's amazing."

"And my daughter? The truth, if you don't mind."

Morgan tipped his head. "She makes light of the pneumonia?"

"She does."

"They caught it early, and I think she's doing better."

William nodded seriously. "I still worry."

"I understand." They shared a grim smile. Parenting had pitfalls. "Well, you're working and we have a flight to catch. Thanks again for receiving the packages."

"You're very welcome. And my sincere congratulations." He nodded to her. "A delight to meet you."

"And you."

On the elevator down she remembered Noelle saying she'd been raised with fear and trembling. Must be nice, though, to know your father cared.

At the congested street, thick with the smell of exhaust and humanity, two assistants stacked boxes on dollies and loaded them into the SUV taxi. Either she had ended up with much more Parisian clothing than she recalled buying, or the hotel had put only an item or two in each box. She looked at Morgan, who offered no comment.

Last night had left no mark on his impeccable appearance. If anything, he seemed to move a little easier, like the tin man lubricated after standing too long in the storm.

He joined her in the cab. "Ready to go home?"

The thought of returning brought a bruising reminder of what she'd run from. "I have a mess to clean up."

"Your house?"

"And maybe my warehouse. I didn't take time to look."

"You can't go back there, can't take the chance of Markham seeing you." Reading her face, he said, "Are you insured?"

She sighed. "Until Vera's I never accumulated much. And I didn't think of the things as mine, because in the back of my head, I thought one day I might have to leave them."

"You knew that before the threats?"

"Markham threatened to make me pay the day they sentenced him." The gleam behind his ice-cold eyes had made it seem there were two different people in one body. She shuddered.

"It's a lot to deal with, and I haven't exactly helped."

"What are you talking about?"

"Laying all that on you last night."

Did he really think silence would be better? "I appreciate you telling me. Noelle made sure anything you wanted me to know came directly from you."

"Were you asking?"

"Only about the panic."

"That's the least of it — believe me."

After glimpsing the rest, she said, "I do."

After landing in snowy Colorado, Morgan transferred their luggage to the Range Rover he'd left at the airport. His anxiety rose with every passing minute. He needed to see his little girl and know she was safe, know she was well. He flat-out needed Livie.

Pressing his speed above the road conditions, he noticed Quinn's — Erin's — discomfort and eased off. He was having a harder time thinking of her in terms of his wife the farther from Paris and nearer they got to home — which wasn't even home, merely a cocoon that provided the illusion of immunity.

He looked at her. "I guess we should talk about what happens now."

She drew her knee up, pressing the heel of her sock into the seat and locking her leg in the bend of her arms. Her shoes nested on the floor. "You said I can't, but I need to get a couple things from my house. A jewelry box and a photo." She tried to hide it, but tears pooled, and her voice thickened. "If they survived."

He watched the change come over her. She'd been almost matter-of-fact about losing merchandise, but those two things mattered. "I'll check it out, once we get a feel for what's been happening."

She blinked the tears back and nodded.

He slowed for a vehicle struggling with the grade, waited for a chance, then moved around it. "I bought Vera's as a halfway house to wean Livie off Noelle. I don't think that'll work now."

"Thank God. I don't ever want to set foot in there again."

"You still haven't told me what happened."

"I did. There's something evil in that house."

"Erin, we were in there multiple times. And in the cellar."

"Call me crazy. I know what I felt."

"Why that time and no other?"

"There were others, just not as awful. No voices or laughter."

He couldn't help staring. "You're serious?"

She nodded. "I don't think it's any mystery someone burned the place."

He gave a slow nod. "Then I don't want Livie there for one more minute."

"You believe me?"

"I know there are angels. Kelsey taught me that. Stands to reason the opposition fields a team."

"So what will we do?"

"Go home to Santa Barbara."

She tipped her head. "Where Consuela is."

"Yes."

"If she's there, what will I do?"

"Erin, you're my wife. You'll do whatever you want to."

"But my part was —"

He squeezed her thigh, and triggered a slight leg jerk. "Forget the cooking equals identity equation. We blew that up in Paris." For better or worse.

She couldn't miss his edgy tone but only said, "I've never been to California."

He tried to picture her there but found Jill instead, looking the way she had the night she went out and got crushed beyond recognition. His pulse raced. His head pounded. The palms of his hands slickened. "Erin."

"Yes?"

"Can you drive?"

Catching his condition, she lowered her knee and shoved her shoes back on. He swung over to the shoulder. While she climbed out and came around, he rested his forehead on the wheel, trying to breathe. She opened the door. Teeth clenched, he got out. This had to stop.

The distance she scooted the seat up made him realize all over again how little she was. Didn't have Jill's hurdler's legs by any stretch. But that relationship was gone. He had to learn how to keep it from interfering. And find a cure for cancer. And bring world peace.

He thanked her for taking over as she pulled into the lane.

"Want to talk about it?"

"I think I've said enough." As the panic subsided, he sighed. "There's just residue."

"I understand."

"I really hope you don't, because it's something you can only comprehend if you've been there." He was creating distance again and couldn't stop it.

To combat the bright mountain glare, she flipped the sun visor down and saw his photographs.

He cleared his throat. "I'm sorry."

"Is that Kelsey?"

"Far right." As though the bald head didn't say it all.

"She looks like an angel."

"Yeah." His voice rasped.

She said nothing about Livie or Jill. Stretching, he pulled the photographs down and slipped them into his pocket.

"You didn't have to do that."

"I can't keep living in the past." As they entered town, he said, "We'll stay at the ranch tonight."

"That's fine, if they don't mind me —"

"You're my wife," he reminded her again. "I bet they kind of expect it."

"Doesn't mean they'll like it." She made the turn up to the ranch, the tires getting sluggish in the snowpack.

"They like you. Rick tried to get me interested the first time he saw you."

"What?"

"At the patisserie."

"No way."

"I don't joke about that stuff. Seriously annoyed me."

She studied him for sincerity.

"That's when I decided to move out. I was crowding them, and they were crowding me."

"And here we are," she said, literally and figuratively, as she parked. "You want to go in first?"

He crooked a smile. "In case of spider webs?"

"In case of flying daggers."

"They'll be aimed at me."

"That's hardly fair."

He preferred it that way. Handing her down from the truck, he stood a moment with his hands on her waist. "Want me to carry you over the threshold?"

"Don't you dare."

He was so tempted. Taking her hand, he went inside, calling, "Livie?" From the kitchen came the patter of little feet. He ran to meet her, swung her up, and tossed her in the air. She came down with a hug around his neck, and he held and held and held her.

The cinnamon scent of snickerdoodles wafted from the kitchen as he at last loosened his hold. He couldn't imagine Noelle baking, or it smelling good if she did. He raised his eyes from the crook of Livie's neck . . . and saw his mother.

"Welcome back," Celia said with a somber smile.

He didn't ask what she was doing there. Either Rick or Noelle must have filled her in. Now he wished he'd let Erin wait outside. "Mom." He turned and drew Erin to his side. "This is my wife, Erin. Erin, my mother, Celia."

Their greetings were stiff.

"This is . . . a surprise." Erin cleared her throat.

"Oh yes. It is."

Erin unbuttoned her coat. "You're visiting?"

"I'm here to learn why two people who just met had to leave the country and marry."

Morgan said, "That was all me."

She pulled a thin, unconvinced smile.

"Do I smell cookies?" He raised his brows.

"Livie's helping Grammy bake." Celia brushed the little girl's arm.

With Livie on his hip, he clasped Erin's hand and followed his mother to the kitchen. Releasing Erin, he snatched a warm confection, bounced it a few times on his palm to cool, and popped it whole into his mouth, talking around it. "Where's Noelle?"

"Upstairs resting."

He swallowed the rich chewy mass. "Rick?"

"Out with your dad."

"Dad's here too? Don't tell me you brought the girls."

"Your father and I flew out."

This was serious if they flew. He handed a cookie to Erin. "No one makes snicker-doodles like Celia Spencer."

"Anyone who follows a recipe can," Celia said.

"No, trust me, there's no guarantee of that." Livie clung, so he didn't try to put her down.

Erin bit in and nodded. "Wonderful."

He knew from experience, their opinion of her cookies meant zip. Nothing stopped a glacier on its course.

"So, Erin," Celia said, "what can you tell me about yourself?"

Erin looked at the firm-faced woman with penetrating eyes and almost said, "Good question."

"You're younger than Morgan."

"I'm twenty-seven." Being small, people thought her younger than she was.

"You're from here?"

"No. I've been in Juniper Falls about six months, a couple other towns before that."

"What do you do that requires moving so often?"

"I have my own business, buying from estate sales and trading on eBay. Different locations keep things fresh."

Celia waited for more with an expression that said nothing less than opening a vein would satisfy.

Erin raised her chin. "I like kids and dogs, drive a truck, and I'm not after Morgan's money." Celia's brows jumped. Morgan straightened as she went on. "For reasons on both our parts, marriage made sense and so here we are."

"I see." Celia looked from her to Morgan.

He pulled a slow smile. "The third degree is a little unfair."

"Maybe so, but it concerns me when one of mine acts uncharacteristically in a life-altering way."

"Your concern is noted."

"How do you intend to make a lifelong commitment with no foundation?"

"Little by little, Mom. Livie needs a mother." There was Morgan, taking it all on himself.

Celia frowned. "I'd have no argument with that, if you'd put any kind of time into the relationship."

Erin tried not to shrink when the eagle eyes returned to her.

"How does your family feel about it?"

Her throat squeezed. "We're not . . . in contact."

"Then an established man who's made a name and amassed some wealth must have been especially attractive."

Morgan was especially attractive, but not for the reasons she'd already denied. She refused to repeat herself. "Will you excuse me? We had a long trip, and I need the bathroom."

"Well," Morgan said. "Guess you got her Irish up."

"This isn't only about you, Morgan. You have a child to think of."

"I think of nothing else." He rubbed Livie's back.

"Then . . ." His mother spread her hands.

If she was looking for logic, good luck. There'd been reasons, as Erin said, that made sense, but they'd left sense and sanity in Paris. "You aren't being fair. You don't even know her."

"Neither do you."

"It doesn't take me long to evaluate people."

"That's fine in business. This is life. Yours and Livie's."

"And Erin's."

Her brow furrowed. "Can you tell me after a few encounters and one holiday meal that you love this woman with all your heart? Because I know you, Morgan. I know how deep you run, how hard you love."

"I won't do that again." Hearing the noise behind him, he realized his mistake.

"I don't expect him to." Erin approached, calmer than she'd been, almost stoic. "Frankly, after all he's been through, it's a miracle he's still standing." She turned her tight face to him. "I'm going to my house."

"Erin, you can't."

She pushed past, grabbed her truck keys off the kitchen wall hook, and stalked out.

With a hard look back at his mother, he set his daughter down and followed his wife.

One thing she didn't do was lie to herself. Morgan's words hurt. Of course he didn't love her, but he never intended to? That cast a different light on things.

"Erin, wait."

She looked over her shoulder. "Go have time with your mother. Really." Her breath made a faint cloud.

"Wait a minute. Please."

Rick had moved her truck over by the barn,

and she made for it. "I just want to see what's left."

"Markham knows that's your place."

She pressed Unlock and turned to face him. "It's been days. He'll think he ran me off."

"Erin, the whole point was to disappear. Your house is the only place he knows you might show up."

That was true. She closed her eyes, barely containing her tears.

He released a slow breath. "I shouldn't have said what I did."

"As I told your mom —"

"I'm in this." He reached for her shoulder, but she shifted.

He lowered his hand. "All right, so we hit a bump. Are you a quitter?" His eyes cut into her.

She looked away. His mother was right about the error they'd made, but quit? She clenched her teeth. No. And he knew it.

"Daddy!" Livie came running out as though terrified he'd left again.

Erin watched them reconnect with a lump in her throat. She had no business in his life. How had she fooled herself?

As he scooped Livie up, Morgan said, "I need to put her down for a nap." He looked back toward the house. "And smooth some feathers."

"Your family deserves the truth. You may as

well tell them. Then we can all stop pretending."

"Erin."

She wiggled Livie's little hand. "Want to come nap with me, sweetie?"

To her surprise, Livie leaned out of Morgan's arms into hers. Rubbing the sleepy child's back, she walked wearily to the cabin.

Morgan watched them go, regretting his careless words, though maybe she was right about the rest. Get it all out there and forget pretending. People married for all kinds of reasons. Theirs weren't the worst.

As he started for the house, Rick and their dad drove up and parked. Morgan gripped Hank's hand and hugged him tight. "Hi, Dad."

"Well, son. You got your mom on an airplane."

"She's shared her concerns."

Hank nodded. "You look good."

Did he?

"Might that mean it's not as dire as she thinks?"

He shook his head. "Nothing's as dire as Mom thinks."

"Marriage is serious business, Morgan."

"We had serious reasons."

"I'm eager to hear."

Rick looked around. "Where's Quinn?"

"Erin took Livie to the cabin to nap."

"Erin?"

"Let's all go in. I'll explain."

His family listened soberly as he laid out the situation. Maybe he should have waited for Erin to be part of it, but this way he took the brunt of their reactions.

"There are any number of ways to help someone hide," Hank said, "that don't involve a lifetime commitment."

His mother crooked a brow. "Did you leave the back door open?"

"We rejected the celibate union option. It was" — he shrugged — "Paris."

Noelle's eyes moistened. "That was Quinn's choice too?"

Did she think it wasn't? "Yes. And please call her Erin. We need a fresh start."

"With a fake name?" She looked pained.

"It's her middle name."

"Morgan." Hank shook his head. "I'd think by now you'd have more sense."

Had to love the irony, a world-renowned problem solver being scolded by his family for his solution. "Erin's side is only half the equation. Livie's taken to her completely. We can be a family."

"How?" his mother demanded. "Without love."

Just because he wouldn't stake himself out on a rock like Prometheus for an eagle to gouge out and feed on his liver every day didn't mean he couldn't make marriage work with Erin. Physical and practical were two good legs to stand on. "I care about her. And I respect her. She's tough and fair and kind. Good qualities for Livie to experience."

"In a nanny."

The lingering scent of snickerdoodles seemed too sweet, even cloying. "I'm not pretending to have it figured out. But it's done, and I'd appreciate your support." He managed to keep the edge from his voice — barely. He was smart, he was sober, and he deserved their confidence.

Rick was the first to reach across the dining room table. "Congratulations. I liked Quinn — Erin — from the start."

"I like her too." Noelle still looked teary. "But I feel responsible."

"Responsibility lies squarely with us." Funny how naturally he spoke of them as a unit. She might be upset, but he'd felt the tensile strength of their joining. They wouldn't let go.

His mother sighed. "Since we're here again, we'll support you as we did before."

Since we're here again? As if this were as irresponsible as getting Jill pregnant? In their eyes it might be. He hoped to heaven it would not be as painful.

Chapter 17

Livie wouldn't let go when she tried to put her in the crib, so Erin snuggled into the extra bed with her and fell asleep breathing her baby scent. She fought consciousness every time it tried to arise, disinclined to face contention and disappointment — theirs or hers — until a hand cupped her shoulder. Having no choice, she opened her eyes.

Morgan's gaze was deceptively soft and warm. "I see she's got your number."

Waking with a squeak, Livie tumbled over her and climbed into his arms.

"That's how it starts, and pretty soon she owns you."

"I can think of worse things." The little monkey held her daddy as if she'd never let go. It hurt to watch.

"I've tamed the dragons if you want dinner. Mom's cooking."

"I'm not hungry."

"Your body clock's off, but we should try to get on track."

"Maybe in the morning." She wasn't tired anymore. It was pure avoidance.

His voice softened. "Do I have to beg?"

What was he talking about?

"If Noelle doesn't see you're all right, she'll worry herself sick."

Faking fine wouldn't fool Noelle, whose doubts were visible from the start.

"At least come and eat."

Livie caught his face between her hands. "Eat cookies, Daddy. Snick-er-doos."

"After real food, munchkin."

"Cookies are food, Daddy. No squirrels." She shook her head seriously. "No giraffes. Cookies."

He squeezed her. "See what I mean?"

Oh, she saw. That little girl had her with that first stolen glance.

Morgan settled his gaze back on her. "Please."

Resigned, she shoved the hair behind her ears. She ought to fix herself up, but she couldn't manage to care. Morgan bundled Livie and planted her on his shoulders. She donned her own coat, one of the only things she'd had before, since it had been on her when Markham had his rant. Even so, the frigid mountain wind bit her cheeks and singed her nostrils.

"Hey." Morgan came up beside her. "What's the rush?"

"Getting it over with, I guess."

"You do take things head-on."

That was not proving the best policy, as her newest scars attested.

In the great room, Rick surprised her with a shoulder hug. "Welcome to the family."

Caught in the throat by his kindness, she barely managed, "Thanks."

Noelle came and squeezed her, whispering, "Are you okay?"

She answered with a reassuring look. Of course she was.

An older version of Rick with whitening hair and Morgan's striking indigo eyes held out his hand, then gave her a gentle, patting embrace. "Welcome, Erin. I'm Hank."

She smiled. "Hi."

By the clattering of utensils and Liam's loud comments, she guessed they'd find Celia in the kitchen. Avoiding her, or simply busy?

"We're about ready to eat," Noelle said. "Want to help serve?"

Her mind filled with Miracle Max in *The Princess Bride. "While you're at it, why don't you give me a nice paper cut and pour lemon juice on it?"* She said, "Sure."

Amazingly, Celia turned from the stove with something like kindness. "I'm glad to have the whole story. And I'm sorry for your trouble."

"I'm sorry for yours." That gave Celia pause, but Erin had meant it sincerely. This decision affected them all. Christmas, for instance. She'd be the awkward stranger they went out of their way to treat politely.

"What can we do?" Noelle spoke gaily enough to disguise nausea, pneumonia, and emotional distress.

"It's ready to serve." Celia handed Noelle a huge bowl of plain pasta. Erin took a platter of chicken, lightly breaded and crisply sautéed, and Celia followed with a tureen of Marsala gravy. Oh yes, she would eat, and bless the hands that made it.

She meant no one any harm, and if she could undo the cause of their concern, perhaps she would have. It was so far from the simple merger that Morgan had suggested, they should be investigated for racketeering. When he seated her with a stroke of his hand across her shoulders, it took all she had to mask the wash of disappointment.

Through the meal, he asked questions about his sisters and other family members — as much to fill her in as to catch up, she guessed. The only questions directed at her were banal. Although everyone worked hard to include her, by Morgan's pronouncement, she was clearly on the outside looking in. As it would be, year after year after year.

She'd answered otherwise, but Noelle sensed Quinn's — Erin's — distress. Understandable with what Morgan had said. Fresh anger flared. Why would he voice such a hurtful thing? And if he didn't love her, or intend to love her, how did he justify what he'd done?

She'd told Erin to trust him, to count on him, to believe he'd do what he said. But her new identity didn't require intimacy, Paris or not. She knew that had been half tongue-in-cheek, but she could imagine Erin entranced by the place and far more by the man. If Morgan displayed even half his charm, how could she not believe it real?

Rick had warned her Morgan might not return to full emotional capacity, but he could fake it with finesse. She looked across and found him reading her. He must see the anger. In fact, she blamed herself just as much for knowing he was vulnerable and pushing them together. His easiest connection was physical, yet Erin must have imagined something beyond that to be blindsided by his declaration.

She'd seen her friend's interest and compassion. Morgan's vulnerability coupled with his beauty and magnetism would have sucked her in like the vortex of a storm. His gaze intensified, but she couldn't give him what he wanted — exoneration.

She shifted her attention to Livie feeding Erin a noodle. Erin ate it with gusto, sparing the child any hint of distress. Morgan said they had developed an uncanny bond. At least that was hopeful.

The thought of Livie leaving caused a hollow ache. But Erin and Livie would bless each other. And maybe Morgan too. She had to believe he could heal. She only wished he'd done that first.

Walking his wife and daughter to the cabin, Morgan was keenly aware of how it should be and wasn't. By telling the truth, they'd eliminated any reason to feign relationship, and what little there'd been had evaporated, as shown by Erin's avoidance of physical or emotional contact.

In the cabin, he went through Livie's bedtime routine, got her down to sleep, and came out to find Erin with a quilt and pillow on the couch by the stove. "Are you cold?"

"No, it's warm."

"The bedrooms are warm too."

"This is fine."

"Erin." He sat on the low table and faced her. "They were careless words." He wished she hadn't heard. "I didn't mean to hurt you."

"I appreciate your honesty more than you know. I only wish I'd known before."

Flames from the stove reflected in her eyes. He got up and closed the iron door so he wouldn't watch himself burn. "We knew going in —"

"And should have left it at that."

He tipped his head back, frustrated. "I care about you."

"I'm grateful."

Grateful? He felt like swearing. He'd never claimed anything but affection and attraction. He'd thought her more resilient than this. Or maybe this was resilience. He said, "You take our bedroom. I'll go in with Livie."

"That bed's too small. And it's your bedroom, Morgan. I'm fine here." Her expression and tone were firm and earnest.

Too whipped to argue, he got himself to bed. And lay awake.

Though he didn't know what exactly they'd pledged, he felt pretty sure it wasn't to love and cherish each other until death. They were joined in a civil union as binding as a contract. By mutual agreement they'd validated the contract. Now she was changing the terms.

He tossed onto his side, wanting what he couldn't have and resenting it. He respected her too much to fake a capacity for love he no longer possessed, yet there must be some way — and then the thought came. He wouldn't let Erin near her house, but he and Rick could go.

In the Tahoe now parked under the balcony behind the A-frame house, Markham dreaded another soul-withering day of waiting. His newest supplies were running out. He was starting to smell. He thought of the mess he'd made in the house, but maybe it didn't matter. He'd survived filth before.

Making up his mind, he stalked inside, picturing Quinn living here, a doll in a doll's house. The spoiling food he'd strewn around her kitchen smelled, but not as badly as it might have, since there was no meat or milk, only bread and vegetables and everything from her cabinets. His shoes stuck to the honey on the floor.

He left them by the broom closet and climbed in his socks the ladderlike stairs to the tiny bathroom. Keeping his ears peeled, he stripped and got into her shower, pleased by the thought of invading her space after the humiliations she'd caused him.

He turned on the water and jumped back, swearing. As he waited for ice-cold water to warm up in the tiny, confined space, he realized he might not hear something downstairs. Having learned to never leave himself vulnerable, he took the blade from his pants pocket and rested it on the pedestal sink, near to hand, should he need it.

The curtain lay in tatters on the floor, but it didn't matter what mess the water made. There was still shampoo in the punctured bottle, and he enjoyed the hot shower until he remembered the one he had shared with the other felons as if he were in some stinking commune. The supposedly nonviolent offenders like himself still found means to deride and dominate. And then there were the guards. Pushing, grabbing, tapping, prodding as though driving sheep who didn't know what direction to go.

He dried himself with the slashed towel, breathing it for a scent of Quinn, but it had been too long. She hadn't returned the whole time he'd been waiting. By the fresh food in the kitchen he had assumed she wouldn't be long. Even if he hadn't thrown it around, it would have been spoiling by now.

Shame came over him. He should not have given in to the violence. She might have come and seen it and fled during one of his absences. A stupid mistake. A rusty man's mistake — a previously caged animal reacting. He was smarter than that, above it in every way.

He pulled his clothes back on and replaced the blade. As he stepped into the bedroom, the rumble of a powerful engine penetrated the thin walls. Creeping to the window, he watched a truck park outside the steel building. Anticipation rose like baking soda in vinegar until he saw it wasn't Quinn.

Two men got out, one tall and western in jeans and Stetson, the other black-haired and sophisticated, maybe a lawyer to the rancher. Adrenaline coursed through him as they slid open the steel door and surveyed his handiwork. A cold drip slid between his shoulder blades.

Fear and fury mingled. Who were they, and what were they doing there? This was Quinn's place, and by extension, his. Trespassers, meddlers beware. Knife in hand, even outnumbered, if he had to, he could make them bleed.

"Thorough, wasn't he." Morgan took in the damage with Rick, the possibility that Erin's warehouse had been spared erased by the sight of smashed and scattered merchandise. Her flat-screen monitor had made a popular target judging from the inky-looking shatter beneath the surface. The tendons in his neck pulled tight when he imagined her working there so conscientiously.

He shook to think mere chance, or God's providence, had her at RaeAnne's when Markham struck. The savage destruction indicated he'd misjudged the threat. Whatever the conviction record showed, Markham's present mood was violent.

Rick looked at him. "What do you want to do?"

"We'll call the sheriff. Let a deputy come have a look."

Snow was coming harder as Morgan scrutinized Erin's home. If she lived this simply, no wonder she'd been overwhelmed in Paris and New York. He told Rick, "I need to check the house for a couple things."

Rick looked over with narrowed eyes. "I don't know, Morgan. Something doesn't feel right."

Maybe not, but he needed to do it anyway. "It won't take long."

"All right. I'll keep watch."

He used his elbow to push open the damaged door and waited. He thought he heard a drip of water, but given the damage, anything could be leaking. Wearing his black leather gloves, he headed straight for the stairs, guessing Erin would keep what mattered near her when she slept. Reaching the loft, he caught the scent of soap and moved quickly. The bathroom air felt damp. Someone had showered.

Adrenaline kicked in. He searched the tiny room. Empty closet. Empty balcony. No one under the bed. He scanned the chaos and saw in one corner an inlaid wooden music box, its lid hanging open by a hinge, no jewelry. He slid the box into the pocket of his black cashmere overcoat.

Moving to the head of the bed, he lifted shredded pillows, blankets, a smashed lamp. And there, between the headboard and the wall, a 4x6 picture frame. Warmth coursed through him with a pang of compassion when he saw Quinn, maybe seven or eight years old, fishing with a man on a riverbank. Standing point beside them, a bluetick hound.

Hearing Livie, Erin waited a moment for Morgan to respond, then realized she was alone with the child.

"Hi, sweetie." She helped her out of the crib, removed her Pull-Up, and led her to the bathroom. Eager to be done showering before Morgan appeared, she used his shampoo on herself, and baby shampoo on the child, then snuggled Livie like an Inuit tot in a thick cushy towel and dried herself with the other.

She wiped off the steamy mirror and had a look. Her long thick lashes needed no help, but for the sake of appearances she brushed a film of plum powder over her eyelids and shined her lips with a wand of gloss. Livie wanted gloss too. She smoothed it over the impossibly small mouth.

With Livie dressed in her magical clothes, she uncovered some magical ones herself in a box just inside the door. As suspected, it held things she hadn't picked out in the boutiques. While she'd been trying on and debating, Morgan must have been buying anything that struck his fancy.

She slipped into fitted jeans and a sweater that felt like woven silk. She pictured a million industrious silkworms in tiny French berets spinning the threads that felt so fine against her skin. Soft and yet warm. A miracle of nature. Before, she had blended modern and vintage clothes from estate sales into her own style. Now she was wearing haute couture.

Erin Spencer, pseudo wife of turnaround genius Morgan Spencer. She carried the rich

— and generous — man's daughter toward the house. At the stable, she saw Hank, not Rick, caring for the horses. Interesting.

Finding Liam in the great room surrounded by oversized Legos, Livie squirmed down to play.

Erin joined Noelle and Celia in the kitchen. "Where's Morgan?"

"He and Rick went somewhere early." Noelle looked her over. "You look nice."

"Thanks."

Celia said, "Would you like some tea?" And sounded like she meant it.

Taking the mug, Erin sipped steaming Earl Grey and remembered that first hot chocolate with Liam and Noelle. She'd left that naïve girl on the streets of Paris, and it was time to accept the choice she'd made. Blaming Morgan wasn't productive, or even fair. He hadn't promised or pretended to love her. She'd mistaken it in his touch.

Livie ran in for Noelle to kiss her bumped finger, then accepted banana slices from her grandma. Liam strode in with boyish energy and strident commentary, receiving a mug of milk and bananas with peanut butter. Into the melee, Rick and Morgan came, Rick in crewneck sweatshirt and jeans, removing his Stetson. Morgan's overcoat was dusted with snow, but he didn't remove it.

She met his eyes, wishing everything in her wasn't drawn to him like Echo to Narcissus.

When he beckoned with his head, she followed him out. "I didn't know where you went, so I showered Livie. I hope that was okay."

"It's great. But I'll show you where I went." He drew her into the great room and took something from his coat pocket.

She gasped, seeing the jewelry box her grandma, now gone, had given her.

He adjusted the lid and said, "It can be fixed."

Of course it could. When he produced the small framed photo, she half laughed, half cried, "Pops."

"I thought so." He clasped her wrist. "Erin . . ."

"Thank you." She pressed her forehead to his wet coat sleeve with a stifled sob. "Thank you."

His arm came around her. "Erin, listen."

Face still pressed to his sleeve, she raised her eyes.

"Someone used your bathroom."

"What?"

"It smelled like soap, and the shower was wet."

Her stomach roiled. "Markham?"

"Can you think who else?"

"No, but . . ." Her euphoria fled. "He was there?"

"I didn't see him. I got out as soon —"

Hank came in with a cheery greeting.

"Breakfast ready?"

"I don't know, Dad." Morgan's tone took the smile from the older man's face. "But we need to leave."

"Trouble?"

"Trouble." Morgan turned. "We'll need things for Livie, Erin. You and I can make do with our carry-ons, and we'll ship the rest."

"Okay." Having a task helped her control the fear. In the back of her mind, she'd known she would have to run. Now, it seemed, she wouldn't be alone.

Skulking on the Tahoe roof beneath the balcony while the man searched Quinn's bedroom had infuriated him, but Markham hadn't moved until the way was clear. If the man had come onto the balcony, he'd have seen the vehicle beneath. If he'd leaned over, Markham would have slit his throat.

But they'd gone. He didn't know who they were. Friends of Quinn's or agents acting on her behalf? It didn't matter. Now that they'd come, his strategy had to change. No more waiting where he might be discovered.

He got into the Tahoe and headed toward town, parking at the general store instead of the grocery mart where he'd shopped for supplies. It looked like a fixture in the heart of town where someone might know everyone. He entered with anticipation and jumped when, just inside the door, a floorboard popped.

"Better than a bell," said the fool behind the counter.

"You can say that again." Markham hid his annoyance.

"What can I do for you?"

Forming his face into the role, Markham played a good-old boy. "I was hoping you could help me out. I'm looking for Quinn Reilly." He held out the photo he'd carried along.

The big guy's face went soft. "Nice picture."

He hadn't asked for commentary. "Have you seen her?"

"Not since Thanksgiving."

Bingo. "She's out of town?"

"Could be visiting family or something."

"Oh, she's not talking to her family. Big blowup."

The man frowned. "That's too bad. When?"

"A while back." Markham plied the lie. "That's why I'm here, to see how she's doing."

"I don't know." The guy had the brain of an ox. "You might ask Rick. He had her at the ranch on Thanksgiving. She cooked the whole meal."

"Did you say ranch?" The pieces clicked into place. She worked for the men — one of them anyway. The rancher Rick. "Where would I find it?"

"It's up that road a couple miles." The man pointed. "Past the only other driveway and all the way to the end."

Markham grinned. "Thanks a lot." He shook the man's hand as if he'd sold him a car. People landed in two categories: suspicious and gullible. He considered it a gift to be able to shift ninety percent into the second group.

Chuckling, he started up the gravel road to the ranch, thinking how it might take only that pawn to capture the queen. As he drew near enough to see the spread — log buildings backing to a minor creek and beautiful pasture stretching up a crag-bordered valley — he imagined Quinn bustling like a little worker bee in their kitchen.

She'd been so diligent, so observant — so suspicious from the first glance. He'd known she'd be trouble, but hadn't imagined how much. He braked at the crest of the rise, debating whether to bide his time or make a bold approach. He decided on the latter, mainly because he was sick to death of biding time.

Erin felt Noelle's distress as she looked from her to Morgan and asked, "Right this minute?" She'd been deeply involved in both their lives the last two years, mothering Livie as she did her own son, who would also be impacted. No doubt Morgan had considered those details when he made his original plan — all changed now.

With his daughter on his hip, he said, "Could you make Livie some car snacks?"

That meant they were driving, Erin guessed, though they hadn't discussed it.

"I'll do that." Celia pressed a hand on Noelle's shoulder. "You finish your breakfast."

They all froze when the doorbell rang. Legs trembling, Erin gripped Morgan's arm, needing the contact she'd avoided last night.

"Anyone expecting someone?" Rick looked specifically at Noelle, then shot a glance at them. "Get your family out of sight, Morgan."

Hank flanked Rick to the door and stayed off to the side as she and Morgan and Livie ducked into the pantry and turned on the light.

"I'm sorry," she whispered.

He put a finger to his lips. Pressing close to him and Livie, she heard the house door open, then the slick salesman voice that turned her stomach.

"Hello. Are you Rick?"

Rick said, "Who's asking?"

"I'm Ken West, a friend of Quinn Reilly. I was told she works for you."

She and Morgan shared a look.

"Who told you that?" Rick sounded vaguely friendly, but nothing like his normal warmth.

"The guy down at the store. Said she

cooked or maybe catered your Thanksgiving dinner."

Rudy. The trapped breath hurt her chest.

Morgan whispered, "He didn't know."

Of course not.

When Rick neither denied nor confirmed, Markham went on. "I'm hoping you can tell me where to find her. I tried calling but can't get service. Must be the mountains."

She pictured Rick standing there, his stoic face inscrutable. As Morgan's hand tightened on her shoulder, she realized she was shaking, but with fear or fury she couldn't tell.

Then Hank's voice came. "Everything all right, son?"

In the dining room, someone silenced Liam when he started to ask what was happening.

Rick said flatly, "He's a friend of Quinn Reilly."

"I've come a long way to see her." Markham oozed sincerity.

"Maybe you should try her house," Hank suggested.

"Sure, sure. Can you tell me where that is?"

As if he didn't know, she seethed.

Rick said, "About three miles east, then north on Arch Canyon Road. Little A-frame." Since Markham had already found it, sending him back to her place might buy them time to get out.

Morgan stroked the nape of her neck, his voice barely audible. "Rudy did us a favor saying you cooked here."

"How?"

"West won't suspect Rick's protecting you."

She looked up. "He's not Ken West. He's Markham Wilder."

His face showed no surprise. "Why the alias?"

"He's a pathological liar. His whole life is one big con."

"All right," the liar said. "Appreciate your help."

She pictured Markham's ingratiating smile. He'd be holding out his hand. It sickened her to imagine Rick shaking it, but not shaking would send a message. Willing Markham to leave, she slumped with relief when the door closed.

Livie said, "We hide-a-seeking, Daddy?"

"Yeah, precious. But now we can get out."

The others were waiting when they did.

"You did the right thing," Celia said. "Testifying against him."

She said *him* as she might *snake.* And it was true, but they didn't know the rest. "How did he look?"

"Like a politician who's done time." Rick eyed his brother. "You want a gun?"

Gun? She blinked at those words from the holy man who raised his hands to pray.

"I'm a lousy shot," Morgan answered.

She shook her head when Rick's gaze shifted to her. The time she'd fired her grandfather's pistol, she'd shaken like a leaf in a bad wind. Grandma Pearl had scolded the laughter out of his eyes, and Pops had knelt down and apologized. "Guess you're a bit wee for it yet."

Morgan pulled her out of her thoughts. "We have to ditch your truck. If he found your house, he might also have the vehicle registration number. Rick, can you handle it?"

He nodded somberly.

"We'll put the bags in the Range Rover." He slid his hand to her shoulder. "You and Livie can take that. I'll drive the Maserati."

She turned. "The what?"

He pulled a slow smile.

CHAPTER 18

Morgan scanned the yard through the blowing snow as he hustled Erin to the cabin to pack things for Livie. Rick had seen Markham drive away, but he could have doubled back on foot to lie in wait. A quick search showed he wasn't in the cabin. "Lock it behind me, and wait until I park outside before you come out. I'll most likely need to jump the Maserati's battery, so I might be a little while."

By now Rick and Hank were armed and patrolling. Noelle and Celia had the kids in the house. They could call the sheriff, but he'd rather get out than wait for one of the county deputies who might take hours to even get there. And what would they say? Could they prove Markham texted a threat? Vandalized her house? Maybe, maybe not. Escape sounded better.

Hurrying to the barn, he pulled open the barn door and moved past the tractor with the plow blade. He stopped beside the vehicle parked along the wall in the black formfitting cover. Softly as a mother cat opening the caul on her young, he lifted the cover off his *rosso trionfale* Maserati Gran Turismo. Driving it was like straddling a cheetah, feeling the restrained muscles and sensing an imminent burst of speed but controlling it with a whisper. It wouldn't be easy to sneak past Markham, but then he wondered if they wanted to. If the jerk was watching, it might be possible to pull a bait and switch.

As the Maserati ground to life like a surly beast from hibernation, his phone rang. Anselm. That gave his heart a hitch. He could count on one hand the times the investigator had phoned instead of e-mailed.

"Morgan, glad I reached you."

"What is it?"

"Did a little more digging on that felon you asked about. It appears that three years prior to his conviction, Markham Wilder was questioned, though not charged, in a couple of homicides."

Fear flared. "Why not charged?"

"The detective couldn't break his alibi, a woman of faith no jury would doubt swore he was working for her the whole day. She called the inquiry a witch hunt."

Morgan swallowed. "Who died?"

"Pair of miscreants related to Wilder. Cousins, I think."

"Case solved?"

"Still open, but they're not working it.

Detective's sure he's their guy."

"Okay. Thanks." He disconnected. Leaving the car running to juice the battery, he went into the house, took Rick's offer, and locked the gun in the Maserati's glove box. He couldn't score a target on the range, but lives on the line might improve his aim.

Inside the cabin, he found Erin zipping the bag of Livie's clothes. "Ready?"

She nodded. "Clothes and diaper bag. I didn't know about books or —"

"It's good enough." He raised her by the elbow. "And I've changed my mind. I want you to take the Maserati to Rudy's. He keeps a shotgun behind the counter. I'll let him know you're coming."

Her eyes widened. "And what, Rudy shoots Markham?"

"Hopefully warns him off. But shooting's okay too."

She searched his face. "Then what?"

"Wait with Rudy until Livie and I get there in the Range Rover."

She forked her fingers into her hair, looking truly scared for the first time.

He went to his closet and took out the colorful ski hat with ear flaps his mother had given him last Christmas. Pulling off the tags, he said, "Can you get your hair in this?"

She looked from it to him. "Probably."

"When you're ready, bind it up and put on the hat. I need to talk to Rick and Noelle."

Her hands shook when she took the hat, but she'd be okay. He went to the house and saw his parents' luggage by the door. Celia looked up from reading to her grandkids. His dad stood at the great room window, one hand in a pocket that probably held a nine-millimeter automatic. Rick and Noelle came down the stairs, wearing matching expressions of concern.

Morgan drew a slow breath. "I just learned the guy hassling Erin is suspected in a couple homicides." He repeated Anselm's information. "For what it's worth, I didn't know until now. When the investigation turned up only fraud and embezzlement, I thought Erin might have overreacted. Not so." He shook his head as a dark mood came on.

Hank frowned. "We should contact the sheriff."

"Do it," Morgan agreed. "But don't say anything about me or our marriage. I want that quiet as long as possible."

Noelle touched his arm. "Can't they arrest him?"

"For what?" He turned to Rick. "Did you hear a threat?"

"No. But her place is trashed."

"Did you see him do it?"

"It's a good guess he did."

Guessing was worth about that. "Get someone out there. Maybe they can find and question him, but that doesn't help Erin get away."

Noelle spread her hand. "So what are you going to do?"

"I'm going to draw Markham off."

"You're doing what?" his dad said.

"I have a plan. It includes Rudy's shotgun."

The three of them eyed him grimly, but no one argued.

Erin tried to look calm and brave when Morgan set Livie down and closed the cabin door.

"You remember what to do?"

She nodded.

"Drive slowly and carefully. If Markham's out there, let him know it's you."

"Then why the hat?"

"You'll see. Get the gas pumping, then go straight in to Rudy."

She forced an even tone. "Okay."

As she hurried through the blowing snow into the Maserati he'd left running, the tiny hairs on her neck rose. Could Markham see her? Every nerve pulled taut as she left Rick's ranch on the one-lane road that only widened out near town. She passed Vera's driveway about two thirds of the way down, a gravel ribbon walled by lodgepole pines. Did Markham lurk there?

Flesh creeping, she came to a stop at the intersection, then continued across the highway, parked at the pumps, and began to fuel. She hurried, heart hammering, over the roughly paved parking lot. Just before she entered, she slipped the wedding band off her finger and into her pocket. The fewer people outside Rick's family who knew, the better.

Rudy met her inside the door with his shotgun and a rueful expression.

"Please don't apologize. You didn't know." She hated that he felt bad in any way, hated that she'd dragged him and the others into her trouble. But with fear still twitching up her back, she said, "Could we wait behind the counter until Morgan gets here?"

"He's not here?" He pressed his hands to his hips. "But that's his car."

"He has the other one."

Rudy's jaw fell slack. "He let you drive the Maserati?"

She should have recognized a shrine. Ducking past when he unlocked the hatch, she took in the relative shelter of the mostly glass counter. A barrier at least.

Beside her, Rudy smelled like a Slim Jim, and its long plastic sleeve clung to the side of the trash can. "You want to get down and hide?"

"Yes. But I think he's supposed to see me."

Rudy groaned. "He looked all right, a little slick maybe, but —"

Someone moved across the tinted storefront windows and came in the door. A jolt shot through her as she came face-to-face with the person she despised. Not a politician who'd done time, though he might have presented that way to Rick, but a maniacal holy man whose brains got too hot in the desert. He knew she saw through him and didn't try to hide it.

"Hello, Quinn." Malice marred the jovial tone he aped, matching the shadow in his eyes.

She raised her chin. "What are you doing here?"

"We need to talk."

"That's why you trashed my house and destroyed my things?" She felt Rudy stiffen.

Markham's face settled into a cold stare. "I don't know what you're talking about. Come out where we can discuss it."

Rudy stirred. "She's fine where she is."

"Listen, you big goob—"

Rudy slid the gun from the shelf where he'd concealed it and held it across his hips.

"Are you kidding me?" Markham's scorn came through every word.

"It's loaded with buckshot. Won't take down a bear, but human flesh is softer."

Erin saw the Range Rover pull up to the pumps and said, "You need to leave."

Eyes narrowed to slits, Markham hissed, "You bought a *Maserati* with my money."

She almost denied it, then realized anything she said about Morgan would blow their cover. "That money belongs to the kingdom."

"You used God's money for a Maserati!"

At the sound of his piety, she couldn't resist twisting the knife. "I have to get around somehow."

He called her a name that would have withered the elders. Rudy raised the gun, still across his body but ready to point if Markham pushed it. "Time to move."

"We're not finished, Quinn." In Markham's mouth her name sounded as dirty as the other. Thank God she no longer used it.

After he stalked out, she drew up to her full five feet three inches. Since Morgan hadn't come inside, she said, "Rudy, would you mind walking me to the door and standing there with the gun?"

"I'll walk you there and use it."

She swallowed a lump. "Thanks."

He pushed the door open for her. "You be careful."

She rose on tiptoe and kissed him on his broad cheek, which instantly flushed. "You too."

Scanning for Markham, she hurried toward the pumps, startling when Morgan reached out the window of the Maserati and caught her arm. When she bent, he tugged the brightly colored hat from her head and put it on his own.

"Get in the Range Rover and stay down until I'm out of sight. Then head west."

She did as he said, slouching so she barely peeked over the doorframe. Morgan peeled out, leaving the smell of burnt rubber and exhaust. Almost immediately, a white Tahoe she recognized by the cross decal on the back window tore out from behind the store. She pressed her hands to her mouth, staring until they disappeared.

"Where did Daddy go?" Livie's plaintive query from the back seat brought her back to reality.

"He took the red car."

"Why?"

"It's faster." And made a flashy decoy. She put the Range Rover in drive. The GPS came on, showing a preprogrammed route. Taking a deep breath, she looked over her shoulder. "Here we go, sweetie. Here we go."

Slowing down for the Tahoe, Morgan took one of the routes leading to Rocky Mountain National Park. He kicked the accelerator, trying to maneuver as Erin might. A little jerkier, maybe, since she hadn't been driving high-performance vehicles for years, as he had. He leaned on the wheel around a bend, laying some rubber.

In the rearview mirror, he watched Markham exit to follow him and leave the way clear for Erin and Livie to stay on the Interstate. At the thought, a surge of fear caught his chest. Thinking of Livie could debilitate him. Concentrate on the road and the plan. Think about Erin. About Markham and the way he'd treated her, the threats, the vandalism. He thought of her courage, her temper, the way she stood up for herself and for him to his own mother. It almost brought a smile, until he remembered what happened next.

Just because he couldn't give her what she wanted, didn't mean he wouldn't give her what he could — starting with escape from the trouble she'd gotten into. The slime bag Markham didn't stand a chance — or did he?

His breath hitched as he took in the situation ahead — road closed for snow. No park admittance. He should have remembered that. The first mistake.

He pulled around the park station and stopped, hoping the structure would hide his vehicle until Markham likewise pulled up. It was his only chance of changing direction without Markham getting a clear view into the Maserati, but if he saw him waiting there, he could block him in.

He heard the other engine approaching and knew his own idle, though amazingly crafted to perform without excess noise, was not silent. Markham would be taking in the situation, wondering where the rabbit had run and if he'd missed a turn. The Tahoe slowed, passed the point where stopping sideways would block the road, inched forward, forward . . .

Morgan hit the gas. The tires squealed. With

the small building between them, he screeched past and flew back in the direction he'd come, the Tahoe coming hard and heavy. Hard and heavy couldn't match raw speed, but on these icy, snowy roads the other vehicle had him.

He fishtailed around a bend, losing seconds. The Tahoe barreled down, reckless in its desire to overcome. Instead of gunning it, Morgan carefully accelerated like a horse pulling away from the pack in the final stretch. Far as he could tell, Markham still believed him to be Erin. He pulled a slow, hard smile.

Back at the highway, with the Tahoe barreling down, Morgan turned toward town, praying Erin and Livie had already passed this spot, heading away. He'd wanted to give her more time, luring Markham in through the park. But sometimes things went wrong. "Just a little help, Lord. Like the Red Sea, Livie and Erin on dry ground, and then, if it's not too much, I'll slosh through too."

Near town, he waited around a bend in the road with double yellow road stripes, then darted around a snowplow. Again with controlled acceleration, he took the curves with speed and precision until he eased onto the small, descending exit that accessed several ranch homes in a low, narrow valley.

He swung around at the bottom, fishtailing onto the frontage road that would emerge on the far side of Juniper Falls. Unless Markham looked down and back in time, he shouldn't notice. Morgan blew out a hard breath, thanking God for that plow and one smokin' chariot.

Hollering in frustration, Markham cursed the snowplow Erin swerved around in her dark red Maserati. His knuckles whitened like wax on the wheel when he thought what she must have spent for it. The tendons felt like lances up the sides of his neck and down between his shoulder blades. Finally his opportunity came.

He gunned the Tahoe, shaking his fist at the plow as he accelerated, then swung the wheel back, exulting, until the tires broke loose. Momentum pulled his front end as the back swung around in a spin. He jammed the brake pedal, and the IBS — so-called intelligent brake system — drummed worthlessly. He cut the wheel into the spin and slid sideways across the oncoming lane and off the pavement.

His shoulder rammed against the door, the belt jerking over his chest as the whole side of the Tahoe crunched into the canyon wall. Everything went still. No airbags deployed. He blinked and opened his eyes, blinked and opened.

With the driver's door wedged against the rock wall, he unbuckled and crawled out the passenger side as a car crept past, passengers staring. They would stop if he signaled. Instead, he slammed the door and kicked a dent in it. He kicked the side panel. Again he kicked, and again. He slammed his fists into the hood. No dents, but it felt good. He grabbed a melon-sized rock from the base of the canyon wall. With a roar, he heaved it at the windshield. Spiderweb splinters stretched across the safety glass.

And finally, gripping the back of his head, he saw what he'd done with dawning dismay. The rage drained, leaving ice-cold loathing. He looked over his shoulder at more faces passing. No one stopped. No one dared.

Erin's neck burned from wrenching around to look. Though she didn't know his plan, she'd expected Morgan to find them by now. Her anxiety must have shown, because Livie's intense little gaze hadn't left her. Mile after mile, the weight of Morgan's trust pressed down as the child's unease increased.

"Where's my daddy?"

"He's coming, honey. Any minute now, he'll find us." The highway stretched and wound, mountains towering on either side. Like the truck she no longer owned, this vehicle was solid and reliable. She'd driven the highway many times. The only difference was Livie.

A half hour, then an hour. She reached Highway 70 and passed Idaho Springs.

"I want my daddy." Livie's voice rose to a heart-tugging pitch.

Erin asked brightly, "Want to sing a song?"

Livie almost refused, then nodded. "Sing 'Sunshine.' "

"Umm . . ."

"You my sun . . . shine, only sunshine."

She started the song, Livie watching her mouth, her eyes, every part of her, seeing if she meant it. "You are my sunshine, my only sunshine. You make me happy when skies are gray."

Her voice cracked. How could she be what this child needed?

"You'll never know, dear —" She looked in the rearview mirror and through the snow saw Morgan's Maserati speeding up to her. Heart rushing, she said, "Daddy's here, Livie. He's right behind us."

She'd expected that to be exciting news, but Livie's eyes pooled. "Daddy." Her wanting grew so big it burst out in tears. She'd been brave, but the thought of him so close and not accessible was more than she could bear. "I want Daddy."

"Just as soon as we can, honey. Just as soon as we can."

She answered the instant Morgan phoned and told him, "Livie wants you."

"Get to Lawson Dumont. Don't stop on the road."

In the five miles to the exit, Livie fell asleep,

but Erin got off anyway. She parked in the first available lot and hurried back to Morgan emerging from his wine-red rocket. "Livie fell asleep. I tried to keep talking so she could see you, but —"

Morgan gripped her arm. "It's okay."

The fear and pressure hit like an emotional avalanche. She started to shake. "Is he gone? Did you lose him? I just kept driving and —"

He hugged her briefly, tight and keyed up himself. "You did great, but we're not far enough to relax."

"Okay."

"You all right?"

An honest answer would bring tears. "I'm glad Rudy had a gun." Her voice betrayed her gratitude and relief.

Morgan cocked his head. "Did I see you kissing him?"

She looked up into his eyes. "He deserved it."

"Ah."

She closed her eyes. "I messed things up for you and Livie. You had a plan —"

"Plans change." He frowned. "I just don't want this hitting her too hard."

The crying had been pitiful. "What do you want to do?"

He strode to the SUV and looked in. "Since she's sleeping, we'll go on the way we are."

"Are you sure?"

He nodded. "She might wake tender, so call

me. This storm system is extensive, but you have good tires. Just don't take any chances."

"I won't. Morgan . . ." She fought to express so much.

He brushed a thumb down her cheek. "You're doing fine. Let's put some miles behind us. Okay?"

The next time they stopped was when Livie woke crying as though her heart had broken in her sleep.

Chapter 19

Any exultation he'd felt at eluding Markham evaporated with Livie's tears. Kissing her head again and again he murmured, "It's okay, sweetie. It's okay." But it wasn't. She had no context for what was happening. It made him weak when she wailed for Mommy Noelle. So much for gentle separation. "Want to call her on my phone?"

"No." She slapped at it, but not hard enough to knock it loose, then clutched his neck. "Hold you, Daddy."

He knew what she meant, but she always reversed the object with that verb, and sometimes he wondered if she wasn't saying exactly what she meant. "I'm holding you, sweetie. I won't let go." Erin had gone into the gas station while he comforted Livie and filled their tanks. With only one of those accomplished, he went in too.

Erin exited the restroom looking wrung out. She said, "I'm sorry. Nothing I did made any difference."

"She's okay. Are you?"

She stared too long at an end cap that held nothing more interesting than tire gauges. "Morgan, you can go back. If I leave —"

"Stop it. We're not splitting up."

"You have to realize he won't stop."

"I know the score." He rubbed his child's back.

Her lip trembled. "Go back and follow your plan for Livie."

"That's not happening."

She splayed her hands. "I'm Erin Spencer now. You gave me what I needed."

"Yeah, well, you owe me the other half of that deal."

"Like I'm doing so great? She doesn't know me. She wants Noelle."

"She's two years old. This isn't her decision." Maybe too many of his choices had been floated in that boat.

Erin stepped close. "I'm thankful for all you've done, but it's enough."

This wasn't only about Livie. It was about yesterday and last night, about Paris and running for her life. He'd found her treasures, but it didn't make up for the rest. She was hurt and she was scared.

Her eyes were a dark force. "I'll find some way to make it right for you. But this isn't it. Please let me take the new name and go."

"You could call yourself Methuselah, and it won't matter the first time you do something that requires your social security number."

"What?" She searched his face. "Then why —"

"I didn't want you to take off."

She processed that with something that looked like betrayal, as if he'd tricked her into this when it couldn't be further from the truth. "We gave you a buffer that allows some anonymity. But that's not enough. He's tracing you through records, and he's better at it than I'd hoped. You need a personal firewall, and I can provide it."

Her face twisted. "Maybe that's true, but I can't stand to have you and Livie in this. I'm going."

"How? Because Livie doesn't ride in the Maserati." He hadn't intentionally deprived her of the truck she might have taken off in without looking back, but he thanked God it wasn't in the mix now. Her realization showed as she slumped. He hitched Livie, who'd stopped crying at some point, higher on his side. "So are you finished?"

She glared at the floor. "I should have kept my truck."

"Well, here's the other news. I need your cell phone."

Her eyes came up, hard. "Why?"

"It's another connection that could leave a trail."

Fighting tears, she took it out. He opened the men's room door and dropped it in the trash, then stepped back out. "When we get there, I'll put another phone on my plan. For now we'll purchase one of those." He indicated the circular rack of prepaid cell phones.

She pressed her hands to her eyes.

"He's playing for keeps, Erin."

"You think I don't know?" Her voice had lost its steam.

He brushed her arm. "So let's quit wasting time and energy on useless scenarios and make this work."

After a moment, she nodded.

Since Livie wouldn't let go, he took her to the bathroom with him. When they came back out, Erin was waiting with a small beanbag teddy. Hiccupping with latent sobs, Livie accepted the comfort of that little toy and slightly relaxed the death grip around his neck.

Erin said, "Maybe for now you should drive the SUV."

She was right. Livie needed him. "Okay. Let's get as far as we can today." He paid for the gas, the cell phone, and an untraceable prepaid Visa for Erin, just in case. "Any plastic you have besides this —"

"I know."

She had to feel stripped. He wished he could make it easier but couldn't see how. He hated turning over the Maserati, and not because he thought she'd take off. The snow worried him, the terrain and Erin's mental and emotional condition worried him. But there it was.

After buckling his daughter into her car seat, he walked Erin to the Maserati and opened the driver's door. "Just like before, okay? Lots of power you need to control." He rested his hand on the small of her back. "Stop worrying."

He could almost see the new facts spinning in her head. Had she really thought it would be as easy as getting married? Had he? The minute he smelled the wet shower in her wrecked place, reality had crashed in. She had to be terrified.

His gaze fell to her mouth, but he dragged it away. "Let's hit the road."

Fear tasted like mercury on her tongue. Morgan's words had penetrated and begun multiplying — splitting and dividing and growing into a life of their own. She had thought she'd been careful, thought she'd been clever. She hadn't even faked careful. She didn't know how to be this kind of careful.

The new person, Erin Spencer, rose up like a clown with fiendish laughter. To keep her from taking off, Morgan had built a house of cards. It collapsed with his admission to Celia, and with a single match from Markham, it could all go up in flames.

Now Morgan promised her a firewall, and

naïvely she believed. Show me another card trick, magic man. She would watch his hands and miss the part where something else disappeared.

She slipped into the belly of the beast, feeling smaller in the Maserati than in the SUV. But she couldn't bear to get between Livie and her daddy, not for a while, anyway. She'd offered to separate, but where would that leave her? No vehicle, no home, no income. She'd be issuing refunds for everything she couldn't deliver with nothing to list in their place. Her eBay store didn't bear her name, but her financial information with PayPal did.

Without a pirated social security number, she could only disappear through Morgan's house of mirrors. She had trapped herself more surely than Markham could have. She just hadn't expected it to hurt.

The snow came more thickly as she drove the narrow twisting canyon out of Glenwood Springs. Her wipers thwacked in a rhythmic swipe and smear that left small trails of snow in their wake. While the SUV muscled through, this rare exotic animal, whose power she nervously kept leashed, tried through elegance to skate upon the surface.

Around a curve, the road plunged down. As the Range Rover dipped down and away, the Maserati chose a new direction, gliding sideways in a graceful arc until the rear side panel smacked into the guardrail that kept vehicles from tumbling over.

Ushered by Rudy's awe and Morgan's certain devastation, tears flooded her eyes.

In his rearview mirror he had watched it happen like a self-fulfilling prophecy. The instant he assessed the road hazard, the Maserati began its slide. Thirty yards ahead, he pulled to the side and stopped. He told Livie to sit tight, and cautiously climbed the sloping Interstate, thanking God the traffic was light.

Erin's hands covered her face as he pulled open the car door. After all the times she'd been strong, her crying now was just wrong. "Are you okay?"

She nodded, but he saw a reddening bump just above her temple.

"I'm so sorry." She cried harder. "It started sliding. And nothing —"

"The tires are practically racing slicks. On that curve and this grade . . ."

Sniffling, she slid her hands off her teary cheeks. "How bad is it?"

He leaned to look. "I'm glad the guardrail was there. Besides that bruise are you hurt?"

"No." Her voice was as small as the real answer was big. She hurt in ways he couldn't even guess. Every relationship had taught him that.

He wanted to comfort her, but the side of the road wasn't the place. He pulled the door as wide as he could before it touched the rail.

"You take the SUV. Livie's okay now."

Letting it idle, she put the gears in neutral and engaged the parking brake. She stepped out into the snow and leaned past him to see the damage. She didn't need to know how expensive it would be to fix and how much value had been lost.

He brushed her arm. "Livie's waiting."

She grabbed her purse and headed to the Range Rover, punishing herself, though this was nothing compared to —

The pain in his chest almost doubled him. *Crushing, screaming metal, the collapse of pliant flesh. "She died instantly. Died instantly."* He needed Livie, needed Erin, out of there. Reaching in, he turned off the engine, engaged the locks and alarm, and shut the door. Erin watched him come.

"Slide in," he rasped.

"Can you drive?"

Better than he could ride after watching her crash. Breathing deeply, he rested his forehead against his hands on the steering wheel. The pounding of his heart made lights blink behind his eyelids. "Buckle up," he told Erin, who seemed to be waiting.

She did. "What about the Maserati?"

"I'll send someone for it." His roadside service would get the Maserati to the nearest garage. At some point Rick could get it from there. With luck no one would careen around that bend and plow into the jeopardized vehicle before that. He raised his head and looked into the back seat. "You okay, Livie?"

Eyes intense, she murmured, "Okay, Daddy," and snuggled the little bear.

He eased the SUV back into the lane and shot a glance at Erin. "It's not your fault."

Her gaze fell to her hands, and his followed. They were small and tense and bare.

"You're not wearing your ring."

She straightened her fingers. "I didn't want Rudy to see."

"Good thought. But you should wear it now." She might be trying to forget, but they were married. Maybe it wasn't all she'd imagined, but reality rarely was.

Leaning, she pried it from her pocket. The sparkle reminded him this was no game. He and Erin were joined. He had to find a way to make it work. His daughter deserved that. And so — he swallowed — did his wife.

Leaving Liam with a friend, Noelle got back into the truck beside Rick. With multiple accidents on the slippery roads throughout the county, it took hours for the sheriff's department to respond to the call they placed after taking Hank and Celia to the airport. Now, finally, someone was available to talk about vandalism.

Rick had wanted her to stay home, but she needed to see what had driven Erin and Morgan into their rash marriage. So together they met the heavy, graying Officer Wentz at Quinn's — Erin's — address. She stood with Rick behind the man as he surveyed the damage from the doorway. She wasn't sure the officer could make it up the ladderlike stairs, but he merely took in the scene from the door.

"The two of you live here?" he said, frowning.

"No," she told him. "It's our . . . friend's place."

"And where's he?"

"She left town. The person who did it is harassing her." This wouldn't be easy without explaining everything, but Morgan had been adamant.

The officer turned. "She's not here to swear a complaint?"

"No, but we are," Rick said. "The warehouse there is as bad as this. I'll show you."

"And I'll take a look, but until the property owner is back —"

"She won't be back . . . soon." Noelle looked from one man to the other. "She received threats, and . . ."

"What kind of threats?" At their guarded expressions, he said, "Did you hear or see them?"

She exhaled. "No, but . . ."

"The guy who did this is here," Rick said. "He came to our ranch this morning, asking for her."

"Have a name?"

"He called himself Ken West. But we think he's Markham Wilder. He was recently released from prison."

"Parole?"

"I don't know."

"Well, I can look into that. But without your friend . . . What was her name?"

"Er — Quinn Reilly." Noelle flicked a glance at Rick, and he nodded.

"I can't do much with threats and vandalism until I talk to her."

Noelle crossed her arms in the chilling wind. "Can't you take fingerprints?"

"With her permission. Unless you think something's happened to her." He looked up with the question in his eyes.

She shook her head. When Morgan called about the Maserati, he seemed certain they'd shaken Markham. And Erin was uninjured.

"Have a phone number for her?"

"Yes." Noelle pulled out her phone and opened her contacts to give it to him, but Rick said, "I don't think that one's good anymore."

The officer tried it and said, "Out of service." He straightened as the matter took on a little more substance. "You have a way to reach her?"

Rick said, "Maybe."

"If you talk to her, have her call. She can make a complaint by phone. But she'd have to appear for court." Officer Wentz looked back inside. "Unless she saw him do this, we'd need evidence to prove it. Without a complaint, I can't really get a tech in here."

It was just as Morgan said.

"Well, thank you." Rick had probably come to the same conclusion. Why would Erin risk her escape to possibly get damages awarded that she would likely never see?

When the sheriff's department vehicle pulled into Quinn's driveway, Markham had left the Tahoe — registered to someone else — under the balcony behind the house and crept around the side to listen. He could have run into the woods if any real search had occurred, but the deputy did as much and as little as the situation called for.

Markham smirked. After losing Quinn, he'd come back to her house, even though, as a hideout, it had been compromised. He'd guessed correctly that little would be done about the vandalism if Quinn had fled. But his position was precarious, so after they left, he made the call he'd been resisting. "Hannah," he said, "I need you to come."

Her silence stretched, until finally, she answered querulously, "Come? You have my car."

"Then use mine." He'd left her his modest Toyota since it was uncomfortable for a prolonged period, during which he would have decided whether to return her Tahoe or not. If he'd found Quinn immediately and gotten what he needed, he'd have been on his way.

Now he needed Hannah, though it would be tricky. At the merest hint of irritation, she crumpled, and especially since his incarceration, he'd struggled to maintain his composure — as today so shamefully demonstrated. "I'll give you an address to enter into the GPS on the dashboard. You should get here with no trouble."

"But . . . why can't you come back?"

"I'll explain everything when you're here. Just know I wouldn't ask unless I needed you." God's honest truth. But she would come. Faithful, devoted Hannah. And the best part was, she looked so much like her baby sister, Quinn.

Around seven, Morgan stopped for lodging at a roadside strip motel that had been renamed but not upgraded by a national chain. He'd have gone on to St. George or even Vegas, but Livie needed food and a good night's sleep. The room was clean and didn't smell, with two queen beds in faded floral spreads and Southwestern prints in warped frames on the walls. He set up a rickety portable crib for Livie and straightened. "Restaurant or fast food?"

Erin looked out the window to the low-slung shake-shingled building with a half-lit neon sign that read — *AURANT.* No fancy name for that eatery. "We can walk to that one."

Probably the best recommendation the place had. While she insisted she wasn't injured, she was shaken, and Livie would fight the car seat if he tried to impose it in search of alternatives.

So holding Livie snugly, he crossed the street with Erin. The restaurant smelled like an old-fashioned cafeteria, canned soup, and gas stove.

The different meals they'd shared, from Thanksgiving, to Paris, to this, made a sort of road map for the course of their relationship. Each stage had high and low points, though he was struggling to find a high point now as he settled into a booth, letting Livie stand on the seat between him and the wall.

Erin slumped into the other side. "I feel awful about your car."

"I know you do." One other booth and two stools at the counter were occupied. Probably travelers, as the waitress talked to them like strangers.

"It isn't as though I can pay for the repairs."

"It isn't as though that matters." He handed Livie the container of sweeteners to sort, and she settled onto her knees.

"But your Maserati —"

"Half yours."

"No." Erin stared, palms flat on the table. "Your things aren't mine just because —"

"We're married? Must have hit your head harder than you thought."

She touched the bump, then realized what he meant and sighed.

Though thin and faded, the napkins were cloth. He spooned a few cubes from the plastic water glass the waitress brought and held the ice pack out to Erin.

"Thanks." She pressed it to her head. "Are you okay?"

He frowned. "Of course."

"After Jill's accident, it can't have helped —"

"Let it go." Her words were like sand in a wound.

"Maybe you should see —"

"I'm dealing with it."

She lowered the ice. "I know. But L-i-v-i-e is starting to notice."

"Don't tell me how to parent."

She jerked back just enough for him to realize he'd said it too harshly. He apologized.

"No, I get it," she said too quickly. "Not my place."

"Erin . . ."

"I need to use the rest room."

He watched her stand, watched her walk away. Neither were at their best, but she hadn't deserved that.

"Daddy? Sing me 'Sunshine.' "

"Sing you 'Sunshine.' " Sighing, he lifted and set Livie on the table directly before him. Softly he sang the song that was both plea and love song. Please, please don't take my sunshine.

Erin ate hot turkey and gravy on a slice of cheap white sourdough. He hardly knew what he ate, but Livie devoured her mac and cheese. The clouds had fragmented, revealing cold, bright stars as they walked back. In the small bathroom, he washed his face and brushed his teeth, gave his little girl a bath, lotioned and jammied her, and then tucked her into the portable crib.

She had the ability to close her eyes and fall asleep. When Erin went into the bathroom to change, he hung his sweater and jeans and got into bed wearing the rest. She came out in soft-looking pajamas and located him, then headed for the other bed.

He followed her with his eyes. "Is this a forever thing, or are you just punishing me?"

"What are you talking about?"

"Separate beds."

"Morgan, we talked —"

"You talked. As far as I'm concerned there are very few things as depressing as sleeping alone."

She sat on the edge of her bed, staring at her hands. After a moment, she looked up. "It's better not to complicate it."

He read the strain in her face and nodded.

"Okay." Sliding under the covers, he rolled to his side. He wouldn't do anything with Livie right there, but it would have been nice to hold his wife. He closed his eyes and begged for sleep.

Somewhere in the night, he realized his face was wet. Now they came? When his biggest feelings weren't about Jill? He ground his palms into his eye sockets. Grief hadn't broken him. But healing might.

CHAPTER 20

Morgan woke angrier than he could remember feeling since Jill told him about Kelsey. He worked hard to hide it when Erin raised her tousled head in the other bed. Since Livie was still sleeping, he got up and power showered.

Then they traded places. While Erin washed, he rallied Livie, eager to hit the road. He hoped Erin wouldn't spend hours coifing but didn't expect her to coil her hair damp into a clip and leave it at that. "You can dry it if you want."

"No need." She packed her things and carried them out to the SUV. If she was trying to downplay her attractiveness it was failing, because every aspect of her appealed to him at deeper and deeper levels. The fact that she tried gave his mood teeth.

"We'll grab some breakfast, then get going."

"Okay." Hands tucked under her armpits, she crossed the street to the same restaurant as last evening. Following with his little girl, he hoped they brewed the coffee strong.

Picking up on his mood, Livie misbehaved to the greatest degree she ever had. He told her, "You're going to be hungry if you don't eat." He could have said the same to Erin but didn't.

Rick called while she was in the bathroom and explained the response from the Sheriff's Department. Not surprised, Morgan said, "Well, at least it's on the record. Erin can decide if she wants to follow up with a complaint." When they were speaking again, he'd tell her.

Loading up, Livie objected to the car in escalating tones. Erin said, "You should sit by her and let me drive."

With a full day's drive ahead, that made sense. The bump on her head looked better, and she'd seemingly slept. Discussion would be superfluous. And just to make sure, he connected his music player to the sound system and chose a playlist heavy on Creed, Rammstein, and Dave Mustaine.

As "Engel" started to play, he tucked his head back. Sometimes he wanted music to hurt.

In the car seat next to him, Livie entertained herself with a zoo book that had finger-puppet animals. Erin drove without comment. After a while, with his hand on Livie's chest and her hand over his, they both closed their eyes and fell asleep.

She'd thought Morgan might expect to drive, but he hadn't even raised the question, or made more than minimal conversation, which would have been difficult anyway with the harsh lyrics, screaming guitars, and drums booming. His playlist sounded like an orc uprising, but Morgan hadn't asked her opinion. He'd gone to sleep.

Around noon, she looked for a place to stop. Even if neither adult had an appetite, Livie needed a break from the car seat and something substantial in her tummy. She pulled into a roadside station with several fast-food options.

For the first time in days, she felt like herself, a woman who stood against what was wrong, who had taken control of a bad situation and paid the price. She felt like Quinn Reilly — except she used Morgan's credit card to fill the tank of Morgan's vehicle on the way to Morgan's home in a state she'd never seen. Okay. That was reality. Deal with it.

Morgan got his daughter out, letting her walk off the traveling stiffness across the parking lot in the chilly but no longer snowy weather. Inside, they ordered food to eat on the road, which meant continued progress and no awkward tableside conversation — or lack of. Erin got back behind the wheel and disconnected Morgan's MP3. Livie balked at the car seat, poor thing, crying when her daddy prevailed, but it was halfhearted and soon she was playing with more things they'd collected on the road.

Morgan didn't sleep again. He worked on his laptop. Nice for him. He still had a business, still had a life, an identity. When they stopped again for fuel, he asked how she was doing.

"A little ragged, I guess." She had driven through the tip of Arizona, the lower point of Nevada, and into California.

"Want me to take over?"

"I think Livie's more secure when you're beside her."

He crouched beside his daughter in the roadside multiplex. "Would you like Erin to sit by you, Livie?"

The child looked puzzled until it clicked who he meant. She grabbed another beanie creature off the shelf and beamed. "Playammals?"

Morgan straightened with a few years coming off his face. "That was her first action verb. I haven't the heart to correct it."

After his wall of silence, that tiny confidence almost brought tears. "I suspected as much." She handed him the keys and got into the back. His laptop lay on a container beside her, and she slipped it into its case and set it somewhere safer. Glancing up, she saw him watching in the rearview mirror.

"You can use it if you want."

"What for?" She settled next to Livie and sighed.

Coming into Santa Barbara in the dark, he felt the acute vivisection once more. The drive had been a sort of torture he didn't want to experience again, but what came next had the potential to be far worse. He hadn't stepped inside his house since the day of Jill's funeral.

Coastal air swept in when he lowered the car window and keyed the code that opened the gates guarding his enclave. He drove reluctantly to the third of five homes perched on the edge of the country. Taking Livie and her blanket from her car seat, he kissed her soft cheek. "How're you doing, sweetie?"

She blinked in the lantern-lit courtyard. "Where is this?"

"Daddy's house. Want to see inside?"

Erin shouldered her purse, waiting. He owed her about a thousand apologies but managed only, "Ready?"

Her face told him little as she followed him across the tiles to the mission-style doors. When he reached for the iron handle, the door flew open.

"Ay!" Consuela's cry would terrify the neighbors. "Señor Morgan! You did not tell me you were coming. Why would you not —"

She saw Erin behind him, her affront increasing. "You bring a guest and don't warn me?"

It would have been an easy phone call to make, and if he had to apply motive to his decision not to, it might have been a little payback for her refusing to come when he summoned.

"Consuela, this is my wife, Erin."

Giving him the evil eye, she pushed past, grasped Erin's shoulders, and kissed her on both cheeks. "*Lo siento* for Señor Morgan's terrible manners. If he had told me I would have prepared something very special. And you." She turned. "This *niña preciosa* is my little Olivia?"

Unused to anyone making so much noise, Livie shrank into him.

Consuela's eyes narrowed. "She doesn't know me. You, Señor Morgan, have broken my heart."

"She just needs a little time." And quiet. Why was Rick's house so quiet? Except for Liam, of course.

Consuela tossed her head. "Erin, you come in. Let me look at the one Morgan has chosen. *Está muy hermosa.* And so tiny."

"I'm a little travel worn." She pulled off the clip, her hair tumbling free.

"Oh, such beautiful hair should not be trapped."

He totally agreed, but Erin only shrugged.

"Come with me. I will make you a bath."

Morgan stopped and instructed her in Spanish to prepare a guest bath and bedroom. Confused, Consuela gave him a dark look but nodded. He shifted his daughter. Livie was tired and needed her bed.

The one that awaited was in the nursery he and Jill had prepared and decorated in lace and flowers. Climbing the stairs, his heart began to pound, his chest closing down as though constricted in a python's coils.

"Daddy." Livie squeezed his neck.

He squeezed her back, drawing strength from her love, his tiny savior. Even though she was only a newborn the last time she'd inhabited the room, the bookcase held a treasure of books, schoolteacher Jill convinced she'd read before she walked. When he flipped on the lamp beside the rocker, Livie squirmed loose and ran to the shelves.

"Read to me, Daddy."

"Of course." They wouldn't consider sleeping without a thorough bedtime ritual.

This nursery adjoined the master suite, and when he kissed Livie the final time and tucked her blanket like a soft cocoon all around, he went through the door into his room and pressed his hands to his face. No way he'd sleep there tonight.

Erin sank into the hot scented water, feeling her body relax. With the tension of their escape, the frost and fire of Morgan's moods, the beauty of his home — what she'd seen of it outside and her trip up the stairs behind Consuela — she'd left the house of mirrors and boarded the Tilt-A-Whirl.

Still at last, she leached every bit of comfort from the bath, then dressed in the soft pajama pants and chemise someone had laid on the guest bed. Guest. She might not be as fluent as Morgan, but she'd caught his instruction to Consuela. She should be glad, yet she suddenly felt lonely.

From her carry-on, she took the photograph of Pops and his two Quinns. With a sharp longing, she set it on the nightstand, then quickly unwrapped the jewelry box and set it beside the picture frame. Putting the carry-on down, she saw a corner of something peeking out of a side compartment. She unzipped it to remove an envelope.

It held a thank-you note written in RaeAnne's bold round script. At the end she included all her contact information — *so you can reach me any way, any time.* Holding the note to her heart, Erin rode the wave of emotion, then called with her disposable cell phone before she realized she was on the West Coast and RaeAnne on Central time. "I'm so sorry!" she said when RaeAnne's groggy voice answered.

"Quinn?"

"I totally forgot the time difference." It was even late in California. The series of cross-country and international flights and two long days of driving had fuzzed her normally keen sense of time.

"Quinn, I'm so glad you called. I've been trying and trying to reach you."

She imagined her phone ringing in the men's room trash. "I had to change my number. Someone was hassling me."

"Don't you hate solicitors?"

"Yeah." She pictured Markham's spiteful face. "Did I wake your husband?"

"He's still out of town. Wish you were here to make brownies."

"Me too." She smiled, remembering.

"And, sugar, any time you call is a good time. I've been wanting to tell you I know who my dad is."

"Is?"

"Yes, he's alive. Raymond Hartley. And the thing is, I know where to find him."

"You've been busy." If it was that easy, how long before Markham was back on her trail?

"I have. And, Quinn, it means, if I want, I could try to see him."

Standing by the dark window, she pressed a hand to her heart. "Do you want?"

"I don't know. It's driving me crazy going back and forth." RaeAnne groaned. "What would you do?"

Erin thought of her own dad. If something happened to him before she made this right, could she live with it? "I wouldn't want something to regret. I think you've been given an opportunity."

"I knew you'd say that. You're so good with relationships."

She expelled a breath. "Why do you think that?"

"Look how nice you've been to me. I feel like I've known you forever."

And she didn't know her at all. Not the facts. Not even the biggest thing she could tell her. Remember Morgan? Oh, by the way, I married him.

"How's your business going? Did you unload the stuff from Mom's cellar?"

The pang was inevitable. "Not yet."

"Morgan doesn't mind?"

"He's in California."

"Oh."

"But back to your dad . . ."

RaeAnne groaned. "I think I have to at least try."

"Will it break your heart if he says no?"

"It'll just prove Mom was right to stick him in a locket and leave him there."

Erin laughed. "I like that."

"So, here's the thing. He lives in Juniper Falls."

"No. Way."

"Yes way. I think that's why Mom moved up there."

Erin sat on the chair. "You can't be serious."

"Well, I don't know, but it's a little much for coincidence."

"You think they reconciled?"

"Maybe."

"Wouldn't she tell you?"

RaeAnne sighed. "Vera wasn't like other people. She didn't just march to another drum, she made the drum and didn't care if anyone marched to it at all."

"But you must have visited."

"We talked practically every day. But I didn't get out there that often. Maybe three times all the years she lived there. She came to see me a few too, but mostly we just talked on the phone."

Not being close to her own mother, Erin understood. Gwen Reilly had been mortified when she got pregnant after the respectable age for those things. She never really connected with her inauspicious daughter.

"The good thing is, I'll get to see you. And maybe you could go with me. We'd meet him together."

Erin pressed a hand to her forehead. "What about your husband? Wouldn't John —"

"No. He travels so much, the only other place he'll go is a beach. And, Quinn, I haven't told him about, you know, the cougar thing. Would you find my father with me?"

"Well, yes, but I'm not . . . in Juniper Falls."

"I'll wait until you get back."

"But, RaeAnne, I'm . . ." All alone in such

an awful predicament.

"Quinn?"

Erin slid her hand down her face. More than anything she hated lies. "If I tell you something, you can't tell anyone else in the world."

"I'm gregarious by nature, but I know when to keep my mouth shut. Got both from my mother." She laughed.

Heart racing, Erin half whispered, "I'm in California with Morgan."

"Morgan Spencer?"

She waited for the incredulity to wear off, but RaeAnne was anything but incredulous. "I knew it. I just had that feeling about you two."

"RaeAnne . . . we . . ."

"I know I sounded like it about Vera and my dad, but I'm no judge and jury, Quinn. If you and that lonely man . . ."

"We're married."

"Whh-at?" The word sounded like wind in her ear.

"He's protecting me from the reason I changed my phone number. And you can't tell anyone."

"Oh. Sugar." RaeAnne was finally at a loss for words.

While terrified at having told, it also felt good to have one person not connected to Morgan in this with her. "I'm praying you're the friend I think you are."

"I would never do something that hurt you." The conviction in her voice soothed the fear. "So . . ." RaeAnne cleared her throat. "How does it work?"

"That —" she expelled her breath — "is an excellent question."

Morgan half expected Erin to come looking for him, even though Consuela said she'd laid out nightclothes and turned back the bed. This was an awkward situation, and she might want clarification — as though he could give any. But Erin didn't come. When enough time had passed, he realized she wasn't going to.

He turned when Consuela entered the atrium. "Do you need anything else, Señor?"

"No, Consuela. Get some sleep."

"Would you like something special for breakfast?"

"Everything you make is special. I've missed your cooking."

She clasped her hips. "You say that so I won't ask why your wife sleeps in another room. Or are you joining her?"

"No. We're still working out the kinks."

"Kink?"

"Issues."

"Oh." Her eyes softened, thinking of Jill, no doubt. Let her think it was grief that made the wedge. Maybe it was.

"There are no ghosts here, Señor Morgan.

I would know."

"Thank you."

"You sleep. And in the morning I will fill your belly." She cast him a critical eye. "It needs it."

He smiled. *"Gracias."*

A fountain trickled down the wall of the atrium he and Jill had designed. Finches, though silent now, sang and flitted about the live trees around the circumference that branched across the glass-paned dome overhead. Jill had loved the space, and while he knew her ghost had no reason to linger, he felt her here, not in a sad and painful way, but happy, as she'd been.

He lay down on the cushioned chaise she called a fainting couch and imagined her nestled against him. Eyes closed he felt the love they'd shared, love he'd known with no one else. Desolation overcame him, but he didn't move. He lay there and took it in, hurting as he hadn't let himself hurt. Here where they'd been happy, he opened the wound.

CHAPTER 21

Erin sat up in the luxurious bed and looked around her. The room was more splendid in daylight than it had been the night before. Persimmon-colored walls that could have been garish were actually spectacular. Broad bands of dark wood trim, a dense pattern of bittersweet on the window treatments, and the dusky sage green bedding made her feel like Thumbelina in a botanical garden.

She went into the amber-tiled bathroom, where a salmon bougainvillea overflowed its pot on the long counter. She washed her face and brushed her teeth. After finger combing her hair, she went back out and heard a soft tap on the door. "Yes?"

"Some clothes for you, Señora."

"Come in."

Consuela entered with an armload of clothing from the boxes.

"I bring you choices."

"Thank you."

The woman laid lighter-weight outfits on

the bed, saying, “It is rainy today, but not cold like the Rocky Mountains. There will be no snow.” She said something under her breath, then added, “When you have dressed, come down to the kitchen and eat.”

“Is . . . Morgan up?”

“I haven’t seen him.” Her face softened, and she looked as though she might say something, then didn’t.

Erin dressed in fawn-colored jeans, a silk blouse that hung to her hips, and a thin, open vest of something shaggy. Where had he found these? She looked in the full-length mirror, taking in the transformation with amazement. If she weren’t Lilliputian, she could have walked a runway in the outfit. But could she walk out the bedroom door?

Her conversation with RaeAnne had grounded her. Quinn Reilly would face it head-on. She hadn’t told RaeAnne she was Erin now, so, raising her chin, Quinn went out.

The house was filled with magnificent aromas. She put on twelve pounds just from the fumes. No wonder Morgan believed food should be an event. Consuela had prepared a banquet.

“Would you like juice?” Consuela held up a bowl of oranges.

She must mean fruit. “Yes, thank you.”

Instead of handing her an orange, Consuela cut them open and squeezed the juice. The first swallow was heaven, and it never diminished.

Consuela invited her to eat, but she said, "I'll wait."

A moment later, Morgan entered in the same jeans and shallow V-neck sweater he'd worn the day before. Seemingly, he hadn't gone to bed. His eye sockets looked hollow, his cheeks sunken, but he said, "I promise not to bite."

"Good." She wasn't up to date on rabies shots.

He started to request coffee as Consuela handed him a mug.

"A cup for you, Señora?"

"Yes, thank you."

Morgan leaned against the marble counter, cradling his mug with both hands and drinking as from a holy grail. At the first sip, she understood why. What possible use had Morgan for her?

"You will eat now." Consuela's half question, half command mobilized them.

She and Morgan sat at the mission-style table set for two. Their chairs were across from each other on the longer sides of the rectangle, and Consuela proceeded to fill both ends with small platters of roasted peppers, a delicious-looking meat dish, some kind of scrambled egg dish, sausage, mild salsa, hot salsa, melon and pineapple and strawberries. Erin looked at Morgan, who shrugged and smiled.

They bowed their heads, and Morgan and Consuela blessed the food in unison. Erin added silent gratitude. What other response could there be to all this? For a little person, she had a good appetite and thankfully a fast metabolism. Morgan didn't comment, but Consuela looked delighted.

He said, "Sleep all right?"

"It's a wonderful room. Thank you."

He drank his coffee.

She took another bite. "I don't know what half this food is, and I don't care. It's amazing."

He picked up a strawberry and bit the end.

"Is Livie still sleeping?" She took a forkful of eggs.

He motioned to the intercom on the kitchen wall. "All quiet in her room."

The unit looked like a command post. "Are all the rooms monitored?" She thought of her conversation with RaeAnne.

"They're all on the intercom system, but the monitor is a manual setting for each room." He set the strawberry on his fiesta-style plate. "We wanted to know Livie was safe in any part of the house."

She chewed the spicy sausage Consuela called *chorizo.* "Are there cameras?" She knew firsthand how innocuous they could be.

"All the houses have one at the door and a monitor that shows the entry gate. I can install one in back if you're concerned."

She hadn't meant that, but it brought reality home. How long before Markham would come knocking on the door? Or had they eluded him? She shook her head. "Not necessary."

Morgan toyed with his strawberry.

"Won't Consuela be sad if you don't eat?"

"She's used to it."

Erin shook her head. "Then why does she make all this?"

"She likes to."

"That's such a waste."

"She takes what's left to the church."

Erin studied him. "How long has it been since you've eaten?" He'd hardly eaten a thing on the drive.

"Don't worry about me."

She laid down her fork. "What am I supposed to do?"

"Enjoy your breakfast."

She rubbed the cloth napkin over her mouth. "Will you excuse me?" She had tried cheerful and positive. Now she headed out the arched French doors that revealed a pool lined in cobalt blue, a terra-cotta patio, and a guest house surrounded by a narrow strip of shrubs and some trees, but mainly an unobstructed view of the ocean.

She walked through the drizzly rain to an opening in the low, white split-rail fence on the edge of the country. It caused a strange feeling in her stomach. Steep stairs built down the cliff wall plunged to a strip of beach with boulders heaped against the foot and erupting every so often from the sand. She started down.

"Take this," Morgan said, catching up with a poncho. "And watch your step. I doubt anyone's been down that way for a while."

The poncho wasn't the yellow plastic kind, but a Lycra-nylon blend, slate blue. A woman's medium. Erin pulled it over her head and started down the steps, needing time and space and a plan. She did not intend to be a guest in his house.

In Juniper Falls there would have been realistic needs for her to meet. Here that seemed impossible. At least —

The stair collapsed under her foot, catching the toe of her shoe and wrenching her ankle as she pitched over and landed on her knees and wrist. Teeth clenched, she shut her eyes and focused on the sound of surf and gulls, the smell of salt and seaweed, willing the pain to stop. She silently groaned when Morgan clambered down the steps above her and reached for her foot.

"Don't!" She gripped her own calf and eased her foot out of the hole, scattering splinters of rotten wood. It felt as if an invisible spiny blowfish had invaded her ankle and was puffing and deflating it with throbbing pain.

"How bad is it?"

"It's not broken." She'd felt the difference when she fell from a ladder as a girl and broke three bones in her foot — a totally different pain.

He looked over his shoulder to the top of the steps. "Can you make it up?"

"Yes."

"Can I help?"

"No."

"Erin . . ."

"I want to be alone right now."

He cocked his jaw. "You know that's crazy, right? Broken ankle or not, you're injured."

The throbbing didn't let her forget.

"All right, you're angry. You can be stubborn and crawl back up, or let me help you. But I'm not just walking away."

She looked down at the gray expanse of water, white ridges tumbling. "I wanted to see the beach."

He frowned, then shifted his position and lifted her.

"Not with . . . I meant alone."

As he didn't let go, she held on around his neck while he tentatively tried one stair step after another. She could tell when he hit spongy ones, but none of them broke. He reached the sand and stood there, taking it in himself. The rain had stopped, and the fog seemed to be lifting as a light breeze pushed in from the water. The sea scent mingled with his, a combination both foreign and right.

"How much of this ocean is yours?"

He shook his head, taking the jibe. "The beach is private for these five houses."

"And guests?"

"You're not a guest."

As she watched, a large gray bird glided across the water, pointed its wings, and dove straight down, coming up a second later to bob on the surface. She couldn't tell if its effort was wasted or rewarded.

Morgan sat down on a flat, pitted boulder, holding her across his lap and staring out to sea. After a while, he said, "I hadn't been back to the house since the funeral."

Her breath made a slow escape. "Are you all right?"

As the sky lightened, the moisture that had pearled in his hair matched the silver strands at his temples. "I needed last night with Jill. I never really said good-bye." His throat worked. "There wasn't . . . Visitation wasn't possible."

She had no experience with that kind of loss, and yet she felt a part of it.

He said, "My, um, bad behavior on the drive was a resistance to facing this, after pretty well perfecting the avoidance."

"And a staunch resistance at that."

His mouth twitched. "I think it was the anger phase."

"My eardrums are still throbbing."

He squeezed her ribs. "It wasn't that loud."

"You were in back."

His attention slid from the water to her at last. "I apologize."

"It didn't even sound like words."

"Some of it was German."

"I thought it was Orc."

His eyes crinkled, then sobered. "Can we try this again?"

"This morning?"

"This everything. I don't want some sham marriage."

But it was. Or not a sham as much as . . .

He slid his hand inside the poncho hood, his palm warm and firm on her cheek. "I want you."

No part of her doubted that, but she shook her head. "That's not the same."

"It's a start."

"It's backwards." The hood fell back.

Sunlight came through the fog, returning the blue to his eyes. "Right now, it's what I have."

A gull made a soulful cry as she absorbed the words and what she saw behind them. Sinking into the place he'd opened up, she pressed her fingers to his lips, then lowered them and kissed him.

It felt like a gift. Instead of covering her mouth and pressing her into the sand as he wanted to, he let her kiss linger like the high note of an aria. He didn't want to drown it out.

With a slow hand he brushed the hair back from her face, reluctant to end this fragile reconciliation but pressed by a growing concern. "I need to check on Livie." He'd have gone right back inside, if Erin hadn't fallen.

Her eyes widened. "Go. I can walk."

Shaking his head, he got his legs under and thrust up. They tipped, then righted as her arms tightened around his neck. Consuela would have paged him at the first sounds of Livie waking, but he wanted to be there when she opened her eyes. His little girl must be exhausted to still be sleeping, but they'd get back on track now that they were home.

Home. He pressed his cheek to Erin's hair as he climbed. *Home.*

"What happened?" Consuela demanded when they stepped inside.

"She sprained an ankle," he said and carried Erin to the atrium, smiling when her mouth fell slack. "It's all right to ogle." He squeezed a little, then laid her on the chaise.

She winced.

"I will wrap." Consuela hurried for the medicine closet while he went upstairs.

Livie heard him enter. She pushed up and sat, blinking at the unfamiliar territory. "Where we are?"

"This is Livie's room. Do you like it?"

That determination would take some time, it seemed. She rubbed her eyes and stood up.

"Which will it be — bath or breakfast first?"

She yawned and reached up. "Cheerios, Daddy."

"Cheerios might be hard to come by. Let's see what there is." He took her to the kitchen to sample the feast and discovered his hunger as well. The two of them had a silly time of it while Consuela doctored Erin. As dark as the night had been, looking at Livie, thinking of Erin, he felt a ray of hope. Juniper Falls and Markham Wilder seemed far away and irrelevant. His simple thank-you hardly felt like prayer, and yet it might be the most sincere communication of all.

In more pain than she'd let on, Erin delighted in the waterfall wall, tiny songbirds, and green and flowering plants of Morgan's atrium. Outside at the beach and in this indoor garden, winter had gone away. It would be easy to believe everything else had gone too. What if Markham never found her?

That possibility sank in and began to swell. This could be her future, and it was bright with possibility. As soon as she was on her feet, she'd find some way to be useful.

Livie came running in and butted into the couch to halt her momentum. "Look." She held out a rock. Erin received the item for inspection as Livie explained, "It round and smooth," though her *th* came out *v.* Erin smiled, liking *smoov* as a description for something that had rolled and tumbled its rough edges off.

"You're right," she said. "Do you know this color?"

Livie lifted her chin and announced, "White and gray spots."

She'd only expected the main color, white, and wasn't sure she'd even get that. Impressed, she touched Livie's tiny nose. "You're so smart." She glanced over at Morgan standing quietly.

His gaze encompassed them both. "Cooking and cleaning is nothing. Keeping my little girl happy when I can't be here is the world to me." He sat down on the edge of the chaise. "My mistake was offering you a job, when what I needed was a wife and a mother for Livie."

"I can't help thinking I limited your choices."

He tipped his head. "I only needed one."

She nudged him with her good foot. "There isn't a woman on the planet —"

"Hypotheticals are useless."

Livie tipped her face up. "Hear the birdies, Daddy?"

He looked up too. "I hear them." Then back down to her. "My business takes me away for chunks of time. That's why I haven't worked in that capacity for two years. Please don't worry about what else you should be doing. Livie's what matters."

"Okay." How would she have reacted at the ranch if he'd come in and said, "I'd like you to be Livie's mother." Her chest made a small collapse.

"What?" His brow creased.

"It's just . . . How can you know I'll be good for her?"

"Part of what I do, maybe the biggest part, more than any numbers my analysts run or strategies I devise, is reading the people I'm dealing with. I'm not even sure it's conscious."

"You've read me?"

"I've watched, listened, internalized."

She swallowed. "What do you see?"

"Someone I trust with Livie." The words might have been disappointing, but not from Morgan, not when the first thing she'd seen in him was his intense love for his child.

"Thank you," she breathed.

"I'll be downstairs working if you need me. You have your phone?"

She touched it in her pocket. "Sort of."

"I'll get the new one ordered. It'll be a second phone on my plan, no name attached."

She nodded, her situation closing in again.

"Need anything else?"

She looked at Livie. "Will she want toys or . . ."

"With the rocks, plants, and water feature, I doubt it." He spread his hands. "I'll have Consuela bring you some books for when she's environmentally saturated, but I don't expect that to be soon."

After a time Consuela lured Livie to lunch with a cinnamon twist she called a churro that looked and smelled much better than the commercially available version.

She said, "I will bring you a tray, Señora, when the little one is settled."

"I can come —"

"Señor Morgan's orders."

Erin settled back in the couch, considering the fact he'd ordered Consuela, not her. Smarter than your average bear. She lowered her foot to the floor, tried the ankle, and flinched. Not a bad plan, keeping it raised. She winced again putting it back where it had been.

"Are you in pain, Señora?" Consuela breezed in with a plate of roasted chicken on a bed of savory rice with crisp lightly charred sliced vegetables.

"I'm all right. Is Livie . . ."

"Señor Morgan is with her. Can I bring you something else?"

"There's an envelope in my room with papers in it." Packing up, she'd stuffed it in her carry-on. Last night she'd dreamed of Vera's cellar — probably a combination of talking to RaeAnne and feeling alienated herself.

If Morgan had Livie, she could take this time to read the history from the professor and try to understand her unnerving encounter.

"I will get it," Consuela said, as though it was her joy.

"Thank you." RaeAnne's mother had lived there twelve years. How had she not been creeped out of her mind? Or had she . . .

Hoarding everything, hiding her treasures in bizarre places. If Vera had been quirky to start with, might something else have twisted her tendencies? The house had felt fortified. But what if the evil lay within, feeding her fear and insecurity until she all but hid among her things?

Nibbling her chicken, Erin removed the file from the envelope and found, as the professor said, a Hauntings section. She slipped her finger in at that divider and stopped, the chicken going dry in her throat. She went instead to Famous Patients.

She didn't recognize the names of the celebrities who had received clandestine alcohol rehabilitation, though people of the time would probably have known them. But halfway down the list, her jaw fell slack. She stared at the name on the page. *Raymond Hartley.* A side note said: *stage actor.*

Erin laid the file across her knees and stared. RaeAnne's dad had been treated in the Juniper Falls asylum for insomnia, rage, and suicidal depression. She closed her eyes and groaned. How would she tell RaeAnne?

She opened her eyes when Morgan entered with a plate of food. "Livie?"

"Wrapping another helpless human around her finger." He sat on the low wrought-iron table beside her, though there were two perfectly good chairs on the other side of that. "Consuela says you're in pain."

"I told her I'm fine."

"She doesn't believe you."

She slanted him a glance. "I've taken care of myself for quite a while now."

"Welcome to my world," he said ruefully.

"Well, you can't take care of yourself."

He fake punched her shoulder but didn't argue.

"Good to be back at work?"

His face softened. "Good to be back."

Unsure of the subtle clarification, she studied him.

With a bite poised, he said, "Not all who wander are lost, but I was."

She squeezed his hand. "Welcome back."

He lowered his fork, his eyes stroking her, but then he leaned away. "If we start something now, I won't be getting back to work. And there's a lot to do before I leave."

"Leave?"

"The consultation. My team went on standby when I took off for Paris. They need a quarterback."

"When do you go?"

"As soon as things are settled here."

She set down her fork. "So . . ."

"Depends on you and Livie."

"How long will you be gone?"

"Five days max. I'll have covered everything I can beforehand."

"You think Livie will be okay with me?"

"Erin, she led the way. If I hadn't seen her gravitate, it would never have entered my mind to marry you."

"You didn't think of it until I told you about Markham."

"I didn't ask until then."

She canted her head.

"It's true. From the instant you made her animals talk."

Her laugh burst out.

"That was a defining moment." He ate the strip of zucchini.

Every time he spoke, she fell deeper and deeper.

She set her plate down. "Morgan, I need to tell you something. You can help me figure out what to do."

"My *raison* —"

"Yes, I know." She nudged him again.

He caught her hand and held it, setting his plate aside as well. "Shoot."

She told him what was in Vera's journal, since RaeAnne had already shared — at length — about the locket. He raised a brow at the age difference, though by his expression he found it entertaining. "But here's the strange part. He was treated at the asylum in Juniper Falls."

Morgan cocked his head. "Really."

She showed him the account. "He's still in town somewhere. RaeAnne wants to meet him, and . . . she wants me to go with her."

He frowned. "In Juniper Falls. Didn't we just make a dramatic escape from there?"

"Yes."

"And your question is?"

"I know. I do. But I feel bad for RaeAnne, and I thought maybe you'd see a way it could work."

"The only way it works, Erin, is by knowing Markham's out of there."

She sighed. "That's the same answer I got."

Chapter 22

Morgan worked solidly for the next hours with a peace of mind that felt like an altered state. With Livie safe and content, and Erin no longer considering him an emissary of the dark lord Sauron, in spite of his playlist, he felt a terrifying contentment. It was completed by the excellence of Consuela's yellowfin tuna caught fresh that day and baked with lime and cilantro, and followed by homemade flan that could grace heaven's table. He'd been forgiven for coming home without warning, for staying away so long.

The only minor concern was that the ankle pain or something else had Erin pecking at her plate. She didn't seem distressed, exactly, but he didn't want her hiding it if something was wrong. After an hour of hide-and-seek with Livie, he let his child unwind with a few scenes of *Finding Nemo* and helped Erin up the stairs.

"Consuela suggested I soak the sprain in salts."

"Consuela's a wise woman." Steeling himself, he led her past the room she'd used and into the master suite. Shadows parted as he touched a switch and the lamp came on.

Erin faltered. "You want me in here?"

"It's a pretty nice tub." One end had a continuous inflow of heated water, while the other drained over an edge and recycled. He helped her sit on the tile platform, then lit Consuela's version of aromatherapy candles, all blessed at the mission. "I'll get Livie to bed and see you in a while."

She definitely worked at her response. Worried about tonight? He should have kissed her on the beach. Then at least she wouldn't be wondering.

When his little trooper was thoroughly cared for, he headed back. After the traumatic drive, he hadn't imagined Livie would transition so well. It reminded him she had a pretty solid core for such a little waif. Like someone else.

Finished with her bath, Erin wrapped in the hotel robe Morgan had purchased in New York. All through dinner, his loss had seeped into her mind. He'd spent the night mourning, and she couldn't imagine how he'd go from that to anything else, even though his spirits had seemed lighter.

"You want to tell me about it?" he said, coming up behind her as she stood before the foggy mirror.

She'd have to get used to him reading her moods. "Just wondering how you're doing," she said.

Turning her to face him he said, "Can I show you?"

He was so at ease, he put her at ease. It couldn't be painless to be where he'd loved his wife, but as he'd said on the beach, this was what he had, and what he had he gave. And tenderly, she gave back.

Somewhere before dawn, he said, "Erin?"

"Mmm."

"You awake?"

Not enough to open her eyes without a compelling reason.

"I've been thinking."

"Should I be worried?"

He nuzzled her neck. It tickled and she tucked her chin, so he tugged her hair. "Are you listening?"

"I'm defending myself."

He ran his hand down her arm. "I was thinking that just because I don't love you as much as I will, doesn't mean I don't."

She turned her face and opened her eyes. "Say that again?"

"You should have paid attention."

She pushed his chest.

Clasping her hand, he held it there. "We've been married six days."

She could hardly believe it wasn't even a

week since they'd been in Paris changing her identity. "So you love me six days' worth?"

He stroked her fingers. "Have to add Thanksgiving — that was great. And hauling that herniating cabinet."

"The talking animals."

"Technically that was Thanksgiving, but I'll give it to you."

"Finding the locket and the journal." Like sleuths in an adventure.

"Psychedelic drugs and shackled beds."

She threaded her fingers with his. "And how about the sink and paper towels for your bloody hand?"

"Unforgettable." His eyelids hooded with the memory.

"It should count twice since you were crabby."

"Oh, I see how it works."

She sobered. "Do we have to subtract wrecking the Maserati?"

"It was just a dent." He stroked the skin above her elbow.

She shoved her hair behind her ear and studied him. "Happy almost-a-week anniversary."

He reached up and freed the hair she had just contained, then drew her in for a kiss. She settled her face in the crook of his neck, warmth and joy communing.

When the sound of Livie crying penetrated her fog, she startled up to see Morgan, dressed impeccably, carrying the child to her. Livie clung to his neck, but he gently extricated her.

"Hey, honey. Hey." Erin drew her in and kissed her wispy hair.

"I'm in meetings all morning, maybe longer." Morgan slipped three storybooks into the bed beside her. "I'll call with an update."

"Did something happen?"

"Belcorp took a downturn. If today goes okay with you two, I'll start the consult tomorrow. There's a lot on the line."

"We'll be okay."

His kiss was minty and long enough to convey a hint more than good-bye. He pressed another on Livie's head and left. Morgan, the success guru, in his glory.

When Hannah arrived, Markham looked as happy as she expected him to be, the role for this minister's daughter one of his very best — scorned prophet. She so admired his forbearance.

Bleakly, she wrung her hands. "I'm sorry for taking so long and —"

"Hannah. None of that matters." He held out his own worthy hands, and as tentatively as she did anything, she took them. "You're here. That's what matters."

Joy and fear stormed her eyes. "But I don't know why, Markham."

"Because I need your help."

Shivering in the cold mountain air, she said, "You really do?"

She was begging affirmation more than confirmation. With a nod he gave both. "You're the only one who can help in this way."

No fear now — only zeal. "What can I do? Tell me."

He formed an earnest expression. "The Lord has revealed that I must forgive your sister face-to-face."

She looked stunned and offended. "But, Markham, how can you?"

"I don't know how I can, only that I have to."

He sent a pained stare to the ground, then back. "Do you know what a wound like this can do? It creates a foothold . . . for evil." He had the timbre just right. This was what he did, his gift, his art, his grand performance.

But there was also a ring of truth. Wounds did create footholds, and nature abhorred a vacuum. Maybe he'd been born vengeful. Or maybe he'd learned it. He only knew it succored him when all the injuries he'd sustained whispered in his ears. "It isn't a request. We are ordered to forgive."

And when the sinner won't repent, put them out and treat them as you would a tax collector or harlot. Quinn had sinned against him, and when she failed to repent he would exact payment in full.

Her eyes filled. “Oh, Markham. I don’t think I can forgive.”

“You have nothing to forgive, Hannah. I was the one she sold for thirty pieces of silver. The burden to forgive is mine.”

She half whispered, “I would do it for you, if I could.”

Simple soul. “I would never ask it.” He led her into Quinn’s house, which he’d cleaned up from his rampage once he knew he’d be putting on the face. All the damaged things were in the Dumpster behind the grocery mart, so it looked as though she’d cleaned out and taken off, leaving only the few pieces of salvageable furniture.

“This is Quinn’s house?” Hannah looked around.

“Yes.”

“Doesn’t she have things?”

He let his face fall. “I’m afraid your phone call gave her the wrong idea.”

Stricken, her mouth fell open. “I only said she should pay for wronging you.”

“I know. But she took it seriously. She thinks I’m out to get her.”

Anger washed over Hannah’s face. “It’s the other way around.”

“Well, she’s convincing. The man at the store turned a shotgun on me before I could begin to explain. Someone else ran me off the road.” He indicated her Tahoe outside the kitchen window. Her father had bought Hannah the large, heavy vehicle because her driving was as challenged as she.

Gulping, she whispered, "You could have been killed."

That hadn't occurred to him in the moment. Only the rage of defeat. "Maybe I shouldn't have brought you here."

"No! You should."

"What if I've put you in danger?"

Her eyes darted between his in a frenzied motion. "Would they hurt me?"

Eleven years older than Quinn, she couldn't hide the weakness leaking through the cracks. He'd recognized a tool at first glance. Simple church mouse awaiting her messiah. Who better than he?

"You're in no danger, Hannah. You're Quinn's big sister. And you're worried about her."

"I am?"

"You're afraid of what I might do."

She flushed. "No. Never."

"You had to come and warn her. What reason would they have to keep you two apart?"

A slow comprehension filled her eyes. "You want me to say that about you?"

"Whatever it takes to lift the burden."

"Oh, Markham."

He closed his eyes, letting some of the real pain show. "I tried to do something *miracu-*

lous, but the Lord turned his face."

"No. It wasn't the Lord. It was Quinn who despised you. I will never understand why."

"Why isn't important." He fought tears. "Only doing this."

She nodded solemnly.

"You'll go to the ranch where she cooks, talk to the people she knows."

Her eyes grew fervent, her heart burning inside her. "Yes."

"Tell them you need to find your sister."

He walked her back out to the Toyota, which was still warm.

"You . . . you want me to go alone?"

"Are you afraid?"

"Yes." Her lip trembled.

He frowned in consternation. "I could ride in back and hide under the blanket, but I can't be seen, Hannah. She's turned these people against me."

"Like last time." Her voice trembled.

The last time he went to prison. This time would be different, very different.

He got into the back seat but didn't cover up yet. It was too demeaning. He gave her directions to Rick's ranch, but as the general store came into sight, gusting wind flapped the tarp up on a car being towed by a flatbed truck. He cried, "Wait!"

Jumping, Hannah almost killed the engine.

The tarp flapped wildly, uncovering the Maserati, wrecked.

"What is it, Markham?"

He stared at the car Quinn had crashed — proof she hadn't gotten far. But where was she? As Rick and the fool with the shotgun got out of the truck and fought the tarp back over the Maserati, Markham hid his face from Hannah, lest she see Satan's own wrath in his eyes.

When the men went inside, he told her, "Pull around to the far side of that store."

She did as he said, sliding to a stop in the slushy lot.

"Listen carefully." He gave the instruction slowly, though there was no guarantee she'd get it right. "Run in and ask what happened to your sister's car."

"My sister's —"

"The Maserati."

Her jaw fell slack. "That car on the truck? How could —"

"She took the money, Hannah. The money I tried to use for God — *she* used for that." He pointed a finger at the graven idol.

"Oh, Mark."

He hated when she shortened the name he'd created but didn't correct her this time. "Go, Hannah. Your sister's in trouble. You want to help her."

The fury in her face might be hard to hide.

"You're afraid for her, Hannah. You'd better be. She could lose her soul."

"She has."

"The only way we can help is to find her. Find her for me, Hannah."

As she walked around to the front, he crept to the store's back door and tried the knob. Finding it locked, he took out a pick and worked it open. Pulling silently, he slipped inside and moved to the slightly open door that separated the store from what appeared to be a small apartment. From that vantage, he watched Hannah enter.

"Please." She rushed to the men, who were looking for something in a bin. "What happened to my sister's car?"

The shopkeeper with the ginger ponytail straightened. "I'm sorry. What?"

"The Mas-erati." Her face broke. "It's my sister Quinn's."

Beside the ponytail man, the tall rancher eyed her. "You're Quinn's sister?"

She nodded vigorously. "She's . . . in trouble."

"What kind of trouble?"

"A man. I'm afraid what he might do. I need to tell her." She sounded like a robot.

"What makes you think that's her car?" the ponytail asked.

"It is, isn't it?"

"No way. That's Mor—"

Rick gripped the man's shoulder and told Hannah, "I didn't get your name."

She gulped. "I'm Hannah. Please, I really need to find her."

"Hannah, I can see you're concerned. But your sister's all right."

"How do you know?"

Good question, but Hannah didn't let him answer.

"I . . . I mean, her car's crashed."

The ponytail didn't contradict this time, but the cat was out. If the car wasn't Quinn's, then whose?

Rick said, "I'm sure if you give her a call, she'll tell you everything's fine."

"I don't have her number. I . . . I did, but then it got disconnected."

The men stood in silence.

"I mean she calls me at home. To the house. I . . . I don't have caller ID."

The woman should be put down.

Rick eyed her so long Hannah squirmed. "Did someone put you up to this?"

"Put me . . ." Her slow brain worked through the implication.

"Are you in danger, Hannah?"

"Me?" she squeaked. "No, it's Quinn."

So much for her getting anywhere he couldn't.

Her voice got shrill. "If you know where my sister is, tell me right now."

"You probably should let this go."

Ordinarily, Rick's tone would have her running for the door, but Hannah stomped her foot. "Do you know who you're protecting?

She took the Lord's money to buy a sports car."

Shut. Up.

"She's not a good person!"

The men looked at each other. Unbelievably, Hannah flew at them, her little fists performing a function they'd never attempted before. The ponytailed one caught her shoulders, and Hannah broke into sobs. "You have to tell me. You have to. She lied. Whatever she said, he isn't like that at all."

Disgusted, Markham let himself out the back.

Noelle blinked when Rick entered the kitchen, for a moment thinking Erin was walking before him. The woman wasn't Erin, only similar.

"Noelle, this is Quinn's sister, Hannah." His expression said Quinn was no slip. "She got stranded at the general store."

"I'm so sorry." She motioned. "Please sit. Would you like a cup of cocoa?" How clearly she remembered serving Erin and thinking she'd make a nice friend.

Confused or dazed, Hannah blinked at her. "I need to find my sister. Your husband won't help. Will you?"

She glanced up. If they were at an impasse, why had Rick brought the woman to the ranch? She said, "I can see you're upset."

Hannah lowered her face to her hands and

cried softly.

Noelle looked at Liam stabbing his marshmallows with a toothpick. Catching the glance, Rick moved their son and his cocoa to the dining room.

Hannah started talking. "Quinn ruined everything. She never listened, never obeyed. She always knew better than everyone, even her own father — the minister." She looked up, shocked and indignant.

Noelle smiled politely.

Hannah's nostrils flared. "She sent an innocent man to jail. Did you know that?"

"I didn't."

"Her lies took away four years of his life."

"Wasn't there a trial?"

Hannah huffed. "A mockery. She said he stole the donations!"

"There must have been evidence."

"From Quinn! She never saw the vision, never believed. Not even our Lord could work miracles in the midst of unbelief."

"This person worked miracles?"

"He was only the tool." Hannah's mouth pulled tight. "The miracle was God's."

"If you don't mind my asking, what miracle?"

"The multiplication of loaves and fishes. If he hadn't been cut down before the miracle came, everyone would be reaping the blessing."

He must have put on quite a show. "But I

don't understand. If you're so angry with Quinn, why do you want to find her?"

Her eyes bulged. "So he can forgive her."

How sadly convoluted. "Is this the man who left you at the store?"

Hannah's mouth fell slack. "It . . . he . . ." Tears welled again. "He wants to do the right thing."

"Then he should return the missing money."

Hannah looked incredulous. "He didn't take it. Quinn did."

Chapter 23

Morgan's morning meetings had stretched into the afternoon, so Erin put Livie down to nap in the crib all done up in Battenberg lace and cream embroidered rosebuds. Uncertain, she'd offered a Pull-Up, and Livie objected.

"Those are nighttime. Not naps." Her serious eyes weren't quite offended, but close. Even though she'd worn a Pull-Up on the drive, Morgan had taken her into the bathroom, so potty training had probably occurred. There were so many things she hadn't asked and didn't know. But they'd work into it, little by little.

Limping only slightly, she closed Livie's door and decided to explore the house. The master suite took a major portion of the upstairs on the ocean side, with Livie's room next to that. Across from Livie's was the guest room where she'd slept and another done in marigold with teal accents. Someone had a flair for color.

A small open parlor area surrounded a

window that looked into the landscaped courtyard, and on the other side of that she found a room furnished as a workroom. One table held clear plastic bins like smaller versions of her own storage tubs. The bins held assorted papers, stickers, scissors, punches — school supplies? The realization dawned. This was Jill's space.

"Señora." Consuela came in with a cordless phone. "Your sister."

Erin came down hard on her ankle, wincing as she dropped into an office chair at the end of one long table. How could Hannah have Morgan's house number?

Fighting a wave of panic, she said, "Hello?"

"Hi, Erin. I hope I'm not bothering —"

"Noelle." Relief rushed in hard. Her sister-*in-law.*

"Are you in a place you can talk?"

"Yes." She assured Consuela with a smile that she could go. "What's up?"

"Well . . . Hannah's here."

"What?" It felt like a reprieve revoked. "What does she want? Does she know —"

"We haven't told her anything."

More guilty relief. "I'm so sorry to have put you in that position."

Noelle said, "Please don't worry about that. I'm calling because I'm afraid for her."

Afraid. "Why?"

"She's with Markham."

Of course that would be a surprise to

someone who didn't know the score. "As long as she kisses the ground he walks on, she's perfectly fine."

"No one connected to homicide is perfectly fine."

It took a moment to sink in. "Homicide."

"Morgan told us about the double murder."

"What are you talking about?" She shoved her fingers into her hair. "And what do you mean Morgan told you?"

"His investigator —"

"Morgan hired an investigator?" She was starting to sound incredulous.

"He doesn't take harassment lightly. Anyway, the investigator said the authorities suspect Markham in two deaths, but they couldn't make a case. That isn't the same as innocence."

No, it wasn't. And she'd had no idea. If she had, would she have dared take him on? She calmed her breath. "What does Hannah want?"

"To find you. So Markham can forgive you."

She dropped her head to her hand.

"Erin, can you believe that?" Noelle didn't ask it scornfully.

"Yes. She's so taken in she'd lie down in front of a train if he told her God asked it."

"He's that good?"

"When he turns it on he can play transfigured Moses on the mount. To my sister he's a desolate, wronged prophet. I think he was trying for slick with Rick, but didn't get much audience participation."

Noelle laughed. "No, Rick can be stone. Used to infuriate me. Actually it still does."

In spite of her rushing heart, Erin laughed with her. None of it was funny, though. Homicide . . . What was Hannah thinking?

"Erin." Noelle cleared her throat. "She said you took the money."

Her throat constricted.

"Erin?"

"That's wrong." The hand in her lap opened and closed like a sea anemone.

"Hannah's convinced you have it. She's on a holy crusade."

"I'm sorry for her. I really am. I'm sorry for all of them." She swallowed the hard dry lump. "But at some point . . . people have to see. You know?"

"See?" Noelle's voice was gentle, but concerned. "Erin . . . does Morgan know everything?"

She closed her eyes. That wasn't only Noelle, it was God asking. "It's complicated."

After a pause, Noelle said, "If there's anybody you can trust, it's the man you married."

"Okay." She thanked her for calling, then held the disconnected phone against her chest. She did trust Morgan. But if it came to it, she needed an exit plan.

■ ■ ■ ■

Morgan strode in just before dinner, shedding his workday as Livie ran into his arms. From his crouch, he raised an eyebrow at Erin. "Up on your feet?"

"I better be. Pretty busy around here."

"Sorry." He spread his hands. "I didn't expect it to go so long."

"We did fine. I'm just realizing I need a checklist or something before you leave, so I know what to do about things like diapers."

"We'll set down a plan after dinner. Was everything okay?" By that he meant Livie, but didn't want to say it aloud.

"We all did great." The words were right, but something in her tone was off.

"Why don't we let Consuela feed Livie, and you and I have a drink outside." The evening — as was the case three hundred days out of the year in Santa Barbara — was clear and temperate. With only minute seasonal shifts, there reigned a sort of timelessness as though residents might live forever and not realize. He knew too well that wasn't true.

He handed his daughter to Consuela, who had fallen deeply in love already. Then to Erin, "What would you like? Wine. Juice. Tea."

"I will have a glass of wine, if you're . . ."

"White or red?"

"White."

He'd stocked a wine room before his change of life, and much of it remained. He opened a bottle of Chardonnay from the cooler and poured her a glass.

"I never had wine before I left my hometown."

"Against the rules?"

"Frowned upon for most of us. Others, I guess, had divine dispensation."

"And some of us divine interference." He got himself a Sobe from the refrigerator. They went out and sat poolside in outdoor furniture designed for comfort. "What's on your mind, Erin? Besides a plan for Livie."

She drew up one knee and anchored that foot behind the other knee. The soft thin pants draped her shapely shin. She took a sip, then said, "My sister's at Rick's. She's trying to help Markham find me."

"Won't happen. Not from Rick and Noelle anyway." And then it sank in. "Wait, she's working with Markham against you?"

She shrugged, a little too casually. "We're not close."

She took another sip for courage or comfort. Though he knew it couldn't provide either, it indicated that something was bothering her. Big time.

She spoke softly. "Noelle said you hired an investigator."

"He's someone I use for vetting companies.

I asked him to look into that phone number when Markham texted the threat."

"He told you Markham's killed people?" She raised her eyes, the starbursts merely tips around the widened pupils in the deepening dusk. "But you didn't tell me."

"He called as we were leaving Rick's. With everything that followed, I forgot to tell you." As lame as it sounded, that was true. He'd left Markham in the dust in more ways than one. The man's reentry at this point rankled. He took a swallow of his Sobe. "It isn't certain. Only suspected on the homicides. He has an alibi."

"I'll bet." She frowned. "Who did he kill?"

"Maybe no one." When he saw she didn't buy it, he said, "Two older cousins."

She pressed her fingers to her temple. "And now he has my sister."

"Has her how?"

"Enthralled." Her voice hitched. "Morgan . . ."

He needed to stop her before she asked something he wouldn't do. "That can't be helped. Not by you, and, honey, right now not by me. I have to complete this consultation. Time is critical."

"So . . ." She released her knee, wincing a little when her foot touched down. "This *raison* of yours is finite?"

"I'm loath to reveal."

She bit her lip. "Maybe . . . after the

consultation?"

"I'm not doing anything that might point in this direction. As far as I know, Markham has no idea I exist. Anything I do for your sister could change that. If he knows about me, he'll learn about us."

She closed her eyes. "You're right." And now her fear showed. It wasn't only about her sister.

"I'll ask the police to keep an eye out here while I'm gone."

"They'll do that?"

"I know a few." And the city was beholden. "Consuela has some guys who can hang around and tend the yard. It needs it." He'd pay a small force to keep watch.

He reached over and squeezed her hand. "It'll be okay." If he didn't make himself believe that, he'd slip back into the paralysis of fear, waiting for disaster to strike once more.

Markham hadn't intended for Hannah to infiltrate the enemy camp, but he could pretend he had. "Hannah," he whispered when she stepped out of the cabin where she'd stayed the night.

She turned hurt eyes to where he barely showed himself.

He motioned her over. She wanted to resist, but every compliant cell in her body obeyed. He saw instantly the little mouse needed building up and said, "Hannah, you were perfect."

"What do you mean?"

"You did exactly what we needed."

"I did?" Her voice trembled.

"You're here, in the enemy's camp."

"I had to come." Her brow furrowed. "You deserted me."

"Never." He gave his next pronouncement forceful sincerity. "Hannah, God is raising you up. The Lord has made you my handmaid."

The hands clasped beneath her chin shook. "Do you mean it?"

"I've never meant anything more." A benevolent warmth overcame him at the thought of her humble service. How pure her devotion. How sweet her belief. He shook himself. "Did they tell you where Quinn is?"

"They won't." She shivered in the frigid mountain air. "They believe I'm helping you."

"You have to convince them you're not. If they believe you've turned against me, they'll help you find Quinn."

"No. I can't."

"You can, Hannah. Tell them you have nowhere else to go." He squeezed her hands. "You need your sister."

She grew still and serious. "And when this is done . . . ?"

He tipped his face to heaven. "In the Lord's time. In the Lord's will."

The rush of pious fervor took him by surprise. Was he believing his own act? What if . . . it wasn't an act?

The rear hoof made a sharp clip on the stable floor as Noelle drew a currycomb down Destiny's russet flank, soothing the stallion as she worked. She'd fought so hard for the privilege of training this horse, finally proving herself to Rick, who took nothing about his stock lightly. One stall over, he picked the hooves of Destiny's dam, Aldebaran.

Noelle smiled. In her early days at the ranch, she had resented riding the mare until she realized Rick's choice was not about hypercontrol of a headstrong guest, but the gift of an animal he cherished. Her mind went to that drizzly day she and the horse took a fall that had broken her bones but, thank God, not Aldebaran's. That near disaster had taught her to listen and trust Rick's lead. Since then he'd learned to listen and trust hers as well — a faith in each other that was nothing like Hannah's blind devotion to a charlatan.

She had prayed last night for the woman's eyes to be opened and knew the Lord would handle it better than she or even Rick could. Destiny tossed his head when the stable door opened and Hannah stepped uncertainly inside. Was this the chance?

"Good morning," Rick spoke over the

mare's back.

"I have to tell you something," Hannah blurted.

Noelle stepped out of Destiny's stall when the shrill tone put the animal on edge. While unafraid, she respected the power he might unleash in a confined space.

Rick rested his hand on Aldebaran's haunch. "We're listening."

Hannah seemed to freeze.

"What is it, Hannah?" Noelle softened Rick's approach.

Hannah looked at her as if she'd only just appeared. Rick had a powerful presence, but he wasn't the only person around.

"Um," Hannah said, "it's Markham."

"He's here?" She shot a glance at the door, thanking God Liam was at playgroup.

Wide-eyed, the woman flushed. "I mean . . . *about* Markham.

"What about him?" Rick's question released a torrent.

"Quinn tried to tell me, but I didn't believe it. She's always been jealous." Hannah gulped. "But she's right. He was telling me . . . lies. Now he deserted me, and I need Quinn."

Could there be a worse liar anywhere in the world? Noelle ached for her. "Hannah, I'm sorry he's left you in this predicament."

Without shifting course, she said, "Please tell me where she is."

"Hannah." Rick leaned on Aldebaran's stall. "Why don't you show us the respect we've given you and stop lying."

In response, her face heated. She shouted, "Tell me where she is!"

At the outburst, Destiny banged a hoof on the stall as he balked sideways. Noelle reached over, gentling him.

"I'm sorry," Rick said. "We can't."

They'd given Hannah hospitality overnight, when her distress and confusion were real. But the hostility coming off her now was tangible.

She cried, "She doesn't deserve your friendship. She's a liar and a thief. She stole Markham's life. Why can't you see that?"

Rick's voice came soft but firm. "You should contact him to come get you."

Her face reddened further, and her mouth worked as if struggling with what to say. "You should have helped him. Now he'll shake your dust from his feet."

Rick took out his truck keys. "I'll drive you to the general store. He can meet you there."

Noelle sighed. Erin said as long as Markham needed her, Hannah would be safe, but she couldn't help wishing they had been able to convince her.

Exerting extreme control, Markham had taken the weepy Hannah back to Quinn's house without losing it. He was not a violent man, despised violent men like the ones who'd raised him, whose greatest intelligence lay in realizing he was less effective with bruises and even so had not been able to restrain their fists and belts.

Thoughts of striking Hannah were like shrapnel in his brain — foreign and destructive. How could he blame her, when his own efforts had failed? It shook him to the core to think he might have lost the ability to sway people. Selling the illusion was his gift. Without it, what was he?

Behind the wheel of his Toyota, he escaped Hannah and sought a way to relieve his fears. How risky would it be to show himself in town? He'd committed no violation they could prove, even if Quinn accused him. He'd only wanted to talk. Was reconciliation a crime?

Confidence swelled his chest. Innocent men didn't skulk. Men with nothing to hide went where they wanted, when they wanted. He donned the mantle of innocence, feeling the assurance like a drug. He had a clue to follow. And every right to follow it.

The Maserati.

Of the two men who had towed it in, he guessed it must be Rick's. He could not by any stretch believe it the other goon's. And if he'd lent it to Quinn, the relationship might be more than the man wanted to admit. That explained how cagey he'd been at the ranch.

It also explained his concern about her house. His wife must be blind.

Smirking, Markham entered the Roaring Boar Tavern. He sat among those lined up at the bar, a hearty lunch bunch who didn't mind a beer or two before noon. After a time of camaraderie, he said, "Shame about that Maserati. You all see the dent?"

As he'd expected, that comment caused a noisy lament. And he'd been wrong. It wasn't Rick, but his brother, Morgan Spencer, who held title. Quite the town hero, Morgan. Quite the legend. And, if they could be believed, quite the gold mine — though, as with any mine, the key was finding it.

Although everyone knew Morgan like a brother, not one had an address. "Oh, he stays at Rick's. Yeah, he's right up at the ranch. Stays up there with his little girl. Too bad about his wife. Awful thing."

Markham tried again with the pockmarked bartender. "Just so I'm clear, Morgan *lives* at his brother's ranch?"

"When he's here, yeah. Been there" — the man shrugged — "around two years."

Hannah had seen no one but Rick and his wife. And their kid.

"When he isn't at the ranch, where does he live?"

Again the shrug. "Somewhere on the coast, I think."

"East or west?"

"Don't know. Maybe both."

"Thought you guys were buds."

The man smiled. "Yeah, Morgan's great. Really gets the place going. Hasn't been in much the last two years, but before the baby, he was a big-time regular. We'd see him every night he was in town."

"And he never said where he spends the rest of his time."

"All over the world, man. Consulting. Wrote some books too. I have signed copies, but I don't read them. All that financial stuff goes over my head."

"You wouldn't have them here, would you?"

"Yeah!" The guy turned to the mirrored shelf showcasing bottles. Just beneath the giant boar's head were two hardcover books. "I put them there since Morgan says the boar reminds him of the nun who taught third grade. Wicked sense of humor."

Markham smiled, sick of this Morgan already. Taking the first book in hand, he recognized the man who'd come to Quinn's with Rick — the suave, compelling expression twisting the knife. "So this is what it takes to get a Maserati."

"Sweet ride. My life flashed before my eyes when he took me out. Worth every minute."

He opened to the author bio, rife with creds and accolades — and no address, even in general terms. No "Spencer makes his home . . ." anyplace. He handed the books back. If Spencer was so important, he'd be on the Internet. More importantly, if he'd lent Quinn his Maserati, she might mean something to him. There could be greater potential here than even he'd imagined.

With Livie playing in the kitchen cabinets while Consuela washed windows, Erin slipped back upstairs to Jill's workroom, drawn by a desire to know the woman Morgan had loved from his early manhood to this day — fifteen years of it spent apart. What kind of person inspired that in someone like Morgan?

When he'd left that morning, he assured her they'd be guarded. But what would guard her from her need to know his dead wife? *"I know how deep you run, how hard you love."* Celia's words were like a taunt, and Morgan's still a spear. *"I won't do that again."*

Was she trying to invade that hallowed bond? Or did what she felt for Morgan lend itself to those who mattered to him? Could Jill fascinate her because she'd fascinated him? And in knowing his wife, might she better know him?

The questions swirled in her head without answers. Maybe it was the curiosity that had stung her time and again, but she wanted to know. With Markham she'd been driven to find the truth and expose the fraud. This was nothing like that. It wasn't a desire to diminish Jill, but to understand.

She went in, noting an organization and order not unlike her own. The books in one bookshelf dealt with early development and educational theory, mental and emotional disabilities, creative learning and classroom management. That, coupled with the storage bins of supplies, indicated Jill had been a teacher. Specific manuals suggested she worked with severely challenged children. Of course.

Erin circled to another shelf unit that appeared to hold albums. They were dated by year, and she pulled the earliest one down and settled into the office chair. The album yielded page after page of children with obvious, and not so obvious, disabilities, learning and interacting singly and in groups. Jill had archived other people's kids who may have passed through her life for only a short time. Yet they lived in these shelves, nine years of her work with them.

Beneath those were undated albums. Erin took the navy blue one farthest to the left and sat once again. Dappled light slanted in the window through the multi-trunk tree Consuela had called a madrone. Supposedly, the tree did not like to be touched or disturbed, and its location on the property as opposed to wild on the hills along the shore was unusual.

Opening the album, she saw what had to

be an elementary-school portrait of Morgan. Even with teeth missing and a bad haircut, he displayed the heartbreaking good looks he'd grown into. She turned the page and found assorted pictures of him in various activities. This album chronicled his growing up, life radiating. With every shot, she fell deeper in love.

The boyhood form lengthened and hardened. Adolescence had been kind to Morgan. She ran her finger over his face.

And then, there she was. The silver-blond beauty had to be Jill. More athletic than she'd imagined, there were several shots of them in sports uniforms, a humorous one in business attire behind podiums as they debated for class president, Morgan obviously playing it for all he was worth, Jill coolly dismissing him. She wondered who'd won.

The prom picture took her breath. Morgan wore the rented tux as though born to it. Jill bore her crown like a true queen. Erin sighed. There'd been no dances at her school, maybe wisely, given what had happened to Jill and Morgan, but she couldn't help a wistful longing.

What if she and Morgan had started out young and hopeful? If she'd never crossed Markham. If Morgan had never known Jill. Stupid thoughts and fruitless. These photos recorded what was real. Jill had loved and been loved by the man who might never truly do so again.

Erin closed the album and shelved it without taking another. Whatever she might learn from the remaining albums was more than she wanted to see.

Chapter 24

Erin couldn't get over how December, at sixty-five degrees, still and clear, looked and smelled and felt like spring. Some trees had dropped their leaves while others had not. Brilliant flowers bloomed without ceasing. The ocean rolled in and ebbed out, as calm and timeless as a dream. After living her whole life where nature had seasonal behaviors, she couldn't quite believe her senses.

Or maybe it had nothing to do with climate or environment. What she couldn't believe was the wonder and magnitude of this life. She knew that, as unexpectedly as it had overcome her, it could all be snatched away. Noelle's phone call had driven that home. It was only a matter of time before her choices caught up with her.

Where would that leave Morgan? And Livie. Her throat constricted.

"Look." Livie ran across the damp sand on the private beach to deliver a piece of sea glass as blue as Morgan's eyes.

"That's special. Put it in your pocket." She helped her secure the treasure, then straightened as a gull waddling by drew her gaze back to the surf. "Oh look, Livie." She snatched the little girl up and pointed to a harbor seal bobbing and diving a short distance out. "It's a seal. Do you see it?"

Livie reached her arms out. "Can I hold it?"

"Only if it flops up here on the beach and gives us a hug."

Livie giggled.

"Think that's funny?"

When Livie giggled again, she couldn't resist tickling just to hear the laugh get high and throaty. Livie squirmed but wanted more because she said, "Want to hug it." And so they tickled and laughed all over again.

Then Livie nearly dove out of her arms. Erin turned, heart leaping as Morgan snatched his little girl and covered her face with kisses. Her arms squeezed so tightly around his neck it was a wonder he could breathe. Then she leaned back and pressed his face between her hands. "We play on a beach, Daddy."

"You sure are."

Erin said, "Consuela had the stairs repaired. Or I wouldn't have risked them with Livie."

"I noticed." He looked back at the work.

"The yardmen had to do something, and we needed a way down."

"Money well spent."

"Glad you don't mind. Because we have important things to do." She wiggled Livie's little hand.

"Such as?"

"Chase crabs, watch gulls, talk to neighbors and their dogs."

He slanted her a look. "Which neighbors?"

"Mainly the voluptuous one who wants to know why you haven't stopped in for a drink lately."

"Uh-huh." He looked annoyed. "She tried that with Jill too. And, in case you're wondering, nothing's ever happened."

"I must admit I was."

"Her innuendoes have innuendo."

"She's very attractive."

"Artificially. She's had a few minor movie roles and done some . . . modeling." When he set Livie down, she danced around him in her little shoes, buoyed with glee at having him home.

Erin tipped her face up. "You said five days, and it's only been three."

"Funny thing, having people to come home to."

"You missed us?"

"Eh, mainly Livie." He shied when she punched him, then caught her wrist and pulled her close, mapping her face with his eyes. "Yeah, I missed you."

He gave her the kiss she wanted, though it

broke her heart just a little.

"I got to thinking I could break it up, kind of punch, counterpunch. I wouldn't be away so long, but . . ."

"But you have to go back."

"I do. Still, this could be the new consultation prototype. At least domestically."

"I think in Livie's world, days are years."

"I think you're right." Threading their fingers, he turned to watch his tot in her hooded jacket prancing in the sand. The damp little divots left by her feet seemed somehow magical, as if they were witnessing elves or fairies dancing on the shore.

"Tell me she missed me a little."

"She missed you a lot. But we managed." At the water's edge a tiny crab skittered out and back in the foam.

"I could see how mournful you both were as I came down."

"That was a little silliness. The rest of the time we said, 'Woe is me — won't Morgan come home.' "

"You're starting to tease as mercilessly as Noelle."

She laughed. "The first time I saw you, I thought she was your wife. Then Rick came in and kissed her."

"He makes sure there's no confusion."

She caught a rueful hint. "Was there?"

He shrugged. "We met her together. I gave it a shot, then Rick came in with the stealth play. A year later, Jill was back in my life." He shook his head. "I don't want to think what a mess it would have been if things had gone the other way."

Erin nodded. "So."

"So." He threaded their fingers. "Does that bother you?"

"I don't think so."

"Good." He let go and ran after Livie, who was chasing a plover, grabbed her into his arms, and tickled her neck and tummy with his face.

Watching, she fought to contain her emotions as ineffectually as the sea contained its waves. She shouldn't be falling in love. She didn't deserve them. And quite possibly —

Their play stopped, and Morgan handed Livie back to answer his vibrating phone. A pelican tossed its shadow over his face as it glided toward the sea. Another shadow passed over her heart as Morgan said, "Anselm. What is it?"

As he listened, the change in his face sent a weight like a stone to her stomach. It could be about work, but somehow she didn't think so. A shift in his demeanor put the walls up between them.

"Okay. Thanks." He pocketed the phone, swept Livie onto his shoulders, and said, "Let's walk."

"What's wrong?"

"That was Richard Anselm, the PI." His

Nikes scritch-scritched on the damp sand. "You didn't mention the FBI was involved in this thing with Markham."

"FBI?" She shook her head. "It was a state conviction."

"Maybe so, but Anselm's search raised a flag. The feds came back at him with questions."

"Why?"

"Never recovered the money. They believe he has an accomplice."

Accomplice. The stone in her stomach turned to ice.

"Erin." He turned and faced her. "Is it your sister?"

"Hannah? No. I swear to you, it's not." Accomplice! That was completely wrong.

"How can you be sure?"

"Because she's not . . . capable." And because she knew the truth. Guilt bore down.

Searching her face, Morgan narrowed his eyes. She watched a grim suspicion rise. "What's going on, Erin? Tell me the truth."

The *truth.* Why would he believe it? Dread gripped her. Markham. The FBI. Now Morgan's doubt.

She had prepared herself to run. *Don't run!*

If he didn't believe her, how would they?

His face darkened. "Were *you* in it with Markham? Are you using me to double-cross your partner?"

Stung, she felt it all crashing in. He could

think that after everything? Drawing a sharp, heated breath, she turned and ran.

Shocked, Morgan hollered after her, but she kept charging up the stairs and disappeared over the top. He'd hit hard, hoping to provoke whatever she hadn't told him, and she'd run. Run!

With Livie in his arms, he made his way to the house and found Consuela staring at the front door, eyes burning. "Where is she going? What happened?"

Handing Livie to her, he hurried for the door. The camera showed the gate closing and a glimpse of her still running. He ran out the door, pushing his legs as he hadn't in too long. Did Erin think she could literally run away? He pressed the button and squeezed through the gate as it opened.

Where was she? There, darting through the undergrowth in a draw dipping away from the road. He sped up, thankful he'd changed into jeans and sweatshirt and especially his Nikes before joining them on the beach. He cut down the way she'd gone, spurred by the knowledge there was no beach on this strip, only sandstone walls dropping into the sea.

"Erin! Stop!"

He could hear her now, rushing just ahead through the vines in the draw. Her cry gripped his heart. He broke through and almost went over as she had. With both hands, she clung to a springy tree trunk, her purse dangling from her neck.

Diving to his stomach, he gripped her wrists. "Stop kicking."

She looked up, her face damp with sweat and tears. Still holding one wrist, he lunged and grasped the hollow of her other arm. Heaving back, he dragged her up, clawing her jeans and pulling her over, then rolled on top of her, furious.

She writhed. "Let me go."

"Yeah, right."

Chest heaving, she pushed and squirmed.

"Stop it." He glared. "What are you doing?"

She gritted her teeth. "Let me go!"

He pulled her wrists up over her head and clamped them one-handed against the undergrowth. "I want answers, and I want them now."

"I can't breathe."

He shifted only slightly.

"I'm not an accomplice."

"Very convincing after this little stunt."

She struggled again. "Get off."

"If you try to run, I'll take you down so hard you'll wish you broke that ankle."

She glared as though unbelieving.

"Did I mention I lettered in wrestling? I can twist you in ways you never imagined."

"You're hurting me."

"Not even close."

"There's a root in my back."
He slid his hand under and felt it, then pulled her up to sit. "Start talking."
"Why should I tell you a thing if you can believe what you said?"
"Forget I said it."
"Forget?"
"Don't turn this around on me. Tell me what you know."
"I don't know anything about the FBI."
"But you do about the rest."
She swiped the back of her hand over her cheek, leaving a dirty swath. Her heaving chest grew less insistent. "I couldn't let them get away with it."
"Them?"
"Markham, the elders, my . . . You can't rub Scripture like a rabbit's foot and make money fall from heaven. It's wrong."
He studied her. "I'm listening."
Still aggravated, she seemed to resign herself. "Fine."
"From the beginning."
"Are you talking or am I?"
"You better start."
Her face flushed with anger. "It started when my dad named Markham his assistant pastor. He'd needed help for a long time, but no one met his standards or shared his ideology. Markham was a perfect fit, as neolithic as my father."
"Neolithic how?"

"Mainly the care and feeding of the weaker sex. It's such an outdated story I'm embarrassed to tell it."

"Plenty of denominations have that focus. It's not always a bad thing."

"Well . . . it was."

"So your father . . ."

"Hired Markham, whom everyone admired. Such a fine young man of God. Such vision, such humility." She made a gagging sound. "I smelled a rat from the start, but no one would listen. The women warned me not to question; the men just smiled as if I couldn't understand."

"Go on."

"He started by collecting for special projects, then missions and disasters, just to warm people up to the joy of giving. *'It is in giving you receive.'* Then he outlined his 'vision,' and I don't mean plan. His was a vision straight from God and no snake handler could have played it better."

Bloody tributaries sprang up on her scraped palm. She glanced down, then looked away. "As the boy had given up his loaves and fishes to feed the crowd, so God would multiply each sacrifice made as soon as the giving was complete."

She shook her head. "People were taking out loans, signing over their IRAs. I think my father had concerns, but he disregarded them when he saw how the people responded to

Markham's prophecy. All the good that could be done if they kept believing that the more they gave, the more they'd get." Her voice wavered. "I want to believe he believed it."

"How did you figure it out?"

"Since no one would listen, I installed monitoring software on Markham's computer. It recorded everything, including keystrokes. While he was being raptured up to the seventh heaven before their eyes, I saw that the money God would multiply was going to an account in the Caymans."

He was getting a bad feeling. "Erin . . ."

"All I did was transfer the funds."

His breath made a slow escape.

"I didn't want him to disappear with the money when the minister confronted him. But when I told my father, he said the account must be intended to keep the donations safe, and that they couldn't stop until the miracle came."

This was not sounding good.

Her brow furrowed. "When I tried to make him face reality, he acted like I was a disobedient child. He refused to believe I could see what he'd missed or that Markham was less than perfection." Her voice broke. "So I told Markham I knew he was a fraud and the software would prove it. Then I went to the authorities and told them what Markham was doing. If my father was caught up, it was out of my hands." She fought back tears.

His heart sank. "What happened?"

Huffing slightly, she said, "They believed the minister naïve and gullible but not culpable."

"And the money?"

She stared at her hands. "I uninstalled the software before I transferred the funds to the other account."

"So they followed the trail to the first account, but then it disappeared."

"I gave them all the proof the software collected."

"But it didn't collect your part."

She looked away. "They asked who knew about the software, and I told them I confronted Markham."

Which pointed right back at him. So why did the feds suspect an accomplice? "Have you used the money?"

"Not one cent. I didn't take it the way they think."

"You didn't turn it over."

The line of her mouth hardened.

"The congregation could have gotten their money back."

"They didn't deserve it back. They played God like a big slot machine in the sky. And guess what? They lost."

It was her father's betrayal speaking. She may have had one intention in transferring the money, but when he sided with Markham it became something else.

"For once in my life, I wanted him to take my side, to be my champion." Her voice shook. "I should have known it wouldn't come from him, but if one person had spoken up . . ." Her eyes teared. "Instead, I had to leave. I couldn't stay in that hypocrisy. And I knew when Markham got out, I'd be alone. No one watching my back."

It hurt to hear it, but he knew it was the truth. Slipping an arm around her shoulders, he tipped his face to the sky, looking not for a shower of silver dollars but a ray of hope.

She felt the tears coming and couldn't stop them. "I didn't mean to get you and Livie in trouble. Let me leave before they put it together."

"You have my name, Erin. How long do you think it'll take?"

She swiped the tears angrily. "You can tell them I fooled you."

"And they'll think me naïve and gullible?"

She shivered, suddenly cold and hurting all over.

"Come on." He pulled her up.

The ankle she'd sprained before throbbed afresh. Her arms felt as if she'd been racked. Her ribs ached, her hands throbbed, and her purse strap had burned the side of her neck.

"You're not indestructible, you know. I sparred with rocks like those. They win."

"Is this a pep talk?" She pushed back a

hank of hair.

"Not really. I'm incensed your first instinct was to ditch me and Livie."

"You said I used you to double-cross Markham."

"You asked for fake ID."

"Because I knew he'd come after me."

He turned and stared her hard in her face. "Don't ever run from me again. I'm not a punk like Markham."

She gulped. "You're a public figure. How will it look for you to be harboring a fugitive?"

"You're not a fugitive. As far as I know, you're not even a suspect."

"Just an accomplice." She grimaced. "With *Markham*."

"I said that to shock you into the truth."

"I never lied."

"You withheld some crucial information."

"I thought if you knew —"

"What? I wouldn't marry you?"

"That was all you." He had to know she wouldn't con her way into his life that way. If he'd gotten her an ID, she could have kept running and hiding without affecting him at all. She took a step and winced. "Am I in trouble?"

He helped her through the undergrowth onto the street. "We'll put a better mind to that than mine."

"Whose?"

"William St. Claire, defense attorney."

She pictured the powerful man, the powerful office. Limping beside Morgan, she felt worse than a fool. She hadn't thought past Markham and her father, past the elders who gambled on God. It had been her chance to prove her mind equal to theirs, and unfortunately she had.

The weight of her bad choices settled as the gate slowly opened. Sensing her letdown, Morgan bent and lifted her. She pressed her face to his collarbone, pinned together after his crash. If he could be fixed after that, maybe this could be fixed too.

"Own any small third-world countries?"

He laughed grimly. "Hadn't realized I'd need one."

As they crossed the courtyard, Consuela opened the door. In his housekeeper's arms, Livie stared at them both. Morgan leaned and kissed the child, then continued past, all the way up the stairs into the master bathroom.

"When you're done washing up, we'll have a look at the damage."

She nodded mutely.

"Don't worry."

Did he think that remotely possible?

On the way out, he paused. "Is there any chance you'll bolt again?"

Where would she go?

"I have a state-of-the-art alarm system to

keep bad things out. Don't make me use it to keep you in."

Swallowing the lump in her throat, she shook her head. Flight had been a knee-jerk reaction. The near disaster of the cliff demonstrated that futility. She could have died. Or been maimed and mangled. "I'm not going anywhere." Except maybe jail.

Chapter 25

Morgan thrust his fingers into his hair. He needed answers, and former special agent turned private investigator Richard Anselm had contacts. Why did the feds suspect an accomplice, and who did they think it was? Erin might be so far off their radar, she had nothing to worry about. They would make it right, but he always preferred offense to defense.

In response to his request, Anselm said, "I'll get back to you."

Knowing Livie must be worried, he retrieved her from Consuela, then went back upstairs. Erin emerged from the bathroom with such a tender expression it stopped his tirade, however softly he might have delivered it.

She said, "I don't want what I did to endanger her. I won't run, but I'll understand if you need me to go."

"What if I need you to stay?"

"FBI, Morgan. And from what you said, Markham's even worse. You have to believe I didn't know that, or I would never —"

"Is he a killer?" He held Livie close.

"I don't know." She looked achingly vulnerable. "But if I give the FBI the money, he has no reason to let me live."

Holding Livie, he felt the fear closing in. He had too much to lose. It was too easy to lose it. His heart pounded. His temples throbbed. He saw Erin's grim determination. She would go if he said so.

Moments stretched. He felt Livie's arms around him. Into his mind came a thought, planted by Kelsey, reinforced in his time at Rick's. "I think we should pray."

Erin's gaze fell. "No."

"No?"

"I won't use God that way."

"Use God?"

"I got myself into this, Morgan. I don't expect God to bail me out. That's just like the rest of them. If I do this, what will God do? When I give this, how much will I get?" She limped to the bed and sat down. "I can't, or I'm the biggest hypocrite of all."

He understood things had been warped. But she was missing the point. "It's a relationship, Erin. You think God wants no part of your life?"

"I worship and believe. I just don't ask."

"Awe is one thing. But there's another side to it." He stroked Livie's back. "This little girl adores me. Do you think I could bear not loving and caring for her?"

Morgan's relationship with Livie was the purest argument he could have made. He'd given that baby life. He deserved her adoration, but it didn't end there. How could it? They'd both be stunted and impoverished.

She felt it herself — the joy of meeting Livie's needs, of delighting her, of sheltering, guarding, and nurturing her. What if she longed to love Livie and the little one refused every overture, if Livie would give hugs and kisses, but shunned anything in return?

She clenched her hands. Letting God care for her felt like proving her own father right, that she was weak and helpless, unable to make her own decisions, that she shouldn't trust the mind he'd given her to get out of her own mess.

"Erin." As Morgan sat down beside her, Livie crawled into her lap. "I spent most of my life doing it my way. It's bogus."

She startled. "Are you kidding? Look what you have."

"I could lose it all and be no poorer than I've always been. What matters are the ones we love. I can't control who lives and dies, but I can give everything I am to the ones I have." He clasped her hand. "Do you think I'm more generous than God? Are you?"

"No! Of course not."

"Needing help doesn't mean we're incapable. It means we're human. And that we have the sense to recognize our limitations."

"Then everything I did, what I tried to make them see, was it all wrong?"

His face softened, his eyes crinkling at the corners. "You recognized a con. The elders didn't see it. Your dad wouldn't listen."

"He should have!"

"No one's perfect."

She pressed a hand to her face. "I thought I knew so much."

He huffed a laugh. "At your age, there wasn't a question I couldn't answer."

"And now that you're old?"

He jabbed her, and when he saw that it tickled, he pushed her down and had at it.

"Stop!"

He caught her face and kissed her.

"Kiss *me,* Daddy."

Morgan kissed his little girl, then turned back with something fierce in his eyes. "I'll do everything I can. But only so much is humanly possible."

Reaching up, she encircled his neck. "Then pray."

Standing at the window of Quinn's A-frame, Markham's jaw felt as though an ice pick had been inserted into the joint. If he heard the tremulous tone in Hannah's voice one more time, he might strangle her. It would be a mercy killing — putting himself out of his misery.

"We have to make plans," she said.

Where had she hidden this trait? The woman had taken his handmaid statement as some sort of proposal and kept prying at him for dates and details. Her persistence shocked and infuriated him.

"I have to go out."

"I'll come with you." She sprang up from the salvaged sofa in Quinn's living room.

"You can't. We might still need you to play Quinn's sister."

"I am Quinn's sister."

"I mean her loving sister."

She blinked big, sorrowful eyes. They both knew that wasn't a role she played well.

"I'll bring you something to eat." He held out his hand. "Let me have your debit card."

Gulping back tears, she gave it. "I don't like being alone here."

He considered the situation, certain he didn't want her coming, but he couldn't leave her crying either. He'd pay for that for sure. "Hold on a minute."

He went out to the warehouse and slipped inside, regretting and yet exulting in the destruction. He searched through the rubble and found the kind of books people put on tables for bored guests to look through. He chose three relatively undamaged and brought them to Hannah.

"Here."

She looked from them to him. "For me?"

"Of course. Quinn left them."

She took the books and sat back down. He went out feeling unencumbered and magnanimous.

The bartender's comment about Spencer's wife had given him a lead. Using a computer in what passed for the town's library, he slogged through site after site to finally find a tribute to Spencer's wife, who'd died in a tragic accident in Santa Barbara County. It was a very big deal. The Fire Department could have been sued, but no settlement was reported — only *Mr. Spencer remains devoted to the community.*

What kind of man didn't seek retribution for his dead wife? Markham rubbed his jaw. He needed to know more, and he wouldn't find it in the business journals. He went back to the Roaring Boar, glanced scathingly at the general store goob eating at the bar, and sat down at the other end.

With Hannah's debit card, he ordered barbecue and beer and another sandwich to go. It would be a splurge, since the allowance her father put monthly into her bank account was meager after the church's financial hit. Had to hand it to a man who could ride that storm and not lose his followers. Never underestimate faithful indoctrination, the lifeblood of his own ministry.

People wanted to be conned. Like the unquestioning housewives in Pastor Reilly's congregation, the whole church had ridden his wave. The fervor of believing, even a lie, lifted them out of the workaday slog to a spiritual plane of sacrifice and expectation.

He took a swallow of beer, the cold malt taste reminding him of the stale breaths and rank urine of the men who'd trained him to lie. He'd honed the skill in self-defense, then wielded it with such skill they'd never seen the final truth until their eyes glazed in death.

When the sandwich arrived, he bit a crisp chip as salt cleaned the malt from his mouth. He had barely initiated conversation with the bartender when he saw the fat deputy come in the door. The man conferred with the yokel from the general store, and a hint of apprehension snaked through Markham's gut. He had nothing to fear, but memories of prison rushed through his mind.

Too much like a guard, the deputy eyed him. Markham returned the stare, something he would never have done inside.

The man sauntered over. "Markham Wilder?"

"Yes, sir."

"Rudy Bauer there says you threatened a woman in his store."

Markham glanced casually at ponytailed Rudy. "He's mistaken."

"You didn't come in looking for Quinn Reilly?"

"I did come looking. But the only one threatened was me — with a shotgun."

The deputy looked over his shoulder. "You pull your shotgun, Rudy?"

"I showed it to him."

"It's called brandishing, Deputy." Markham could hardly hide the glee. "But I'm not pressing charges. I'm all live-and-let-live."

The deputy braced his wide hips. "You have anything to do with her house?"

"Her house?"

Deputy Wentz looked annoyed. "Did you mess it up?"

"It didn't look messed up when I visited her sister."

The deputy frowned. "Her sister lives there?"

Markham shrugged. "The family had a falling out. Hannah's trying to reconcile with Quinn but hasn't been able to find her."

"Guess I should go talk to her."

"I'll ask you not to."

"Why not." He put the law-enforcement edge on the words.

"She's mentally delayed. It would upset her."

He backed off instantly. "What part do you have in this?"

"Me? I'm her sister's keeper." Maybe he shouldn't have chosen the odd phrase, as the deputy's brow lowered. He quickly added, "I look out for her." He reached into his wallet and took out his Doctor of Divinity ordination card. "As I said, Officer, I'm not the troublemaker here."

Making sure he had some privacy, Morgan took the call in his home office. If the news was terrible, he wanted time to process it before he brought Erin in.

"Here's what I got," Anselm said. "During the trial, allegations connecting Markham Wilder to the same or similar church scams in other states got the feds involved. Because the monies appeared to be rolled over from one scam to the next, the investigation focused on discovering what he did with the accumulated funds after Quinn Reilly blew the whistle."

"Makes sense. Why adopt the accomplice theory?"

"Jailhouse informant. A blue-collar embezzler looking to shave time came forward with comments Markham made. According to the source, Markham claims the money was stolen by someone he intends to take out — as in permanently."

"Did he say who?"

"No name. But they got intent to commit murder and a line on the money."

"Did this guy get credit for the information?"

"He did. And not only that — Markham received time off his sentence."

"The feds wanted him out?"

"The informant provided cause to monitor Markham when he got out, not that they wouldn't have anyway, but it looks better when you have it. So, Markham tracks down this other person, the agents track him, they get the money. Only problem, he went off the grid."

"How?"

"My guess? An accomplice."

He immediately thought of Erin's sister. "What would that entail?"

"Someone paying his bills."

"That's all?"

"It's not like he's on the FBI's Ten Most Wanted list."

Morgan frowned. "If he gets the money he could disappear altogether."

"Happens more than you want to know." Anselm cleared his throat. "You want to tell me your interest in this?"

"Someday," he said. When it was over.

He went upstairs and, bearing Erin's weight to spare her ankle, led her through the kitchen, still redolent with cumin and roasted peppers and cilantro from lunch. They walked across the yard to the fence along the cliff, overlooking the Pacific. A rare afternoon mist nearly shrouded Santa Cruz Island, making it look like a long, brooding prehistoric beast.

He paused, as always, taking it in. In some ways the view never changed, yet it was always changeable.

Erin leaned, maybe unconsciously, into him.

"How are you feeling?"

"Like I've been through the tornado and landed in Oz."

Standing there, one arm around her shoulder, a part of him felt the strangeness of Erin beside him, but more and more she was feeling so right.

"Do you think I'll go to jail?"

"No."

"What if they believe I stole the money? This could all come crashing down."

"Like Dorothy's house on the witch?"

She turned and jutted her chin. "It's not funny."

"I'm looking for the lighter side. Besides, you did steal it."

She groaned. "That's the lighter side?"

He turned and threaded the fingers of both their hands. "William's defending a case right now. As soon as that's completed, we'll bring this to him. There's no one better."

"Will that . . . damage your relationship?"

"With William?"

"I saw how much you respect each other. If your wife —"

"I respect you too, Erin. And so will he. What you did was misguided, not evil. And we can make it right."

She shook her head. "I told Noelle the one thing I hated was dishonesty. And here I am. Poster child."

He drew her in. "Let it go for now."

"Better take me to the wizard."

He grinned. "Follow the yellow brick road?"

"And watch out for flying monkeys."

"One of cinema's true horrors."

Her laugh warmed him as only Livie's could have in the past. And not only her laugh, but her expressions, her conversation, her humor, her overdeveloped conscience — in spite of one significant lapse. He sensed her anxiety beneath her stalwart front and wanted to help. "Let's go out."

"On a date?"

"We've had a honeymoon."

"And a cliffhanger."

"Could have done without that."

"Me too." She grimaced.

"What do you say?"

"Well." She shrugged a shoulder. "I'll try to find something to wear."

He laughed. "The place I'm thinking of won't require dolling up, but the food's excellent and the ambience is one of a kind." He couldn't wait to see her reaction. "Local celebs sneak away there for an evening out."

"Okay. I'm intrigued."

"You will be."

"Any clues?"

"Don't wear stilettos."

"With this swollen ankle?"

He kissed her. "I won't say it serves you right."

"Oh, but you'll think it."

She absorbed every detail of the San Marcos Pass as they climbed into the Santa Ynez Mountains. They made the drive early enough to enjoy the landscape dressed in pale grasses and clumpy scrub oak that wasn't much different than lower elevations of Colorado. "I thought it would be tropical, like the palm trees along the shore."

"Those are imports for the hotels. What you see here is indigenous. The central coast is pretty ideal, moderate temp all year, and it's . . . real. Around the other side of these hills are vineyards and horse breeders."

"What kind?"

"Andalusians, Friesians, Blue Roan Percherons. Livie will be riding before I know it."

As long as she didn't have to do the same. "How did you end up here?"

He sped smoothly into a curve. "One of my first consultations — a little company with a big idea it didn't know what to do with. They gave me stock to show them the ropes. That stock put me on the financial map and is still the best investment I've made. More than that, it planted me in Santa Barbara."

"I can see why you love it. No snow-peaked Rockies, but everything else."

"Once this place gets into you, others are great, but they're not home."

"I get the impression Rick feels that way about the ranch."

"Sure. We vacationed in Colorado growing up, and it got inside him."

"Do you think everyone has a place that fits?"

He glanced over. "I hope this one fits you."

She stared out. "I don't know what fits. I've been so busy making whatever place I'm in work for the time I'm in it."

"Maybe it's time to settle."

She frowned. "There's the little issue of a sociopath with a grudge."

"We're not discussing Markham tonight."

"You know, I'm good with that."

He turned onto a narrow road that tucked up into the forest. Shady trees and airy shrubs crowded the curving pavement.

"What are these trees? They smell good." She'd opened her window to fully experience it.

"Sycamore and bay laurel. Very native."

As they crept to a stop in a dirt lot, she stared at the wood-plank, and stone-chimneyed shacks that looked like a Western hideaway. "What is this place?"

"An old stage stop. It was built as a way station in the 1860s."

"You mean it's real?"

He gave her a hand out and supported her past the first building with a porch framed and upheld by forked and knotted saplings. An iron street lantern illuminated a rickety, raised wooden walkway between the first and second structures. The ivy-covered building with red-and-white-checkered café curtains bore an old-style hanging sign that read *Ye Cold Spring Tavern* in complete incongruity with the scattered Harleys and leather-clad bikers gathered around a roaring fire pit one building over. From that one came sounds — she thought — of a live rock band.

She slanted him a look. "You didn't tell me to wear leathers."

Morgan's eyes crinkled. "Wish I'd thought of it."

He pulled open the door beneath the sign, and she limped into a space lit by kerosene lamps and a blazing fireplace. The rooms were filled by a small number of white-vinyl-draped tables and wooden chairs. A deer head that hung over the fireplace looked as though it could have been lopped from the first meal served in 1860. The coyote over the long wooden bar appeared to have needed that meal as much as whoever got it. The mangy bobcat head just made her shudder.

She could not for the life of her believe this was Morgan's kind of place. Where were the tuxedoed waiters, the chilling champagne?

The chairs were hard, the walls planks. She could smell kerosene, though where they sat it was only a whiff. Still, she had to wonder if he was playing a practical joke.

"Morgan." The approaching waitress beamed, warm brown eyes under thick black brows, and broad toothy smile all his. "I hadn't heard you were back."

"Only just." He glanced across the table. "Tam, this is my wife, Erin."

Surprise and disappointment moved through her face.

Erin smiled. "Hi."

Planting her hands behind her hips, in a pose that presented her assets, Tam asked what they'd like to drink. Morgan deferred.

Erin said, "Just water, thanks."

"Two." He smiled. "And start us with the tiger prawns."

"Sure." Tam cast her one more glance and went into the kitchen.

Erin tipped her head. "It's a little unnerving being sized up by everyone you know, especially when you know everyone."

"I hide out here a lot."

Either he was serious or he'd win an Oscar.

He jutted his chin. "Look out the window."

She took in the cool forested slopes in the last of the light. "Imagine we've just arrived by coach. It's a relay point where we'll take on extra horses to make it over the newly completed pass. Word is they serve the most delicious meals in all the West."

"I can't help thinking one of them is hanging on the walls."

"Forget the trophies. They're just character."

"Okay." If she limited her view to his face, nothing furry and long dead interfered.

"One of the buildings out there was the bunkhouse for the Chinese road crew that built the pass. Another's the Ojai jail. The four little shacks out back are all that's left of the ghost town of Gopherville, California."

"I didn't know you were a history buff."

"As a rule, I like new and shiny."

"You bought the old asylum medicine cabinet."

"An experiment to see what you were made of." The corners of his mouth twitched.

"I knew that sale was fishy, just didn't guess it illegal. Shoot, what if they add that to the other charges?"

He sent a glance out the window. "Your accommodations will be better than Ojai's."

"All I ask is no mangy critters."

He pulled a slow smile. "Better keep you out of jail, then."

Someone brought their water, and shortly thereafter the waitress came with broiled tiger shrimp on skewers. One taste and Erin realized if she and Morgan did nothing but eat out the rest of their lives she'd die happy. She only hoped it wasn't soon.

CHAPTER 26

With Livie clutching her finger, Erin limped behind Consuela from the parking lot to the squatty stone fountain that stood in the plaza of the Old Mission Santa Barbara. On tippy-toe, Livie peered through the lily pads, looking for fish, as Consuela continued the lesson she'd begun on the drive over.

"The mission was established on the feast day of Saint Barbara, who got beheaded by her father for becoming a believer."

That put things in perspective.

"It was built to serve the Chumash Indians but became the center of life for the whole town."

Erin looked up at the flat Romanesque façade with twin bell towers, imagining a simpler time, and then realized there was no such time. Political squabbles, power struggles, and human and natural forces arrayed against it from the start. Yet the mission had served more than two hundred years in spite of two terrible earthquakes and a fire, a testament to charity and resilience.

Bearing a crate of "extra" food she'd prepared the last couple days, Consuela started across the plaza.

While the Chumash were no longer a distinguishable group, having intermarried in the course of things, the affluent city still had its homeless, its hungry. Erin had seen them on the streets, in the parks, on the beach — castoffs people passed like ghosts while scrutinizing the fine offerings in shop windows. She had chided Morgan for Consuela's wasteful cooking, when really it was a collusion of generous souls. How many other things had she judged without comprehending?

"In May," Consuela said, "they make chalk paintings on all the piazza. It is called I Madonnari festival. Italian street painting. Magnificent. You'll see." She nodded. "We will come and watch the artists."

Consuela had no reason to suspect, come May, things might not be as they were. Erin's stomach formed a hard ball of worry. She wanted so much to be part of this life, but what if she couldn't? What if it all got taken away? Livie hugged her neck, showing an uncanny awareness that both comforted and increased the angst.

As Consuela delivered the food to be distributed, Erin stepped into the ornate historical church and smelled wood oil and candle wax. Beautiful as the surroundings were, it wasn't the building that mattered. It was the heart, the purpose behind the beauty. A celebration of love? The yearning in her heart said yes.

Believing God loved and cared for her wasn't weakness. It was grace. Cradling Livie, she dropped to her knees and formed a prayer that was neither praise nor thanks, but bald supplication. *Please help me make it right.*

Back outside, she took the call that had begun vibrating in the church. "Noelle, what's wrong? Is it Hannah?" Bracing for bad news, she sat quickly on the steps, settling Livie beside her.

"No. I haven't seen her since Rick took her to Rudy's store. Presumably, she rejoined Markham."

"Are they gone?"

"I don't know. I'm not getting out much right now, so I haven't even heard."

Erin stared across the courtyard to the vast rose garden, as verdantly blooming in December as any other month, and suddenly felt desolate. "How did Hannah seem?"

"Well, to be honest, she seems bitter and troubled. And forgive me, but is she learning impaired?"

"I'm not sure. She passed her classes in school, but it was the church-affiliated school and our father the minister. It would have looked bad to hold her back." For an instant she wondered what someone like Jill might have accomplished with her.

"We tried to get through, but Markham has her thoroughly snowed."

Erin groaned. "She's happy to stand in that blizzard." Hannah had dreamed of life with Markham and believed so completely in his miracle. If anyone had corrected her earlier, smaller mistakes, she might not have been so susceptible to gigantic ones. "Thank you for trying. I hope . . . I pray she'll be all right."

Noelle's voice softened. "Rick and I join you in that. He regrets turning anyone away, but Erin . . . the hatred."

A lump formed in her throat. "I know. It's always been that way. When I was little, she'd break my things and tell my parents I shouldn't have toys if I couldn't take care of them." She often wondered if that was why she never got a pet, even though she begged so often.

Livie examined a fallen leaf, unfurling the brittle skeleton that resisted her determined fingers until its spine snapped.

"That explains the spitefulness I saw when she talked about you."

"She's not that way with anyone else. Usually she's kind and sweet."

"That makes it harder, doesn't it."

"Yes."

"But," Noelle's tone brightened. "I was calling to see how you and Morgan are."

Erin shook her head. Any answer would be so inadequate. "We're good." She could barely get her mind around it all, from the moment they'd met to now. "Morgan changes lives."

"You don't have to tell me. Without Morgan, Rick would have sent me packing."

"What?" She found that impossible to believe.

"Rick had a strict policy against lodging single women in the house. I don't know what I'd have done if Morgan hadn't changed his mind. He's a people whisperer."

"He's exactly that." Erin pressed a hand to her heart.

"And trust me, with Rick that's a feat. Of course, his rigidity formed in reaction to Morgan's . . . oh. Forgive me."

Erin laughed. "Morgan's incorrigibility?"

"Well . . . yes." Noelle laughed too.

"What does it say that I love even that?" Silence fell between them as she realized what she'd admitted.

"It says you're exactly who I hoped you were."

Markham smiled when the overperfumed Lydia Patterson led him to her desk. He'd met her at the grocery mart and, seeing the *Ask Me About Real Estate* button on her lapel had done just that.

Motioning him to sit, she said, "I'll brew us

some fresh coffee and warm some scones for a little snack while you peruse the MLS."

"You're an angel," he said.

"You should know . . . Pastor." Her lashes fluttered. "Just holler if you need anything else."

Besides the use of her national database, he couldn't think of a thing. This was how he'd found Quinn since she couldn't resist telling her mother she'd bought a house, even if she wouldn't say where. He had nearly blown a gasket, until Hannah explained Quinn had bought the cabin with her own precious savings — a bargain basement deal at a bankruptcy auction, perfect for a junk dealer.

His fingers moved on the keyboard. He'd destroyed pretty much everything she owned when he trashed the property, although the house was still livable. Maybe he'd burn it when they were done — symbolically.

His focus now was not Quinn but Morgan Spencer. Unfortunately, this search did not yield immediate results. Santa Barbara County showed no property titles for Morgan Spencer, not even a transfer of title, since he might have sold a home after losing his wife. He searched the county records for titles in the name of his corporation, and under the Kelsey Foundation.

He'd read more than he wanted to know about both of those entities in the exhaustive Internet search he'd conducted for days. All the articles and images he could stomach, but no real estate. Just as he considered heaving the monitor into the wall, Lydia returned with their snack, all glowing smiles. "See anything you like, Pastor?"

He ran his eyes over her. "Why yes, Lydia." With a touch of his finger, he closed that search, returning to the multiple listing service.

She flushed and fanned her hand, suddenly acquiring a southern accent. "Doesn't flirting break one of your ten commandments?"

"Merely appreciating God's creation."

They shared a wholesome laugh with a naughty undercurrent. He'd played her perfectly, and his confidence swelled. "Do you know the Spencers?"

The change of topic took her by surprise. "Rick and Noelle?"

"And isn't there a brother?"

"Oh, Morgan. He's the big fish."

"Really."

She exploded with excitement, telling all she knew about the man, none of which was new. "I could not believe he bought Vera's old place, even if it is right next to Rick's ranch. What would he want with that place built on an old, haunted cellar?"

"You're confusing me, Lydia."

"Oh you." She laughed. "I'm saying Morgan Spencer bought a dumpy little house, when he could have had any listing on there."

She motioned to her computer. "Of course, he didn't consult me."

"Then how could he buy something?"

"Oh." Her voice sailed up at the end. "I'm not the *only* way. He went straight to Vera's daughter. I don't think the sale's recorded yet." For an instant her face looked hawkish. "I do wonder what he paid."

Realizing he was in her chair, Markham jumped up. "Where are my manners?"

"Oh, don't worry. I sit there all day."

"No, please. I hope you made yourself something." He indicated the food.

"Well, I did." She smiled. "Probably don't need it."

"Everyone deserves a treat." He pulled the plastic chair from the corner and sat down across from her like old friends or . . . How did she see him? Client? Love interest? Both? "You were saying Morgan lives in a house by his brother's ranch?"

She frowned. "I don't know that he lives there yet. I think he had some furniture delivered, but he must be somewhere else for the holidays. Frankly, I can't envision him living there at all." She shook her head. "Maybe he bought it for someone else."

Markham went completely still. Of course. Spencer saw the wreckage at Quinn's and bought her a new house. "Would he do that?"

"Oh, he's that way." She took a loud sip of her coffee. "The more I think about it, the more sense it makes. He stays at Rick's when he's up here. He wouldn't need Vera's."

"Who would he buy it for?"

Lydia shrugged, thought a moment, then set her cup down deliberately. "Well, I heard one thing. I hesitate to tell a minister, since it could be gossip."

He waited past her hesitation with a genial if not overly encouraging expression. Let her conscience decide.

"There's a gal, Quinn Reilly. Bought a cute little place six months ago, on a steal from the bank, but I guess she had some trouble there. Rudy from the general store said someone broke in and messed the place up."

That store might burn too. He sat back. "I hadn't imagined crime up here."

"Oh, no. People don't even lock their doors."

"Was it personal?"

She took a bite of her scone, catching crumbs with her fingers. "Deputy took a look, but who can say?"

He knew all about the deputy. "What relation is she to Morgan Spencer?"

"Oh, no relation. Friend, maybe."

"He buys houses for his friends?"

"I'm only speculating. But if he knew she needed a place and Vera's came available . . ."

"Quite a guy." Markham sipped his coffee.

"Real estate's a great investment. The house might not be much, but it has good property.

It's on the same road as Rick's ranch." She raised and dropped her shoulders, making her bosom quake. "Maybe Morgan's renting it to her."

"Would your records show that?"

"As I said, it's probably too soon."

"But she . . . lives there now?"

Lydia sipped her coffee. "To be honest, I haven't seen her since she closed our deal."

He pursed his lips, coming full circle to his reason for being there. "Tell me, Lydia, how would someone hide property?"

She blinked. "Hide it?"

"Is it possible to have property without people knowing you have it?"

"Oh. Of course. The easiest way to hide a property asset would be a land trust. That excludes your name from the public records. No one will know who owns the property but you, your attorney, and the trustee. Are you . . . wanting to buy in secret?"

He wasn't wanting to buy at all, but it felt so good to have her on the hook after fearing he'd lost the touch that he couldn't resist. "People expect men of my calling to live simply. You're saying if I bought something extravagant, in a land trust, no one could find me out?"

She gave him a broad smile. "Oh, Pastor. It would be our secret."

Since Morgan had the weekend before diving

back in with Belcorp, they were making the most of it. Last evening had been theirs, and today was for Livie, the first stop the antique carousel where children lined up to ride with a troop of Muppet-style puppets — and puppeteers — who'd come to town. Elves and reindeer and toy soldiers and dolls, and somewhere in there a "life-sized" Santa Muppet gave an original twist to an age-old tradition.

She made a good effort to hide her discomfort, but Morgan missed little. He brushed her arm. "Hurting?"

Her ankle and pretty much every other part hurt worse today from body-slamming against the cliff than yesterday, but she wanted to do this for Livie. What better time than their first Christmas season to start making memories — even if the beautiful day felt summery. "I'm all right."

He eyed her purplish foot in the sandal. "Maybe you should have that looked at."

"I'd know if it were serious. I broke it once, picking apples with my sister. She accidentally knocked the ladder away from the tree."

Morgan raised his brows. "Accidentally?"

She opened her mouth and closed it. Uncanny how perceptive he was. "Everyone said so." She edged Livie forward. "Hannah's the good girl. A perfect product of indoctrination, skilled in awe and obedience."

A preschool girl in front of them reached

into her mouth and stretched a long string of chewing gum. It snapped like a rubber band and stuck to her cheek, earning her a scolding from her mother, who should have known better than to give her toddler gum.

"The same indoctrination you received." Morgan ran his thumb up and down her spine. "Where's the awe and obedience?"

She glared. "That meal was served, but I didn't eat."

"Ah." A smile tugged his lips. He crouched and lifted Livie, who had turned toward his leg and pressed in with her little torso. "Almost there, punkin." He smoothed her wispy hair.

Erin counted the children between them and the carousel. With the carousel ride, and then conversation and photos as the Santa Muppet heard each rider's heart's desire, it would take a while. The little girl with the gum must have wanted something. When her mother said no, the child proceeded to pinch the woman's thigh with vicious little fingers. Instead of pointing out the inadvisability of pinching in front of Santa Claus, the woman yanked her daughter's arm and pulled her out of line.

Morgan raised a brow as they stalked off. "One down."

Erin giggled, but having counted, she knew that one meant Livie would make the cut this round.

Morgan rested his palm against her back. "So what's wrong with your sister?"

"What do you mean?"

"She knocks a ladder out from under you. She swallows the party line and falls for Markham."

Erin sighed. "She's . . . impressionable."

"That's all?"

"Maybe a little challenged."

"You don't know?"

"It doesn't matter. Once she sets her mind, she's as stubborn as . . ."

"You?"

"I'm reasonable. I went to Paris and married you."

At the mention of Paris, his eyes hooded, his hand coming to rest lower on her back than Santa would approve.

"Morgan."

He shifted up an inch. "I wonder how much your sister's limitations shaped your dad's precepts."

"What do you mean?"

"Maybe he extended the necessary care and protectiveness beyond one individual to help that individual blend in. To make that level of care the norm."

She'd never considered it that way. "That's the kindest thing you could have said."

He shrugged. "I get it — that's all. If Livie had a disability, I'd change the world around her."

Her chest warmed. "I love . . . that about you."

He pulled a slow smile. "Careful. You might say something you're not ready to say."

Her heart raced. How could she not say it, and yet . . .

He leaned in and kissed her. "Doesn't matter. It's all over your face."

The rat. She tugged his shirt sleeve.

Grinning, he lifted Livie onto the carousel. With a full heart, she followed them aboard.

Buckling his daughter into her car seat after several enchanting hours at the zoo, Morgan asked Erin, "Do you mind sitting in back to keep her awake?" If she slept now that was all the naptime they'd get.

"Sure." She took her position — not in awe and obedience but as part of a team working in sync, one mind, one intention. He'd seen her ability to adapt, to either take charge or support. Good qualities. With training, she could be a force in the corporate world or anything else she chose. Was it fair to assume she wanted nothing more than to love the child who'd come with the marriage?

Livie was half asleep as he laid her down, his heart swelling as it did every time. He'd thought Erin followed him inside but didn't see her when he left Livie's room or in going downstairs. He went out to the courtyard, where she pointed to a spray of lavender-colored blossoms springing from the gray-skinned branches of the jacaranda.

"It's blooming in December."

"A minor flowering. The leaves will fall off in the spring, and in June the whole tree will burst with blossoms."

"So here you have fall in the spring and spring in the winter."

"For this variety of tree." A memory came in so piercing it caught him in the ribs. He recalled standing here, giving Jill the same explanation, and her amusement that Christmas was coming and this silly tree thought it was spring.

No panic came, but such sadness. He realized it showed. "I'm sorry."

"It's okay."

He dropped his gaze to the ground. "Sometimes it just comes. Everything's great, and then . . ." He shook his head. "It's the stealth of it, creeping in for no reason."

"There's a reason." She rested a hand on his arm. "You didn't give me a date, but if Livie's birthday's in September, and she was three months old . . ."

He closed and opened his eyes. "December 7th."

"Morgan, that's tomorrow."

He nodded. It wasn't as though the date could pass without his realizing, though it was astute on her part. "It's supposed to be the rainy season. But it was dry that year, and temperatures were high." He swallowed. "One of the freakishly hot sundowners blew over the mountains, rushing down like the breath of hell." He shook his head. "Wrong place, wrong time. Three young mothers. The other two survived." He slanted her a glance. "I'm thankful for that."

She nodded, believing him, then slid her hand down his arm and clasped his. "Could we visit her grave?"

He felt a sinking in his chest, as though the bones turned to wax and collapsed. He'd avoided all thought of it, and yet it had been there. What kind of man walks away from his wife in the ground and never once looks back? Sorrow graveled his voice. "You want to?"

"Livie can bring flowers to her mother."

Another collapse. "She doesn't know. I didn't see the point, when she was too little to even realize a loss."

"You were right. But now she could know. If you want her to."

Erin could have pushed for a clean break. Two was little still, and her position would solidify with more time. But this was Livie's reality as much as his, and Erin recognized that. He simply nodded. Tomorrow they would go.

The rain fell straight and neither warm nor cold in the Santa Barbara cemetery, the grass a moist green carpet on the gentle slope and level ground with grave markers laid flat and only a few raised stones and scattered trees in the portion where they walked. Her heart had stirred when Consuela asked to come and Morgan welcomed her. Now Livie walked on tiptoe just in front of the three adults, maybe because Morgan explained this wasn't a playing park. It was a praying park.

Erin carried the small bouquet she'd brought for Livie to give her mother. She didn't know how much the little girl would comprehend, but Morgan needed this. At the grave, in khaki slacks and black leather bomber jacket, he crouched down and encircled Livie between his knees, speaking softly into her ear. Erin's throat swelled.

Consuela surprised her by squeezing her hand. She whispered, "*Gracias,* Señora Erin. You do his heart good."

After a time, Morgan parted his hands and Livie slipped free, rushing over. "May have my mommy flowers?"

Erin dropped down and placed them in her little hand. "Here you go."

Livie turned and walked somberly to the plaque that bore her mother's name. Crouching like a grasshopper, she put them on it. "Here you go, Mommy."

Morgan's face twisted, silent sobs shaking him as he remained crouched, wrists draping his knees, hands slack.

She stayed beside Consuela as Livie wandered a little among the graves. The rain lessened, more mist than drops. A car drove slowly along the near road, heading as they'd done for a name on the ground. Morgan rose and came to them. He looked into Consuela's face without speaking. She held out her hands and he squeezed them; then she went around him to tend Livie.

Erin stared into his eyes as Morgan drew her in. She turned her head against his chest and pressed in, embraced by grief and solace. Long minutes they stood, as he raised a hand and stroked her hair.

She tipped her face and said, "I love you."

His next breath seemed to deepen. He pulled her tight again, pressing his cheek to the crown of her head. "Let's go home."

Chapter 27

Not even trying to keep up with Liam, Noelle climbed the stairs to the small town library. He gripped the door handle and leaned back to pull it open as someone approached from inside. Noelle blinked. "Hannah. Hi."

Hannah recognized her and flushed. "Oh. Hi."

"How are you? I didn't know you were still here."

"I'm fine."

In fact, she looked better than the last time, Noelle thought. Her heart quickened. Had Hannah split from Markham?

"I wanted a book to read, but they won't issue a card to nonresidents."

"That's no problem. I'll check it out for you."

Liam took that as his cue to dart inside, and Noelle caught the door starting to close. She felt certain Hannah would refuse, but Quinn's sister said, "I like to read."

"Have you picked something out?"

"Yes." She went back in. "He has it at the counter, waiting to be shelved again."

Noelle headed to the old ornately carved counter where Pike Gregory looked sorrowfully insistent. "I don't make the rules," he said to Hannah beside her. "Just follow 'em."

"I'll check it out for her." Noelle laid her card on the counter.

"Your responsibility."

"That's fine." She loved how seriously Pike took his job. He'd been watching over the library since he was born — when dinosaurs roamed the earth. She handed the card over, and he actually ran it and Hannah's prairie historical under a scanner, a wonderful mix of ancient and current day.

When Hannah thanked her, she said, "You're welcome. Hope you enjoy it."

"I like these old stories. I mean stories about old times."

Noelle nodded. She'd have guessed as much, since Hannah didn't seem to fit the present world too well. She wanted to ask about Markham but held back. Liam came running over with a big shark picture book, and while she told him it was a great choice, Hannah slipped out. Noelle moved to the front window and saw her get into a white Tahoe with a smashed windshield. She had to climb in through the passenger door.

Noelle pressed a hand to her chest with a

pang of sorrow and also regret. Maybe there would be a way to help her yet. At least she could have asked where Hannah was staying.

"What's that?" Markham leaned over to see what Hannah held as she sat primly on the damaged sofa that was also serving as her bed.

She started to speak, then her eyes grew large.

Since he'd spent the past few days ingratiating himself at the Roaring Boar, trying to learn anything that would lead to Quinn and Morgan, he'd paid little attention to Hannah's activities — though he'd assumed she stayed at Quinn's except to buy food. It appeared he was mistaken.

She gulped. "It's a library book."

"How did you get it?"

Again the big gulp, the worried eyes. "Noelle checked it out for me."

He frowned. "Noelle?"

"R-Rick's wife. She was happy to help . . . me. . . . With the book, I mean."

"What did you tell her?" As hard as he tried, he couldn't keep the edge from his voice.

Her lip quivered. "I said I liked stories about the past."

"I don't mean that. Does she know we're staying here? Together?"

She shook her head. "That's all I said."

Eyes pooling, she half whispered, "I would never make trouble for you, Markham. God made me your handmaid."

A phrase he wished he'd never uttered. "I don't want you talking to anyone in this town."

She retreated like a turtle to its shell, but instead of keeping still, said almost defiantly, "Then I'm glad I have my story. For all the time I don't have you."

"You think I like being out all day, trying to find Quinn?" He lowered his voice. "I *have* to do this." For once the importance of his mission seemed lost on Hannah.

"But I'm alone. Why can't I go with you when you're out?"

"Are you questioning me? Maybe you no longer believe I hear God. Maybe you think —"

"No, Mark. Please don't say it. Of course I believe. I know you're trying to do what God requires."

"My name is Markham."

She blinked without understanding.

"You called me Mark. Don't do that again."

Her face crumpled. "Oh, Mark-ham."

"I'm not —" he breathed through his clenched teeth — "angry." A bald-faced lie. If something didn't happen soon, the anger would build up. The anger would come out. But what could he do?

There'd been no sign of Quinn or the

fantastic Morgan Spencer in town anywhere. As far as he could tell, there was only one location — thanks to Lydia — that might prove useful.

Morgan gave Erin a hand getting off the Bowflex home gym. On the ride home from the cemetery he could tell that she was unsure about what to expect after visiting the grave. As cathartic as that had been, he couldn't dwell in sorrow. He'd lost his wife this day two years ago. That was a fact he'd live with every year. But there were more hours in the day than tears, even if those were the first he'd shed at her grave, even if each one had come from a place aching to be made whole.

Erin had raised her brows but not questioned when he suggested a workout. If she'd known him before, it wouldn't surprise her. His fitness had lapsed these past two years, but it was an essential part of him. Chasing Erin and this workout showed it was time to take it seriously again. Healing in mind went hand in hand with a healthy body.

He'd hoped by going gently on the machines, Erin might work the soreness from her strained muscles, and it seemed to have done that. They were both sweaty and her cheeks were flushed.

He hung a hand towel around her neck without relinquishing the ends. "Not bad for a sprite."

"Watch it. I have all my teeth."

"Even wisdom teeth?"

"Mm-hmm. They came in perfectly and make one effective bite."

"Let me see." He tipped her face and looked into her mouth. "Huh."

"You?"

"Had mine out. Got a dry socket, but I manned through."

"Wonder if your mother would agree."

"To Celia I walk on water with Michael, Patrick, and all the saints."

"Oh right. I forgot."

He studied her. "Tell me something else about you."

She gave a little laugh at his silliness. "I won every spelling bee I entered."

"I'm not surprised."

"There were only three. In first, second, and third grade. Then my father thought it inappropriate for the minister's daughter to compete."

With his fist holding the towel, he chucked her chin. "Knew the others had no chance."

With a shrug, she wrapped her hands over his. "Now you."

He paused, then went with the obvious. "I had my first kiss at eleven."

"Now *I'm* not surprised. Who was it?"

"I can't kiss and tell."

"You probably don't remember." She pulled

the towel out of his hand. "I want to know something that isn't physical."

He rested his forearms on her shoulders. "When I was a kid, maybe four or five, I wandered off at a stock show. I kept going stall by stall, barn by barn, corral after corral, thinking I'd see my parents and Rick, or someone I knew." He remembered the enormity of the fair, the smell of the animals, the dung, the sunbaked hay.

"Were you scared?"

"I must have been, but I didn't cry. I kept looking until this cowboy stood in front of me and asked who I belonged to." He pictured the man in tan shirt, Stetson, and chaps. "I told him I belonged to myself. He thought that was funny, but I didn't know why. Even then I had this sense of identity."

"What happened?"

"He asked my name and I said Morgan Spencer and told him my family got lost."

Erin drank it in, amused. "What did he do?"

"He put me on his horse and walked us to a microphone, then asked the announcer to call the lost Spencer family to meet Morgan at the bandstand."

Her whole face lit. "Livie has that. She not only knows exactly who she is, she's sizing up the rest of us as well."

He leaned in and kissed her. "I love that you see that." He kissed her again. She had told him days were like years to Livie, but now it seemed they were putting years into days, learning each other at a feverish pace and a cellular level.

She brushed his cheek with her fingertips, her eyes shiny and mysterious, her puckish features adorable. "When I was little I wanted a horse. Some of the people in the church had land and animals, and I wanted a horse so much I could hardly stand it. I read stories about them, drew pictures of them, dreamed and begged. And finally my dad took me to see one that was for sale.

"I was so excited I almost cried." She rested her hand on his arm. "The mare was brown with a white blaze, and I already knew all the promises I would make if I could only have her."

He tipped his head, sensing a twist.

"As I drew close, I realized how big she was, and being — as you incorrigibly observe — diminutive in stature, it gave me pause. As I stood, the mare stomped a hoof and tossed her head, that giant muzzle coming up. All of a sudden, I was afraid. It was like someone opened my head and poured fear in like sand. It sank down and stuck my feet to the ground, froze my hands to my sides. I was terrified of the thing I loved most in the world."

"And?"

"My father turned to me and said, 'Be careful what you wish for.' "

Morgan hissed a breath between his teeth.

"He should have put you on her back."

She formed a faint smile. "It was more important to make his point."

"That natural affections would endanger you?"

"That I couldn't trust myself to know best, even about my own heart."

"Are you still afraid of horses?"

She shrugged a shoulder. "Haven't really explored it."

So, yes, but the lesson hadn't kept her from wishing or taking chances. She'd followed her conscience and found her own two feet. That strong, feisty woman he'd first seen was the real deal, her core, in spite of misunderstandings and questionable judgment. Quinn Erin Reilly Spencer had more substance than her diminutive stature suggested.

Erin hurried out of the shower to answer her phone. Swabbing that side of her head with the towel, she raised the phone to her ear and answered without concern since almost no one had her number.

"Quinn? Hi, it's RaeAnne. I hope I'm not getting you from something, but I just haven't stopped thinking of you and had to call." She spared a second to breathe, then, "How are you and that hunky husband?"

Erin laughed at the impossibility of expressing the strides they'd made, even since Noelle had asked her the same question. "It's kind of amazing, actually."

"Oh, honey, I'm so happy. And his little girl?"

"She's wonderful. I thought she'd miss Noelle so much, and she does, but Morgan's been so integral in her life, it's not as painful a separation as he'd feared. It's like he's her true north, and even at two she's navigating by his constant love."

"Oh." RaeAnne sniffled. "You made me cry."

"I guess that was sort of a Hallmark commercial." She laughed. "How are you?"

"Oh, you know, still wanting answers or closure or whatever."

It hit her that she hadn't told her about Raymond Hartley's asylum file. Toweling dry with one hand, she strode to the bathroom and hung it, then pulled on her robe. "Well, are you sitting down?"

"Ye-es. What is it?"

"You remember those historical accounts of the asylum your mom's house is on?"

"You were getting up the gumption to read them when we finished Mom's journal."

"Well, except what Dr. Jenkins and I read at Thanksgiving, I hadn't read any more until I got out here."

"And?"

"RaeAnne, your dad was treated there."

"At the mental hospital?" She took a long indrawn breath. "What for?"

"These are stories, not actual files, so remember it's hearsay."

"And I'm not a court of law."

"They treated him for rage and suicidal depression."

"Wow," she breathed. "Didn't see that coming."

"Maybe it's how he wound up in Juniper Falls, and then your mom came as well."

"Makes all kinds of sense."

She thrust her fingers into her wet hair. "If it was really bad, that might be a reason Vera didn't tell you more about him."

"There you are again, making everything better."

"I wish I *could* make it better, or at least help you see him." But she told her about Markham and her sister being in Juniper Falls and a little of why that wasn't a good thing.

"Your own sister?"

"Afraid so. But they can't stay there forever, and as soon as it's clear, we'll go meet your dad."

"Please do not put yourself at risk."

She pressed a hand to her heart. "Morgan won't let me."

"I'm so happy you have him."

"Yeah," she breathed. "Me too."

Having come so far, she really had no excuse for her mind's continued nagging. But when Morgan slept, wrapped in dreams that made his eyelids tremble, she slipped out and moved silently down the hall. She turned on the light, took the three remaining albums from the shelf, and sat cross-legged on the floor.

The first album held wedding photos. After a gap of fifteen years from that prom picture, the two tenacious lovers reunited, every moment, every smile, every kiss chronicled. Other faces and figures filled out the scenes, but only Jill and Morgan held her. Photo after photo, she felt drenched in them, drunk in them.

The next album showed them in various places, engaging activities — and throughout it all, Jill's lithe beauty, Morgan's charisma. In the third, she watched Jill's belly swell, saw them outfit the nursery, attend birthing classes, the list of names considered and rejected. And then, Olivia Joy.

She heard a sound and saw Morgan in the doorway, hair spiked, features edgy.

"I hope you don't mind," she said, in a voice like a wraith, then realized the stupidity of that remark. "Of course you do. I won't —"

His gaze lifted and moved around the walls. "I forgot this room." He came and sat on the floor beside and against her, his angled knee, shin, and thigh forming a backrest for her, one hand resting on her far shoulder, the other hand on her near arm. In almost every way, he encompassed her.

Looking into his deep blue eyes, she said, "I needed to face my fear."

He looked down at the album in her lap, the pictures of mother and daughter. He saw the other albums lying near, surely knew their contents had been revealed, scrutinized, absorbed. His voice was soft and thick, but steady. "She had none of Noelle's issues. Pregnancy, like everything else she did, came easy. Livie's birth, a breeze, though I didn't say that to her."

"Smart man."

"She'd have been a great mom." Sawdust filled his voice. "She loved kids so much, fought for them, bled for them." He glanced at the shelf. "Did you see her students?"

"Yes," she whispered.

His brow tightened. "It killed her giving Kelsey up. I think that's why she didn't marry, couldn't . . ."

"Replace you?"

He squeezed her arm. "When Livie came, all that fell away. She might have finally . . . healed."

She could imagine Livie healing any ill. She'd fallen in love with his child before she knew she loved this man.

"I'm sure women hate to be compared. But your way with Livie reminds me of Jill." He glanced over to gauge the impact. "You're hardly alike in any other way, but in that . . ."

He ran a hand down her arm, his eyes getting dark and serious. "You know what I want?"

"What you usually want?"

His voice got husky. "I want babies with you."

Her heart skittered.

"I know that probably feeds into the whole gender manipulation issues you've escaped, but there it is."

She searched his face for hints of insincerity. As always with Morgan, he meant what he said. "Because I'm like Jill?"

"What I saw and loved in her I can see and love in you, and it doesn't mean I want you to be her. Deep inside, so deep it's more than visceral, I want children with you."

She drew a ragged breath, amazed it came at all. She pushed her hair behind her ear and managed, "Someday?"

He whisked the hair back where it had been, then bunched the unruly stuff even closer around her face. "Unless you're taking measures your chastity in Paris would seem to rule out, we haven't exactly prevented it."

She felt her eyes widen as that truth sank in. In this whole heart-searching, mind-bending whirlwind, she'd poured herself into caring for Livie, healing Morgan, and guarding her heart. She felt callow, infantile to have not considered that ramification.

He stroked her cheek. "For what it's worth,

I'd want it this way — God's time without our interference."

"Even after . . ."

"Kelsey?"

She nodded.

"I was an irresponsible kid when Jill got pregnant. A lot of people, her own parents, thought that mistake should be erased." Anger stirred in his eyes. "But as painful as it turned out for us, any other baby at any better time wouldn't have been Kelsey. She wouldn't have been on this earth to impact so many lives, to bring hope to dying kids and restoration — to her mother and me." He swallowed. "Someday look up her Web site. She was the miracle we might have thrown away."

He sent his glance around the room. "But that, and all of this, is before." He returned his gaze to her. "This thing between us — it's not only physical. And it's not just how good you are with Livie. Sometimes when I look at you . . . it feels preordained."

Chapter 28

Standing in Morgan's well-appointed home office, Erin admired his efficiency as he prepared to leave early the next morning. But he stopped everything when a wasp-waisted woman in a fitted gray suit entered through the outside door without escort or announcement from Consuela.

With only a hint of surprise, he said, "Erin, this is my assistant, Denise."

In moments like this she realized how much about Morgan's life she still had to learn.

The other woman's surprise was even greater when he said, "Denise, meet my wife, Erin."

This was news, and Morgan was enjoying it.

"Hello, Erin." Denise had porcelain skin, but a faintly indented line across one cheekbone and another on her jaw suggested scarring. Some kind of accident, maybe.

"Hi." Erin smiled, amazed it hadn't occurred to her that Morgan had actual people working for him. He had talked metaphorically about teams and quarterbacks, but Denise didn't fit that mold, and she had access to the house. Consuela he'd mentioned, so why not Denise?

The sharp-featured blonde gave him a pointed look. "Private ceremony?"

"We married in Paris."

"Oh. The delay for Belcorp. And the purpose of your current restructuring?"

"I also have a two-year-old."

"Yes. Of course."

He looked at his watch. "I thought we were meeting at the airport."

"There's a complication." Her stance softened. "Glen Conyer had surgery at three o'clock this morning, an emergency appendectomy."

Morgan lowered his hand. "Is he doing all right?"

"It had ruptured, so recovery won't be routine."

Morgan considered. "I don't think we can delay. Who do we have who can come in as support?"

Waiting while they discussed names and business issues, Erin studied Denise. Her corn-silk blond hair pulled into a twenties-style twist appeared natural, her figure a human equivalent to the original Barbie dolls, before social concerns reduced the bust and expanded the waist.

Morgan said, "No, I'm not replacing him. They can work in tandem when he's back on his feet."

"The analysis doesn't require two."

"Well, I won't bring someone in and then ditch him or her. And when Glen's ready, his position will be there."

"Or we could have another project queued up."

He quirked a brow. "Have one in mind?"

"I have."

"Okay. We'll talk about it on the way." He took his briefcase and came around the desk. Leaning in, he kissed the wife he'd failed to mention to the likewise unmentioned assistant and murmured, "*We'll* talk tonight."

Feeling strange, she wandered back, past Consuela's apartment and the home gym and into the kitchen, pondering the rather vast office with two desks and an assistant who carried a key. Consuela must have read her mind — something she did as eerily as Morgan — because she said, "You met the assistant."

She laughed. "That obvious?"

"She is not as hard as she seems. It is the . . . face she wears." Consuela hung the towel she'd used on the dishes and slid the plate onto the stack.

"No one would doubt she's indispensable." If unmentionable.

"She has been with Señor Morgan for

years. For some of them, she lived in the guest house." She motioned to the cottage at the opposite side of his property from the pool.

"On the premises? Why?"

"The boyfriend. Señor Morgan said choose the emergency room or him. If she wanted to die, he would find a new assistant."

She pictured the ghostly scars on Denise's flawless face and felt dreadful. "She chose Morgan."

"In the work," Consuela emphasized. "It was never personal. Too much . . . bad feelings."

"Why did she move?"

"Señora Jill, she was not so . . . confident. There was —" Consuela made a motion with her hands — "friction. So Señor reopened his office downtown and made a place for Denise."

"And the boyfriend?"

Her face darkened. "He's a bad one. Still he bothers her. But I think there is money."

"From Morgan?"

"It keeps the wolf from the door."

Hitching a ride with Denise hadn't been the plan, but it worked well since they needed to resolve the personnel situation. As she drove to the Santa Barbara airport in Goleta, he called his first choice of accountants who came close to Glen's proficiency. Before they reached the airport parking, Alyssa Vogler had joined the team and would meet them in LA.

Denise's heels clicked beside him as they processed through the new terminal and boarded their flight. They were actually airborne before she said, "Your wife?"

"My wife." He smiled.

"You could have texted me that your personal emergency included a honeymoon."

"I could have. But time was limited, and now you know." Their relationship was starkly professional, yet she'd resented his first marriage and might his new one as well.

"At least you won't worry about Olivia while we're on task."

He smiled slightly. "At least."

"Of course, you had Consuela."

"Yes."

"So it isn't only for the child, is it."

"No."

She nodded. "Good. Once word is out, it will ease any lingering concerns about your state of mind."

"Good thing."

"I'm serious, Morgan. Perceptions rule."

"Indeed."

"Wouldn't you rather have people congratulating your marriage than condoling your loss?"

He swallowed. "I would."

"We should plan an event. Introduce her. Get the word out in all the right places."

"No."

She cast him a glance. "Why not?"

"It's not good timing."

"It's excellent timing. We'll get press."

"Yeah, well, not right now."

"Are you back or aren't you?" She eyed him critically.

He only smiled.

Markham brought Hannah with him, not only to prove his devotion, but also to have her aboard in case they were questioned. Poor Hannah, still looking for her sister and no one will help. He turned up the road toward Rick's ranch.

She gripped the armrest, clearly concerned. "Why are we going here?"

"It's not where you think." Instead of proceeding to the ranch, he took a narrow driveway that cut diagonally through pine trees and aspen to a house not nearly as unremarkable as Lydia had said. It was larger and more livable than Quinn's other. She must have been touched and amazed by the gift.

He climbed out of the car, and Hannah tentatively followed. At the locked front door, he searched for the key and found none. The back door was likewise locked, contrary to Lydia's assertions about the town. But he'd come prepared. From his wallet, he took a pick and worked it carefully until the lock released.

"How did you do that?" Hannah's awe was tinged with fear. Why would a holy man have that skill?

He lowered his chin, then gave Hannah a reluctant yet confidential look. "I don't tell many people this. In fact . . . I've never told anyone."

She fairly trembled with the honor and responsibility.

"My poor mother had a head injury. Often — I am sorry to say — she forgot I lived there, caring for her. The paranoia made her change the locks every time she suspected intruders, so learning to use lock picks helped both of us through a difficult time."

"Oh, Markham. What a hard, hard thing."

"It's in the hard things that God reveals himself."

Her eyes widened. "Is that when he called you?"

He couldn't have said it better. His face showed the radiance of her understanding.

Even so, she seemed hesitant to go inside. "Whose house is this?"

"It's Quinn's."

"But I thought —"

"Hannah." He smiled. "Don't trouble yourself." She was proving such an asset he actually felt affection. No one could doubt that Quinn would allow her mentally challenged sister a place to stay in her absence.

Taking her hands, he said, “Come,” and together, they went in.

Markham frowned. The house didn’t appear to be lived in. No mail addressed to a resident. No computer. Furniture but no basic living supplies, no books or magazines. The refrigerator and pantry were empty. If the house was Quinn’s, she hadn’t moved in.

Maybe that was timing. She’d fled Rick’s ranch, where she must have been staying until this one was ready. But just because she hadn’t come back yet, didn’t mean she wouldn’t.

He looked around the kitchen. The furnishings in the other rooms were new, but in here, one old cabinet had something inside. He tugged the antique knob. Locked. Through the milky glass he saw bottles of what could be medicine. A worthless antique, though it matched the rest of Quinn’s junk. Maybe he’d smash this, just for consistency.

Then he remembered Hannah and turned to find her quaking.

She said, “Why does Quinn have two houses?”

“She was moving from the other one to this. Someone bought this house and gave it to your sister.”

“Gave it to her?”

“Or is renting it. Who knows.”

“This one has furniture, but not really things.”

"Very observant, Hannah. I don't think she's moved in."

"Because she ran?"

"Apparently."

"But she'll come back?"

Now, that was a good question. "I think she might." Especially if he and Hannah laid low for a while. He went over to the sink and tried the water. Since they also had heat in this wintery place, her utilities must be on. Maybe she'd be back sooner than he'd thought. "In the meantime, we'll make good use of Quinn's *blessing*."

As he said the word, something stirred uncomfortably.

Sitting beside the wooden toy kitchen they'd bought to keep Livie out of Consuela's cabinets, Erin enjoyed watching her play. With the high-quality miniature cookware and educational food products, Livie had taken to it like a miniature chef. Extending the minute spatula, she offered a sample of her wares to pretend eat, emphasis on pretend.

"Mmm. Best I ever tasted."

Her phone rang, and Morgan's first words when she answered were, "Is Livie close?"

"Right next to me."

"May I speak with her?"

"Of course."

She put the phone on speaker and set it on

the miniature stove while daddy and child conversed in mildly frustrating spurts and pauses. When she heard her name, Erin took up the phone, brushed Livie's head, and wandered a small distance to talk. "How is the man who had surgery?"

"He's out of the woods. Thanks for asking."

"And everything else?"

"Denise wants to throw you a coming-out party."

"A what?"

He laughed. "She wants the world to know I've cast off my sackcloth and ashes and donned the wedding garments of the blissful and invincible success guru."

"I see." Although she didn't.

"Unfortunately, the timing of this press release is decidedly inopportune."

It all hit home. "Decidedly."

"The good news is, she thinks you're beneficial."

"I'm touched."

He chuckled. "As I knew you'd be."

"Consuela filled me in."

"As I knew she would."

"Why didn't Denise find Jill beneficial?"

"I think it ruined my international playboy image. You know, the enigmatic Bruce Wayne?"

"The Dark Knight." She slid her hair behind her ear. "That fits, you know."

"Not by my performance in our gym yesterday. All the *bams* and *pows* would be my face with stars around them."

"Well, the knight part anyway."

"Don't get sentimental. I have to stay focused. I just wanted to tell you, the *gardeners* will be back. With the reshuffling of my team, I could be gone all week."

"Our weekends are pretty awesome."

"Yeah." His voice thickened, and then he growled. "Now look what you've done. I'll have to force my head back to the game."

"You can do it, Caped Crusader. Go defeat the villains of the underworld."

"If only it were that easy." He gave a low sigh. "What are you taking on in my absence?"

She thought a moment. "How about asylum lore? I ought to find out if there's anything else I can tell RaeAnne."

"Ugh. Happy hunting."

"Thanks. I think."

After putting Livie to bed, Erin climbed into her own with the professor's tales. Maybe it wasn't wise to read alone in the dark, but it wouldn't happen at all with Morgan home. This time she went, as if drawn, to the Hauntings divider.

Taking a deep breath, she began with an account written by one of the asylum directors. The first thing the woman did was establish her credentials.

I am not doing this to prove my importance, but rather my sanity. Someone who has studied as I have and mastered many fields is not inclined to imaginative flights.

Quinn swallowed, pretty sure she wasn't going to like this imaginative flight, and too afraid she might recognize it.

What I will tell here was first brought to my attention by one whose veracity I had not judged entirely sound, so my response was unequivocal: "Do not speak of this again." In time I would see, whether spoken of or not, some things are what they are.

I have striven to resist any bias that attaches good and evil to any condition that brings a soul into our care. A defect in the mind is no punishment from God or whatever universal force may rule this world. But I have come to believe it might provide a channel by which evil may take form.

Herein you will find a recounting of not one, but many instances of this phenomenon that can be called by no other name than hauntings.

"Okay, I'm creeped out." She took her phone and called RaeAnne. It would only be nine o'clock central time.

"Hi, Quinn!"

"Is John Carter home?"

"Yes. Watching the football game or the after-show or something. Please, take me away."

"I'm reading the professor's file. The . . . Hauntings section."

"Oh my. Anything interesting?"

"I don't know. I'm too scared to read on."

"Want to read it together, like we did the journal?"

She half laughed. "Maybe that's why I called. Are you sure Vera never mentioned weird goings-on?"

RaeAnne thought. "No, I just can't remember anything like that."

"She must not have been susceptible."

"There was the hoarding."

Erin nodded. "I thought of that too. But lots of people do that, and she wasn't saving pet bones or anything."

"Weird you should say that. There was something about pets. Every time she tried to get one, it ran off."

"I've heard animals are perceptive."

"Well, let's hear it."

Erin picked up the paper-clipped sheets and read, " 'The first incident of my experience occurred on the heels of a darkly restive night.' "

"Quinn, I swear you should do voice-overs. You just put chills down my back."

She laughed. "I'm so glad you're doing this

with me. I'm putting chills down my own back."

The tale was more disturbing than scary, though. The patient, whom the director declined to name except as patient 1, had begun her therapy session as normal, then begun speaking in an altered voice and foreign language. " 'It was especially notable that patient 1 had no recollection of the event.' "

"That sounds demonic, Quinn. Are you telling me my mother's house is possessed?"

"I don't think places get possessed. Only repossessed."

"Thanks for the humor. But I'm serious. Did I sell Morgan one of those houses they show on TV where everyone runs out in the night and never goes back for their things?"

She quivered, recalling the menace in the cellar. "Will you think I'm crazy if I tell you I felt it?"

"No. But I'll think you're crazy if you ever set foot in there again."

"I never intend to."

"So tell me what happened."

She did.

"And neither Morgan nor the professor felt anything."

"No. But I'd spent quite a lot of time there by that point. Maybe it takes a while to make an impression."

"Maybe. Do you want to read some more?"

"Yes, but you don't have to listen."

"As long as John Carter's watching TV, I may as well."

"Okay, then." She raised the pages once again.

"Our janitor was a solid sort who applied himself to the job with methodical competence. When he came and stood before me, his face like chalk and one hand badly seared, I feared his recounting. He'd gone to the cellar, he said, to check the boiler. He'd been certain it had failed because the temperature in the cellar had dropped severely. Upon approaching it, however, he felt a great heat and was compelled to lay his hand upon it."

"Good heavens," RaeAnne cried.

"Or hell."

"My Lord," she breathed.

"Saying the name of Jesus lightened the oppression I felt. I didn't even realize what I was doing."

"Quinn, you are never, ever to go back there, and neither am I. When we go meet my dad, we'll find somewhere else to stay."

"I'm sure we could stay at Noelle and Rick's."

"That's right. You're family now. I still can't believe all that."

"I'm starting to."

"You should write *your* memoirs. They'd read like a romance novel."

She smiled, hoping it wouldn't be a jailhouse romance.

RaeAnne sighed. "John Carter's turned off the TV, so I guess I should go."

"Thanks for listening. Hope it wasn't too disturbing."

"I'm eight hundred miles away."

She was more than that, but looking at the pages after she hung up, it seemed that maybe alone wasn't a good way to read the notes after all.

Chapter 29

"You're not serious," Erin said with a pallor in her cheeks that shouldn't have been possible in the hot tub, even though he'd lowered the temperature to accommodate Livie.

"Oh, come on." The corners of his mouth pulled. "It's Christmas."

"At your parents'?"

"That's the tradition."

"Why can't we do it here? Or at Rick and Noelle's?"

"Because my mother birthed us."

"Not me," she muttered.

Bright red sand verbena and chaparral lotus scented the air around the tub without sweetening Erin's mood. He'd flown in just hours before, his part of Belcorp's rescue in the bag, his team in place and functioning. Relaxing now with the positional jets hitting just the right spots, he watched Livie paddling in her tiny life vest. Clearly his child was in paradise. His wife, not so much. "Rick and his family will be there."

"They like Rick's family."

"Erin."

She closed her eyes — probably imagining hours of inquisition and full-fledged shunning.

Maybe it wouldn't be the easiest time for her. But Livie needed it, and so, surprisingly, did he. "You're making this worse than it is. Relax."

"I'd rather face Markham and the FBI than your unhappy mother."

He grinned. "Celia's a warrior, I'll give you that. Like Old Testament Deborah. Fierce and faithful."

"It's the fierce part —"

He gripped her shoulder. "Just be yourself."

"And that would be?"

He thought a moment. "Ruth."

"Ruth?"

"Loyal. Devoted. Brave. She's listed in the lineage of Christ."

She cast him a perplexed look.

"What?"

"It surprises me you know these things."

"Thank the Jesuits."

She searched his face. "I can't reconcile that with . . ."

"My carnal nature?" He pulled a wry smile.

"Your Bruce Wayne."

He toyed with a strand of her hair. "What picture of heaven did Jesus present? A feast. A *wedding* feast. Or in this case" — he tapped her nose — "Christmas dinner."

She groaned. "That will not be heaven."

He pulled her legs across his and encircled her shoulders. "We're not leaving for several days and we'll only be there a week."

Livie leaned off one of the seats into the deeper water. "Look, Daddy. I a harbor seal. Look, Mommy Erin."

He turned with widened eyes. "When did that start?"

A smile softened Erin's face. "After the graveyard."

"Do you mind?"

"How could I?"

He stroked her cheek, then kissed her. She'd be just fine, wherever they spent Christmas or anything else.

As much as she had tried to pretend it wouldn't happen, it was. The moonscape of the earth below proof she was being carried irrevocably toward the dreaded holiday gathering she'd envisioned.

"We see Grammy?" Livie queried.

"Yep." Morgan cradled his daughter's head where she sat between them.

"We see Gramps."

"That's right."

"We see Mommy Noelle?"

"Yeah, sweetie." He smiled. "We'll see Auntie Noelle."

"We see Liam?"

"Liam and Uncle Rick and all your aunties."

Ruth, she thought. Your people shall be my people.

Their choppy landing fit her frame of mind, but there was no use pointing out the omen. Morgan didn't realize the calm seas he floated on were the eye of the hurricane. All the wind would be aimed at her.

When Rick arrived in his truck at the airport, she helped Morgan load their bags and gifts, along with half the house that had to be hauled when traveling with a child. She would have climbed in beside Livie's car seat, but the guys motioned her into the front, where she slid to the middle. Morgan rested his arm across her shoulders and asked Rick when they'd gotten in.

"Couple days ago."

"And the rest of the horde?"

"Present and accounted for." Rick glanced at her. "Ready for this?"

"I'm light on combat training."

"Aw, there won't be hostilities. You might get smothered, though."

Morgan tweaked her hair. "She's pretty sure Mom will swallow her whole."

Rick pulled into the traffic lane. "Celia's no dragon — unless you threaten her treasure."

"That would be her brood," Morgan added darkly.

The whirlwind of nerves kicked up to a

small tornado in Erin's stomach. With Celia's disapproval of their marriage, Christmas loomed like a Salem witch trial.

"Breathe," Morgan whispered in her ear.

Easy for him to say. He wasn't wearing the noose.

She had to admit the idyllic snow-covered farm shone like a Thomas Kincaid canvas — lanterns on the porch and barn, strings of icicle lights on the rooflines, and colorful Christmas bulbs draping shrubs and trees and pristine white fences. As Rick and Morgan grabbed armloads, she freed Livie from the car seat, murmuring, "We're here, sweetie."

The little girl squeezed her neck when the house door flew open and people piled out to the shoveled porch and path. Their combined greetings made clouds of white in the brisk twilit air.

Squealing, a high-school or college-age girl flung herself at Morgan, who dropped the portable crib and two bags to hug her.

"How could you!" she demanded. "How could you pull a Rick and get married without me?"

"Two words, Tara. Life happens."

"And in Paris!" Punching him, she made a noise of extreme frustration.

Morgan laughed. "I know. Insult on injury. But look —" he turned — "I brought my bride."

With Livie plastered to her like lichen on a rock, Erin took a step forward. As excited as the child had been to see them all, in this moment they shared a mutual apprehension.

"I'm Tara," the young woman said.

Erin freed a hand and offered it. "Erin."

With dark brown hair and indigo eyes in a heart-shaped face, Tara was stunning. "Guess you're madly in love with my brother. Everyone is. I spent nineteen years fending my friends off."

Morgan crooked a brow. "Since the day you were born?"

Tara didn't miss a step. "That pink bundle in the nursery beside me? I gave her a piece of my mind."

He gave a hearty laugh and hugged her shoulders.

Other young men and women crowded him, and in the doorway Hank and Celia appeared. Celia's attention slid off Morgan. It was undoubtedly Livie she was looking for, but as they were interconnected, the gaze landed squarely — and surprisingly softened. A clinging grandchild will do that.

"It's okay," Erin whispered in Livie's ear.

"Don't let go me." Livie's voice was small.

"I won't."

From the center of the melee Morgan assessed the situation but seemed to think she had it covered. She found his confidence questionable.

Tara circled around to Livie. "Hi, monkey. Remember me?"

"Hold me, Mommy Erin." Livie buried her face.

"It's a little overwhelming," she told Tara, and then Celia was there, pressing a kiss to Livie's head.

"Here's my little girl."

Livie transferred her hold, and Celia took over. "We'll be in the kitchen, Erin." The light touch on her shoulder could have been an invitation or dismissal.

Morgan took her hand. "Everyone, this is Erin. Erin, my sisters Tiff and Steph. You met Tara, and that's Therese over there with her husband, Stephen, and their twins." The twin boys looked about three.

"Don't know those two guys." He indicated the young men who appeared to be connected to Tiff and Steph. Luke and Danny introduced themselves.

Erin got handshakes and hugs, some more exuberant than others. Therese, who looked like Rick, seemed to reserve judgment, and Erin guessed she and Celia had close communication. Then Noelle came outside with Liam, and those hugs were heartfelt.

"Thank you for being here," Erin whispered.

Noelle squeezed her hands. "You look beautiful."

"I do?"

Noelle's smile glowed. "And happy."

Erin drew a shaky breath. "That part, yeah."

"Morgan even more."

Erin nodded, warmed again by what she felt for him.

Liam tugged her jean leg, and she crouched down. "Yes, Liam?"

"Where's Livie?"

"In the kitchen with your grandma."

"Come on." To her surprise, he took her hand and tugged.

She raised her brows to Noelle. "I guess we're going in."

As the family moved inside, Morgan moved with them. Watching Erin bear up reminded him of Thanksgiving, how she'd not only prepared the meal but celebrated it with four virtual strangers, with such good humor and compassion. She'd awakened dead feelings, feelings that now came as naturally and essentially as breath. He hoped his mother would see Erin's substance.

Not a harsh woman, Celia simply loved with a ferocious love, not cast in a broad net but endowed individually, unwaveringly. She needed to know the ones who mattered would not be injured. And if they were threatened, she made no excuses for her defense.

The house smelled of cinnamon and roast meat, probably his mother's pork chops with spiced apples. Her down-home cooking was different from Consuela's, hearty and nourishing without the sizzle. He moved into the family room, where the tree looked like a commercial lot specimen, more evenly shaped than the ones they'd cut themselves. Adorned in mostly homemade ornaments, its pine scent mingled with the kitchen aromas.

"You look good," his dad said.

Morgan nodded. "I am."

"Praise God."

"I am."

They shared a shoulder hug. Hank eyed him. "The marriage is working."

Working seemed an understatement. "It's working."

"Well, Morgan. You've never done things typically."

"Orthodox I'm not."

"You always land on your feet."

"This was a long drop."

Hank sobered. "I know it, son. For all of us."

Morgan nodded, looking around. Jill hadn't been a part of enough family gatherings that he saw her in everything, but a little of her lingered, especially the grief of last Christmas. He'd spent so much energy the past week encouraging Erin, he hadn't shored himself up.

Celia called her brood like the Little Red Hen who made no bones about who would share her bounty. Seating Erin, he checked her for damage. So far so good on that front.

She told Livie, "Fold your hands, sweetie." And when Livie's little voice joined in the blessing, he looked over. "We've been practicing," she said.

"I say grace, Daddy."

"I heard you, punkin. You were perfect."

When she beamed her chipmunk smile, he realized another tooth was coming in. Before he'd noticed every minute detail, his life in orbit so tightly around his child, she had her own gravity. Now Erin had done something with her he hadn't realized, and a physical — albeit tiny — change had escaped his notice.

"Morgan."

"Thanks." He took the bowl of mashed potatoes from Tiffany on his other side. He put some on his plate and Livie's and passed it on to Erin. A savory gravy followed, then Brussels sprouts and cauliflower. He doubted Livie would eat either but gave her a portion anyway. At the ends of the table, his parents each started a platter of pork chops that would be moist and tender and delicious.

Tara had commandeered Erin's other side and plied her with questions about Paris. Like Tiffany, the kid was a Francophile.

Erin said, "We were only there a day and a half."

"But you went shopping." Tara touched the sleeve of Erin's blouse, the layered vest. "I know this didn't come from Macy's."

"We went to some boutiques, but you'd have to ask Morgan where. It was a blur to me."

He let the names of the couturiers slide from his tongue, and Tara squealed. "I'm dead. You stabbed me through the heart."

He didn't tell her he planned an extended tour of France for her college graduation gift. Three years in the future would be painfully long for her to anticipate. Maybe his parents would consider a semester abroad for their youngest, but he doubted it. She was too impulsive, too driven by emotion, too much like their oldest son. He didn't think her small college had an overseas program anyway. He gave her an indulgent smile. Someday.

Seeing him across the table, Noelle hardly recognized Morgan. There was a lightness in him, as though the leaden grief had lifted. And Erin had a confidence and ease with him and Livie that was heartwarming to see. She'd been so worried about their rash marriage, but it had become this. What wondrous ways God had.

After the meal, Celia and Therese handled food storage, Tiffany and Tara cleared, and Steph loaded the dishes. Knowing they'd be extraneous, Noelle took Erin into the family room. "Have you settled into Santa Barbara?"

"Getting there. Morgan loves the place, and it's hard not to."

"I was afraid the memories . . ." She paused, not wanting to make Erin uncomfortable but imagining the awkwardness of Jill's shadow.

"Of course they're there. In the house. In his eyes." Erin looked into the fire, then back. "We went to Jill's grave."

She raised her brows. "He asked you to?"

"I asked him. I thought it would help both of them. Consuela came too. It rained."

"It rained at her funeral." She pictured them there, and the images overlapped, Morgan as gray as the rain, insubstantial as a ghost himself. "Did he grieve?"

"Yes."

"Thank God."

"Yes."

"How did Livie do?"

"Remarkably well. For such a tiny elf, she has amazing gravitas."

Noelle smiled. "I could say that about you. I don't think either of them would be doing too well out there on their own."

"Well, we've found a fit. I just hope it doesn't all blow up."

"You mean Markham?"

Her brow furrowed. "And the FBI."

"What?"

She listened, dismayed, as Erin explained. It was so much worse than she'd known.

"What does Morgan say?"

"He's hoping your father will keep me out of jail."

"Oh, good. I was going to suggest it, if he hadn't already asked."

"I don't know that he's asked. But he plans to. Morgan's going to interview a potential client in New York, and while he's out there he'll discuss my situation with your dad."

"You'll be in good hands."

Erin sighed. "It's so humiliating. What was I thinking?"

"You were only twenty-three."

"Still . . ."

Noelle pressed a hand to her mouth and laughed softly. "I wish I'd seen Morgan's face when you took off running."

"It was not fun when he pinned me to the ground and threatened wrestling moves."

Again she laughed.

Erin braced her hips. "You heard Markham. How would you like being accused of partnership with that rat?"

"It would be appalling." But then she sobered, picturing the woman in exactly that position. "I'm so sorry for your sister."

Erin's face fell. "I know. I think, maybe I should call, maybe try again to help her see. But I'm the last one she would listen to."

"Why is she like that?"

"I really don't know. I told you before she didn't accept my arrival. I guess it's worse than I even knew."

"Well, I'm very glad we're sisters now." She reached and Erin clasped her hands.

"You have no idea how glad I am."

Morgan gazed at them, aglow with firelight. Even though Noelle's beauty was epic, it was Erin's that caught him in the throat. He hadn't intended to love like this again. He knew the potential for loss, his fragile ability to prevent it. And yet like spring, it came, breaking through the frost.

He approached and hugged her from behind. "Surviving?"

She laughed. "So far."

He glanced at Noelle. "Thanks for guarding her flank."

"She holds her own."

That she did. "I came to say Hank and Rick and I are going out."

"Now?" Noelle raised her eyebrows.

"We're picking up something Hank didn't want around too early." He nodded his head toward the kitchen.

"Oh," the women said together.

He squeezed and released his wife. "Shouldn't be more than an hour."

"Okay."

As he started out, Livie ran in and hesitated, confused to find both Erin and Noelle. He crouched, scooped her up, and said, "Have a hug for Auntie Noelle?"

Livie lunged into Noelle's arms, tucking her head into the crook of her neck. She should have been Auntie all along, but he'd never planned on another mommy for her. Again the pang of love and fear. Maybe they'd always mingle. Maybe they always did. He walked out into the cold, frosty night.

Hank unlocked the truck and said, "I'll keep it in the barn until Christmas morning. But the Turners are leaving town so I have to get it tonight."

The new range and rotisserie oven would thrill Celia, who was eking every last breath from her old one. Rick climbed into the front, so Morgan got in next to Livie's car seat. He noted it with a jolt. What if she had an emergency? If they transported her unsecured — *Boom.* The pounding heart, the beading sweat, his airway constricted. How long had he gone without this?

"Wait, Dad." Forcing strength into his voice, he disconnected the base and carrier parts.

"Morgan?"

"Let me take this in." He hoisted the seat with slippery hands. Where could his daughter be safer than in the heart of this home on a still winter night? But the panic came hard, not driven by reason. He practically stumbled.

Erin met him at the door and grasped the seat. "Good thinking," she said, ignoring his shaking hands. Her eyes reflected him, pale and terrified, but she leaned over the carrier and kissed him. "She'll be safe."

Their gazes locked. He took her assurance like a drug. "Thanks."

From the first attack she'd witnessed at Vera's, her nonjudgmental, sometimes humorous responses were more of a tonic than any sedative. His shoulders relaxed. His hands released the seat. Panic subsiding, he went out.

Setting the car seat by the door, Erin turned and saw Celia in the entrance to the dining room. "He's leaving the seat for Livie, just in case. Is this okay?" She indicated its position by the door.

"That's fine."

She started back to Noelle and Livie, but Celia said, "Would you have tea with me?"

No. Thanks. Really. "Sure." She turned to Noelle. "Are you . . ."

"We're fine. Go ahead." She settled into a chair and lifted a children's book from the table. Liam must have been somewhere with his cousins, and Livie would like alone time with the woman she still missed.

Erin entered Celia's lair. The scents of dinner had been replaced by the steamy, soapy scent of the dishwasher, the water whooshing inside.

"I already heated the kettle," Celia told her.

"I have a loose-leaf British tea, or would you prefer a caffeine-free herbal?"

"Herbal's probably better before bed."

Celia held out a basket with choices. Erin fingered through them and selected chamomile, which she didn't really like but hoped would work its calming magic. Celia prepared and handed her a mug, then motioned her to a seat at the kitchen table. Erin breathed the steam, willing the herb to dull her senses.

"Would you like anything to sweeten that?"

"Nope. Thanks."

Celia took her seat on another well-worn wooden chair. Her cup released a matching scent of chamomile. Calming her own nerves? Holding the tag, Celia gently swished the bag in her mug, and said, "I haven't seen the Morgan at the table tonight in many, many years."

Confused, Erin said, "I thought he always came for Christmas."

"Not always." Celia looked up. "But I didn't mean he wasn't present. Although essentially that's true. Tonight he looked the way he used to when everything was possible."

Erin removed the tea bag and set it on the holder. Celia must have seen him with Jill, happy at last to have the woman he'd longed for.

"You're thinking of Jill."

Erin raised her eyes, startled.

"Jill was a warm and caring woman, but what they went through in high school, and all those years later with Kelsey, impacted everything." Celia sighed. "With time, they might have overcome it."

"They didn't have enough," Erin murmured, raising her cup. Steam dampened her nose and lip as she carefully tested the temperature.

"A year and a half" — Celia sat back in her chair — "of brittle love."

Though not spoken harshly, the descriptor still grated.

"A dream," Celia said, "they'd held on to because they didn't know what else to do."

"It survived fifteen years of separation." How could she not see the power in that?

"Much of what they had," Celia said gently, "was what they imagined they might have had."

Erin didn't want to contradict, but she'd sat in Jill's room, seen the pictures of their life. Yet snapshots couldn't show it all. And maybe losing the potential could hurt as much as losing Jill.

"It's a terrible loss. I'm not minimizing it." Celia set her cup aside. "But what I saw just now, what passed between you and Morgan at the door, the way you took his fear inside yourself, the way he let you . . . That's something not even I can do."

Her heart quickened.

"I want you to know" — Celia reached over and squeezed her hand — "this family is blessed to have you."

Amazed, Erin blinked back tears. "I'm blessed to have you."

Chapter 30

Hannah would not stop crying. Even though they were far more comfortable and she should be content, from the time they'd moved into Quinn's other house, his every move, every word made her cry. It corroded his self-control until ungodly thoughts filled his mind. Biting, cutting words caught in his mouth. He held them back, and still she cried.

"It's almost Christmas. I've never spent Christmas without my family," Hannah sobbed.

He paced the living room. *Stop it. Stop it. Stop her.*

"My mother needs me. She's calling every day."

Take the phone. Break it. Smash it. Smash her.

He couldn't. He needed her. If anything could make Quinn come, it would be her poor, poor sister.

"Oh, Markham," she wailed. "Just for

Christmas."

Only one thing would make that happen. "Will Quinn go home for Christmas?"

Her eyes widened. "I don't know. Maybe."

"Did she last year?"

Hannah shook her head.

"The year before?"

"Not since she went away. No one's seen her since she left."

"Then why would we go?"

She burst into fresh tears.

He shot a burning glance into the kitchen. Saw the cabinet. Maybe there was something, something to make her sleep. *Make her stop, make her sleep, make her stop.*

He walked stiffly in, tugged the knob. Locked, still locked. Moving as though something else animated his arms, he gripped a chair and drove the ladder-back knob through a milky pane of glass. Hannah shrieked. *Make her sleep, make her stop.*

Reaching through the hole, he cut his arm. Blood pearled and streamed. He grabbed a bottle, a teeny tiny bottle. He read the label, one part standing out. LSD. *Yes . . .*

Standing on the large wraparound porch with a mug of hot chocolate braced between her gloved hands, Erin swelled with gratitude. All the Spencers, plus three spouses, four grandchildren, and two significant relationships had stretched the Spencer hospitality to breaking. Squeezed with Morgan in the music room's sofa sleeper, Livie's portable crib right beside them, and surrounded by all the other guests and family, last night had felt like Livie's storybook about a mitten stuffed with so many animals the seams finally popped.

But gazing through the lacy icicles jeweling the eaves and banisters, to snow-covered shrubs and laden tree boughs, snowfields stretching to an icy pond rimmed in sugared cattails, she thanked God Morgan hadn't given in to her concerns and stayed in Santa Barbara. How could it feel like Christmas on the beach with soft sand and gulls? Although she supposed they'd make it Christmas wherever they were.

Sipping her chocolate, she looked toward the large white-and-gray stable and saw a man with a horse. Morgan. With a dim concern starting inside, she lowered the mug to the rail. He approached sedately, leading an animal larger than himself with no more than a word and a rein.

Six feet from the porch, he stopped. From her raised viewpoint, it seemed she looked eye to eye at the horse, a brown mare with a white blaze, two white socks, and a black-tipped tail.

She dragged her gaze to Morgan and made herself speak calmly. "I know you mean well."

He smiled. "Come here."

"I'm over it, Morgan. I can appreciate horses from a distance. They're lovely."

"Erin."

Stuck to the porch by the same sand that had held her frozen before, she chewed her upper lip. He held out his hand. No, no, no, no, no. His draw was irresistible. Her feet moved. Leaving the cocoa on the rail, she took one step down, then another. The horse grew taller.

She said, "I'm just not . . ."

"Sure you are."

She reached the snowy path and paused, eyeing the horse. It didn't stomp. But it could. Didn't toss its head. Though it might.

"She's very well behaved." He reached farther and caught her fingertips.

Heart tripping, she eased her hand into his. "What's her name?"

"Maple Sugar."

"Maple for short?" Her voice cracked.

He drew her to his side. "Stroke her neck. She likes that."

Her hand no longer obeyed her brain. It was connected to his voice. Maple's hide was smooth but not soft, her mane thick with stiff strands. Disney princess eyelashes framed her large, gentle eyes angled to take in the stranger making contact. Morgan brushed his hand down the mare's long bony face, patting her cheek and stroking the velvety nose.

Erin looked into his face, imagining the boy who'd told the stockman he belonged to himself. It wasn't true. More than anyone she'd ever known, Morgan belonged to everyone. She touched the mare again, feeling her warmth, the solid mass of her, the patience. Breathing the horsey scent, she put both hands on the mare, letting that satisfaction flow into her.

Morgan watched without speaking. She slid her hand to the horse's face, drew it down to the soft, soft muzzle. As a child she'd imagined kissing such a nose, imagined jumping astride and riding like a shooting star through the sky — dreams crushed by fear and an object lesson.

"Put your left foot in the stirrup," Morgan said.

He couldn't be talking to her.

"Take hold of the pommel and pull yourself up."

She took a step back, and there was his hand against her spine, steadying her.

"You can do it."

"I don't want to. Really. I'm over it." The mare slow-blinked.

"Hold this." He pressed the leather reins into her hand. Stepping around her, he gripped the saddle and swung up behind it, settling easily astride. It seemed as though he and the horse had joined forces. Bending, he took the reins and held them to the far side of the mare, who stood calmly as though nothing had changed.

"Left foot in the stirrup."

She closed her eyes.

"Swing yourself up. I'll catch you."

Her chest quaked as she stretched one shaky hand to the pommel. She raised and tucked her foot into the stirrup. Pushing up, she felt Morgan guide her leg over as she landed in the seat of the saddle.

"Tuck the other foot into the stirrup."

She opened her eyes to find it. With his arms on either side of her, he touched the reins to the horse's neck, turning the mare slowly. She held her breath, getting used to the strange sensation of an animal bearing her and praying Morgan knew what he was doing.

Except for the time she'd seen him care for Rick's stock, she'd never thought of him as a horseman. Now she realized he'd grown up on this farm, and even if it hadn't become his career, it was part of him. Slowly her spine relaxed. Morgan brushed a kiss on her jaw, speaking no other encouragement. She needed none.

At first she thought they'd go to the stable and be done. Instead, they rode toward the pond, the still morning spreading out around them, hooves muffled by snow. Clouds puffed from the mare's nostrils. Morgan sat solid, and yet fluidly, behind her, guiding the horse by almost imperceptible means.

After a while he murmured, "What do you think?"

"It's wonderful."

He tightened his arms. "Couldn't let anything hold you back."

"I'm supposed to be careful what I wish for."

"What could you wish for that you shouldn't have?"

She sank back into him. "I love you."

"I know." He laughed softly in her ear.

"Is it crazy?"

"Yeah. But inevitable. I swear I fell in love before you served the pumpkin pie."

Her heart swelled. "Do you think Rudy knew?"

"He saw it flashing like a neon sign." Morgan eased the mare down and up a narrow ditch.

"Were you really afraid for me to leave, or was that strategy?"

"I really did panic. But having you there opened something inside me. It was like that skeleton key hidden away until one day it turns a whole new lock."

"You do recall that lock secured dangerous illegal drugs."

She felt him stiffen and said, "What?"

"I just realized we never took care of that. I was going to when you came and dragged me off to Paris."

She giggled. "Like that took dragging. I think you meant it when you proposed. Or you could have handled it like Denise and who knows how many others."

He was quiet so long, she turned in the saddle. "What?"

"It's just sinking in that you're right. Rick told me to offer a job, but I didn't want that. I tried to meld the two into that ungainly proposal, but once the vows were spoken, I couldn't pretend."

She sank back against him. He'd called it preordained. "God made this happen for us, didn't he."

"Seems that way."

"That's . . . amazing."

He tightened his arm around her. "Yeah."

They rode in silence until he circled the mare back around toward the farm.

"We're going in?"

"This being your first time on a horse, if you sit too long, you'll get sore. These haunches aren't feeling any too good to me either."

"Oh."

"Don't worry. You'll have other chances. As I said, Livie needs a horse, and you may as well be able to mount up with her. I might look around for a nice spread with an ocean view somewhere in the Santa Ynez Mountains or the hills of Montecito. Get some champion stock — Andalusian, maybe."

"And sell your wonderful home? Why?"

He pressed his cheek to her head. "I don't know. Maybe that's who I was. Who I tried to be with Jill. But it's us now, and you were a girl who wanted a horse."

Listening around the words, she guessed it wasn't as much about a horse as it was about them. A new vision. Their own prototype.

Back at the house, she slid off awkwardly and let Morgan stable the mare.

Tara leaned on the porch railing. "First time riding?"

"Is it that obvious?"

Tara flashed her perfect white teeth. "Everyone starts sometime."

"I suppose you were about two."

"Eight months. As soon as I could sit up without falling over."

Erin gaped. "That's crazy."

"Mom's a believer in natural instincts. The sooner a girl bonds with a horse the better."

She was rapidly re-envisioning Celia, and realizing how different this family was from hers.

"Just get a good instructor. You'll catch up."

As Erin climbed the steps, Tara took in her jeans and fitted coat, Hermes silk scarf, mohair hat, and mittens. "Paris again?"

"I'm afraid everything I have is Parisian."

"Everything?"

"The clothes I had before got . . . lost."

"Lost?" Tara crooked a brow in an expression very like one of Morgan's.

"Someone broke into my house and trashed everything."

"That's horrible! Who do people think they are?"

She knew exactly who Markham thought himself.

"I'm always afraid someone will break into my dorm, but it has security doors, and it's a small school." She crossed her fingers. "So here's hoping."

"What are you studying?" Erin picked up her deserted mug of chocolate. The skin at the top was starting to freeze.

"Well, everything, since I'm a sophomore. Core subjects, you know. But I want to major in theater, and if I don't become a famous film star, then I'll teach musical theater to underprivileged kids."

Erin smiled. "Two good alternatives." Tara had the beauty for film but seemed too pure for that industry.

"Polar opposites, I know. Fame and riches or penniless service."

Amused by the dramatic tone, Erin said, "Musical theater must mean your talent is broad."

"Acting, singing, dancing. Noelle taught me piano — for a little while — and then I had to take regular lessons. You'll hear me tonight. Everyone, actually."

"Everyone plays piano?"

"Different instruments or singing. Everyone performs something for the talent show. It's the rule."

A rule no one — most notably Morgan — thought to mention. "I can barely hold a tune."

"Nuh-uh. I heard you singing to Livie."

Now, that was an idea. Partner with Livie and let her steal the show. "Speaking of Livie, I better go see how she's holding up with those rowdy boys."

"Grammy's watching."

"Your mom might be more than ready for a break, especially since she's trying to bake."

"Okay." Tara pushed off the rail and bounded down the steps. "See you."

Erin carried the remains of her cocoa to the kitchen and set the mug down. Livie's rush into her arms warmed her heart — and Celia's apparently, no doubt relieved that not only Morgan but his little angel had opened to her. "How you doing, sweetie?"

"I doing great. Want to play animals?"

Noting the big-girl version of the question, she felt a tiny pang of loss. "Are there some?"

"Soft ones with bean stuffing."

"Well . . ." She cocked her head. "Do they talk?"

"They do talk!" she insisted, tugging.

Erin sent Celia a smile before settling in at the toy box, where she entertained herself as thoroughly as Livie. Every now and then the boys barged in, their attention and energy wholly different and overwhelming. She laughed when all three "captured" her, tumbling on like a munchkin football team.

When Livie joined in, Erin fought back with tickling until Morgan and the other men came in. Perceiving rescue, she collapsed onto her back, arms outstretched as the various dads complied. Morgan extended a hand and got her to her feet. "I leave you alone for a minute . . ."

She planted her hands on her hips. "You have some *'splainin'* to do."

He crooked an eyebrow.

"The matter of a talent show?"

He tipped his head in mock compassion. "No talent?"

"Maybe not." She narrowed her eyes. "But I have a secret plan."

He laughed. "Of course you do."

Markham sat up on the kitchen floor with a slight itching pain from the cut on his arm. He looked up at the broken pane on the cabinet door, remembered reaching in. Beside him, a tiny glass vial had rolled up against the foot of the cabinet. He remembered breaking it open. He'd intended it for Hannah, but the liquid spilled on his hand, down his wrist, and into the cut.

Dizzy and restless, he'd staggered around the kitchen, Hannah wailing in the other room. Or maybe it hadn't been Hannah. It had seemed like a multitude.

He remembered sinking to the floor in a wonderful intoxication, his stimulated mind bursting with fantastic shapes and kaleidoscopic colors. But then everything he saw began to waver and stretch, distorting in horrifying parodies of themselves, Hannah's face twisting and morphing monstrously.

He couldn't move. He'd felt paralyzed, glued to the floor, while the cabinet loomed and threatened to fall on his head. Screaming beside it, Hannah became a witch with green brushy hair and a mouth as wide as a door.

He'd shut his eyes and kept them shut, losing all sense of time, unable to tell how long the horror lasted before the colors returned, alternating, spiraling in and out, exploding fireworks of color. Every sound transformed the vision, creating a new and wondrous landscape, until at last exhaustion brought sleep.

Now, when it seemed he should have felt a dreadful aftermath, he woke refreshed, clearheaded, as he hadn't been for days. A euphoric sense of renewal and well-being brought him to his feet.

Seeing Hannah asleep on the couch, her face puffy and streaked red from distress, he rushed in and dropped to his knees beside her. "Hannah."

Her eyes flew open. "You're awake!"

"Of course I am."

"I tried and tried to wake you."

"It's all right. Everything's all right. It's wonderful."

"It is?"

"Yes, don't you see? It's all going to work. I saw it."

"In a vision?"

"Oh, Hannah. Such a vision."

Her eyes pooled. "Then we can go home? For Christmas, Markham?"

For a moment the exhilaration dimmed. "You know what I have to do, Hannah. It hasn't changed."

Her face fell. "Isn't it enough to forgive her in your heart? You don't have to tell her face-to-face. God knows."

"Of course God knows." His mind still seemed accelerated and fresh — brilliant even. "But Quinn will have no peace. Quinn can't go home until I have forgiven her. She'll keep running and running. Only I can stop her. Only I can give her peace." And deep eternal rest.

Hannah sank into the couch and said in a tiny voice, "It's always about Quinn."

"Hannah." He clasped her hand between his. "How can we begin anew with this Sword of Damocles over my head?"

"Sword of —"

"Never mind." He stared into her bloodshot eyes, her red swollen nose, her splotchy cheeks. Unable to hate her, he wondered if what she wanted might be good. Quinn had changed her number, and no one Hannah asked admitted having the new one, but might she not call at Christmas? If they were there together, if he announced his desire to marry their daughter, their simple daughter . . .

"All right, Hannah. For you, we'll go home for Christmas."

Her whole body shook. "Do you mean it?"

"I do. We'll go right now."

She jumped to her feet, hands clutched beneath her chin. "Oh, Markham!"

As she ran to gather her things, he imagined finding Quinn and all the money she'd stolen and all the money he might add to it from Morgan Spencer and the life it would buy him. No more cons, no more being what someone else wanted, only what he wanted. Enough money to be nothing at all, or even . . . himself.

He had to make that happen. But how? And then he saw the door behind the hutch.

Chapter 31

One of these days they would need to move the baby grand to the family room for the holiday talent show, but so far they fit. Barely. Morgan looked around the music room. Stephen had been through the drill several times, but it was new for Luke and Danny. And for Erin.

His parents started with a duet to break the ice, then Noelle played something exquisite from memory that made Tara groan with envy. So, of course, she brought the house down with her "Santa Baby" on Hank's knee. The world had better prepare itself for his baby sister, Tara.

Morgan motioned her to the piano to accompany him singing "I Want a Hippopotamus for Christmas" to Livie. And for Erin it had to be "All I Want for Christmas is You."

It was embarrassing to see the tears in his family's eyes, but he didn't care. He'd fallen in love with a woman like no one else —

except maybe Livie. Bright spirits, both of them.

Dabbing her eyes, Erin scooped Livie up and took his place on the tall stool. She detached the microphone — feeding their talent to the computer for posterity — from the stand and said, "This isn't a Christmas tune, but I don't think anyone will mind." She held the mic to Livie's mouth and whispered something.

His heart swelled when his little girl, with gentle promptings from Erin, sang the song he'd sung to her since the day she was born. "You are my sunshine, my only sunshine."

When the last sweet "please don't take my sunshine away" faded, applause filled the room. Erin hung the mic, lifted Livie, and moved back toward her place. Unfortunately for his wife, everyone started chanting, "Erin, Erin, Erin." So much for her secret plan.

She shot him an ocular plea. Laughing, he drew her back to the mic, whispered in her ear, and when she nodded, told their choice to Steph, who'd taken Tara's place at the piano. Together he and Erin sang "I Saw Mommy Kissing Santa Claus." At the end, he gave a thorough demonstration, to laughter, boos, and hisses.

Coming back up, he saw Noelle crying. She had doubted, but she must realize now that the radical proposal she so opposed had saved his life.

After a midnight celebration of the Savior's birth and a few hours' sleep, they all packed into the family room around the tree. Caught in the crush, he cocked his head at Erin. "What?"

"Are you kidding? This has to break every fire code known to man."

The rooms of his parents' old-style farmhouse were boxy and small, but the tree had always occupied the family room corner, and what did it matter if some of the young guys had to stand and most of the girls were on the floor? Pressed into the lower branches with Livie between his knees, he had Erin almost in his lap as well. Sure, it was snug, but who cared?

Although it seemed chaos reigned, in fact the activity had time-honored order, alternating youngest to oldest or oldest to youngest, with time to see each gift opened before the next. Purchasing small, as opposed to ungainly, gifts had entered the tradition as the family grew and space diminished. Hank's present to Celia this year broke that rule — as would what Erin received. While not overly large, ungainly certainly applied.

They'd made the rotation several times when the doorbell rang. People looked around until Morgan nodded at Danny. "Can you get that?" No way was he getting through to answer it himself.

A couple minutes later, Danny returned

with a very round woman holding a half-grown Australian shepherd with worried eyes staring and shaggy legs dangling. Erin's jaw fell slack as Morgan slid her a glance. "You said you were thinking of getting a dog."

"Morgan," she breathed.

"That blue merle on her coat was as close as I could get to bluetick, but the breed's instincts are good for herding and guarding, both of which you seem to need."

"That doggie mine, Daddy?"

"That doggie is Mommy's, Livie." *Mommy's.* He'd said it without thought.

"Well, clear a way," Cleo from the shelter told them and proceeded through to settle the animal in Erin's lap. "She had a good home until her companion changed jobs and moved to a city apartment. Broke her heart to let Bella go, but that's no way for this active breed to live." Cleo looked into Erin's eyes. "You'll love her, won't you, dear?"

Erin stroked the soft fur as Bella licked her hand. "I already do."

As the crowd was a little intense for the animal, Erin carried her out to the kitchen. He followed with Livie, who was expressing in her charming way how the doggy was hers *and* Mommy's. She'd seemingly transitioned into the term as automatically as he.

Erin set Bella on the floor and filled a bowl with water. He'd contacted Cleo a week ago, describing what he wanted. They'd agreed on

Bella since she hadn't been mistreated, and with Livie that was essential. An animal that knew pain and cruelty could misinterpret a child's innocent mistakes.

Now when Erin and his little girl went down to the beach or off on walks, there'd be someone keeping watch all the times he couldn't be there. At five months, according to Cleo, Bella already showed the instincts of her breed. When Livie could stand it no longer, she buried her face in Bella's side. Bella turned and licked Livie's cheeks with a dripping muzzle fresh from the water bowl. Yeah. Morgan laughed. This would work.

"I can't believe you did this." Erin looked into the sweet, sweet face of the worried young dog, trying to give what comfort she could. "How did you know I thought about getting one?"

"Noelle mentioned you might bring a dog on Thanksgiving." He shrugged. "Then you didn't."

"I checked the shelter, but it was especially for damaged animals, and my situation had the potential for unrest." As, she had to remind herself, it still did.

He crouched down. "Hey, Bella. Don't look so worried. You're going to be just fine with us." He scrubbed his fingers through the fur behind her ears. Bella grinned.

Watching them, Erin screwed up her courage. "I haven't given you my gift."

He looked over his shoulder toward the family room. "We'll never get our places back."

"It isn't under the tree." She ducked into the music room, where they were staying, took the small package she had just wrapped, and brought it to him. "It's hard to know what to give the man who can get everything."

He sat back on his heels. "Somehow I think you've managed."

She chewed her lip as he stood up, untied the ribbon, and untaped the paper. From it, he withdrew the plastic stick with the blue plus sign. She watched the realization dawn. His eyes found hers.

She shrugged a shoulder. "Paris has that effect."

Letting out a whoop that sent Bella to the corner of the kitchen, he grabbed her so hard she didn't try to breathe until her feet came back down to the floor.

"Daddy, why you crying?"

"It's okay, Livie. It's okay, Bella." His assurance came hoarsely. "Erin, Erin . . ." He pressed his face to her neck, squeezing her again.

She held him just as hard, only now absorbing her own reality. He kept breathing "I love you" into her hair. She held him laughing and crying until she realized his holler had brought the others. She bent and scooped

Livie up as they pressed in, Tara leading the charge.

"What? Tell us."

Again Morgan held her eyes. "There are no secrets." He held up the wand.

"You're pregnant?" Noelle blurted.

Rick laughed. "Nothing like jumping in with both feet."

Erin turned, worried until she saw Steph had knelt beside the dog, gently stroking and reassuring her. Then she gave herself up to the congratulations.

When they'd all cleared out again, taking Livie and even Bella, Morgan threaded her fingers with his. "How are you?"

"Fine. So far."

"What made you take the test?"

"After we talked I realized I was late. I only took it this morning so we'd know at almost the same time." She'd never have hidden it otherwise. "There are sunglasses under the tree, in case it was negative. Livie pulled the earpiece off your Oakley's."

Grinning, he rubbed his hand up and down her arm. "Both thoughtful gifts. Thank you." His eyes creased deeply. "It's great we were here to share the news. They've gone through a lot with me. This . . . this is extraordinary."

That seemed too little a word for it.

"You know, Erin." His voice softened. "Something like this, your family should know."

Tears burned. He had to know how much she wanted to share it, to tell her mother, Pops, her father, even Hannah. She was having a baby. And they didn't even know about Morgan.

"How can I? They'll get my number, and if it gets to Hannah it will get to Markham and we'll start all over again."

"In a couple days I'll be taking what you know to William. Once he works the deal, the FBI will step it up on Markham. He'll have more to worry about than getting back at you."

She considered that. The phone wasn't in her name, or even Morgan's, only his company. And if Markham got it, she could change the number. "If I tell them I'm pregnant, I have to tell them about you."

"Fine. Just no names."

She pressed a hand to her heart, fear warring with longing. She couldn't bring herself to dial her parents. No, if she could tell one person in the world, it had to be Pops. It was Christmas, and hearing his voice would be such a gift. She looked into Morgan's eyes and said, "Pops can't stand Markham. He'd never help him find me."

"Tell him Merry Christmas from me." He bent and kissed her.

Trembling as much with concern as excitement, she keyed the number. When her grandpa's voice came on, her chest swelled with tears. "Pops? It's . . . Quinn."

"Quinn, darlin'. It's been so long."

"I know. I'm sorry." Sorry for time she'd never get back — time that, at ninety-one, her grandfather might have little of. She caught a tear in the corner of her eye. "Pops? I have some news."

Hannah looked almost pretty. No, Hannah did look pretty in her Christmas dress, with her hair done up and her face aglow.

Standing in the family room of her father's house, Markham watched her, amazed, as she shared the wonderful news in a buoyant voice with none of the tremulous hesitation. For the first time in her life, she had something worth sharing and shared it proudly. "Markham and I are going to be married."

"With your permission, sir. I apologize for not asking first, but . . ." He waved a hand at Hannah as though she were explanation enough. He cleared his throat. "Hannah's faith and devotion humble me."

With a strange feeling in his stomach, he recognized in Hannah a belief no one else had ever placed in him. Hundreds had been swayed to belief by his act, by his lies, by his cons, but no one had believed *in him.* Crazily, he imagined himself married to her. Did he have something with her he would never find again?

The minister looked at him with mingled

sorrow and joy, probably thinking of how his people had suffered from the loss of their retirement funds, the loss of their great hypothetical riches, the loss of hope. Did he believe, as he'd testified, that Markham Wilder acted in good faith, believing a miracle of abundance would come to those who gave generously from the heart? Or would he condemn him now?

Markham bowed his head. "I pray you'll consider my request. I've been tempered by trials in the furnace of tribulation and emerged chastened and stripped of all worldly hopes but one. This one I set before you — more, I know, than I deserve." His gaze slid briefly to Hannah's tearful face, still amazingly lovely. Why had she never adorned it with joy before?

Thomas Reilly turned to Hannah, his face concerned and tender. "Hannah?"

"Oh yes. I want this." The tremulous tone returned, but for once it touched him.

Thomas held her aching eyes with wells of kindness in his own as he told her, "Markham may not be embraced by the others, by those who struggle now or are financially ruined. You could be shut out."

"It was Quinn who did that, Daddy. By her unbelief. Quinn not Markham who brought ruin. Markham paid the price, and he only wants to forgive her, Daddy."

The minister's wife came and stood in the

doorway between the family room and kitchen. Four years had aged her, and he wondered briefly if it was true, as Hannah said, that Quinn had not been home and had spoken to them only a handful of times in those years. He forced all rage and animosity from himself as he thought of her. Nothing must mar this moment.

"You're younger than Hannah, Markham," the minister said. "In fact, I expected it would be Quinn who caught your interest."

Did he see the effect his words had on his daughter?

"And yet you've recognized the purity of Hannah's spirit," the man continued. "That speaks to the character I saw in you, the trust I placed in you." His gaze went soft as cream, landing on Hannah.

The man loved his daughter, but Markham wondered if he understood either of the women he'd fathered.

"Markham, I give you Hannah's hand and my blessing. I call you son."

His wife's eyes closed as she lowered her face, gathered herself, and found a smile for her daughter. Hannah rushed into her arms. "Oh, Mama. It's the best Christmas ever!"

A loud banging at the door interrupted them. Thomas moved to answer, pulling the door open with surprise. "Da." The minister's voice was clipped.

"Merry Christmas, son, Hannah, Gwen."

Markham held himself stiffly. Seeing him, the old man's face purpled. Markham returned the scowl. He'd expected no less from the man, but his fury was hot and immediate.

"What's this?" Corlin Reilly gaped at his son, a storm on his brow. "You'd have this felon here and not your own girl? What's wrong with you?"

"Not now, Da. As always, your timing is terrible."

"My timing, is it? Do you know your daughter's married? She's having a babe."

The room fell silent, all but the rushing in Markham's ears. Hannah shriveled in her mother's arms. Gwen's face clouded and shone and clouded again.

Thomas drew himself up. "It does not surprise me that Quinn, named by you, married and conceived — if it was in that order — with neither my knowledge nor my blessing."

It didn't surprise, but it saddened the man. Markham saw it come over him like a heavy cloak, bowing his shoulders. Did he love his troublesome daughter, even after what she'd done?

"My . . . other daughter, my Hannah . . ." his voice rasped, "will also be married, and Markham has asked and received my blessing."

Corlin's eyes widened. "This . . . is God

laughing at me. To blind my son with such piety he lies down with fools and liars."

For that, the man would die.

"Watch your tongue, Da. You'll not insult Markham in my home."

"Markham, is it? Were you born with that name, man? Or is it yet another mask you pull over your true face?" Turning once again on his son, he dug the phone from his pocket. "Call Quinn. Tell her to come home. To bring this husband of hers for your *blessing.*"

Thomas stood rigidly, his spine a testament to resistance. "My daughter knows where to find me."

"Aye." Corlin cocked his head back. "But why would she?" He shoved his phone into his pocket, turned with one last glare, and left.

Standing in the yard while Bella sniffed out the most special spot to relieve herself, Erin almost jumped out of her skin when her phone rang. Her nerves had been live wires since calling Pops, but she exhaled with relief and delight when she saw who was calling. "Merry Christmas, RaeAnne."

"And to you, Quinn. I couldn't let the day go by without wishing you a great one. How's that peach Morgan?"

Erin laughed. "I can't wait to call him a peach."

"You sound happy, even happier than last time."

"Well, I'm in love. And we're having a baby."

"Oh . . . my . . . *goodness,*" RaeAnne screamed. "Congratulations! With my busy job and then John Carter's taking him away all the time, we never really made that work, but I'm just as happy as can be for you."

Maybe it was hearing RaeAnne's voice or something in the words, but Erin suddenly imagined Vera, pregnant, with the love of her life walking out. No wonder the woman never said his name again. No wonder she hid the journal where it would be forgotten and stuffed the locket in a mousehole. That wasn't crazy, it was just sad.

"Quinn?"

"I'm sorry, I . . ." She cleared the emotion from her voice. "RaeAnne, I'm wondering if we did the right thing, reading the journal, learning who your dad is. I'm not sure Vera wanted that."

"I'm sure she didn't." RaeAnne sobered. "But I'm in this too." Emotion came thickly through the phone. "You know how many Christmases I spent wondering what my dad would have given me? I even made him presents in school. In case that was the year he'd show up."

"Oh, RaeAnne."

"My mother couldn't keep him in real life,

but where I was concerned, she kept him all to herself."

She hadn't thought of it that way.

"Maybe he didn't want me. Or maybe he didn't have the chance. But all these years later, I still want him. Or the possibility of him." RaeAnne sniffled. "The truth is, not having him, not understanding what happened between them, is the real reason I don't have kids. I couldn't see how to do it right when I didn't understand what went so wrong."

Erin closed her eyes, getting it so deeply it hurt. "We'll do it, then. Just as soon as we can."

"You're situation's still messy?"

"Close to a solution, I pray."

"Me too, sugar. And, Quinn . . . ? I am *so* happy for you and Morgan. And the baby. Don't let anything get in the way."

"I won't." If she could help it.

Disconnecting, she continued to the stable, where Rick had guessed she'd find Noelle. With Bella curiously sniffing everything, she went inside. It smelled sweet with hay and looked as clean and orderly as Rick and Noelle's, everything in its place, tended and tidy. She felt the wholesomeness and understood how people loved the rural life. Maybe it touched that old desire for a horse of her own, though now she also understood why her father didn't want to take it on. If only he hadn't left her afraid.

At one of the end stalls, Noelle ran her hand over a stately horse's jet-black cheek, talking sweetly, as if she didn't get enough horse time at home. In the last month, she'd started to show but still stood tall and slender, her hair a silky veil over her shoulders. It slid to the side when she turned her head and smiled. "Lots of excitement this morning."

Erin smiled back. "I expected Morgan to be happy but hadn't anticipated quite that enthusiasm."

Noelle's eyes warmed. "No one's crazy for babies like Morgan. Oh!"

"What?"

"Put your hand here."

Erin pressed her hand on Noelle's sweater and felt a tiny flick. She drew in her breath. "Was that —"

"It was." Noelle beamed. "Wait until you feel it from the inside."

Still astonished by the test results, even though pregnancy happened all the time and was the normal course of things, she couldn't help feeling that someone living inside her was too weird to think about. "I guess I'll ease into the whole idea."

"Hmm." Noelle's smile turned knowing. "Hold on to that dream."

Laughing, she said, "Ludicrous, right?" Thinking of Morgan's face as the gift sank in, she suspected few things would ever be humdrum. "It almost feels like my own life is just beginning, as though everything before was a strange dream, and now I'm awake."

"And Morgan's awake. But his was a nightmare. Thank you for healing him."

"I only pointed the way. He and God did the work."

CHAPTER 32

Morgan leaned against the kitchen wall as Rick and his dad disconnected the old range and attempted to install the new. It didn't require three, and he'd have been little use anyway. He allowed the experts in their fields to perform those tasks. And given the difficulty they were having, he saw no reason to change that policy.

"Have anything to offer?" Hank crooked his head toward him.

"No. Looks like you two have it covered."

"His mind's on one thing only," Rick said.

"Pretty much." Hours later, it was still sinking in. These two thought it preening, and sure there was a little, but every time he thought of Erin carrying life inside her, it nearly brought him to his knees. Livie was proof enough of that miracle.

It also exponentially increased the stakes. His meeting with the CEO of the Asian company Denise had selected for their next consult wasn't scheduled for two days. But the guy was in New York the whole week. Maybe they could move it up. And then he'd see William sooner, and resolve Erin's trouble sooner. He didn't want his child experiencing her fear and uncertainty, didn't want Erin bearing anything more than she had to.

Though it was Christmas, he called Denise and, sadly, reached her.

"Yes, Morgan."

He didn't apologize for interrupting anything that might not be happening, just said, "Any chance we can move my meeting with Mr. Funaki to sometime tomorrow? I'd like to handle some things in New York as soon as possible."

"I'll see what I can do."

Before his mother's stove was installed, she called back. He would meet Mr. Funaki over dinner tomorrow night. Reservations were made. She had sent him all pertinent details. He said, "You know you're the greatest, right?"

"You know it too. Merry Christmas."

Laughing softly, he checked the information she sent shortly after. His morning flight might give him enough time to meet with William first. He didn't expect clear sailing, but he'd breathe easier when all this was behind them.

"You're talking to him tomorrow?" Erin said with a hitch in her diaphragm when Morgan explained his change of plans. She appreciated his motivation but regretted his losing time with his family. They'd scarcely finished Christmas dinner, and she knew his sisters wanted the next few days to reconnect.

She bit her lip. "Should I go with you?"

Morgan tipped his head. "You can if you want. But it might be better to let me present the situation first. Let William take a look at it all before we involve you."

"I am involved, Morgan. It's you who shouldn't be."

He smiled. "I'll be there on business already. Talking with William will simply get the ball rolling." The words came too lightly.

She narrowed her eyes. "What aren't you saying?"

Realizing she wasn't fooled, he drew a slow breath. "Worst-case scenario, when he contacts the FBI, they could issue a warrant for your arrest. As an officer of the law, William would be obligated to produce you."

Her mouth fell slack. "Seriously?"

"I said worst case. If you're not there, it's a nonissue."

She slumped against the piano in the music room, where last night she'd felt radiant with joy. Suddenly, missing family time seemed small.

"I don't think that will happen. William is highly respected and feared. If the feds can get what they want without having to engage him in court, it would be the better part of valor."

"What will he do?"

"I don't know exactly. I need to give him the Cayman account information, and he'll use it to your benefit."

Respected and feared or not, how much could he do? She took a pad and paper from the bookshelf drawer, wrote the account number, passwords, everything.

He raised his brows. "You memorized it?"

"Anything else would have been careless." She tucked the hair behind her ear. "The money was God's. I didn't want anyone finding it before I made it right."

"You're a marvel."

"Well, go keep your marvel out of jail."

"Yeah." He took her hands and kissed her. "I'm a bit of a marvel myself."

Learning Quinn was married and expecting obliterated the beauty Hannah had briefly revealed. She'd become a whining shrew even her mother tolerated with difficulty. Thomas had walled himself off in his study to prepare a sermon he hoped would still the waters of the storm that could arise. Markham had no intention of weathering it. He didn't need their acceptance. All he needed he could get from the old man — access to Quinn. *Take it. Take him. Break him.*

He shook his head, surprised to hear the

voice outside Quinn's house where it first insinuated. Maybe a half-life on the drug. Didn't they claim it caused flashbacks? Or had the voice come before he broke the glass? That seemed the order when he thought back, though it didn't matter.

"Markham?" A sweetness entered Hannah's tone when she said his name.

She was trying. Part of him understood there was simply too much bitterness, a critical mass that became undissolvable by even floods of tears.

"What are you doing?"

He said, "I have to go out."

"Why?"

He forced the irritation out of his response. "Have I asked you to explain every move you make?"

"No." She shrank in. "I'm sorry."

As though sorry mattered. "I won't be long." *Take him. Break him. Make him pay.*

It was almost a serenade as he drove, when he parked, and while he closed in on his quarry. Why had he hated hunting? There was no exhilaration to compare — when it wasn't dumb animals, but a deserving prey.

What had he done to earn the old man's vitriol? Nothing. He'd spoken no harsh word, taken not one cent from the skinflint's fist. The old rebel had formed an opinion from his own wasted soul — and Quinn's whispers no doubt. How close they were, the outcasts, misfits, miscreants. *Break them. Break them both.*

He shook the voice away. What he did now must be his choice, no one else telling him what to do. No orders. Never again. Sweet silence seeped in and with it a clarity of purpose on this cold, clear day.

As retribution coursed through him like quicksilver in his veins, Markham crept up behind the old man hunkered on the shore between his small house and the Fall River. A fishing pole hung idly in the half-frozen flow, as Corlin hollered into his phone. "Quinn, darlin', your father's a horse's rump and your mother never grew a backbone. If you don't speak sense to your sister, she'll marry that rotted soul. And mark my words, he'll be acting the maggot and her too simple to see."

Cold fire turned the silver to steel as Markham slowly bent and gripped a rock.

"I've tried, lass. You know I have. On your grandmother's sainted soul, I've tried. They have less an ear for me than you." As the old man listened to Quinn on the phone, Markham raised the rock.

"Aye, well, the devil takes his due. You're well away from here, my girl. And maybe you should stay. But know I love you with all my heart." He dabbed a tear. "Aye, lass. Aye."

As Corlin closed the phone and held it loosely in his palm, Markham tightened his muscles and struck.

■ ■ ■ ■

Wishing badly that Morgan was there to discuss it, Erin pocketed her phone and looked across the kitchen at Celia.

"Something wrong?"

"Yes, and I don't know what to do."

Celia listened, head cocked, while her daughters worked around them in a synchrony of kitchen chores. They all heard as she explained her grandfather's request, but they seemed to realize it was Celia's opinion she sought. Erin spread her hands. "I want to help, but I'm the last person Hannah would listen to. She truly hates me."

Surprisingly, Celia didn't offer a typical rebuttal, like "Surely not." She said, "Frustrating, but you can't walk through closed doors. From what you've said, Hannah locked this one a long time ago."

Erin looked at Morgan's sisters. Although they worked quietly — amazing given their normal volume — there were looks and murmurs and genial interplay she'd never had with Hannah. And what about her parents? If Morgan was right, and they built a world around Hannah's limitations, where did that leave an eager, precocious child?

She began to suspect they not only hadn't planned the interruption of their myth, they hadn't wanted her rocking Hannah's boat.

Why else would every argument have gone Hannah's way, even when it had to be obvious she'd been at fault? She remembered times when her grandparents pointed out inequities and were brushed aside or silenced. After Grandma Pearl went to heaven, Pops kept up the fight, fueling the war.

"My father gave his blessing on their marriage," she told Celia, feeling hurt and bewildered. "Even now." How could she penetrate a myopia that saw no further than his own mindset?

"Erin, to recognize Markham's guilt, he'd have to see his own. How much easier to believe God's miracle got blocked by unbelief than to admit he was wrong."

"But the court proved it."

"A worldly institution that sometimes gets it wrong. Jesus was tried and convicted and put to death as a criminal."

"Markham probably thinks it's one and the same." She sighed. "I hate feeling helpless."

Seeing her distress, Celia said, "If you'll forgive me another maxim, when water can't flow one way, it finds another."

In the bacon-and-onion-scented kitchen, she thought about that. She could do nothing for Hannah, but knowing Markham and her sister were with her parents, preparing to wed, there was someone she could help. "Celia, could Livie stay with you if I left for a couple days?"

"Yes, of course, but I thought you couldn't do anything."

"I can't help my sister. But there's a friend who needs something in Juniper Falls, and I may not get another chance." Morgan had left for New York not an hour before, but she had the prepaid Visa cards he'd given her. "If I get this coordinated, could someone give me a ride to the airport?"

Celia looked troubled but nodded. "I'm sure someone could."

Erin went into the music room and phoned RaeAnne. "I'm buying you a plane ticket. Get ready to meet me in Denver."

Morgan tried calling Erin to say he'd landed and was on his way to meet William. There was no reason to talk to her. He simply wanted to reassure her one more time. Or maybe he only wanted to hear her voice. When she didn't answer, he called Noelle.

"How's Livie?"

She laughed. "Three hours, Morgan? She's fine. Loving time with Grammy and Gramps."

"Naturally." He hadn't been worried, only interested. "Is Erin close? She called earlier but didn't leave a message, and she's not answering her phone."

"She's probably on the plane by now."

"The plane?"

"She flew to Denver to meet RaeAnne. I'm

sure that's why she called you."

Adrenaline surged. Through clenched teeth he said, "In what world did that make sense?"

"Markham's with her family, Morgan."

"How do you know?"

"Her grandfather told her. He called this morning to say Markham's marrying her sister. After everything."

He drew a solid breath. "You're saying Markham's not in Juniper Falls?"

"He and Hannah are at her father's house. Her grandfather saw them."

If that was true, Erin hadn't exaggerated her dad's obstinacy. And it did give her the opportunity she'd been hoping for. His heart rate calmed, the panic subsiding.

"She took the chance to help RaeAnne meet her dad, Morgan. You know how much that means to her."

"Yes, I know." The worst layer of shock peeled away. "Do you know when she's landing?"

"They're meeting at DIA around one o'clock Mountain Time and driving to Juniper Falls."

"Okay. Thanks, Noelle." He might not have advocated it, but he knew how RaeAnne's situation was weighing on his soft-hearted wife. As soon as he finished in New York, he could meet her out there. Pocketing the phone, he reminded himself Erin wasn't Livie. She could make decisions on her own, and did. He settled in for the drive.

The last time he'd been to William's Long Island estate he'd been reuniting Noelle with Rick after their heartrending split. Now William's firm handshake drew him inside, where Ellen's two-handed grasp was as familiar as she got. Decades as the watchdog assistant to William St. Claire, Esq., created a formality she'd never shed, even though she had been his wife for the last five years.

"Wonderful to see you, Ellen." He squeezed her hands in return.

"How is your new and controversial wife?" William asked with a gleam in his eye.

For a moment he thought someone had exposed her legal woes, then realized Noelle must have filled him in on the family strife. "Words can't come close." He tried not to look like a lovesick goon. "And actually it's Erin who brings me here. A legal matter."

"Oh?" William paused at the library doors. "Would you like something hot, or will brandy do while we talk?"

"Coffee would be great," he told Ellen. "Keep me from glazing over when William gets technical."

"You mean boring," William said.

Laughing, they entered the library. Over cups of Costa Rican wet-processed Arabica, Morgan laid out Erin's situation as clearly as possible, then asked, "Is it serious?"

William answered gravely. "It's not inconsiderable. In essence, she withheld information during trial and discovery and thwarted the recovery of funds she misappropriated."

"She hasn't used the money."

"Then the better word is stole."

Morgan frowned. "Will they push this accomplice angle?"

"Her blowing the whistle and testifying argues against collusion, though partners have been known to take the other down. I've seen it a few times myself." He pulled a wry smile.

While seeing the humor, Morgan had to work at enjoying it. "All she wanted was an apology, for someone to admit she'd done the right thing. She was twenty-three and idealistic."

"Not a legal defense."

Morgan frowned. "Then what do we have?"

Every inch the top-tier criminal defense attorney, William said, "We have the money."

RaeAnne squeezed her hard, laughing and crying when they met at the baggage claim. "This is it. This is really it."

Erin squeezed her back. "Not Christmas Day, but close enough?"

"Oh, Quinn." RaeAnne kissed her cheeks. "You are the best friend. But, oh, I forgot to ask. How are you feeling?"

"So far, so good."

"That's great. I know a gal who got sick the

day she got pregnant and stayed that way until she pushed her baby out."

"Delightful." Erin shouldered her carry-on. "Noelle's still not doing all that great. But I felt her baby kick. It was . . ." She laughed. "I'm sorry. This isn't about me, RaeAnne. It's about you and your dad. What's the plan?"

"You're asking me?"

"Ye-es."

"Well, I have an address. So I . . ." She fanned herself with her hand. "Do I just go?"

Erin smiled. "First, we'll get to the car rentals."

"Oh good. Baby steps."

"Hold on." Erin fished her phone out. "It's Morgan."

RaeAnne took three steps backward and raised her fingers in a wave.

Drawing a deep breath, she answered. "Morgan, I tried to call, several times. I left you a message when I landed, and —"

"Erin."

"Yes?"

"I don't need excuses or explanations. You assessed the situation and used your judgment. I just want to make sure you're okay."

Warmth filled her. "Really?"

"You're bright, decisive, and you care. Good combination."

Her eyes burned. "I have a feeling this is going to be a tearful pregnancy."

He laughed softly. "One thing, okay? I don't want you anywhere near your old place."

"We're planning to stay at the ranch, in your cabin."

"Okay. But he knows that connection."

"He's not there." Everything Pops told her poured out. "I'm sure they're making wedding plans, and God only knows what. He'll have the whole church believing I'm Jezebel and he's weeping Jeremiah in the well." She was mixing prophetic stories, but whatever.

A team of teen girls and four adults in matching warm-ups went noisily past.

"I know that hurts."

"I should be used to it."

"Well, as you said, it gives you this chance. I trust your judgment, but if anything seems off, pay attention."

"I will."

"Now, listen to me, and I don't want you to argue." His tone grew so serious it slowed her heart. "There's a gun in the Maserati glove box."

She pressed a hand to her chest. "I don't —"

"Just have it in the cabin in case. The car's in Rick's barn." He told her where to find the spare key he hadn't grabbed when they left and gave her the alarm code. "I didn't lock the glove box in case I needed quick access."

She listened half disbelieving. "I had no

idea it was there."

"I didn't want to scare you." His voice thickened. "But I want you to have it ready."

"Then I will."

"Okay," he said. "Good luck to RaeAnne. Hope it goes well."

She smiled. "I love you."

"Love you more." She heard the sincerity in his graveled voice.

Holding the phone to her chest for a moment, she sighed, then she and RaeAnne joined others getting the ground-transportation shuttle.

RaeAnne studied her as they rode to the lot, and then as she got behind the steering wheel. "You all right, honey?"

She told her what Morgan said. RaeAnne brushed off the part about the gun and focused on the heart of it. "I'm glad he wasn't angry about not knowing."

She was still riding that wave. "It's the first time anyone's trusted my judgment."

"Well, it's about time. You're like a catalyst for all sorts of good things."

And yet Morgan was in New York trying to keep her out of jail. She hadn't even asked if he'd met with William. Her concern notched up. They shouldn't waste any time. "Let's go directly there, RaeAnne. Let's meet your dad."

She drew a shaky breath. "All right. It's only been forty years. Why wait?"

His address was in one of the two small condominium complexes in Juniper Falls. While not a specified retirement community, it apparently catered to seniors. The walkways were ramped and the outer doors equipped with automatic switches at handicapped level. The lodge-style buildings were surrounded by spruce and Douglas fir trees, snow cleared from the walkways but lying unmelted on the shaded lawns.

They entered the building and walked to his unit. At the door, Erin turned to RaeAnne. "Are you ready?"

"I think so." She squeezed the hand Erin rested on her arm. "Thanks for being here."

Erin rang the bell, a little anxious, though nothing like what RaeAnne had to be feeling.

The man who answered had aged from the locket photo, but his features still had good lines in spite of puffy bags under his eyes. His hair was graying in the way that made blond seem faded. He looked from her to RaeAnne and said, "Can I help you?"

She had prepared to make introductions if necessary, but RaeAnne said, "Raymond Hartley?"

"Ray, yeah."

"I think you're my father."

A furrow the width of an earthworm formed between his brows. The slack skin of his neck pulled with the rise and fall of his Adam's apple. "I'm not sure why you'd think that, but you may as well come in."

He ushered them into a small room, sparsely furnished with a pale green couch, holding several days of newspapers, an ivory coffee table with an unfolded pile of laundry, and a flat-screen TV that had to be sixty inches. No mystery how Ray spent his time, although there were shelves of books as well.

He indicated they should sit on the couch, then pulled the table back and perched beside the clothes. "You're Vera's girl."

RaeAnne's mouth fell open. "How'd you know?"

He smiled wryly. "You look just like her."

Erin felt RaeAnne's excitement but also the control she exerted.

"You knew she had me?"

"Sure. She talked about you."

Hurt and surprise found her eyes. "When?"

"When we started talking again. When she came up here."

With an effort RaeAnne held the reins of rejection, since her mother hadn't mentioned him to her. "R-Ray. Why don't you think I'm your daughter?"

"I don't have kids. I . . ." He brushed his hand through his hair. "I have some mental health issues, so I got a vasectomy."

"When?" RaeAnne all but whispered.

"At twenty-one. So you see . . ." He spread his hand.

"My mother was pregnant when you left. I

have the locket you gave her. We could have the hair tested if you don't believe me."

His hand slowly lowered to his thigh. He searched her face, putting it together. "But . . . she never said. I-I mean all these years."

"Well . . . join the club." RaeAnne's own face twisted.

Shaking, Markham tried to get through to her again. "You had Christmas with your family, Hannah. As you wanted. And once again Quinn couldn't be here."

"It doesn't matter. She's married. She's having a baby. That's her family now."

"My mission hasn't changed."

Hannah's hands writhed like puppies in her lap. "Why do you care? She doesn't."

He paced back toward her in the tiny study of her parents' home. "Hannah. You're going to be my wife. I'm telling you we need to go. That's all there is." He had thought Quinn headstrong. Hannah took passive-aggressive to new lows.

"Mama and I need to plan my wedding. There are so many things to do. Why are you thinking of Quinn? Why can't you think of me?"

"Hannah." The jaw pain reached inside his ear and shot into his temple. "I thought you were ready to leave your parents and cleave to me. I see I was wrong."

She looked up, wary and tearful.

"Of course I won't take you from your mother." He rested his hand on her head like a child's, letting her see his distress. "But I have to go." He turned toward the closed door.

"Markham, please. Wait. I want to be with you. I don't know why it has to be today, but . . . if you say so."

He looked over his shoulder. "I'm no cradle robber."

"I'm thirty-eight. That's a grown woman."

"You haven't behaved like one. I think I was mistaken." He might still need her, but there was no time to argue. He had to get out before the old man was discovered. The deed clung to him like tar. He couldn't clear his head. He needed the drug that helped him see so clearly, that made him invincible. "We've wasted too much time. As it is, we won't arrive until dark."

"We could wait until tomorrow."

"No, Hannah, we can't."

"Then I'll come with you. Please don't leave me behind."

He searched her face for sincerity, for the loyalty he'd taken for granted until envy made her as sharp as vinegar. "All right, Hannah. If you're sure."

"I'm sure."

Relief washed over him, but when he opened the door, the minister was there.

"A word, Markham."

"Sir?" His heart rushed with such violence he swayed. Had they found the old man? He gripped the doorframe.

"Please come out and close the door. I don't want Hannah to hear."

They couldn't have connected him. No way he'd been seen. He stepped out and closed the door.

Thomas Reilly spoke softly but firmly. "Markham, I can't allow you to take Hannah."

He stared, baffled. "But . . . you . . ."

"I've given my blessing, yes. But she is too innocent to grasp the temptations involved in this situation. If you intend to take her with you now, I'll perform the ceremony before you leave this house."

"She wants a wedding, Thomas."

"When you've resolved matters with Quinn, we'll have a reception. The congregation will see we're all united. Until then, you can leave my daughter or take her with you as your wife. There are no other options."

This was the man who'd built his own following, whose judgment they trusted. Utterly. He'd thought him weak, but it was the opposite. He wasn't getting Hannah past him. Markham bowed his head. "It'll be my honor." The pain worked in behind his eyeballs before he thought to unclench his jaw.

CHAPTER 33

At the grocery mart, Erin purchased meat and bread and produce for a few meals, unsure how much they would need. She'd bought one-way tickets so she and RaeAnne could individually return home whenever they each needed to. She was sure Rick and Noelle wouldn't mind RaeAnne using the cabin if she stayed longer. Forty years was a lot of catching up. Four years would be a lot — if that ever happened.

Climbing into the rental car, she imagined her mom and Hannah, making plans, dreaming dreams. Hannah's wedding would be a special event for the whole church, and if Markham was the groom, blessed by her father, their shepherd, then someone else must be responsible for the collapse of their miracle. She blinked the tears and shrugged. Hannah wouldn't have made her a bridesmaid anyway.

She dried her eyes with her sleeve and drove to Rudy's store. She parked and went in, remembering all too well her dash inside with Markham on her trail. Rudy looked up from the stool behind the counter and grinned. "Hi, Quinn. I didn't expect to see you back here."

"Only for a day or two. I had to say hi and thank you for last time."

"You sort of did." He touched his cheek.

She smiled. Morgan's eyes had smoked a little when he asked about that kiss. "You haven't seen Markham lately, have you?"

"He was hanging around the Boar for a while, asking about the Maserati when your sister thought it was yours."

She frowned. "How did Hannah know about the Maserati?"

"She saw it getting towed. Had a fit about the dent like something bad happened to you."

Erin groaned. "I'm trying to forget that dent."

"It's not that bad. Back quarter panel."

"A couple grand, you think?"

He blinked. "I'm no expert."

Meaning way worse. She covered her face.

"Hey!" Rudy rose from his stool. "You're married."

"Oh." Her ring glittered in the clear winter sunlight as she lowered her hand. "We're trying not to let Markham find out."

"Who's we?" He searched her face. "You and Morgan?"

She nodded.

"I thought you'd just met."

"Uh-huh."

He pulled a slow, goofy grin. "Another Morgan legend."

"No, please. You can't tell anyone. Not until we figure out this other thing."

"Don't worry." Rudy raised his hands. "I'll just laugh about it myself, sitting by the fire and toasting you two." He looked at her hand again. "But if that's the case, you better take off the ring."

"Markham's not here now."

"Well, people talk. That bling could be seen from space."

A laugh caught her. "Did you say bling?"

"Hey, I read magazines. What do you think I do in here all day?"

All laughter aside, she hated to remove the ring that meant so much more than the first time she'd slipped it off with hardly a thought. But she put it in her pocket and said, "I'm glad you know, Rudy. And thanks for keeping the secret."

"So where's Morgan?"

"He's in New York." Another pang of apprehension caught her. She needed to know what was happening. "I'm here with Vera's daughter, RaeAnne."

He frowned. "You sure it's okay?"

"I know Markham's somewhere else right now. But I guess if you see him, I could use a heads-up."

"I don't have your number."

When he pulled out a thick, old flip phone, she told him her new number. Likewise, she keyed Rudy's number into the new smartphone Morgan had given her, assigning a speed dial. If she needed to call Rudy, it might be in a hurry.

He smiled ruefully. "I'd have asked for this under other circumstances, if it were anyone but Morgan making moves Thanksgiving night."

"Making moves?"

"He's so smooth, you didn't even know."

Morgan claimed he fell in love before she served the pie. And he'd conveyed that to Rudy. How had she missed it? And then she realized — Livie ran interference.

Her gaze fell to the fishing flies. "Do you tie these?"

"Sure."

"They're excellent. My Pops ties his own flies. I always thought they were too pretty to hang on the end of a line for a fish to swallow."

"They don't actually swallow it if you set the hook right."

"I know, but it's still been in that fishy mouth and all drenched and drowned in river water."

"Sounds like you fish."

"Not for a while." She couldn't help the

wistful tone that came with thoughts of Pops. If Markham married into the family, would she ever go home?

"Ever ice fished?"

She shook herself back to the conversation. "No."

"Want to?"

"Well . . ."

"I'm going out in the morning. You haven't fished until you've fished on a frozen silver mountain lake."

She looked up at Rudy. "What time are you going?"

"Meet here about six thirty. Be on the lake for sunrise. It's a ways off the beaten track."

"That sounds wonderful." It was not part of the plan, but RaeAnne and her dad would want time without her around. And who better than Rudy to be with? "Yes. I will."

His broad smile spread. "Great."

"Well, I guess I better get back to RaeAnne. See you in the morning."

"See you, Quinn." Being called that by him and RaeAnne jangled a little, but also felt right. She'd been Quinn here. She'd been Quinn everywhere she wasn't Morgan's wife.

When she got back to Ray's condo, RaeAnne joined her in the kitchen to make sandwiches for supper.

"Quinn, it's like an ocean of stories I'm trying to pour into a thimble."

"You don't have to learn everything now.

You have your dad. You can make time together, talk on the phone, write e-mails."

"He doesn't have a computer."

"Letters, then. Old-fashioned letters."

RaeAnne could hardly keep the smile from her face. "He said I look like Mom, but I feel like there's some of him too."

"Of course. And have you noticed Vera named you after him? Ray, RaeAnne."

RaeAnne pressed her fingers to her lips. "She did, didn't she."

Watching the truth unfold for the daughter who'd made presents for a dad she'd never seen, felt as good as anything could. "How does he seem — you know, mentally?"

"He takes some meds, but nowadays who doesn't?"

"Would he mind if I ask him about the cellar?"

"No. I told him you found Vera's journal down there and started me looking for him. He's not self-conscious."

They brought the sandwiches into the other room. Ray had turned on the TV to the America Movie Classics channel but kept the sound off. He smiled when they returned.

"You know what your mom loved?" he said. "Silent movies. The old pitted, jerky silent movies. We'd put them on here and laugh and laugh." His eyes got misty. "I miss her."

Erin said, "How did she end up living in

that house, Ray? The one built on the asylum cellar."

He shrugged. "Just a fluke, I guess. It was selling cheap, and she wanted to be up here."

"But did she know . . . ? You know . . . about . . ."

"Sure she did. I told her. But she was Vera."

"And there wasn't any reason she . . . wouldn't want to? Be there, I mean?"

He stayed quiet a while, then rested his hands on his knees and rubbed slowly. "I wouldn't go there. That's why she always came here."

Erin gave it a second, then said, "Because . . ."

He studied her. "Not great memories for one thing."

"Were you there at the end? When it burned?"

He looked down at his large but somehow delicate hands. "You'd think they would have known. With so much else, they should have known."

"Known what?"

He stood up and searched the couch for the remote, then set it on the arm and sat down again. He looked at her. He blinked. "RaeAnne said you felt the bad stuff."

Her chest quivered. "I felt something in the cellar, maybe heard something."

He nodded. "Then I guess it's still happening. I hoped it got burned up with . . .

Brandy."

RaeAnne sat perfectly still. Erin felt a dread, but couldn't stop wanting to know. It wasn't morbid curiosity; it was the same compulsion that made her seek answers from the professor. It seemed important for reasons she couldn't explain.

"Ray, what happened to Brandy?"

After six hours of weepy Hannah, Markham wanted to run off the road. The simple rite had not been the wedding she'd imagined. No matter how many times he told her they could do it over, she kept coming back to the same refrain. "But we're married. It won't be the same."

"Listen to me, Hannah. Do you know what a wife does?"

"Of course. Love and cherish and obey."

The simplicity of her words made him wish anything in life was that basic. "Those were the vows, but do you know the physical responsibilities?"

She flushed scarlet. "Of course I do." Her lip quivered.

He spoke softly. "If you stop crying, we'll wait for that until you have the ceremony you want."

Hannah blinked wet eyes and gulped. "You would do that?"

He would do anything to shut her up. "It's right and good for us to be joined, but to soothe your tender heart, yes. It'll be as if we're not married until you have your special wedding." Why was that so easy to promise? Because he didn't want her, or because something bigger was taking place in his mind?

"Oh, Markham."

"But I'm serious, Hannah. You'll stop crying, you'll stop whining, and unless I address you, you'll stop talking. Understand?"

"Yes, Markham," she answered in tremulous tones. Then silence.

Oh, the peace. He hadn't really intended to marry her. At least he didn't think so. He didn't care what words the minister spoke. He'd played the role as he had so many others. Gwen cried. Hannah cried. Thomas looked stern, yet proud. Maybe in a small part somewhere inside, he felt gratified. Their delusion had no end.

Or did they see something he hadn't fully grasped? Maybe it wasn't a con. Maybe somewhere in the process, what he pretended became true. What was the line between faith and illusion? He had done little more than the Reverend Thomas Reilly to form the thoughts and behavior of his flock. While the divinity credentials of Pastor Markham Wilder were phony, wasn't it possible the calling was true?

It would explain his flawless performance, the fervent response. When he called on God,

God appeared. The visions, the prophetic words were God's own. Was it possible that if Quinn hadn't interfered, the miracle would have come?

And maybe, with her elimination, it still could. He imagined leading Hannah back into the church, the minister at his side, the hush of the confused and wounded crowd. He saw himself raising his arms and calling out to heaven and the money Quinn stole multiplying in baskets until they overflowed.

The roar of the crowd. The holy ecstasy. Wasn't it possible — if only Quinn was brought low. He saw her being dragged in and cast down to the floor. He had forgiven, but the others cried for blood. *She must pay for her sin. Like the woman caught in adultery. Stone her. Strike her.*

He gripped the wheel. No. He couldn't desire such violence. Not anymore. Not ever again. He had exacted his final retribution. And yet there must be a reckoning. Quinn must repay not only what was Caesar's but likewise what was God's. She must acknowledge him, and beg *his* forgiveness. Now, that was a vision to contemplate.

Soon they'd be in Juniper Falls. He considered the plan he'd formulated before his awakening and found it sound as far as it went. The first order had to be recovering the funds, and then, of course, the multiplication. With Hannah as bait, he could lure

Quinn anywhere. But he liked the symmetry of bringing her back to the place he'd found her, the place she'd eluded and embarrassed him. This time he would have complete control.

They entered the sleepy winter town where he and Hannah would stay in the house Morgan Spencer bought for Quinn. Again the symmetry. He and his wife in place of Morgan and his. Pure and chaste Hannah and her prophet. A pregnant harlot and the worldly mogul. A white queen and a black queen, and a knight to defend each.

He took the road to the ranch and once again turned into the narrow drive. Quinn might have fled without living there, but the house was hers, he was sure. When he checked back with Lydia, there was still no name attached to the title. Spencer had hidden the sale the same as all his properties. For Quinn, his wife and the mother of his "babe."

Another flash of anger caught him. Four years he'd been imprisoned and demeaned because of Quinn's interference. He wanted her to know that suffering, to suffer it herself. He didn't have years, but he could make each day seem like a year. It would be purification. He formed a deep, satisfied sigh.

Morgan stood and shook hands with the striking Japanese CEO whose bearing, drive, and apparent integrity impressed him as it had Denise. Once again she'd proved indispensable as a screener, with a thoroughness and natural instinct for people that made her choice of boyfriends baffling. And, though he'd rather have the lout in jail, since Denise would not testify, paying to keep the barrier in place was well worth it.

He called to tell her the initial contact with Mikio Funaki had intrigued him enough to arrange the more in-depth scrutiny that would take most of tomorrow. She was especially impressed by his ability to recognize hers. He disconnected with a smile tugging. It was good to have people who honed you. He and Denise would never be flint and steel, but they were definitely steel on steel.

The meetings would also take his mind off William's upcoming conversation with the FBI. He believed what he'd told Erin, that they were in good hands — the best. But she had committed a crime, however naïvely, and the piper must be paid. From what he'd been told before reviewing the files Anselm provided, William expected a grand jury hearing at the least.

Alone in the elevator, Morgan prayed that was the most. If Erin had a chance to explain herself, they'd see her sincerity, her decency, the things he'd been drawn to from the shadows. Her bright spirit had breathed life into his flagging soul. He wanted nothing more than to live in peace and raise his children with her.

After cabbing over, he entered the hotel where he and Erin had stayed on the second tumultuous night of their marriage. He was tempted to call her again but had to trust that she'd let him know if anything happened. From the little she'd shared, her father and the other men in her life had undermined her intelligence and resourcefulness. He wasn't going to be one of them.

Instead he phoned his baby girl and filled his heart with her chatter. Then he settled into the creative stream of professional energy he tapped to prepare for tomorrow.

In the mountain condo, with the night settled hard and cold, the lines of Ray's face grew long as he sent his thoughts to a time he'd clearly avoided visiting. He had taken so long to answer, Erin thought she'd overstepped in asking so directly about someone he'd obviously cared about.

But after a while he said, "The Juniper Falls Mental Hospital started out way back as an asylum for real head cases. The stuff in the cellar is mostly from those days. By the time I got there it was an exploratory, transcendental sort of drug and alcohol rehab center. A treatment facility for anger management and depression, where celebrities came to get their auras smoothed with acid and rituals. It was sort of a badge of achievement to have done a stint at JFMH."

"No electroshock?"

"A decade or two before. Then it went to progressive, experimental treatments."

Erin listened intently, aware of RaeAnne doing the same, as he described therapies that sounded more like rites — maybe dark rites — to her.

"Brandy arrived in the last year of operation. Well, she sort of saw to that," he added with a shadow entering his eyes. "A young starlet with every kind of issue you could imagine." He shook his head. "She immediately attached to me, which was all right, except she wanted something romantic, and I just wasn't into young women."

RaeAnne made a sound in her throat that brought a ghost of a smile from Ray.

"Maybe it was her addictions, or her insecurities. Maybe she went looking, or was merely susceptible, but she reacted to whatever was there in a terrifying way."

RaeAnne jumped in. "What do you mean 'whatever was there'?"

Ray looked from one of them to the other. "Brandy wasn't the first to have weird episodes, things that got people hurt or scared them silly. Sillier. We were all a bunch of nutcases."

"That's not true," Erin said. "Every person in there was dealing with an emotional or physiological condition. It doesn't make you less human."

He spread his hands. "Just a figure of speech."

"Go on," his daughter said, caught up now.

"Stuff had happened there as far back as people remembered. But Brandy's was the worst I'd heard of. They started finding her in locked places, places she shouldn't have been able to get into. And there were always some marks on her, bruises or burns, hand marks around her throat, cuts when there wasn't anything sharp in sight. She didn't know how she got there or what happened."

Erin thought of patient 1 in the asylum director's account not remembering the strange voice and foreign tongue. Of the janitor not understanding why he touched the searing boiler.

"All the staff was questioned and even took lie detector tests. No one was doing it. I told Brandy to leave, that it was no place for her. I'd have left myself if she agreed, but she wouldn't. She seemed to . . . thrive on it." He shook his head. "People said she wanted attention. And she did. But this was something else. This was something . . . evil."

Erin swallowed. In hardly more than a whisper, she said, "Brandy lit the fire?"

It was minutes before Ray spoke. "That's what they say."

"You think it was someone else?"

"Some*thing.*" The skin around his eyes reddened. "Something was there before Brandy." He fixed her with a blue stare as serious as a stroke. "Sounds like it still is."

Leaving Ray's condo, Erin did not feel like talking. For once RaeAnne seemed to agree. Processing his story about Brandy along with the rest of the visit, they drove silently to Rick and Noelle's ranch, where she let RaeAnne into the cabin, then went herself to get the gun. She took it from the glove box, knowing it was loaded and dangerous. Morgan had briefly explained its operation, the safeties, etc.

It was lighter and smaller than the revolver she'd shot with Pops. It might not buck and smart as that one had, but she didn't want to know. Next, she used the key hidden where Noelle told her, and went into the big house to get her truck keys. Rick hadn't sold it yet, she discovered when she disarmed the Maserati's alarm. That way, RaeAnne could use the rental car, and she'd have her own transportation.

She put the gun and the keys on the nightstand in Morgan's bedroom, where she'd refused to sleep the night they spent here. She'd been right then, but she sure wished he was with her now.

In the other room, she smiled at RaeAnne. "Well?"

"He's kind of sweet, don't you think?" Rae-

Anne's eyes looked hopeful.

She pictured Ray. "He's more than sweet. He's kind and good and humble. He's everything a dad should be."

RaeAnne's tears flowed. "I can hardly believe it. Yet as happy as I am, I'm so angry too. How could Vera have done this to me? To him? Why would she keep us apart and never let us know?"

Erin shook her head. "I think you said it. She wanted him all to herself."

Markham had thought about giving Hannah a dose of the drug but decided not to share the experience. His visions were private, between him and God, and though the mountain air was frigid, freezing even, he went outside to experience the quest without Hannah hovering.

He wanted to know what the stars and trees would look like when the effects began. He had dripped it from an ampule onto his tongue, and it seemed to take longer to take effect. Once it began, he would return to the house before the imagined paralysis made him unable to move. For now he wandered between the trees in the slicing moonlight.

With only the first hints of dizziness, he followed a path packed into the snow and relatively visible. It shouldn't have surprised him that it came out at Rick's ranch. They did share the road to the area, the only two properties on it.

His steps seemed to labor and fly at the same time, as though he covered a great distance without moving at all. Astral projection, he told himself with a laugh that made no sound. One of the cabins had lights on, and he moved toward it, feeling invisible and no longer cold — overly warm, in fact. He crept up beside the window and looked in, stunned by what he saw.

On her back across the bed lay Quinn, talking on the phone. He watched as she twisted her hair, her face sweet, then animated, serious, then amused. It had to be her husband she was talking to with such emotions playing over her face. Markham's eyes narrowed when she rested her hand on her belly. What would the man pay for his wife *and offspring*?

Still talking on the phone, Quinn closed her eyes, a look on her face he'd never seen on Hannah's. With such similar features, he should have. His breath grew shallow and sharp — the drug, he told himself, knowing he had to get back. Hannah worshiped him. He was not merely a prophet, but a god.

The sky exploded into colors, the stars praising him as he moved along the path. He was great and marvelous, deserving of praise. Not only a divine messenger, he was himself divine. So why had he never seen the look on Quinn's face in Hannah's eyes for him?

CHAPTER 34

Before dawn, Markham opened his eyes to Hannah beside him on the bed, staring like a farm animal. A woman in the congregation, the midwife, had told him Hannah's birth had been complicated, cord issues, oxygen deprivation. She'd approached him in reverence to intercede on Hannah's behalf. Maybe another small miracle? If he had the time?

"Are you awake?" Hannah's voice trembled. He wanted to pump air into her lungs and force it out robust and lively — like her sister's. *"I expected it would be Quinn who caught your interest."* Oh yes. But she'd been shrewd and suspicious, never giving him an instant's encouragement, whereas Hannah . . .

He frowned, less euphoric than the last time he'd awakened from the drug. "What are you doing in my bed, Hannah?"

"You were so cold and confused. I tried to warm you."

He had no memory of her. Obviously he'd

been lucky to make it back.

"Thank you, Hannah. God is dealing with me in new and fearful ways."

"I was afraid. You weren't yourself. It didn't . . . sound like you."

He smiled. "My sweet Hannah. It wasn't me."

Her eyes widened in amazement — and fear. He rose and went out. Tracing the path he'd taken the night before, he found a place in the trees and watched. After a while, Quinn came out and went into the barn. Moments later she drove out in a black truck. He had no need to follow. He only wanted to make sure he hadn't hallucinated last night and imagined her altogether.

Now that he knew it, he made his way back to the house and let himself in. Hannah waited at the door, a little confused, but — he was gratified to see — still devoted. She would need that for this trial. "It is good you're here with me, like the widow for Elijah."

"I don't want to be a widow. This house scares me."

"No, precious Hannah. Not a widow. But you too have been chosen."

"Your wife and handmaid."

"Yes." He laid his hands on her head. "And you remember your vows. They mean even more for us than a typical marriage. We've been set apart."

"You have, Markham."

He smiled. "But like Esther, you're here for a time such as this."

She blinked with awe and wonder.

"Are you willing? No matter how hard it might be?"

"I am," she breathed.

"Then come."

She gaped when he put his shoulder to the hutch and pushed it away from the hidden door. She had no idea where it led. But he did.

Erin slid with anticipation into Rudy's oxidized Wagoneer. The narrow lake was remote, tucked into a valley with steep evergreen slopes rising to a slate gray sky. Breathing air so cold it pinched her nostrils, she watched, shivering, while Rudy bored a hole with a four-foot corkscrew he called an auger. When he'd settled beside her, wrapped in a blanket that matched hers, she said, "It's so peaceful."

"Yep." Rudy handed her the pole and tackle that included a speckled grub he wanted to compare with the Phelps Glow Spoon on his. "I like to try out the equipment," he said, "and this is a good chance to go head to head on the lures."

She butted fists with him. "May the best fake bug win."

The valley was almost wholly silent, the

gray dawn broken by a cold silver sunrise behind a veil of clouds. Across the freshly glowing sky an eagle soared. A bull elk stalked majestically to where the water flowed beneath a thinner crust of ice. With its powerful hoof, the elk crushed the ice and drank. It reminded her of the bugling she and Morgan had laughed at, one small vignette in their storybook romance.

Before she would have expected it, her pole dipped. She glanced at Rudy, who had noticed it too. When she got another tug, she jerked up, feeling it snag something in the dark gray hole. That something pulled back. With both hands she held and reeled the line in, Rudy watching without a word. The fish had heft and spirit for having pickled in ice water, but she hauled out a pale yellow, gray-speckled cutthroat trout longer than her forearm.

Sliding her the pail with a huge grin, Rudy said, "If I took you fishing first, Morgan wouldn't have stood a chance."

"Probably." She tipped him a sidelong glance, smiling back.

"That'll make you a nice dinner."

"It will. Want to join me?"

"Would, but I've got a Scout troop meeting tonight. Lots to get ready."

"You're a troop leader?"

"It's slim pickin's up here."

She shoved his knee. "I'm sure you're great.

What don't you know about scouty stuff?"

"Scouty?" He shook his head, chin down. "Scouty."

They sat a good while, but nothing else decided to bite, and it was time to check in with Ray and RaeAnne. Carrying the bucket, she felt a little bad for the fish, but it would be put to good use. Even split three ways, it would make a tasty treat, and Ray, for one, might enjoy hearing how her speckled grub won the contest.

Back at her truck, she thanked Rudy for what really had been a special time — different, yet sweetly reminiscent of those spent with Pops.

As he pulled out in the Wagoneer with a wave at the window, her phone vibrated. She dug it from her pocket, noting eight new messages. That little valley must not get a signal. With the exception of one from Morgan, they were all from Pops. She pushed Talk. "Hi, P—"

"Quinn!" her sister gasped. "Please come."

What? Her thoughts stalled. Why did Hannah have her grandfather's cell phone? "Hannah? What's wrong?" If something had happened to Pops . . .

"It's dark and —"

She sensed motion and started to turn when a jolt struck her back beneath her left shoulder. Her muscles twitched with uncontrollable spasms. She couldn't move her arms. Millions of tiny needles shot through her body as confusion and dizziness filled her mind.

Something big moved behind her, then around to the side. Her arm pulled back but not by her own muscles, or her will. A hard shove pushed her over, and her other arm jerked back. The sound of something ripping moved through her mind, but she didn't make sense of it until the stickiness wrapped her wrists.

She was flying — no, someone lifted her off the ground and tossed her behind the driver's seat into the cab cargo area. A terrifying helplessness overwhelmed her, even though the hard spasms were lessening. Dazed, she lay at an awkward angle on her shoulder, her cheek pressed into the utilitarian truck carpeting.

Where was her phone? Where was the gun? She didn't need to ask who or why — only what was he doing here?

Her head cleared as the truck moved, slowly first, then stopping, then accelerating. She could think, but she couldn't seem to act on anything. As the last of the contractions tapered off, the truck stopped. The door opened, and before she could even cry out, another jolt arched her back, as a hundred hammers pounded up and down her spine. Her limbs jerked, then froze, and on a terrible wave of vertigo, she lost the last thread of thought.

On his way to meet Mikio Funaki, Morgan tried to reach his wife again. This time instead of going instantly to voice mail, as it had before, it rang. It rang, but she didn't answer. Any other time, he'd balance all the reasons for that. Now, disquiet seeped in like sarin gas invading his lungs and sinuses.

Answer the phone, Erin.

William's meeting with the assistant deputy director of the FBI had already begun. After studying Markham's conviction and Erin's testimony as well as the current case the feds were building, he'd sounded confident of her chances for a plea and cautiously optimistic about no charges at all. She could deliver what they needed and connect it to Markham — leverage in William's hands that worked like magic.

Morgan wiped the sweat from his palm. Before he got locked into this meeting with the Japanese CEO, he wanted to tell Erin things looked good. He wanted her to know she'd be fine, everything would be fine. Yet he couldn't shake the disquiet.

Cell service worked well at the ranch, though he didn't know what part of Juniper Falls RaeAnne's dad lived in, and there were spotty areas. That gave him a thought, and he called another number.

"Hi, RaeAnne, this is Morgan," he said.

"I'm trying to reach Erin and not having much luck."

"Erin?" She voiced real confusion. "Who's Erin?"

It baffled him for a second; then he said, "Didn't Quinn tell you she's going by Erin?"

"Why would she do that? Quinn's a great name."

He gave her the succinct version.

"Well, I knew about most of that, but she's still been Quinn to me."

He rubbed his eyes. "I guess it doesn't matter. Is she there?"

"No. I'm at my dad's. She said she might join us later, but she went ice fishing with Rudy."

Ice fishing. In the valley Rudy usually fished, there'd be no service. He blew out his breath, relief clearing his head. "Is there a plan for later?"

"She said we'd talk. I'm actually thinking of staying the night with my dad. There are so many things I'd like to do here at his place before I go."

"Okay. But if you don't talk to her soon, would you go by the ranch and see what's up?"

"Sure. Of course. Is everything okay?"

He frowned. "Probably."

"Well, I'll let you know as soon as I hear."

He thanked her and hung up. Erin would see his calls when she got service. She'd call and tell him she was fine. Maybe at that point he could tell her the same from his end.

Dizzy and disoriented, she opened her eyes to darkness and Hannah weeping. Feeling the cold metal clamp on her left wrist, she realized the tape that had bound her was gone. She shifted on the hard surface, rolling from her hip to sit up against a metal bed frame she recognized by touch. Groping, she found Hannah's hand in the other cuff on the same bed and said, "Are you all right?"

The noise Hannah made was not speech. Fear, fury, loathing.

"Hannah, are you hurt?"

"No," she wailed.

Erin let go of her sister and felt her pocket. No gun. Either it fell out when Markham manhandled her and it was on the ground somewhere . . . or he had it.

She didn't feel her phone either. Then, as if her mind willed it, the phone rang. But not in her pocket.

It was Morgan's ring tone from the modern metal opera he loved. An organ blast, then "What good this deafness if this prattle I must hear."

She had laughed so hard the first time she heard what he programmed for his ring. She couldn't laugh now.

In the nearly complete darkness, Markham touched her phone. The face of it faintly illuminated his features as he said, "We'll let it go," and touched Ignore.

His appearing like that in the darkness creeped her out — as he intended it to. She waited him out, but when he laughed softly, she said, "You're scaring Hannah." Her sister hated the dark.

"Are you scared, Hannah?"

She whimpered.

"There, see? No complaints."

"This is between us. Let her out of here."

Laughing contemptuously, he lit the camp lantern from the kitchen and eyed them. "You still think you have control. It's hard to imagine you don't. There's no point of reference for the sort of helplessness you're experiencing, so your mind spins scenarios of escape. If you do this, or you say that . . ."

She didn't respond. Let him play out his fantasy.

"Then comes an incident, an action that cracks the veneer. You grasp the possibility of chaos. You conceive a state of helplessness in which you have no control. Can't talk your way out. Can't fight your way out. Can't. Get. Out."

Glimpsing his anger, she trembled. She knew he wanted to punish her, just hadn't imagined it like this.

He said, "That moment hasn't occurred . . . yet. The action that drives you over. But it will." He lifted the lantern from where he'd set it and started up the stairs.

She wanted to holler out everything he needed to get the money, but it wasn't about that anymore. As with everything else, Markham would make this a show. Though Hannah whimpered when he reached the top, he didn't turn back, just went out and closed the door, plunging the cellar into utter darkness. Hannah let out a high-pitched cry, like a banshee fading into the wind.

Erin counted the beats of her heart until she was sure he wouldn't respond to Hannah's scream. Then she felt inside her coat for the zippered pocket and pulled out her small, super-bright LED flashlight. She pressed the switch and a piercing bluish light streamed out. Gasping, Hannah stared at her.

"There," she said. "Don't be afraid." As though the words ever made it so. She studied her sister, truly confused. Could Pops have gotten things so wrong? "Hannah, why is he doing this to you? I thought you were getting married."

Hannah started to sob. "He wanted to forgive you. He had to forgive you so you could stop running. So we could be married without a sword between us."

As usual, Hannah didn't exactly make sense, but his bald-faced lie was clear enough. Erin hated him with a purity she wasn't certain she'd repent. She said, "If that was what he wanted, why didn't he do it?"

"I don't know." Hannah cried for long minutes before she could go on. "Maybe he can't forgive until you give back the money you stole. When he gets it, God can work the miracle."

"Markham told you that?"

"God revealed it. He's going to multiply the money. And then we'll have our real wedding."

"Real?"

Hannah gulped. "Daddy already did it, but we're not counting that."

So they had been there, six hours away in Hot Springs, South Dakota, as Pops said. She hadn't imagined her father would marry them on the spot. What was he thinking, that a show of faith would erase everything else?

"Hannah, why does Markham have Pops' cell phone?"

"What?"

"The phone you called me on. It belongs to Pops."

Hannah scowled. "He came to the house. He told us you're having a baby. Are you?"

Erin pressed a hand to her stomach as though that could shield the life inside. "Did Markham take his phone?"

"Of course not. Pops hollered at our father and left."

Her chest constricted. "He has it now, Hannah. How did he get it?"

"I don't know," she whined. "How would I know?"

"You weren't with him?" She tried to calm the building terror. "When he got the phone, were you with him?"

"I don't know that he has it. Only that you say so."

And why would she ever believe the sister she despised? She tried to remember any good times they'd had, but the things that stood out were the accidents.

The ladder Hannah knocked down — resulting in Erin's broken ankle. The hot water Hannah spilled — burning Erin's arm. The bicycle Hannah lost control of — Erin's equipped with training wheels, plunging over the embankment.

A deep sadness worked into the fear and discomfort of the moment. "Did you ever love me, Hannah? Even a little?"

Hannah sniffed. "How could I?"

"But why? What did I do?"

"Everything. Everything I couldn't." Bitterness came off her like a scent. "Even the day Markham asked our father for my hand. You weren't even there, and it was still about you."

"How?"

"I told you. Pops barging in, telling us you're married. You're having a baby. Always first. Always better."

Erin closed her eyes. So Markham knew Pops could reach her. He knew she'd take his call. But . . . oh, God, how did he get the phone?

She felt a crushing sensation in her chest, a grief that she might be responsible for what happened. If she hadn't called Pops, hadn't shared her joy — No. She didn't know anything. She couldn't give in to despair. Markham wanted to break her, but she wouldn't let him.

Without her phone, she couldn't tell how long she and Hannah sat without speaking. The last she'd eaten and drunk was a bottled water and trail mix Rudy provided while they fished. Her haunches ached from sitting on the cold, hard cement. Whatever position she shifted to, her shackled arm hurt. The stun gun didn't seem to have left any damage, but the baby?

Like nothing else, that thought almost made her weep. Their child must be so tiny, so protected by God's amazing design of her body. She had to believe she'd kept the shock to herself. Still, she breathed, "I'm so sorry, little one."

After a while, Hannah crawled onto the linked-spring support that once held a vinyl pad. Erin sighed. She had probably disposed of it in the Dumpster, never imagining they might want it. When she heard Hannah sleeping, she turned off the flashlight, since she didn't know how long they'd need the batteries. In a more thorough search, Markham would have found it too. He must have been too thrilled to find the handgun and her phone to look further.

Having the light was a small defiance but enough to encourage, even turned off. While it was worse for Hannah, she didn't enjoy sitting in complete darkness either. At least it was quiet.

How much of the whispers and laughter had been the power of suggestion? Professor Jenkins thought so. She thought of his face and swallowed a lump, thought of RaeAnne and swallowed another. If she pictured Morgan, she'd cry.

The pressing issue was needing a bathroom. She'd been in the wilderness with Rudy, and then Markham launched his attack. She shifted the position of her bladder. Whatever Markham endured in prison, at least he had a toilet.

Lord. Was this her penalty for punishing the people who preferred Markham's lies to the plain truth? She pushed up onto her knees, careful not to jostle the bed, and tried to understand.

Reverend Reilly had embraced Markham, therefore Markham was embraced. He believed Markham, therefore Markham was believed. Markham's con became their credo.

"The believers gave over the fruits of their labor, so God's miracle would satisfy all. Give, that you may be satisfied with more left in

scraps than what you gave up.”

She thought of Morgan rubbing Livie’s little back. *“Do you think I’m more generous than God?”*

The same message with such different intentions. Morgan modeled a father’s love she’d never felt herself, but now she’d seen it, now she understood when he said, *“Could I live without loving and caring for her?”* There would be love for their new baby too. What their hearts held for Livie would not be diminished by opening to another. No baby would hunger as she did.

Morgan had asked her to call on God to do what wasn’t humanly possible. Her heart broke to think he might lose another wife and child. With that aching thought, she breathed, “Help me, Lord. I need you. This baby needs you. And Morgan needs us. Please, please, help.”

In the dark and dreadful cellar, grace surrounded her. She knew with stark clarity that Markham could kill her. But God would be there, as fierce for her young as Celia, as generous as Morgan, as pure as Livie. She would not die in doubt, even if it was in vain.

CHAPTER 35

Markham pressed his palms to his temples. Hannah was crying again, though admittedly with good reason. He'd originally intended to use her as bait, then let her out while he contacted Morgan Spencer to ransom Quinn. Unfortunately for Hannah, the relief from her incessant need proved irresistible — that and the fact he had no key for the shackles.

He had left them both in darkness while he took a psychedelic journey. A lower dose limited the paralysis and exhaustion, but he still experienced the psychedelic thrill and some euphoria on waking. Maybe at some point he would drug Hannah to ease her suffering.

He studied the cabinet with one shattered pane, the ampules nestled inside. The liquid only needed to touch her, but he hesitated. She might not have the mental capacity to handle the effect. Hadn't she screamed and screamed his first time? He couldn't risk making it worse. She understood the importance of his mission, yet still she cried when he lit his way down the stairs.

"Please, Markham. I need a bathroom."

He wasn't heartless. In his first exploration of the cellar, he'd found a few useful things. From a small rubbish heap, he provided a bent and dented bedpan. "It's the only one," he said. "You'll have to share."

Hannah's face seemed almost sweet in sacrifice. "She's here, Markham. Isn't it time?"

She wouldn't understand the complexity and magnitude of his plan, remembered only the small lie he'd told, as though forgiveness could ever be extended. "God's ways are not ours, Hannah. I must listen and obey — as you have promised to."

By Quinn's glare, he thought she would dispute that, but she only said, "We need water."

"Yes, please, Markham," Hannah implored.

Why was Quinn not begging? Would she if he only cared for Hannah? If it were up to Hannah, Quinn would go thirsty.

Leaving the lit lantern on the floor, he went up the stairs and out to the garage, where several cases of bottled water awaited an emergency. He supposed this qualified, at least in their minds. He went back down with a water bottle for each. "Better just sip or the bedpan won't be enough."

■ ■ ■ ■

Erin seethed. Hannah had relieved herself while he was gone. Now he was back, and though she desperately needed to go, she'd wet her pants before she'd give him that satisfaction. While he stood, pondering God's ways, her phone rang in his pocket. With a twitching smile, he pulled it out. "Who's RaeAnne?"

She clenched her jaw. "My friend." If she didn't take it, RaeAnne would worry. She might —

He held it out. "If you let on that anything is wrong, I'll cut Hannah and let her bleed." From his pocket he pulled a knife, and with a *whht* a razor-sharp blade shot up. Lethal as it was, it couldn't cut Hannah more deeply than hearing his threat.

Erin took the phone, and said, "Hi, RaeAnne."

"Did you have fun fishing?"

"Yes. I caught a cutthroat —" Her voice almost broke on the word. "How's your dad?"

"I think he's really happy I'm here. Would you mind very much if I spent the night? I'd like to get his place as clean as you got Vera's."

She wanted to scream she was trapped at Vera's and to send help, but Markham's voice had been bloodless. His eyes showed the duality she'd seen before, a cold vacancy and fiery zeal.

"We're going to watch some movies," Rae-Anne said. "The old ones he watched with my mother."

"That's a great idea." She didn't want Rae-Anne sucked into her mess. "I'll talk to you soon." She pressed End and clung to the phone.

But Markham said, "Slide it over."

Dread filled her as she relinquished her connection to the world. She'd just bought him time. Unless Morgan . . .

Hannah sniffled. "I'm hungry. Markham, please let me come up."

The problem was obvious, but if he didn't have a key, he could get bolt cutters at Rudy's store. Somehow she didn't think it was high on his list.

"I'll see what I can find for you to eat," he told Hannah, and went up. While she could hear him moving around the kitchen, Erin used the bedpan with burning relief. The smell of mingled urine almost made her retch, and she prayed he'd take it out and dump it. By the look on his face when he came back down, Markham had no intention of doing so. He brought them partly stale French rolls.

"Bread?" Hannah gaped. "Dry bread, Mark?"

His eyes turned to flint. "What did you call me?"

"Markham. I . . . I mean Markham."

When Hannah started to cry, Erin stifled a groan. She wanted to feel compassion, but instead she felt like kicking them both really hard.

Clearly Markham intended this to drag on, to maximize the terror in some twisted game, but she refused to play. The minute he went up and took the lantern with him, she lit the flashlight. Before anything else, she had to get out of the shackle. The chain was old, the metal possibly fatigued. Even so, her flesh was too tender to apply that kind of pressure to metal. She needed something else.

The rubbish she'd left to be discarded later provided the best possibilities. Some kind of bar might pry open the chain or even the shackle itself. She couldn't reach the pile from where she was, but the bed wasn't fixed to the floor. Though heavy, it was movable.

"Hannah, I want to find something to undo these cuffs."

Hannah sulked. "It's your fault we're in them."

"Help me move the bed to that pile."

"It's not God's will."

Supreme frustration swelled like a volcano. "How can you still think he speaks for God? Look at us."

"Paul was in chains, Joseph sold into slavery. Sometimes that's how God works."

"Did Markham tell you that? When he chained you to this bed?"

" 'We glory in tribulations.' "

Erin let out her breath. "Okay. Fine. We'll do it Markham's way." She turned off the flashlight.

Hannah shrieked.

"If your screams bring him back, I'll give him the light." Not.

"Turn it on," she rasped.

"I can't. We have to see if he's coming."

Sure enough, Markham opened the door. "Hannah?"

"I . . . I heard something. It scared me."

He shined the lantern on their faces.

"Markham," Hannah cried. "Please leave the light on."

It was senseless cruelty to keep them in the dark, but he closed the door without a word. Before she employed the flashlight, Erin said, "If I drag the bed myself, he'll hear it. We have to lift it together." Hannah might not be much use, but she was attached. "We can lift and set it down. As long as it doesn't make noise."

Hannah whimpered. "Turn on the light."

Erin pressed the switch and held the flashlight between her teeth when she stood up. She showed Hannah how to hold the frame. The first try, Hannah only lifted it inches and they went nowhere.

Erin took the light out of her mouth. "You help me do this, Hannah, or I swear I'll smash the flashlight."

She hissed, "I can't."

"You'd better." As kindly as everyone before Markham had treated her, the only thing that seemed to motivate now was cruelty. Not that this even touched cruel. "Again." She bit the light and gripped the frame.

They lifted and moved one foot. Then another. Hearing something, she doused the light. The whispers stilled. *Lord.* There was nothing in the cellar that could hurt them. She turned on the light. They moved forward with the bed. She felt like Hercules next to her sister, but it didn't matter. They were getting there.

Scanning the heap with the flashlight, she considered and rejected two flimsy metal strips, rusted bedsprings, the bar from a file drawer that couldn't bend a chain. But that rod might. Crouching and stretching, she walked her fingers and touched, then grabbed the thick iron rod.

Holding the chain in place with her foot and shackled arm, she angled it into the link. No way the link would spread, but she noticed a crack at the base of the hasp. Of course. The welding would be the weak spot. Weak, she thought grimly. She could only pray.

She took the light out of her mouth. "We

need to move it back."

"Why?" Hannah whined. "What difference does it make?"

Not daring to bring Markham back into it, she said, "We just do."

Hannah's efforts diminished on the return trip until it seemed they would drag it after all. When they got close enough, Erin went back to work, forcing the hasp in one direction and then the other. The rod proved a good tool for the job, but it could take a very long time — if it worked at all.

Hannah watched sullenly. Erin didn't try to talk. What do you say to a sister who admits she wishes you were never born? She only had to exist to be despised. No point hoping for reconciliation. Anything that came out of this would be bittersweet.

After a while Hannah said, "Why did you do it?"

"Do what?" Sweat beaded her brow and slicked her hands as she strained to separate the hasp from the bed frame.

"Spoil the miracle."

She wedged in the rod and pulled up with all her strength, feeling the strain in her shoulders, the skin on her palms tearing. What she wouldn't have given to be pushing through a snowdrift with Morgan at the other end. She pictured the look in his eyes when he eyed her snow-packed clothes, little Livie calling her a snow *girl.* She needed them so much.

"Why?" Hannah demanded.

"There wasn't any miracle, Hannah. I don't expect you to believe me." She released the rod and pressed her palms painfully together, then took it up again. The miracle would be getting out of Markham's trap alive.

Morgan had told Mikio Funaki there were two calls he'd have to take when they came. Neither had come. When they broke for lunch, he got no answer from Erin. He tried Rudy with no luck. Maybe they were still somewhere out of service. Rudy knew the wild territory well, and that likelihood allowed him to refocus on Funaki until they finished.

In the late afternoon, just as the meeting was breaking up, William called with the news he wanted. The FBI would deal. Relief rushed in like a river, filling the deep roots of worry he'd tried to ignore.

"I'll give you the details over dinner," William said. "Our house, Ellen insists."

"It sounds good," Morgan said, entering the down escalator in the business complex.

"You can tell your bride the monkey's off her back."

"I'd love to, but I haven't been able to reach Erin. I know it's earlier there, but I'm a little concerned."

"Did she know you were conducting business today?"

"Yes." He paused and slipped on his overcoat for the sleeting rain outside.

"Then she probably wasn't expecting to hear from you."

He knew beyond doubt that would be true for William, whose focus on each case was epic. Erin may have made that assumption. Stepping into the rain, he motioned for an available limo cab.

"Well, if she went somewhere after ice fishing —"

"Ice fishing?"

"Yes. The person she's with is a real mountain man and a good friend." He climbed into the cab. "I probably shouldn't worry." He only wished she'd given him a heads-up before she went off the grid.

"You don't have the corner market on worry. But it sounds like she's in good hands."

If only he could be sure she was.

"See you this evening," William said. "Seven sharp."

"I'll be there." He wished Erin could too. Why had he thought it better to leave her? Because she was supposed to stay put.

Markham paced the kitchen, his attention snagging on the gun he'd taken from Quinn. His lip peeled up. Had she intended to use it? Of course she had. He could still see the fight in her eyes. She had not admitted defeat, had not felt the helplessness he wanted her to know all the way to her bones.

Would she have shot him? Could she have? He glowered at the gun, jerking with memories. Another dark-haired woman.

Shots. The body falling. The blood. *"You saw nothing, kid. Got it?"* The stench of his cousin's breath and her blood had stayed in his nose for years, dulling the flavor and aroma of food, of flowers and fresh air. It had made him throw up at night, and the smell of that joined with the rest.

Quinn had carried a gun. He'd taken it, but even now she was plotting against him. He knew her. She wouldn't stop unless he made her feel powerless, helpless, hopeless.

He turned on the crackling flooring and started back the other way. What would it take? He could defile her.

Something stirred like shadows shifting.

He'd said it himself. An inciting incident. Chaos. Defeat. *Make her. Break her.*

He turned back toward the cabinet, stared through the broken glass like a toothy maw. He could drug her, incapacitate and force her.

It stirred again. Swirling darkness. An acid flashback? A trick of the senses.

He paced the other way, brooding. She had to pay — not only in money, but in fear and humiliation. He wanted her powerless, hopeless. And he could do it. He felt a surge inside, recalling what he'd seen on her face when she talked to the man who spirited her away. *Break her, take her, break her.*

Then he remembered Hannah. Even if he could violate Quinn with Hannah looking on, he would not do anything to diminish himself in her eyes. It stunned and touched him that she still believed. And he vowed as long as she did, she would live.

He stopped pacing. His mind cleared. Hurting Quinn must wait. It was time to implement the plan.

Cabbing to Oyster Bay for dinner with William, Morgan could no longer pretend he wasn't afraid. With no answer from Erin, he tried calling Rudy again — and got him. "Rudy!" he all but cried.

"Morgan, you sly married dog."

In no mood, he snapped, "Rudy, is Erin with you?"

"Who?"

"Erin. Quinn. My wife." He white-knuckled the phone. "Is she with you?"

The limo sedan smelled of something Eastern eaten for dinner, but the back seat smelled of fear.

"No. I haven't seen her since fishing this morning."

His heart made a slow thud. "Did she say

where she was going? What she was doing?"
"Something about Vera's daughter and her dad."
Except she wasn't with RaeAnne. They'd spoken but weren't together. Neither had seen her since the morning. "Rudy, can you do something for me?"
"Wh—"
"Wait a minute." His call waiting beeped. He looked at the caller and switched. "Erin, thank God."
"Who?"
It wasn't the question that chilled him. It was the voice. Markham Wilder's voice saying, "Who's Erin?"
Cold adrenaline shut the panic off like a faucet. Every part of him went still. Markham using Erin's phone meant one thing. Jaw clenched, he said, "If you touch my wife, I'll hunt you down and kill you."
The driver flicked a glance in the mirror.
"Given that I have the blade at her throat, you're in no position to make threats." Markham's tone set his teeth on edge. "Tell him, Quinn."
He heard a sucked-in cry.
"Hear that? Just a little prick with the blade."
He had never known if he could kill, whether some barrier would prevent him. Now he knew. But sinking to Markham's level would cancel his advantage. "What do

you want?"

Another soft whimper went straight to his heart. Erin would be fighting the sounds with all she had, furious and humiliated. He heard sobbing, but it wasn't Erin, at least not as he'd ever heard her. "I said what do you want?"

With a voice like the devil, Markham rasped, "I want her to suffer."

The pit of his stomach liquefied.

"To know what it's like having someone else in total control. To know I can hurt her. I can kill her."

Desolation opened like a chasm, but he slammed it shut with the force of his will. "What will that get you?"

"Satisfaction."

"Then what? Back to prison?"

After a pause, Markham laughed. When he spoke again it was a different person. "Have a better offer? What's your wife worth to you . . . ? Oh, wait. It's wife and kid, isn't it?"

Morgan flinched. "Name your price."

"What fun is that? Let's bargain. What will you give for one prime, pregnant woman — a twofer."

Another sound from Erin shot all sorts of images to his brain, but he let Markham keep talking.

"What is it, a million-dollar baby?"

"If you say so." The man wanted power.

"So Quinn must be worth two. That's three

million if you can't do the math. A full return on my investment."

"Take the blade away from her or you don't get a cent."

Markham laughed as if they were two frat boys being cool and getting wasted. "You still think you have power here. You're used to that, I know. But the truth is" — the other voice came back — "you have no idea what I'm doing to her, what I'm going to do in the time it takes you to get the money into my hands."

He was not playing this sick game. "This is the way it's going to work. You want the money, I'll get it. If I find . . . Quinn completely untouched, you'll get transportation. A private jet to take you anywhere you choose." He could almost hear Markham salivating.

"How do I know it's not a trick?"

"We'll drive to the airport together. There's a small one not far from Juniper Falls."

The silence stretched.

"I'll have two million in hundred-dollar bills with me. The third on the jet waiting to take you out of there."

Breathing heavily, as though fighting a great resistance, Markham spoke in a strangled voice. "It's a deal."

"Where's my wife?"

"Old dark hole in the ground. No sniper windows. New bolt on the door, and I hold the key."

The cellar.

"I took the precaution of stocking it with propane tanks. Besides the blade, I have a gun — your wife's to be precise. You bring law enforcement, we'll have fireworks."

He closed his eyes. "I want to talk to her."

"You got your proof of life. You have until noon tomorrow to get the money here. Or the deal's off."

"That's not enough time." He didn't have that kind of cash readily available. Liquefying assets, converting and transporting the money would take much longer.

"Noon tomorrow." The line went dead.

His chin fell to his chest.

But then Rudy's voice came on. "Morgan? What's going on?"

He quelled the panic rising. "The guy who chased Erin has her."

"Markham Wilder?"

"I think he's keeping her in the asylum cellar at Vera's."

"I'll get the sheriff."

"No. He's rigged the place with propane."

Rudy swore.

"I need to be there by noon tomorrow with ransom money. Can you watch the house without being seen and let me know if anything changes?"

"You know I can," Rudy said. "What if he takes her somewhere else?"

"In a perfect world, you'd follow."
"My world's pretty perfect."
Morgan swallowed. "Thanks."
The limo pulled into William's compound. Entering without knocking, he found William in his library.
William tipped his head up, all joviality fading.
Morgan said, "The Satan-spawn has Erin."

Giddy, Markham released Quinn's hair and drew his blade away. He was going to get more than he'd dreamed when this was done — a miracle of multiplication, just like his vision. He pulled a paper and pencil from his pocket. "Write it all down. Everything to access the account you funded."
With a shaky hand, she did.
"I will check it upstairs and know if one digit is wrong." He had no way to verify it, but she didn't know that.
"It's not. That's everything you need to get the money. Please let us go."
"You weren't listening. That's only half of what's coming."
Looking into her face, he felt a burn in his gut as it slowly sank in he'd been outmaneuvered. Morgan's offer had surprised and dazzled him. The cash *and* transportation. A jet to take him anywhere.
And all he had to do was leave Quinn unharmed. That was the razor in the apple.

She wasn't weeping like Hannah, afraid of the dark. She looked at him with judgment and loathing. He'd heard her cry when he pricked her with the blade, yet she still glared back. Maybe he should take Hannah out and leave Quinn in the cellar alone, but then he'd have to deal with Hannah.

He had to think. There had to be a way to have it all. He'd rigged the cellar with propane tanks as a deterrent. He didn't need to blow it up. And now Morgan was doubling the take — more money than he'd ever make in scams. If he killed Quinn, he'd have to kill Morgan.

Then he'd lose the jet and a chance for freedom he'd never experienced. The black knight had guarded his queen admirably. But it twisted the worm inside.

Markham stared into the darkness past the illumination of the lantern. What was that shifting and stirring? *Kill her, kill them, kill her anyway.*

He'd exterminated his cousins and left the world a better place. Could he say the same about Quinn? What did it matter if he left her alive? He clenched his hands, resisting. He wanted the jet to take him away. So Quinn would live. But he could still make her suffer.

"By the way." He fixed her with a stare. "Your grandfather sends his regards."

He saw her stiffen.

"Or would, I'm sure, if he could."

Chest heaving, her voice came in breathy bursts. "What did you do?"

"Nothing that old degenerate didn't deserve."

"Markham?" Hannah blinked, and for the first time he saw doubt and accusation.

"He was bound for hell, Hannah. Your father said so himself. Only Quinn, here, held out hope and affection. Pity." He blinked. "Your last conversation provided the cover and distraction this 'rotted soul' needed to get close."

She pressed her hand to her mouth, tears swarming her eyes.

"Never fear, Quinn." He raised her chin with the flat of the blade. "He'll be in hell to greet you."

She slumped in the dark, head in hands when the door closed. Hannah whimpered but didn't ask for a light. No cruelty Markham could inflict compared to knowing she'd gotten Pops killed. Agonizing guilt drained her will to fight. Somewhere in her mind, she knew Morgan was coming, but this sorrow would not end.

"Stop it," Hannah said.

"Stop what?" she barely answered.

"Whispering. Stop whispering about me."

Through her fuzzy head, thoughts flickered.

"Don't." Hannah's voice cracked. "Don't

say that."

"I'm not talking, Hannah. Whatever you hear it's not me."

"It is. You hate me."

"I don't hate you." Tears clogged her throat. "But Pops is dead. And we're responsible."

"No." Hannah clamped her hands to her head, the chain jangling. "Stop it."

A dim awareness grew. Jerking her head up, she saw the shadows shift. "Think of your favorite psalm, Hannah. The one hanging on your wall." The most commercially available psalm in the world because of its beauty and consolation. " 'The Lord is my shepherd . . .' "

" 'I shall not want.' "

"That's right. Keep going."

As Hannah recited it, Erin pushed up to her knees in a wash of anger and sorrow. She stuck the rod into the weakened hasp, bent but still clinging to the frame. Her hands were a misery of torn and swollen skin. The pain nothing, compared to her heart. Oh, Pops.

And then she seemed to hear him say, "What are you crying for? Put some muscle in it and get your wee self out." Clenching her teeth, she forgot the pain. She pressed the rod as hard as she could and broke the weld, freeing the chain from the hasp.

She was free. She could get out. She could use the rod as a weapon and get past Markham. She could escape before Morgan put himself in danger. Except the cellar was rigged with propane.

The thought of starting over on the other shackle brought tears to her eyes, but she rasped, “Your choice, Hannah. Are you staying here for Markham or coming with me?”

Chapter 36

Markham had said noon. With William's help, he'd be there an hour before. Aboard the law firm's jet, Morgan read the file Anselm had compiled. He read it to know his adversary, to learn exactly who Markham was.

Born to an addict who didn't live past his first month, the infant Mark Withers was placed into the care of a cousin, Leon Gaines, who lived with a woman of low character for the first four years of the boy's life. She disappeared under suspicious circumstances, and Withers and Leon moved in with another male cousin, Hugh Bower.

While sympathy escaped him for the man Markham became, Morgan admitted the boy had stepped up to the plate with a broken bat. Lying probably saved his life more than once, if the arrest records for the cousins were any indication. For the next fifteen years, the three worked scams together until both men were found dead, at which time Mark Withers was questioned and released — with grave misgivings.

Billing himself as Markham Wilder, the young man perfected his prophetic show, swindling small homegrown churches with his visions of abundance. The file held account after account, yet he was never blamed, never suspected. Suspicion always fell on someone in the church — probably someone he set up.

Would that have been Erin? Had he started casting doubt, stirring unrest? Maybe sensing that led her to investigate him. Markham wouldn't have expected resistance from the minister's daughter, not when the older daughter was so pliable. Morgan formed a cold smile, thinking the man had no idea what pixie he was provoking.

He read on. As the proceeds accrued, Markham learned how to shelter the money offshore and rolled a portion of that into each new scam, the ripest plum being Erin's father's church, for which — thanks to her — he got charged, prosecuted, and incarcerated. Four years for his grudge to grow.

The knot in his stomach hardened. Markham killed his cousins, but assuming he'd kill Erin would paralyze him. Predisposed by loss to expect the worst, Morgan fought it with everything in him. This time he would not be impotent. This time the reckoning was his.

Within the hour, he joined Rudy in the trees and stared at the house he'd bought with such different intentions. "Any activity?"

Rudy lowered the binoculars. "Not outside. I've seen him walking around the kitchen. He's been walking all night, talking to himself."

"No one else?"

"Seems to be alone, but he goes through that door and comes back."

"That's the old asylum cellar." Where Erin had gotten so spooked she never wanted to be in that house again.

Rudy blew a long breath through his lips. "Quinn's in there?"

He swallowed. "Rudy, do you mind calling her Erin? It's her married name."

"No. Sure. Sorry."

"I'm just trying to —" What?

"I get it."

Morgan stared back at the house. His nerves were so fired up, his skin felt prickly. He needed this to happen now. He activated his radio and told the head of William's security team he was moving.

Duane Bow replied in the affirmative. "Go."

With the cellar a potential propane bomb, they couldn't risk shots fired. Given the near certainty that Markham wanted to live, avoiding gunfire should be utmost in his own mind. He took out his phone and called Markham. "I'm here with the money."

"Where?" Markham left the kitchen. "I don't see you."

"I'm going to drive up with it now." He was already heading to where he'd left the sedan that had been waiting at the airport. He pulled up outside Vera's garage and removed two sports bags weighing twenty-two pounds each and holding two million dollars between them. Through his bank William had facilitated the transaction more swiftly and smoothly than had seemed possible.

Praying that grace would continue, Morgan walked to the open space outside the front window, not too close to the house but where he could be easily seen. He set the bags down on either side. This was half of his part of the bargain. If Markham shot him dead, he wouldn't get the jet or the third million. Might be an option for a madman, but he was counting on greed.

When he saw Markham in the window he said into the phone, "Here's the money. Bring me Quinn."

Markham had intended to accept the deal, but looking at Morgan standing there, smug and confident, and everything Mark Withers once wanted to be, he felt a swelling rage. *Break him, kill him, kill them all.*

He turned and stalked to the cellar, yanked the door open, and descended. He hardly looked at the women. He wouldn't think of them as anything but collateral damage.

"You didn't consider the collateral damage."

The blows rained down. *"You cost us, you pathetic ingrate."*

He cost them, and he paid them in full. Nineteen years of collateral damage. Carrying the battery-operated lantern, he moved from position to position, opening the propane valves. Something opened inside him, releasing poisons equally flammable. *Burn it, burn it.*

"Markham?" Hannah's doubting voice fueled his fury.

Quinn stared through him as though he didn't exist, as if he were nothing. She'd see. Once and for all, she'd see.

With all the tanks releasing a slow stream, he shot one look at them and stalked back up the stairs, leaving the door open for a draft. In the garage, he filled a quart jar from the gasoline can and shoved a rag into the mouth. Even without the drug, his mind was working more sharply and clearly than ever before. This was his prophetic call, his vision from God — to rain fire upon the unbelieving harlots, the grasping tycoon. *Burn, burn, burn.*

Holding the jar and lighter behind his back, he drew Quinn's gun and stepped around the side of the house. "I want to see the money."

Morgan turned, surprised. "Okay." He bent and unzipped the bags.

It looked real and impossible to believe. "Step away." He circled behind as Morgan moved toward the house.

"Two million there," Morgan said, as though it were nothing. "The third on the jet. I only want Quinn."

"Then go and get her."

Morgan looked behind him, then back. "We'll go together."

Markham raised the gun.

Morgan spread his hands. "The pilot won't take off without my order. Don't screw up your chance."

Markham laughed darkly. Amazing what a pilot would do with a gun to his head. He could see it so clearly. An airport near Juniper Falls. A private jet. A reluctant pilot seeing the light.

With that very gun held up, he said, "If you want your wife, you better get her before I change my mind." He could see the man's fear, reveled in it. "I left the cellar open for you."

Burn, burn. It didn't matter how much money Morgan Spencer made, how many books he wrote, how famous he was. Markham's chest swelled. All he had to do was sacrifice both queens and the power was his — prophet, hand of God. God.

As Morgan disappeared inside, Markham shoved the gun into his jeans. He flicked the lighter and ignited the rag. Behold the instrument. He rushed toward the house and felt a punch that spun him half around before he heard the shot. The last things he saw were the oaf from the general store with a hunting rifle and the ground bursting into flame when he fell.

Hearing the report of gunfire, Erin jammed the rod once more into the hasp of Hannah's shackle, yelling with the effort that ripped her palms open. "Pull, Hannah!"

"It hurts."

"Pull!" she screamed.

With both their strength and what felt like another pair of powerful hands, they broke the weld on the hasp as a man charged down the stairs. With her lips drawn back on bared teeth, she shouldered the rod to swing, then saw him in the flashlight's beam. "Morgan!"

"Come. Now!"

Choking in the propane that felt like lead in her lungs, she gripped Hannah's arm and yanked her toward the stairs. They tripped and staggered over each other in clumsy haste as she pushed her sister ahead and Morgan followed. In the kitchen, he propelled them out the back door, pushing them as they ran.

The air seemed to gather and suck in. Then a force threw her off her feet and onto the ground, rolling and skidding. A blast of heat roared up behind her as she shielded her face and eyes. She didn't have to look to grasp the destruction. Through hollow ears, she heard

Hannah crying, heard Morgan hollering, "Erin."

She tipped her face to see him. "I'm okay."

He hauled her up from the ground, searching her, feeling her, clutching her.

"It's all right." She held him, stroked him, gripped his face, and kissed him. "We're all right." They held on, his chest against hers, their hearts beating fast and strong.

Behind them, the fire crackled and spat, shooting flames into the sky as emergency vehicles arrived. They had to have been en route to be there so quickly. But if she'd waited for rescue . . .

She closed her eyes, her chest heaving, and thanked God for the strength he'd given. Then she dropped to her knees by Hannah and held her stunned and sobbing sister.

Flakes of ash fell like soiled confetti. The smoke and stink of burnt materials and chemical agents stung his nostrils as Morgan ushered Erin and Hannah around the burning house. The flames, the fire equipment, and most horribly the billowing smoke bombarded him.

He braced for panic, but with Erin under his arm, he felt only bone-deep gratitude. They'd alerted local fire and police as soon as the plan was in action, but he hadn't wanted anyone causing this exact thing, if there was a chance he could lure Markham away peaceably. Right up to the moment he entered the house, he'd hoped. The second he hit the door, he knew better.

Reaching the front of what used to be the house, Hannah broke his hold and flung herself at the charred remains on the ground, screaming and thrashing as firefighters pulled her off. In a weird dissociation, Morgan looked from the body to the big man who resembled Evander Holyfield, holding the two sports bags.

"I couldn't get the body," Duane said. "I only had two hands."

The sheriff arrived with two deputies, but before explanations could begin, the FBI's Critical Incident Team moved in and took charge. Morgan surveyed the scene as from a distance, hearing Duane and Rudy's statements. He hadn't realized Rudy took the shots. Justified, certainly, but it couldn't hurt that before he left New York, the FBI had issued a warrant for Markham Wilder's arrest.

In that moment, Rudy became a legend at the Roaring Boar and elsewhere, but by the look of his friend when they wrapped his rifle as evidence, that was far from his mind.

"You okay?"

Rudy gave a slow nod. "It's not the same though. Can't field dress it. I mean, the guy was nuts, but . . ."

"Think soldier, not hunter. This was war."

Duane Bow approached. "I'm cleared by

the FBI to return Mr. St. Claire's funds. Will you be needing the jet?"

Morgan told them to go ahead, then looked at Erin giving her statement to the agent in charge. He saw her glance worriedly at her sister, who must have been sedated to control the hysteria. Seeing her sister for the first time, he could not miss the similarities, yet they were only skin deep. Hannah looked like a leaf that had blown off a bonfire, brittle and singed.

Erin — also battered, with her hands bandaged where she'd torn the skin getting free of the shackles — had a substance and clarity he could hardly take in. Pure and piercing, like rarified air, and yet so exceedingly breathable.

"Have you been checked over?" Sheriff Ingram asked. "Medically?"

"I'm fine. We got out."

"You know, as an alternative, there's always law enforcement for these kinds of things."

Morgan nodded. "Sometimes you just act."

"I'm not saying it would have ended differently, but you put yourself in harm's way."

He nodded at his wife. "They were already in harm's way. If he'd taken the offer, they would have been safe and . . ."

"Then the agents on the jet would have nabbed him."

"That was the plan." Morgan ran a hand through his hair. "Didn't foresee the Molotov cocktail." He shook his head. "It seemed everything he did was motivated by greed."

"I don't know," the sheriff said. "With con men there's power and manipulation in it too."

And maybe something more sinister. Morgan directed his gaze to the flames the firefighters were knocking down with hoses. That was one house that would not be rebuilt.

Erin joined him with a look over her shoulder at the same awful scene. "Makes me wish I hadn't done all the patching and painting."

He formed a soft smile. "That felt like an act of kindness for Livie and me."

"It was." But then she shuddered.

"That goodness, the way you cared about RaeAnne and the people treated there — and me — protected you the whole time you were working in it. Whatever evil was there couldn't get a hold."

She looked into his face. "I'm not crazy, then?"

"When I was running down the stairs, it felt like hands were pushing against my chest, trying to keep me from you."

"The hands on my side were greater by far." She frowned. "But Markham . . ." Her face twisted. "Morgan, he killed Pops. After I called. He killed him and took his phone." She shook as tears came. "I thought it was Pops calling."

Dismayed, he gripped her shoulders. "He's a liar."

"I saw the bloody phone. And he knew exactly what Pops said to me. He snuck up because Pops and I —"

"You had nothing to do with that."

"If I hadn't called —"

"No. It was Markham. Not you." But it shook him, too, to think their decision to reach out to her family might have ended the old man's life. They couldn't have known. But it hurt. He held his wife as the sorrow moved through her. So much destruction, for what?

Holding tight, he looked over her head at Hannah, the piteous piece of the puzzle. "Will your sister be okay?"

"I don't know." Erin looked up, pulling herself together as she must have done so many times already. "Could we take her home?"

"With us?"

"No, I mean, to my family." She wiped her tears and swallowed.

Anger clenched his hands. "Are you ready for that?"

She looked back at her sister, wrapped in a blanket and staring. "She needs her dad."

"But I was asking about you."

She shrugged a shoulder. "Markham's gone. If not now . . . when?"

He made his hands relax. They didn't

deserve her, but he said, "As soon as we're free to go." They'd be untangling it for some time. He rubbed her arm. "Could we restrict any future rescues to small children and animals?"

She gasped. "Bella! Livie!"

"Relax. Your only problem there will be convincing Livie that Bella isn't her doggy. She's talked of nothing else, and I mean nothing."

Erin pressed a hand to her chest. "I miss her so much my heart hurts."

There was nothing else to say to that.

The drive to Hot Springs, South Dakota, with Hannah crying would have been awful. The same drive, silent, broke her heart. With Morgan behind the wheel because of her bandaged hands, Erin glanced back at her sister lying in the back seat of her truck, mute, staring. She wished so many things could be different. But where would she even begin?

When she turned back to study Morgan in profile, a quality of feeling rose inside that was more than emotion. It was as though he were inside her and she in him. The beauty of that made her hurt all the more for Hannah. The cruelty of what Markham had intended would hurt far longer than any physical injuries. Probably forever.

How had her father let that happen? Had

his pride and the inability to admit he was wrong jeopardized the person he loved most of all? She understood what Morgan said about building a world for Hannah, but why invite the serpent to the garden?

Or was he merely a fallible man, trying like the rest of them? She sought the right spirit and mindset to face him. *Lord.*

They had washed up at the ranch before heading out. She'd helped Hannah into and out of the shower and borrowed clothes for both of them from Noelle's closet. They had not tried to eat, even though the last she and Hannah had was Markham's bread and water and a Gatorade from the EMTs.

In darkness, they entered the community she'd left four years ago in righteous anger. That anger stirred again as she passed the homes of people she'd known her whole life — church members who lived in close proximity to the minister like a flock around their shepherd. It seemed they would get their money back, once the FBI sorted it out.

She shuddered, doubting these people would ever be told the full extent of what he'd actually done. One tiny bright spot was that she wasn't going to be charged or have to testify again at Markham's trial. She was free to live her life. Or almost free. Her stomach shrank in when Morgan parked outside her father's house.

Pops had described her parents' insipid reaction to her news — in their last conversation before he died. His cell phone must have blown up in Vera's house, or burnt up on Markham, destroying evidence of that crime. She trembled with grief.

Morgan looked over. "Ready?"

She glanced back at Hannah, still lying there. "I'll let my father get her."

She and Morgan went to the door. Since her cell phone was also destroyed, they hadn't called ahead. She could have used Morgan's, she supposed, but what would she have said?

It took a long time for anyone to answer the doorbell. Then her father, still mostly brown-haired with white along his hairline, stood in pajamas and a green velour robe, taking them in with bewildered annoyance. "Do you know what time it is?"

She wondered how long those first words to her in four years would linger. "Hannah's in the car, Dad. She needs you."

His visible transformation hurt.

"Dad?" She caught his arm before he passed by. "Markham's dead."

Stunned, he looked immediately at Hannah, his heart in his eyes. As it should be. She let go of his sleeve.

"Quinn?" Her mother's voice brought her around.

"Mom." She went into her arms, needing that touch more than she'd let herself know, then turned. "This is my husband, Morgan."

"Oh," Gwen murmured. Knowing nothing of his fame or worldly success — though he did cut a striking figure in the smallness of her parents' front porch — her mother's eyes widened nonetheless as she took him in. Erin shook her head. As much as she loved and respected him, she hoped she never looked at him that way.

"Morgan, my mother, Gwen Reilly."

"Come in," Gwen told them. Had she always been so whispery? She was a puff of wind next to the mighty redwood Celia, though it wasn't fair to compare.

"We brought Hannah home." Erin rested a hand on her mother's arm, her birdlike bones frail beneath her skin. "I'm sorry, but Markham's dead."

"Dead?" She seemed more confused than hurt by the news. "How?"

"We'll wait for Dad, if it's okay. I only want to tell it once."

"Yes, of course. He should be the first to hear."

She hadn't meant that at all, only that emotional exhaustion would only carry her through one explanation.

"I should see what I can do to help your sister."

Erin nodded, witnessing once more the way of things.

As her mother went to help her husband with Hannah, Erin leaned with Morgan against the spotless Formica counter, standing on the freshly mopped linoleum. The cabinets retained a scent of Murphy Oil Soap. The pink chintz curtains were pressed right up to the crisp gathers. Gwen Reilly loved keeping house.

Leaning there, Morgan closed his eyes, fatigue catching up. Neither of them had slept in more than a day. He and William had spent the night meeting with the FBI and lining everything up.

In the Bureau's version, the critical incident team would have been first on the scene handling the hostage situation with the other agents waiting on William's jet, if it went that far. But Morgan and William privately agreed he had a better shot at a positive solution by going in under the radar and working with Markham's demands.

In the end, Markham went off the rails altogether. She wondered what pushed him over, but it didn't matter. Though she hadn't wished the end that came, he'd chosen it. She asked Morgan, "Do you want to sit?"

For an answer he put his arm around her, sensing the fine tension keeping her upright. "Nope."

"Should we drop Hannah and run?"

Eyes still closed, the corners of his mouth deepened.

She said, "I don't think they'll miss me."

He opened his eyes, angling his face to her.

"The problem is, you don't fit here. They probably had no idea what to do with you. The best they came up with was hiding your light under a bushel."

She stared into his face, touched and heartened by his perception. "Are you tired of hearing I love you?"

"Try me in forty years or so."

From the bedroom, she heard Hannah crying. It was going to be a while. "Let's come back in the morning."

He searched her face, then straightened off the counter. "Okay. Where to?"

Her chest quaked. "Pops' house."

"Erin."

"I know." She suppressed a sob. "I just want to be in his place. To say good-bye."

Morgan released a breath. "Okay."

They drove the short distance to the tiny turn-of-the-century house by the river they'd fished. She couldn't stop the tears as she climbed the porch stairs and turned the old knob. Pops had never locked it. How she wished now that he had.

The house smelled of lemon oil and shirt starch and faintly of fried chicken. It seemed impossible she'd never see him with an iron skillet at the stove again. A wave of pain closed her eyes, twisting her brow like a hook in her forehead.

And then a voice broke the silence. "Stand right there. By Patrick and all the saints, you'll not catch me unawares again."

"Pops?" Her legs gave out.

Morgan caught her going down. The light came on. All the emotion of the whole horrific affair burst from her in sobs.

Morgan said, calmly, "Is there somewhere she can sit?"

A bandage wrapped his head, and Pops moved jerkily as he ushered them into the parlor, but his voice was strong, his tone insistent. "Be still, lass. Be still."

She dropped to the velveteen sofa. "I thought you were dead. Markham said —"

"And that should have been your clue. Take more than that scurvy weasel to crack this Irish skull. Did more damage to the rock."

She caught the amusement in Morgan's eyes, a matching high spirits in Pops's.

"This isn't funny. I've been in agony over you."

"Well, about time," he said. "If it takes bumping my head to bring you back, I'll do it myself. And a better job of it."

She dropped back against the couch with a hint of exasperation.

Pops shifted his attention. "You must be Morgan. Great name, that. Welsh bones in it."

Morgan rose and offered his hand. "Morgan Spencer."

"Corlin Reilly." Pops returned Morgan's

firm grip. "You're a lucky one, getting my Quinn."

"Don't I know." Morgan took his seat again. "But . . . she goes by Erin now."

She studied her grandfather for a reaction.

"Oh?"

"We changed it when we married to elude Markham, but . . . I like it that way."

Pops gave Morgan a long stare, then said, "Just as well. I only gave her Quinn to nettle my son. Erin, though. That came from the heart."

Morgan shot her a look that said he'd told her so.

She raised her chin. "Pops, tell me the truth. Are you really fine?"

"A wee concussion. My neighbor found me almost right away, got me off the river shore into my kitchen. We had a stiff drink and toasted Markham straight to hell."

She couldn't help thinking he'd gone there. But she raised her brows. "I thought you didn't believe in hell."

"No, lass. I believe that right well."

"Then, why are you so against God?"

To her surprise, he pondered it. "It's not so much I'm against God as I don't think he's got much use for me."

"But, Pops . . ." Surely there was hope in this.

He gripped the chair arms with his gnarly hands. "I did things in my youth. Killed a man in a bar fight. He had it coming, but it turned me somehow. Never saw myself the same again." His brow furrowed. "Lately, though, and maybe while I lay there, contemplating my demise, I thought there might be room for conversation. God and I."

She crossed her hands beneath her throat, tears brimming. "I'm sure you'll have plenty to say. Both of you."

"Aye." He pressed his palms to his knees. "But I've said enough for now. Take your pick of the rooms upstairs . . . Erin. Just don't keep me up all night."

She drew a sharp breath.

But Morgan stood and took her arm. "We'll hold it down, Pops."

She held her peace all the way up, then hissed, "Hold it down?" when he closed the door behind them.

Morgan laughed out loud.

Epilogue

"May I ride the horsey, Daddy?"

"Well." Morgan lifted Livie onto the pristine white fence of the corral, perching her next to the equally pristine white mare with soft gray muzzle and rippling creamy white mane. The purebred Andalusian might have been over the top as a first horse for a not-yet-three-year-old, but as Erin said, he just couldn't help himself. "Let's ask Mommy."

He turned as Erin approached, one hand resting on her protruding belly. Nowhere near as pronounced as it would get in her two remaining months, it still amazed him watching their child grow inside her.

His glance shifted to Noelle walking beside her, his infant nephew tucked under her chin. He had a feeling these two babies would be as close as Liam and Livie, even if they didn't live in the same house. The amount of time they spent in one place or the other would keep them together enough.

"Ask me what?" Erin said.

"May I ride the horsey, Mommy?"

Bella trotted up and put her paws on the fence rail as Erin stroked the horse's head. "I think the one you need to ask is Princess Snowflake."

His mouth pulled. That was what came of a two-year-old naming a horse — not quite the registered version.

Livie put her face almost onto the mare's. "May I ride you, Princess Snowflake?"

"I definitely think she says yes." Erin's eyes gleamed. "As long as Daddy rides too."

He leaned his forearm on the fence. "You know Celia would disagree. She'd put her on bareback."

"Yes." Erin stroked the dove-gray muzzle. "But you asked Mommy."

He sent a glance to Noelle, who shrugged. "Rick would agree with Erin. Especially when you buy a sprite a war horse."

"She's a show horse."

Erin stretched up and kissed him. "It's your call."

Which meant he'd saddle up and take Livie for her first ride on Princess Snowflake — an opportunity he wouldn't miss since he'd be flying out in the morning.

The spread they'd found comprised scenic acres surrounding an hacienda-style house that immediately gained Consuela's approval. It was farther from the mission but closer to her heritage. Erin and Livie didn't seem to mind the seven-minute drive to the sparkling shore they viewed from their large, arching windows, and Bella thought anywhere they ended up heaven.

With an arm around Livie on the fence, he pulled Erin up and kissed her longer. The baby would be born before their first anniversary, but it was good spacing for Livie, and Erin glowed. He hadn't seen this coming, might have missed it, locked in his gloom. But Erin and Livie had conspired, with a little of Rick and Noelle. He felt pretty sure Jill and Kelsey approved. And he no longer wondered but was wholly convinced the matter was God ordained.

"You know as soon as this one's born, it'll be you in the saddle."

"Can I nurse the baby first?"

He nudged her. "Wise guy."

"Wise *girl,* Daddy."

"Wise woman." Erin looked into his face, the essence of her — like Livie — catching his breath as it might for the rest of his life.

His chest expanded. "Definitely." His mouth found hers with a will of its own.

"Kiss *me,* Daddy!"

He and Erin broke their kiss and as one covered Livie's cheeks and neck with all the kissing she could bear.

ACKNOWLEDGMENTS

Many heartfelt thanks to the people who helped make this book:

My editorial team at Bethany House, Karen Schurrer, David Horton, and all those who took a pass at this. Thanks to marketing, production, cover design, and all of you behind the scenes. Such a joy to work with you.

My agent, Donald Maass. Fantastic insights for unrelenting improvement, solid representation, and great advice.

My readers, Jane Francis, David Ladd, Kelly McMullen, Melodie Fry (don't talk to me; I'm in Paris), Devin Heitzmann, Jessica Rae Lovitt, and my husband, James. Every one of those comments, questions, and answers made it that much better.

A most special thanks to Everleigh Grace Lovitt for inspiring Livie and putting the wonderful in every day. And for little Greyson, whose turn is coming.

As always, profound thanks and praise to

God — Father, Son, and Spirit — all for your glory.

ABOUT THE AUTHOR

Kristen Heitzmann is the bestselling author of historical and contemporary romantic suspense novels, including Colorado Book Award finalist *The Still of Night* and Christy Award winner *Secrets*. She lives with her husband, extended family, pets, and wildlife in the Rocky Mountain foothills.

Visit her at: www.kristenheitzmannbooks .com

Facebook: Author Kristen Heitzmann
Twitter: Kristen Heitzmann

The employees of Thorndike Press hope you have enjoyed this Large Print book. All our Thorndike, Wheeler, and Kennebec Large Print titles are designed for easy reading, and all our books are made to last. Other Thorndike Press Large Print books are available at your library, through selected bookstores, or directly from us.

For information about titles, please call:

(800) 223-1244

or visit our Web site at:

http://gale.cengage.com/thorndike

To share your comments, please write:

Publisher
Thorndike Press
10 Water St., Suite 310
Waterville, ME 04901